THE DUKE'S FALLEN ANGEL

Prelude to the Devilish Dukes Series

by

Amy Jarecki

Rapture Books

Copyright © 2017, Amy Jarecki

Jarecki, Amy
The Duke's Fallen Angel

ISBN: 9781725876538

First Release: October, 2018

Book Cover Design by: Dar Albert
Edited by: Scott Moreland

To Grace Burrowes, a brilliant woman and author who is also generous and giving in everything she undertakes. She has done so much to help emerging authors gain a foothold in this industry, I am truly amazed at her altruism. This is a woman who knows how to give back just as she assisted me with *The Duke's Fallen Angel.* I thank Ms. Burrowes for helping me to grasp the Regency/Georgian voice. And especially, I thank her for an abundance of thought-provoking opinions.

Chapter One

London, 5th April, 1833

If a man was capable of spontaneous combustion, Drake Chadwick, Duke of Ravenscar, teetered on the verge of bursting into flames. Bad news came often enough but this topped the charts as the most calamitous complication of the Season.

No, not the Season; of his lifetime.

In fact, he didn't believe a word.

Drake leaned forward, grinding his knuckles into his writing table. "Repeat yourself, sir. *If* there is the remotest truth to the blather you spewed, not only is Chadwick Theater ruined, my reputation will be smeared for the duration of eternity." His stomach roiled to the point of losing his breakfast. Either that or he was about to commit murder.

Mr. Howard Perkins, theater manager, raised his palms, stepping back as if he sensed his life was about to be smote. "Your Grace, I am simply the bearer of regrettable news."

"Regrettable?" Drake growled. "Profoundly catastrophic is more apt."

Perkins lowered his arms. "I concede our situation is gravely dire, but we must face the fact that Mademoiselle Taglioni was not on the ship. Furthermore, I'm told she has signed a continuation of her contract with the Paris Opera and refuses to come to London."

"Good God, are the French angling to start another war?" Despite that the disaster was egregiously infuriating, he'd been deceived on an international scale. How the devil was he to explain this to his patrons, to all those ticket holders anxious to see the opening of a grand spectacle? "Who else knows about this?"

"No one. I met Monsieur Travere and the troupe at the wharf, marshaled them into carriages and took them directly to the theater."

"And you left them there?"

"To come here, Your Grace."

Drake picked up the program he'd saved from the performance of *La Sylphide* in Paris. The cover featured a rendering of the famous ballerina for whom he'd paid a premium. A payment for which he would be seeking recompense.

"We have collected ticket revenues. The premiere is sold out. I spent countless hours entertaining benefactors with the promise of Marie Taglioni's London debut." He faced his man while solutions rifled through his mind. "Tell me, who have they sent in her place? Fanny Essler? Emilie Bigottini?"

Drake gave the globe a spin though, of course, when it drifted to a halt, bloody, bedamned Paris was facing him. The debut of his new theater had been years in the making—represented the culmination of his dreams. Drake's greatest passions? Theater. Opera. Ballet. Shakespeare. But dukes did not appear in operas, ballets, or plays. Dukes became benefactors and theater magnates.

In Paris he'd found the perfect ballet for the grand opening of Chadwick Theater. Marie Taglioni had stunned the world with her performance of *La Sylphide* and Drake had salivated at the chance to be the first to introduce such talent to England. Nothing like the diva's ethereal dancing had ever been seen in Britain. He'd promised all of London a phenomenal performance, an extravaganza, a display of epic brilliance.

"Ah…" Perkins looked to his shoes. A very bad sign. "Monsieur Travere extolled the competence of Taglioni's understudy."

"Understudy?" Drake boomed so loudly, his voice cracked. Without wasting one more tick of the clock, he marched for the door. "Do not tell me I have paid an outrageous sum to present the most acclaimed ballet of this century, and the Parisians had the gall to send an *understudy!*"

"That was exactly my response." Perkins scurried behind as Drake bounded down the stairs of his town home.

Pennyworth, Ravenscar's butler, met them in the entry with gloves, hat and cane at the ready. Drake took them, giving a nod of thanks while a footman opened the door. "And how did Travere suggest his troupe repay the hundreds of Londoners who purchased advance tickets?"

"He didn't."

Before descending to Half Moon Street, Drake shoved his hat atop his head and tugged on his gloves. "That's the first offense I must remedy."

By the time they'd marched the two-thirds of a mile to his new theater on Haymarket, Perkins was wheezing with beads of sweat streaming from his brow. Drake patted the man's back. "Stand straight, old friend. We need to don our battle armor for this confrontation."

Taking a deep breath, Drake glanced to the brass placard above the door bearing his family name gleaming in the afternoon sun. At the time, Chadwick Theater had a delightful ring, if not a tad vainglorious. He'd dreamed of elite members of the *ton* referring to Chadwicks over a cup of tea:

"Will I see you at Almacks tonight?" asks one.

"I could not possibly entertain attending a ball," responds another. *"No one can miss the debut of some-or-other ballet at*

Chadwicks…you haven't tickets? Oh my, that is a quandary. Opening night has been sold out for over a month."

With a grumble, he pushed inside. There would be no Chadwicks if he didn't sort out this dilemma posthaste. He'd be ruined. Even more abominable, his mother would be devastated, possibly forced to endure the rest of her days in far less comfort than she was entitled. He bristled, imagining the shock and disappointment on his mother's face when he broke the news. After the death of his father, the duchess' care and wellbeing had been Drake's first priority. Disappointing her with a black mark against the Ravenscar legacy would send her to an early grave.

Inside, the place was embroiled in chaos with hammers pounding above the relentless clatter of the pianoforte. The curtains were drawn on the stage where bedraggled dancers, still clad in traveling attire, queued in rows as they practiced *pliés* rather than rehearsing *La Sylphide.*

Drake planted his fists onto his hips and scanned the mayhem for their leader.

"There he is," said Perkins, pointing and leading the way toward a rather short gentleman who was in dire need of a shave.

"Travere, is it?" Drake asked in a low voice, eyeing the deceiver.

Appearing affronted, the man sneered. Unfortunately, Perkins stepped between them before the duke could brain the imbecile with a swing of his cane. "Monsieur Travere, allow me to introduce His Grace, Duke of Ravenscar—"

Drake grasped Perkins' shoulder and ushered him aside while he stepped so near the dance master, the man was forced to crane his neck. "Exactly what do you think you are about, coming to my theater with an understudy after I, in good faith, contracted Mademoiselle Taglioni for the Season?"

"I must—"

"She wasn't on the ship." He didn't like that he was growling at the Frenchman, but nothing save the famous ballerina would be astounding enough for the London crowd. How in God's name did Marchand expect him to meet the first payment due his lenders with an understudy?

"*Mais non*, but—"

"And you thought it was but a trifle to bring a substitute with no experience in her place?"

"Your Grace, you must—"

"Do you believe the English to be daft, uncivilized, and uncultured? Exactly how do you plan for a mere understudy to compensate me for my losses? You received payment in advance for Taglioni, the most famous ballerina in the history of dance, and you send me an untried, inexperienced, clumsy—"

"Your Grace!" Travere had the audacity to stamp his foot.

Annoyed by the man's arrogance, Drake stiffened before the dance master continued, "If you will allow me to speak, I shall ease your concern. Our replacement is every bit as talented as Mademoiselle Taglioni, possibly more so."

At the surge of blood thrumming at his temples, Drake took in a deep breath. "I doubt your claims are true. I saw the diva's performance at the Paris debut of *La Sylphide* and it was nothing short of stellar, hence my invitation for the privilege of opening what will become the most acclaimed theater in Britain." Drake threw up his arms, gesturing to the tiers of boxes festooned with gilt filigree and red brocade drapery. Even the ceiling had been painted with the final scene from *Romeo and Juliet* by England's own Thomas Webster. "No expense has been spared. Damn it all, sir, I paid for a grand spectacle!"

"And that is what you will receive." With an upturned palm, Travere curtly gestured to the aisle. "Please, if you will allow me to return to my duties, I have little time and much to accomplish."

Gaping, Drake exchanged flabbergasted glances with Perkins. Was the Frenchman completely dicked in the nob? Did he know he was addressing not only a duke, but the man who held his future success by the cods? Drake could ruin Travere—see to it the only position he could hope to attain was that of a dance master in an Australian penal colony.

"If I must remind you," he seethed through his teeth, "I am holding the purse to this production and I will remain where I stand until I have my due." He slammed the silver ball of his cane into his palm. "I ought to call an end to this sham and send you back from whence you came."

"Ahem, I'm afraid that would leave us in a quite untenable situation," Perkins edged in.

Drake folded his arms and gave the dance master a pointed frown. No one needed to tell him he was in a scrape with no place to go. If he sent the Parisians back to the Continent and demanded damages for the loss of his investment, he doubted he'd see a halfpenny. If he allowed the performance to go forward without Marie Taglioni, his self-respect would be damaged beyond repair. Mother had no idea the Pall Mall mansion had been put up for collateral. A matriarch of the *ton*, it would destroy her to move into a lesser home. And to add salt to the wound, Drake's wager with Percy would be forfeit.

He looked to the stage where three dancers halfheartedly marked their steps, doing nothing to calm his ire. "I'll need to see this fledgling whom you deem remarkable."

"I'm afraid that is not advisable." If Travere could pose any greater a buffoon, he'd just crossed the line. "Mademoiselle LeClair has been a day on a rocking ship in foul weather and before that, two days riding in a carriage from Paris to Calais. She will not be in ideal form until she has had a night of rest."

About to swallow his spleen, it took five and twenty years of practiced restraint to keep from wrapping his fingers around Travere's neck. "If I do not have the pleasure of witnessing a performance by your prodigy within the next quarter-hour, I will have you and your band of miscreants escorted off the premises with no passage home."

"All right then." Travere scratched his head, making his hair stand on end. Most likely, the man needed a good tot of rum, given these circumstances were presumably not of his doing. Nonetheless, he was the responsible party who had been sent to ensure the ballet was fit for the premiere opening of a grand theater. "If you will take a seat, I shall arrange for a demonstration."

"Thank you," said Perkins, though Drake wouldn't have wasted his breath.

"Mind you," the dance master added, "there will be no costumes and we will be working only with a rehearsal pianist."

"Good God, man!" Drake's spleen had finally burst. "Stop spitting excuses and see to your obligation."

Marching across the parterre, he opted not to sit in his second-tier center box. Rather, he stood at the back of the pit with his arms crossed. Mr. Perkins followed suit. Together, they waited without a word between them while Travere waved a baton and shouted orders in French, making dancers scurry about. The rehearsal pianist fumbled through pages of music as if he had no idea what he was doing. The stage had cleared by the time the accompanist flipped out his coattails, sat erect, his fingers at the ready, his gaze focused on the dance master.

Travere gave the man a nod and, after a few measures of introduction, a circle of ladies *bourréed* from stage left, their arms swaying above their heads like wheat. A cascade of scales accompanied each dancer as she, in turn, bent at the waist emulating the opening of a flower until only one remained in the center, her arms held in first position. Without the illumination of the gaslights, details blurred into silhouettes. The shadowy and remaining figure was smaller than the others and wore a dark traveling dress. The outline of her hair was disarrayed as if she had returned from the midst of a tempest.

"The unveiling of a dormouse," Drake growled behind his fingers.

Disastrous. If my mother suffers one day from the consequences of Marchand's backstabbing, I will call him out and show no mercy.

The music paused for a moment, then continued into another set of tumbling scales while Miss Dormouse appeared to float forward, opening her arms. Admittedly, her *port de bras* was reminiscent of the graceful revealing of a peacock's tail.

Drake ignored the whisper of tingles along the backs of his arms. He even considered calling a halt to the performance until his jaw dropped. With a whirlwind of notes, the ballerina commenced a mesmerizing display of twirls on the tips of her toes as Taglioni had done in Paris. However, Miss Mouse extended her leg so high in the air, Drake reached forward as if to prevent her from snapping in two. On the dance continued with a flurry of effortless grace. Then his heart stopped as she leaped so high in the air, it was as if a breeze had captured the woman and took her sailing aloft until she elegantly descended and performed a *glissade* into an *arabesque*, finishing with a *pirouette*.

When the music ended, a void spread through Drake's chest and refused to stop expanding until Perkins began to applaud. Suddenly realizing he'd just watched a woman dance so passionately that polite society would consider her movement lewd, he elbowed his theater manager in the arm.

"Did Travere mention the ballerina's name?" he whispered.

"LeClair, if my memory serves." Perkins waggled his brows. "She is astounding."

"Shocking is more apt."

The man grinned, deviousness filling his eyes. "Yes."

"But she's still plain."

"I disagree. I would classify the woman as perhaps…" The theater manager adjusted his spectacles thoughtfully. "An *enchantress.*"

"Hmm." Drake shifted his gaze to the ornate painting on the ceiling which alone had cost a fortune. *It's a damnable risk, but such beauty deserves to be seen.* "Lord save us, I will allow the premiere to go on as planned."

"Shall I inform Monsieur Travere?"

"It may lead to my ruination but do so." Heading for the door, Drake intended to slip home and drown his misery in a bottle of brandy. A theater bearing his name was opening four days hence with a young woman who danced like Beelzebub's mistress and who looked like… *Not a dormouse.*

Who knew what the gaslights would reveal come opening night?

Damnation, I am doomed.

***

Before he made it outside, a man dressed in full-length trousers and a woolen doublet stepped from the shadows, his neckcloth uneven and hastily tied as if he could ill afford a valet. "Yer Grace, Maxwell with the *Morning Post* 'ere."

Drake stopped. Wonderful. The vultures had already begun to descend, posturing to pick the remains of his carcass.

"Is it true Marie Taglioni gave ye the slip?" The meddler sounded as if he'd just arisen from the bowels of the East End.

Drake should have ignored the impertinence and kept going but he didn't. "Where the devil did you hear that?"

"Sailors off the ship, Yer Grace. Said ye're in more trouble 'an King Charlie at Whitehall."

"They are mistaken, I assure you."

"I've seen the passenger manifest. Taglioni wasn't aboard. Wha' ye aim to do? Will Chadwicks still open come Tuesday?"

Well, the bird had already flown and a day hadn't yet passed. *May as well set things in motion and cause a real stir.* "Did the sailors not tell you?" Drake leveled his gaze with the journalist's.

"Can't say they did." Licking his lips, the man leaned in, clearly hungry for a scandal and all too eager to report the news of His Grace's impending ruination. Once Drake's lenders caught wind of imminent disaster, they'd be pushing for early payment, eager to claim the premium real estate occupied by Ravenscar Hall.

"I'll only say this once." Drake tapped the tip of his cane on the floor. "Chadwick Theater will open as planned, debuting a mystery ballerina."

"Cor." The man gaped with wide eyes. "But people 'ave paid to see Taglioni."

"They have, and I will not honor one single request for an advance refund. If, after the performance, Chadwick's patrons are not satisfied, the theater will consider any reasonable appeal for reimbursement."

"She's that good, eh?"

"We shall find out Tuesday evening, shall we not?"

"If ye please, can ye give us 'er name?"

"Mademoiselle LeClair. I tell you here and now, London will be dazzled with talent never before seen on the stage." Drake tugged up his gloves. "Good day, sir."

He strode away, swinging his cane as if he hadn't a care. Unfortunately, the tempest swirling in his chest was as ominous as the thunder overhead. And droplets slapping his face served as dancing pixies sent from Satan come to laugh at his demise.

Chapter Two

Bria dropped onto a chair in the backstage dressing room and rubbed her neck. Traveling had taken its toll, but she mustn't give in to exhaustion. For the first time in days, she was finally able to stretch her legs and dance. Being confined in a carriage and then the steamer packet across the channel had all but suffocated her. And then Monsieur Travere had been cajoled into giving a demonstration for the Duke of Ravenscar and Mr. Perkins. Did they not know dancers couldn't step off a ship and deliver their best? Goodness, she'd spent the entire sea leg of the voyage on deck with her head over the rail.

To her chagrin, she'd given the worst performance of her life. At least it felt miserable. Wearing soiled traveling clothes, weary, and half-starved, who would not feel miserable? She'd been astounded afterward when Mr. Perkins came forward and told them the ballet would open as planned. Throughout the demonstration, Bria was convinced the duke would make good on his threats and send them away. And all because of her. The man had spoken harshly when he'd confronted the dance master—had judged her before she'd been given a chance to rest and perform at her best. Of course, His Grace couldn't know dancing the lead role was her life's ambition.

Neither did he know she would expel every ounce of strength she possessed to ensure the theater's debut was a success.

If Chadwick Theater failed, she would fail, and Britannia LeClair had worked too hard and fought too many battles to be humiliated and sent back to Paris as a national disappointment.

Removing her slipper, she massaged her toes. She should have realized the proprietor of Chadwick Theater would be angry, though neither Messieurs Marchand nor Travere had indicated the Duke of Ravenscar had not been informed that Marie had decided to stay in Paris. No wonder His Grace was furious. But his fury burned as if a flame had burst inside her. His words instilled doubt in her abilities.

And he'd made her so self-aware standing in the parterre looking as noble as the King of England—no doubt passing judgement like a king as well.

Somehow, in the next four days she needed to recondition and regain her polish lest she not be ready for Tuesday's debut. If Ravenscar had truly been deceived, then she had naught but to give a performance as never before seen on the stage either in Paris or London. If he sent her home, her dancing career would be ruined—a travesty that would crush Bria to her very soul.

What would she do then? Without a reputation behind her, if the London debut of *La Sylphide* failed, all hope would be lost. Thespians without prestige and notoriety were not trusted anywhere in Christendom. They were looked upon as vagabonds and thieves. She'd end up destitute, lucky to find a position as a serving wench in an alehouse, destined for a life of poverty.

"Ah, here's the *fille* who kept us from a wretched disaster," Pauline, Bria's only trusted friend, walked into the dressing room, her arms filled with gossamer and tulle costumes.

Florrie, who danced the part of Effie, flounced in behind, carrying nothing, of course. "*Oui*, if it weren't for your *grand jeté* at the end of the sequence, I think the duke would have sent us away before I got to know him better." The girl was forever prowling about for a benefactor. Bria believed the only reason Florrie continued to dance supporting roles was to find a wealthy nobleman to set her up in lavish style. In truth, most of the girls in the troupe were waiting for opportunities to charm a gentleman into establishing them in comfortable accommodations.

She switched feet, working her fingers from the arch to her toes. "I cannot believe he spoke to Henri Travere disrespectfully. I've never seen anyone be so bold before."

"I agree, though it was rather fun to watch," said Pauline. "If His Grace weren't such a large man, I believe Monsieur Travere would have escorted him outside. Besides, did you see that weapon he was carrying?"

"His cane?" Bria asked. She'd noticed the piece, elegantly finishing off the duke's pristine appearance. In truth, every dancer on stage had audibly sighed when the man boldly strode through the parterre, elegant beaver hat in hand, elaborately tied neckcloth, well-cut coat and skintight pantaloons trimmed by a pair of gleaming Hessian boots. Pity he wasn't a danseur as such a masculine specimen would command the stage in any performance.

"It had a silver ball on one end." Pauline drew Bria from her thoughts. "A gentleman's weapon for certain."

Florrie licked her lips. "Do you think it was pure silver?"

"Of course," Pauline insisted. "Ravenscar footed the bill for Chadwicks. Did you see the painting on the ceiling? Word is the duke is one of the wealthiest men in England."

"Then I'm doubly glad he was amenable in the end," Florrie said, waggling her shoulders, the tart. "Did you see him? He looked like the prince of darkness."

"The prince of dreaaaaams." Pauline twirled in place.

Florrie clasped her hands over her heart. "I want him. Do you think he already has a mistress?"

Looking to the ceiling, Bria jammed the heels of her hands against her temples. "*Mon Dieu*, you're not here for an entire day and you've already set your sights on a duke."

"And why should I not?"

"Because his class looks upon us as fallen women," Bria replied. "We have absolutely no chance of marrying anyone from polite society."

"Your vision is full of stardust." Rolling her eyes, Florrie snorted. "Who said anything about marriage?"

"Perhaps you should keep your options open," said Pauline. "We'll all need benefactors of some sort sooner or later."

"I strongly object." Bria shoved her feet back into her slippers and stood. "I did not come to London to become someone's mistress."

"Is that so, Madame High and Mighty?" asked Florrie. "Thespians do not marry outside their class and, in ballet, women outnumber the men three to one. You will not be nineteen for the rest of your days. And it is unlikely you'll be dancing past six and twenty."

Bria arched her eyebrow, giving the fortune hunter a purse-lipped frown. "Whyever not? Gardel came out of retirement at thirty."

"For a year." Grumbling, Florrie plopped her makeup valise on an open toilette. Brand new and smelling of lacquer and fresh paint, the dressing room for the principal women contained five toilettes with mirrors, which allowed for the three leads and two understudies.

Glancing to Pauline for support, Bria stood her ground. "A woman can aspire to other pursuits." She tried to sound convincing, but everyone knew if her stage debut was not a success, there would be little chance of ever being anything but a member of the *corps*.

"Why are you so contrary to the notion of becoming a gentleman's mistress?" Pauline asked, the turncoat. "Truly, all the great vocalists and ballerinas have benefactors. 'Tis the way of things, and come Tuesday you will be in the starlight. Men will be interested."

"Wealthy men," Florrie added. "Excepting Ravenscar. He is mine."

Noticing a tear in one of her slipper ribbons, Bria fished in her sewing kit for a needle and thread and set to mending. What would she do if she were forced to leave the stage? Change her name? Forge references and become a governess? That might work until she was found out and thrown into prison. Still, if she didn't set the bar high for herself, no one would—and nary a soul would give a fig.

"I want no part in charming a man merely for his wealth. What happens when the dancer loses her looks or the gentleman grows tired of his mistress? She ends up out in the cold without a single silver coin in her reticule."

Rouge pot in hand, Florrie leaned closer to the mirror. "That's why a girl must strive to please her benefactor, then she'll have nothing to worry about. If you continue to keep your legs crossed, you'll be finished by the age of six and twenty with nowhere to go."

But Florrie hadn't been abandoned at the age of fourteen. In the past five years, Bria had scratched and clawed for her hard-won success, learning the brutal lesson not to rely on others for anything. "Who knows, perhaps someday I'll be lucky, fall in love, and marry." If there was one thing Bria craved more than dancing, it was to have a family of her own. But she wasn't about to say that in front of Florrie—who knew how the girl would use such information against her at the most inopportune time? Goodness, she hadn't even told Pauline about her dreams to be a mother, have a hoard of children to love and cherish, to no longer be alone.

"I'll always have somewhere to go," Bria added, trying to sound self-assured. Bless it, she would struggle for the rest of her days if she must.

"I wish I had your confidence," said Pauline.

"I'd call it arrogance," Florrie added.

Bria didn't care to argue. Was she confident? Yes, she had to be in order to withstand Messieurs Travere and Marchand. Toes bleeding, she had worked hard every day to ensure she kept a place in the *corps de ballet,* and it was no windfall last year when she'd earned the right to be Taglioni's understudy. What would she do when she was six and twenty? Heaven's stars, that was seven years away. How could she think that far ahead when there was so much to concern herself with now? She tied a knot and snipped the thread. A woman of six and twenty was still in her prime. Bria practiced more and worked harder than any of the others. Why would she not be able to continue dancing at least until she found a decent man with whom to raise a family?

Still, doubt pulled at her insides. What if something happened? What would she do if she were gravely injured?

I know what I would not do.

"Come." Pauline tugged Bria's arm. "We're all tired. Let's go see the boarding house we'll be calling home through August."

"You go ahead with the others." She pulled away. "I must rehearse."

"You cannot be serious," said Florrie. "Everyone is exhausted. You have dark circles under your eyes. If you stay any longer, you'll make yourself ill."

Bria held up her hands. "I disagree. My legs are stiff from traveling and I'm not about to step on stage for our premiere without being in peak condition."

Pauline looked her from head to toe. "No one is in better condition than you."

"That's because I practice more than everyone else." Bria sighed, giving her friend an appreciative smile, grateful to have someone who cared.

Pushing to her feet, she headed for the stage while the other two followed.

Florrie tapped her shoulder. "It isn't safe to venture out alone."

"The boarding house is only three blocks away. I'll be fine." Stretching her arms over her head, Bria bent from side to side.

"Very well, *mon amie*." Pauline gave her a peck on the cheek. "But do not stay for more than an hour. Someone needs to look after your care and, since you're averse to it, I'm taking a stand."

"Thank you." Bria squeezed her friend's hand. "I do appreciate your concern."

With a snort, Florrie flounced out behind Pauline, much the same as she had flounced into the dressing room. Bria shook her head. Truth be told, Florrie, a daughter of two principal dancers, had loads of natural ability but the girl was lazy. Both Pauline and Bria had to work like beasts of burden to earn their places in the company, though even Pauline had a better pedigree. Her father was a composer.

Honestly, Bria had no idea what her pedigree might be. Once she'd started earning a meager wage, she had made inquiries and was still clueless as to the identity of the woman in the miniature from the wooden box she'd found the day before she'd been mercilessly turned out of the home she loved. The box had contained no memorandum, only a brass plate engraved with one name, "Britannia". Not long after she'd arrived in Paris, she asked Monsieur Marchand what he knew about Sarah Parker and had only learned that the woman she'd once believed to be her mother had, indeed, been a member of the *corps* and was the daughter of an English vicar and had been well educated.

***

As Bria moved to center stage, she looked over each shoulder to ensure she was alone, then she slid down until her legs were stretched as far to the sides as humanly possible. She lay her stomach on the floor, holding the position, willing her mind to embrace the pain. No, sliding into this pose was not ladylike for a female dancer but, in private, Bria worked through a number of exercises of her own design to improve her flexibility and strength. Some she'd learned as a child and others she'd copied from the male dancers and made them her own, each intended to give her an edge against her competition.

After four years in the *corps de ballet*, Bria had fought her way past protégés like Florrie, though she'd only stepped in for Taglioni a few times at the famous *Salle Le Peletier*. This trip to London was Bria's chance to prove she was worthy— worthy in her own right. This was her opportunity to prove she was as good as everyone else out there who knew who their parents were, who had a sense of identity. Bria's mother—the only mother figure she knew—had introduced her to dance, and she'd embraced it with every fiber of her being. Ballet had become her sole master. It possessed her, drove her, consumed her.

After stretching and already warmed up from rehearsal, she started in on *changements*, one hundred of them, followed by *grands battements* then leaps, one after another in quick succession around and around the stage as she breathed life into her limbs and willed away the stiffness caused by the past days of traveling. Her last *grand jeté* took so much effort, she landed with a huff. Crouching, her hands on her knees, she panted and fought to catch her breath. "*Merde, je suis fatiguée.*"

"*Je comprends porquoi*," said a deep voice from the wings.

Britannia jolted upright, her heart racing. "Who's there?"

The Duke of Ravenscar meandered from the abyss of black curtains and onto the stage, his gaze trained on her. Bria clasped her hands under her chin and scooted back as he neared. The man was nearly twice her size, black hair, startling eyes—vibrant blue like the color of a shallow sea. When he'd been speaking to Monsieur Travere on the parterre, he'd appeared poised and severe but now, looming so near, he was nothing short of dominating. "*Parlez-vous anglais?*" he asked, his French practiced, but not Parisian.

She stood her ground and lowered her arms. She must not show fear, not to the man who held her future in the palm of his hand. Bria had faced powerful men before and the only way to earn their respect was to project an air of confidence no matter how much her insides quaked. "I do, Your Grace. Latin as well."

"Surprising for a…" His voice trailed off as he rubbed his neck and glanced away. Goodness he was imposing and, as everyone had noticed, well-formed.

"A ballerina?" she ventured, too aware of the poor opinion society harbored for artisans. Truth be told, the Paris Opera Ballet was infamous as being the "nation's harem". Nonetheless, what was true for some did not apply to all, and Bria's love of her craft would not be sullied by falling victim to the wiles of men.

"Yes," he agreed, "women in your profession are not known for their…ah…intellect."

Her spine shot to rigid with a jolt. "I emphatically disagree with you on that point. To be proficient one must be shrewd and learn quickly."

"Ah…perhaps that's why you're dancing the lead role. Forgive me if I was unduly coarse." Dark, expressive eyebrows drew together. Heavens, his gaze disarmed her. "Your English is very good."

"'Tis better than your French, if I may speak boldly, Your Grace."

Full lips formed an "O" for a moment before he bowed his head. "Why not? And generally speaking, I do not believe I've ever met a dancer who was well-versed in Latin."

"True. I am an oddity in many ways." Bria's stomach squeezed while she studied him—virile, confident, aloof. *Commanding.* What was he up to? Hadn't he already left the theater? "Forgive me, but have you come to see Monsieur Travere? I'm afraid he has retired for the evening."

"Actually, I was hoping to gain an audience with you, if I may." The duke took a step forward, his cane tapping the floor.

"Me?" She gulped, eyeing the weapon before she shifted her gaze back to His Grace. He had the stature to wield the silver ball on his cane like a medieval flail—pillaging his way through England, winning the hearts of damsels who fell victim to his smoldering gaze. She could imagine him as a black knight riding an enormous stallion, leading his army in the crusades—

"Indeed," he said, drawing Bria from her musings. He seemed not to notice any trepidation on her part. In fact, his lofty demeanor relaxed a little with a half-smile...well, at least she didn't *feel* threatened—a tad muddled was more apt.

"Whilst I was walking in the rain," he continued, "it came to me that I needed a meaty tidbit of information about you to dangle before society to include in Tuesday morning's papers. Something to make them salivate."

"I hardly see lords and ladies salivating."

"Madam, we are about to open my new theater with ballet billeted to be the London debut of the most famous dancer in the civilized world and, as of tomorrow, all of society will find an understudy has come to perform in her place." Those vibrant eyes grew dark, his countenance serious again. "The nobility to whom you refer are like dogs to a bone when it comes to gossip. And they will be gnashing their teeth to see me fail. I need something upon which to direct their attentions. What about your parentage? Are you the daughter of a great choreographer perchance?"

Her mouth dropped open. What should she say? *Help!* "I am not," she squeaked.

"A famed composer, a renowned danseur?"

Bria shook her head, lead sinking to her toes. She couldn't lie, but the truth might mean the end of her dreams.

"What about the offspring of a count or someone of note?" he continued, oblivious to her discomfort. "That must be it. Your English is far better than most Parisians I've met on my travels. Come now, you must give me something— something astounding."

She backed away, shifting her gaze to her toes while her lowly birth hung on her neck with the weight of an anvil. "I'm sorry to disappoint you but my life to date has been rather dull. I was raised by an Englishwoman and her merchant husband in a provincial French village."

"Raised, did you say?" His eyebrows slanted inward. "Who were your parents?"

Praying His Grace wouldn't do something rash like cancel the premiere, Bria raised her chin and squared her shoulders. If she didn't tell him, someone like Florrie would be all too happy to impart the brutal truth. "I never knew them. I thought Monsieur and Madame LeClair were my parents until their deaths, whereupon I discovered I am a foundling."

"Foundling?" With a grumble, he chopped his cane through the air "That simply won't do."

Bria's stomach chose this moment to growl loudly. Feeling a bit lightheaded, she started to slide toward the wings while Ravenscar paced and raked his fingers through his thick black hair. "Dash it, you could have at least been raised by an abbess…or a king from the Orient. That would have been exotic."

Watching the silver ball on his makeshift weapon, she stole another step toward the exit. "Is the truth not scandalous enough?"

"It is not," he said as if she'd just failed her exams. "I daresay, 'Come see the new mystery ballerina, progeny of the Duke of Anjou,' would be far more interesting than, 'Come see the foundling who was hidden in provincial France by an English woman for fourteen years'."

"When you put it that way, I think my past does sound mysterious and scandalous. In truth, I much prefer the latter to your conjuring of Anjou."

His eyebrow shot up. "Opinionated are you not?"

"I'm told 'tis my most annoying trait."

"Hmm. But I'd still like something more." Stroking his chin, his dark gaze spilled all the way from her head to her toes. "Tell me about your education."

"*Maman*, er, Madame LeClair was from a gentle family. She taught me everything from mathematics and languages to history and dance. When I entered the Paris Opera Ballet School, I continued my studies when I wasn't dancing, of course."

Ravenscar resumed his pacing. "Well, that's about as exciting as reading *The Mirror of the Graces*."

"*The Mirror of the…*?"

"*Graces*. It is a lady's journal of correct form and, by my oath, the person who wrote it must have been a humorless crone."

The man was insufferable. "I'm sorry to have disappointed you. I hope my dancing will be far more inspiring." Bria curtsied. "If you will excuse me, Your Grace, I'm very tired."

"Apologies." He bowed, his action every bit as poised and controlled as a danseur. "I have been thoughtless. I shouldn't have kept you."

For a moment, she tried to think of a witty remark to prove her determination. After all, they both had a great deal riding on Tuesday's debut. Wishing him well would sound trite. Telling him she would do her best might come across as pallid. What if she let them all down? What if the London crowd detested her?

"Good evening," she managed before spinning on her heel. Bria hadn't intended to swoon. But having expelled a great deal of energy throughout the day after enduring a bout of sea sickness on the paddle-steamer that ferried them from Calais, her fortitude wasn't what it should have been. The stage spun. Unable to clear her vision, she raised the back of her hand to her forehead.

The next thing she knew, the Duke of Ravenscar swept her into his arms. Surrounded by warmth, the power in his embrace imparted succor she'd seldom experienced. Kindness, human touch, tenderness—things she'd once taken for granted but hadn't been blessed with in years. Turning her head toward him, she inhaled, swathed in the scent of fresh linen and exotic spice. Too overcome to push away, her eyes fluttered closed as she took one more blissful sniff of heaven.

***

Drake recognized the ballerina was slight, but when she fell into his arms, she seemed as if she were made of gossamer and lace, and fragile as a bird. *A foundling?* How did this delicate creature manage to survive among the snakes who infested the world of ballet? "Good heavens. Are you unwell?"

"Forgive me." Miss LeClair's eyes rolled back as she brushed lithe fingers across her hair. "I suffered sea sickness, and I haven't eaten in two days."

Two days? Who the hell did Travere think he was, starving his dancers? Not daring to set her on her feet, Drake carried the woman to a chair, practically swooning himself as he breathed in the heady scent of female. Delicate, floral bouquets in a myriad of varieties made him dip his nose and inhale more deeply. "Why didn't you leave for the boarding house with the others?" he asked while identifying wisteria as the most potent flower in her potpourri.

"I needed to practice. You said yourself, the theater's patrons will be angered when they discover Mademoiselle Taglioni will not be performing. I cannot let them down. I must not!"

Stepping back, he straightened his cuffs. "Well, you won't receive any ovations if you swoon on stage and are unable to dance."

"Please do not think ill of me." Miss LeClair pressed a dainty hand to her cheek. One he wished to touch to see if it was as silken as it appeared. "I've never actually swooned before. When the ship arrived, the thought of food soured my stomach. I'm sure once I've eaten, I'll be fine. I promise I will."

He shook his damnable thoughts from his head. His dreams might possibly crumble around his feet and there he stood musing about soft cheeks and heady fragrances. For the love of God, if this dancer did not regain her strength, he could kiss his venture goodbye. Dash Travere, where was the theater's hospitality? "Mr. Perkins hasn't fed you? What about the others? I must order food to be catered at once."

"No, no. Luncheon was served. I was too queasy to eat."

"Let it not be said the Duke of Ravenscar ignores his performers' basic needs. Especially the ballerina responsible for the lion's share of my investment. I will personally see you suitably fed."

"Oh, no, thank you. I'm certain they'll have a warm meal at the boarding house." Miss LeClair scooted to the edge of the chair. "In fact, I must make haste before I miss supper."

"Absolutely not." He held up his palm to prevent her from standing. "I forbid it. I will take you where you can find a proper meal."

"I beg your pardon? You may be the owner of this theater, but it is not your place to dictate where I choose to dine." Squaring her shoulders, the imp swayed on the seat. A bit outspoken, but she demonstrated a backbone. Usually people held their tongues when confronting a duke. Miss LeClair seemed quite oblivious to the norm.

"At the moment, I disagree. You are not the only one who will be ruined if *La Sylphide* is a failure." Planting his fists on his hips, Drake leaned toward her for added emphasis. "And I'm not accustomed to failing."

"Nor am I."

"I am glad we agree. Come now, as your employer, I insist."

She met his gaze with an indignant strength he rarely ever saw in any woman—she might be petite, but he guessed she had the heart of a lion. *How else did she end up playing the lead in my theater?* Drake swallowed, studying the power of her will as it radiated about her. *The foundling who should be queen.*

The light on stage was rather dim, but the woman had the most soulful eyes. Were they brown? Unable to ascertain for certain, he offered his elbow. "I'll hail a coach."

She hesitated.

The corner of his mouth ticked up. "Or I can simply toss you over my shoulder."

She didn't bat an eyelash. "That won't be necessary, thank you."

Drake never asked his groom to hitch a carriage or saddle a horse for a casual jaunt of less than a mile. A man needed fresh air and exercise daily. He had friends who walked little, and they were all growing thick around the middle. But at the moment, he rued not having a town coach in which to make a stealthy exit.

It couldn't be helped. The papers already had their story for the morrow, and it certainly would provide society with interesting conversation over Easter dinner. Perhaps in hindsight, it was a boon to have scheduled the premiere of *La Sylphide* for the day after the holidays. The *ton* would have less time to gossip.

Chapter Three

Shaking from hunger, Bria accepted Ravenscar's hand and alighted from the hackney. Though he wore gloves, the power beneath the leather made gooseflesh rise on her arm. She stole a glance at his profile—a bold nose, chiseled chin, and black hair that brushed his nape.

If only he were old and crusty, she might be more comfortable sharing a meal with a man of his station. Shabby from her travels, she was in no state of dress to be parading about town, especially with a duke. But Ravenscar had promised a simple meal after which he'd see her to her accommodations. How could she refuse such kindness from the gentleman who owned the theater where she was to perform for the next four months, especially when he'd caught her mid-swoon? *I swooned, for heaven's sake.*

At least her reasoning to accompany him was sound until she realized he hadn't taken her to a tearoom or even an alehouse. They stood on a residential street lined by rows of elegant town houses. She took a step toward the coach which had already started away from the curb. "Wait!"

The coachman didn't bother to turn, blast him.

Pleasing to the eye or not, she whipped around and faced the duke. "Your Grace, you said you were going to take me to a place where we could eat. Clearly this is a residence." She flung her hand toward the door. "Is this not your home?"

"Indeed, it is. One of them, anyway. The Dowager Duchess of Ravenscar occupies my mansion on Pall Mall. This humble abode suits me, however." Swinging his walking stick, he started up the steps. Did he oft bring unmarried dancers to his home just to feed them? What if he tried to take advantage of her behind closed doors? Duke or not, she mustn't allow him liberties.

Bria pressed her palms to her face to stop her lightheadedness. "I cannot go in there."

His Grace stretched his arms to his sides. "Whyever not? You'll eat better here than at your boarding house."

Because I'm not about to let you charm me into thinking our association can be anything other than dancer and theater owner. "It wouldn't be proper."

"Pardon?" A pinch formed between his brows. "Earlier you told me you are a foundling from a village in provincial France. Clearly you're not a debutante being cosseted by a mother hen. Are you worried about your reputation?"

She raised her chin and straightened, though stretching to her full height was fruitless. "I am very concerned with how I look in the public eye. I do not want people to think me a woman of easy virtue."

"Then I suggest you should have opted for another profession. A governess, perchance?" He chuckled while he gestured north and south. "To ease your trepidation, allow me to say this; all of society is embroiled in Easter preparations and festivities. There's nary a soul about this eve. Besides, not but a quarter-hour ago you collapsed in my arms and admitted to being starved half to death. I'll not be accused as the duke who turned his back on his theater's hungry ballerina."

Groaning, Bria clamped her fingers around her cloak's collar, squeezing the neckline taut. "But you didn't say you were taking me to your home. You said you knew just the place."

He grinned—good heavens, he could make the entire cast of *La Sylphide* swoon when the corners of his mouth turned up—straight white teeth, eyes sparkling like stars. "That is because I do. My cook is one of the finest in London. My table mightn't be as formal as my mother's, but I assure you, when my carriage returns you to your boarding house, you will be sublimely satiated."

Bria pursed her lips. Obviously, since she was a mere artisan, Ravenscar thought nothing about how it might appear for her to be entertained alone…within his town house. True, she was of the working class, but she still had values. "If anyone in the troupe discovers you have dined with me privately, they will assume the worst, especially Monsieur Travere."

"Well then, we'd best hasten inside before someone happens past."

She brandished her reticule while she scooted away.

Tall, bold and entirely insufferable, he stepped very near. "Miss LeClair, presently no Londoners have any idea who you are and, therefore, anyone who may be hiding behind a lamp post will have absolutely nothing to gossip about unless it is that I am keeping company with a housemaid."

"A housemaid?" If only she had a weapon as sturdy as His Grace's cane, she might thump him with it. "Do you think insulting me will aid in your effort to coax me into your home?"

"Dash it all, that's not what I meant. I was referring to our master-servant status." His expression softened while his gaze slipped to her skirts. "Forgive me. My housemaid comment was unfeeling and brash, though I imagine you are not wearing the finest gown in your wardrobe."

Bria followed his gaze. She'd been wearing the same traveling dress for nearly a week. Not that she could afford many dresses, but this one looked the worse for wear. Wrinkled, stained, the hem muddied. For days she'd been hankering for a bath and a change of clothes.

"Now, shall we proceed inside? You have my word that I will ensure you enjoy a substantial meal after which my coachman will take you home. Allow me to also add; on the topic of your esteemed virtue, you have nothing to fear from me." He bowed, gesturing up the steps, looking every bit the composed and cocksure duke. "Shall we, or would you prefer I call for a tray to be brought out to the footpath?"

Ravenscar's argument only served to make Bria's head spin and the last thing she needed was to collapse in front of His Grace once more. What if he decided she was unfit to perform? Then Florrie would dance the part of the Sylph and she was hopeless at toe dancing. Good heavens, if Bria fainted, she might again end up with those brawny arms wrapped around her or, worse, carried upstairs to a bedchamber while the duke called for a physician. Notwithstanding of the circumstances, far more calamitous for her debut, bedrest might be ordered, and she'd never be ready for opening night.

Florrie will not dance in my place, I swear it!

Bria took in a reviving breath, grasped her skirts, held them to the right and only high enough to ascend the steps. Thank heavens *Maman* had taught her something about how to behave amongst polite society, lest she be completely flummoxed. "I thank you for your concern. But please understand I am accepting your hospitality because you put forth a convincing argument and assured me of your honorable intentions." She would enjoy a simple meal then hasten to the boarding house with no one the wiser.

"What is it about you?" he asked, opening the door, those vibrant blues growing dark again.

"I beg your pardon?" Watching him, she stumbled forward. She, a ballerina about to debut in London managed to trip her way into the Duke of Ravenscar's town house.

"'Tis naught but a trifle." He ignored her clumsiness. "Only…" Squinting with one eyebrow arched, he studied her as if she posed an unsolvable puzzle.

"Yes?"

"You are nothing like what I expected."

She clutched her reticule with both hands. "With all due respect, you cannot say something like that and assume I will brush it under the carpet. What, pray tell, were you expecting?"

"I anticipated you might be more tractable—a bit of a shrinking violet."

"Hardly. I have been on my own for five years and if I cowered to powerful people, I would presently be no more than a street urchin," she said, stepping further into the entry, still shaking and starved.

Vaguely, Bria noted the opulent simplicity of the duke's abode as he guided her through the entry. The immediate impression was that of masculinity. An enormous portrait of a black stallion greeted them, stark, dark-wood furniture, green and white striped wallpaper, tasteful, unpretentious wainscoting. The décor was simple, exquisite, and uncluttered.

"Pennyworth," Ravenscar said to a man in black coattails and white gloves who could be none other than the butler. "This is Miss LeClair. She took ill on the voyage from Calais and is in sore need of sustenance. Please tell Cook we must be fed immediately."

The man's gaze shifted to Bria but revealed no judgement on his part. "Straightaway, Your Grace." He had gray-streaked, thinning hair atop his head, which seemed to have migrated down to his hedgerow of eyebrows—a long nose, hollowed cheeks. He wasn't quite as tall as his master. After bowing, the butler left them.

Bria glanced from the closed door to the very large, devilishly handsome and domineering duke who owed her a well-prepared meal. "Shall we?"

***

Seated at the dining table with ample light, Drake studied the ballerina from behind his wine glass. He hadn't expected Miss LeClair to be so young, but then performers were usually young unless they were well established in their professions. Upon their arrival, she'd asked to freshen up, emerging from the withdrawing room with her hair smoothed, her face and hands washed, and a darling smile— one worthy of a halo of wisteria. Now that she'd also imbibed in a few sips of sherry, a bit of color had sprung in her cheeks. As a general rule, he preferred more full-figured women. But there was something about this dancer he couldn't put his finger on and he had a blasted time preventing himself from staring at her.

Whisky. That was it. The color of her eyes was that of aged whisky. Soulful, expressive, and luminous, they were wideset, but not too wide. And the lady's hair wasn't brown. It was more like cinnamon with wisps of fairer blonde framing her face. Her eyebrows were expressively defined, and her eyelids drooped a tad as if she were tired, which anyone would be after an arduous journey. A straight nose suited her face. But was it her mouth that enticed him? Her lips weren't thin as were many of the constant stream of heiresses introduced by his doting mother. On the contrary, Miss LeClair's lips were full, and the corners turned up a tad in repose.

She held her glass in a dainty hand and took a sip. Those whisky eyes met his for the briefest of moments before she blushed and set the glass down. Seeming to study the cut of the crystal, she traced her finger along the stem. "I mustn't drink any more."

As if on cue, a footman arrived with pastries and a soup tureen.

"Ah, sustenance. This will set you to rights." Drake sat back while they were served, pleased to see Miss LeClair select the largest pastry on the platter, take up the correct knife, slice it in two, then try to look well-mannered while she shoved it into her mouth.

"Mm," she moaned, her eyes losing focus.

Good God, the dancer's enraptured face looked as erotic as a woman pleasured. Drake shifted in his seat. Miss LeClair posed a picture of feminine innocence, not one of Aphrodite. He would stop staring this instant.

"Coming to London when so many patrons have quite high expectations must be unsettling," he said.

She gulped down her bite. "Somewhat, though I am thrilled to be given a chance."

"How long have you known you would be dancing in Mademoiselle Taglioni's place?"

"I was only told two weeks before we left Paris, though I have been Marie's understudy since *La Sylphide* opened last March."

What was this? She was advised a fortnight before, yet Monsieur Marchand hadn't bothered to send word ahead? The man most likely had known of Taglioni's intentions months in advance. The bloody backstabber had set him up for failure. Well, Drake wasn't about to lie down and allow a Frenchman to take advantage. First thing after the holidays, he planned to have his solicitor renegotiate the contract at the very least.

If only Miss LeClair had given him some tidbit of information to make patrons curious, he might be able to assuage a riot before opening night. "Tell me about your childhood."

She took two spoonsful of soup before she said a word. "Must you know more? I've already explained my past."

He watched the candlelight flicker in the reflection of his silver knife. "Taglioni is the daughter of a renowned choreographer. She pioneered toe dancing. That, in and of itself, would have ensured Chadwick Theater would be sold out for the Season."

With a turn of her head, Miss LeClair's chin rose, delicate eyebrows arched pridefully. "As you saw, I dance on point as well. We've worked to reinforce the slippers to make dancing appear more effortless. In fact, I'd like to think I was instrumental in perfecting toe dancing."

"Interesting point. But what else? Go back to your time in Bayeux."

"As I said before, I didn't even know I was a foundling until the couple who cared for me died."

"Both passed at the same time? Was there an accident?"

"Smallpox. Those were the darkest days of my life." Her shoulders fell a tad. "I was the only one in the village who would tend them—not even the physician would come."

The memory of Miss LeClair in his arms weighed on him. She'd seemed frail. Though he suspected her will might be forged from iron. Drake's gut twisted. Her past had been haunting, and it made him want to cradle her to his breast and vow to be her protector from this day forward. "How awful for you, and at such a young age. 'Tis a miracle you survived."

"A miracle, perhaps, but the people of Bayeux branded me a demon." She took another spoonful of soup, leaving a tad of moisture glistening on her lip.

"Is that when you went to Paris?" Drake's tongue slipped to the corner of his mouth. What would it taste like to kiss her? Would she respond with the same passion she showed on stage?

Good God, I will stop forthwith!

"*Oui*." She glanced away as if there might be more to her woeful story.

Drake thought of more important matters while the tureen was cleared and replaced by a roasted goose and leg of mutton. At least he tried to think of more important matters.

"Another course?" Miss LeClair asked.

"There will be three. Eat your fill."

Drake stared at the candle flame, pondering the possible headlines for Tuesday morning's paper. *Ballerina and toe dancer extraordinaire who escaped the grips of the Angel of Death? A foundling who rose from the bowels of Paris like a shooting star?* He tapped his fingers. Such statements would whet the appetites of the curious. He would dispatch a letter to Mr. Maxwell at the *Post* straightaway.

Drake finished his wine, suddenly curious to know her given name. Was it something exotic like Brielle, Evlina, or Alegra? By the way she danced, lively Alegra would suit her ideally. But he wouldn't be so bold as to ask. The mystery would be solved as soon as Mr. Perkins had the programs reprinted.

A footman bowed with carving knife and fork in hand. "What is your pleasure, miss?"

"A bit of both, please."

Drake held up his glass to be filled. "I'll have the same."

"With a side of cauliflower?" asked Pennyworth, giving a nod to a footman who'd just entered with the vegetables.

"Thank you," Miss LeClair mumbled, her mouth already full. For such a diminutive person, the woman could eat like a prize fighter.

Entranced, Drake hardly touched his food, watching her consume a goose leg, a quarter of a breast, three slices of mutton, and the entire bowl of cauliflower. "Fascinating." He only realized he'd spoken aloud when she glanced up.

Her eyes enormous, she drew elegant fingers over her mouth. "I beg your pardon?"

Food certainly had a way of brightening her complexion.

"I do not believe I have ever seen a small woman eat with such robust abandon."

"Oh, dear." She swallowed with a gulp. "Forgive me. I was so hungry I forgot my manners."

"Not at all. 'Tis refreshing to see a lady with a healthy appetite."

"Truly, I never shovel food into my mouth like a starved dog. I have no idea what came over me."

He offered her the last slice of lamb. "I think anyone who dances as vigorously as you must need more sustenance than, say, the daughter of a nobleman who sits in her withdrawing room and embroiders or reads all day."

Miss LeClair frowned. "I cannot imagine such idleness."

"Quite." Drake couldn't imagine the lady at his table doing anything but dancing with the vigor she'd demonstrated that day.

Vigor that could make any man's loins stir. He ignored his own inopportune ping of desire. His loins stirred fifty times a day, just like any red-blooded Eton graduate. Lustiness was part of being male, which was why God created Sunday service...to be reminded they were not barbarians. The Duke of Ravenscar had the responsibility to be a gentleman. To respect others just as he commanded respect. And Miss LeClair, possibly the most gifted dancer he'd ever seen, would receive his respect tenfold.

Clearing his throat, he finished his second glass of wine while he pondered the differences of the fairer sex. Drake abhorred the idea of entertaining a mistress. He'd tried it once. Never again. On the other hand, his mother was unduly anxious for him to marry, a topic that detracted from appreciation of any female, including the feminine form sitting beside him. In truth, now he'd spent a bit of time with Miss LeClair, she was far prettier than a dormouse.

Far prettier.

The final course arrived—stewed plums with cream and brandy sauce, and the ballerina showed no signs of slowing down. Holding her spoon like a practiced duchess, she took the tiniest of nibbles, closed her eyes and moaned. Well, so much for being duchess-like. Nonetheless, Drake preferred Miss LeClair's unfettered expression of delight to any of the debutantes his mother had introduced.

A grin stretched the corners of his mouth. How refreshing to see a woman display such unabashed pleasure. Such a simple thing, eating. But Miss LeClair brought to the table a new sense of passion for well-prepared food.

Her gaze lazily shifted until it collided with his. "This is so good, it must be sinful."

Drake picked up his spoon and tasted, not quite able to look away. "Cook is a master at tantalizing the palate, but I assure you, nowhere in the Bible does it say that eating stewed plums is a sin."

"I will trust your word, then," she said, a bit of mischief dancing in her eyes as she scooped a larger bite. "You said your mother resides in a grand mansion. Do you live here alone?"

"I do, though I keep a small staff of servants."

"In Bayeux, we had a housekeeper and a cook which was ample for the three of us."

Drake employed hundreds of servants, but he considered his Half Moon Street town house to have a modest staff. A stable manager, a coachman, two stable boys, a valet, Pennyworth, who went with him whenever he moved houses, two scullery maids, a cook, two footmen, and a housekeeper. If Miss LeClair grew up in a manor with two servants, he wasn't about to tell her his smallest estate merely supported twelve.

When nothing remained of her dessert, Drake asked, "Are you still hungry?"

"Not at all." She clutched her palms to her midriff. "In fact, I can barely breathe beneath my stays."

"See? I told you I would ensure you were filled to the brim before I took you home."

"Thank you for your kindness." Sitting back to allow the footman to clear her bowl, she dropped her hands to her sides. "I do have one question for you before I go, however."

"And what is that?" His heart stuttered as he met her whisky gaze with curiosity. Pretty wasn't the right descriptor for Miss LeClair. Beautiful? Remarkable? *Both good, but not precise.*

She clasped her fingers and regarded him with a sober expression, luminous, yet ever so astute. "I want you to know that I understand how important the opening of *La Sylphide* is to your reputation. If there is one thing I can do to endear myself into the hearts of Chadwick's patrons, what would that be?"

His answer took no time to ponder. "Your opening performance must be flawless. You have no name, no pedigree upon which to lean, and yet you'll be dancing in place of a woman who has both. People will be looking for reasons to discredit you. Do not let them."

Chapter Four

Enjoying a game of billiards, Henry Somerset up-righted his cue stick when his man entered the salon. A chill always managed to charge the air when the former Bow Street Runner made an appearance. With a gaunt face and dark features, had beheadings still been a form of corporal punishment, the runner would have fit the bill for the king's headsman.

"Your Grace." The man removed his hat and bowed. "My informant has advised that Miss LeClair will play the leading role in *La Sylphide.*"

"God save us." Henry pounded the butt of his cue onto the floorboards while heat flared up the back of his neck. "Why didn't your people stop the imp in France?"

"There wasn't time."

"There never is. Damn it all, this should have been avoided years ago. You assured me the child would be brought up to become a governess or at least something respectable."

The man's Adam's apple bobbed while he stood at attention, saying nothing.

"Fie and double fie," Henry continued, "I blame Sarah Parker for the girl's disgrace. You never should have trusted her. Thespians are banes of society, women of ill repute."

"Agreed," the headsman's features grew even darker. "They are all debauchers of the worst sort."

Henry slapped a billiard ball, watching it slam into the bumper. "And *you* let that foundling come here, blast you."

"She knows nothing."

Inclining the cue stick toward his man, Henry's eyes narrowed. "Mind you, your duty is to see it remains that way."

"Nearly twenty years have passed." The runner showed no inkling of fear. "King George is dead. The trail is wiped clean."

"You'd best ensure it remains so, else we must take matters into hand." Henry lowered his voice. "You know what I'm saying."

"I hope it doesn't come to that, though I am and will always remain your servant. Meanwhile, rest assured I shall continue to be vigilant whilst LeClair is in London."

"Good. And find out what she really does know."

"Yes, Your Grace."

Returning his attention to the table, Henry reached for the billiard rack. "I have avoided a scandal all this time and I am not about to sit idle while the ugliness of the past rears up and smears my family's name. I am fifth in line to the throne. My daughter has moved on—married a peer, a good man. I will not see her ruined in his eyes."

***

"Where have you been?" Pauline jumped off her bed and thrust her fists into her hips. "I was about to inform the stage manager that you'd gone missing."

Bria's jaw dropped. "How could you think of doing such a thing?"

"I expected you back hours ago. For all I knew, you'd been kidnapped by an English highwayman or worse."

"I don't think there are any highwaymen in London."

"Well, there are plenty of scoundrels."

Bria spotted her portmanteau on the bed across from Pauline's. "Oh good, my things have arrived. Have you been to the bathhouse?"

"I was waiting for you. And you haven't told me what happened. For heaven's sake, we've been here less than a day and I'm already at my wit's end."

"Forever the mother hen."

Pauline tapped her foot. "Britannia."

Groaning, she locked the door, took Pauline by the hand, and pulled her onto the bed. "Very well." Thank heavens only they were sharing the room together. Some of the girls in the *corps* had to share four to a room. They may have chosen an attic chamber all the way up on the fourth floor, but at least they had privacy. "You mustn't tell a soul."

"Do I ever?"

"No," Bria stood and opened her portmanteau. "But this is different."

"*Mon Dieu.*"

"Um…" She took out a clean chemise, trying to think how she could omit as many details as possible. "When I was practicing on stage I grew so hungry I managed to fall into the arms of the Duke of Ravenscar."

Pauline's eyes practically popped out of her head. "You did what? How? Didn't he leave the theater?"

"He came back." Rolling the chemise around her hands, Bria explained all to her only friend, including the reason why Ravenscar had returned, the unbelievably delicious food and what he'd told her she needed to do to be successful. The entire time he'd acted gentlemanly and had been rather annoyed when she'd asked his coachman to leave her a block away from the boarding house. He'd allowed it, though he did insist on riding along and watching until she was safely inside.

When Bria finally took a breath, Pauline was gaping like she'd just opened a present filled with gold coins. "You were invited into His Grace's town house? Scandalous!"

"*Tais-toi!* Who sided with Florrie about the virtues of being promiscuous?"

"You know I was teasing." Clapping her hands, Pauline giggled. "What is it like? Is he as handsome up close as he appeared from the parterre?"

"Ah…the house is very stately, but not overdone— masculine décor."

"He is a bachelor, I suppose one would expect the interior would appeal to manly tastes." With a rapt glimmer in her eyes, Pauline clasped her hands. "But what about *him*?"

Bria gulped, not wanting to divulge too much. Good heavens, she couldn't admit that the man set a new standard for attractiveness. Though they had no secrets, this once it might be prudent to be vague. "I imagine with a face like his, the duke has a mistress for every day of the week."

Hopping up and executing *piqués* turns until her head nearly collided with the sloped ceiling, Pauline laughed out loud. "You are awful."

"I am practical, and let me make it perfectly clear, he did not indicate he might harbor an interest in me whatsoever."

"And why not?" Pauline spun back to the bed. "You are darling—one of the loveliest women I know."

"Not at all. I'm too thin, and too headstrong, and too independent."

"But—"

"No! Absolutely not. We are no longer having this conversation."

"All right then, neither of you seemed to be inordinately attracted to each other…"

Bria chewed her lip. Pauline's assumption wasn't exactly precise, but it was best not to correct her. After all, it didn't matter if she'd found Ravenscar to be magnificent in a very masculine way. A man like His Grace would never look twice at a foundling from Bayeux. Their classes alone were so far apart, she might as well sprout wings and fly to the moon as to think he would entertain pursuing a woman with no pedigree who had fallen so low as to perform on stage. Thank heavens nothing had come of their meal together. She wouldn't want to pine for a duke—a man she could never have and who could never fall in love with her.

"But tell me," her friend continued, "Do you think he can help you with your quest?"

A little squeeze flitted in Bria's stomach. She'd had no success in France. "I wouldn't want to bother him. He'd consider me impertinent."

"Perhaps not." With a blink of brown eyelashes, Pauline pointed her toes. "After all, we've already ascertained the kerchief bears the coat of arms of the Prince Regent."

"Who became king and passed away three years ago." Bria crossed herself to honor the deceased. "If only he were alive, I could have had someone ask his Royal Highness to identify the woman in the miniature."

"Someone must know who she is. Even after nineteen or twenty years."

"But she mightn't be English. When I was born, England was still at war with the French."

Pauline stretched her leg upward, executing an elegant *developpé*. "We've been over this before. In 1814, the House of Bourbon was briefly restored while Napoleon was in prison. England and France were amicable until the emperor's escape in 1815."

Bria pulled the miniature from beneath her chemise and held it in her palm. The woman in the portrait had a familial likeness and now that Britannia had grown into a woman, she was even more convinced they were related. Ever since she'd found the painting, she'd dreamed the noble lady with porcelain skin and clad in blue satin was her mother. "But she could be Spanish."

"She doesn't look Spanish," said Pauline.

"Dutch, then."

"You need to find out who the *Grande-Duchesse* is, whether she is in England or Holland or the Holy Roman Empire. Imagine, you might be a princess." They'd oft referred to the woman as the *Grande-Duchesse*—it was akin to their secret code.

"Foundlings are *never* princesses," Bria insisted. "Besides, I honestly have no idea if the kerchief or the miniature have any significance. As I've told you before, after the LeClairs died I found these keepsakes in a box with my name engraved in the top. Before that, I'd never laid eyes on them."

"Even if she's not your mother, the beauty in the picture might know something about where you're from."

"And that's why I keep looking." Sighing, Bria replaced the miniature inside her bodice, then fished in her portmanteau for a bar of rose soap. "We shall be in London four long months. Perhaps after *La Sylphide* opens I might happen upon someone who can help me find the *Grande-Duchesse*. But right now, we have more things to worry about than an elusive painting. And the first is a bath."

***

On Easter Sunday, Drake sat across the carriage from his mother and gazed out the window while they ambled from Westminster Abbey toward the family's Pall Mall mansion.

Esperanza? No, Miss LeClair doesn't have the right coloring for a Spanish rose. Darcia? Amaris? Perhaps Serilda—a maiden in battle armor? Possibly. Parthena? She does seem pure. But I think I'm partial to Bernadette. Yes. Bernadette is French and reminds me of a dancer. I could wager on it.

"Whatever are you thinking about?" asked his mother, her gloved hands primly folded in her lap.

Though his stomach leaped, Drake shifted his attention to Her Grace, projecting an image of utmost composure. "Hmm? Not a thing."

"I know you better than you think. You have that contemplative look in your eye. Something is weighing heavily on your mind."

He released a long breath he hadn't realized he'd been holding. Mother always could read him like a book. "I'm concerned about the opening of *La Sylphide*. There has been a development." Which was an understatement. Instead of dreaming up names for Miss LeClair, he should have been thinking about how to ensure an entire Season of strong ticket sales to keep Chadwick Theater's doors open and the lenders away from Mother's favorite home.

"Oh?" she asked. "Did the cast arrive safely—yesterday, wasn't it?"

"The day before." Bless her for not paying attention to the gossip columns. And with the morning service, Drake hadn't had a moment to tell her the news. "Unfortunately, the most important and only woman who made *La Sylphide* a sensation did not sail from France."

Mother's prim lips gaped in astonishment. "You cannot be serious? Marie Taglioni is not in London?"

"Nor will she be."

"Good heavens, this has the makings of a disaster."

"My thoughts precisely."

"What will you do?"

"They've sent an unknown in Taglioni's place…"

Mother drew a palm over her heart. "It grows worse."

"The woman is quite good, but—"

"Yes?"

Drake tapped a cushion tassel, trying to think of the exact word. "Vigorous."

"Unusual epithet for a ballerina."

"Quite, and I'm not certain if London is ready for her."

"But you said she has talent. Will it not be refreshing to see something new?"

"That is exactly what I keep telling myself." He stretched his legs to the side and crossed his ankles. "Perhaps it would be better if you wait to hear what the critics say before you came to the theater."

"One moment." Mother held up her finger. "Let me see if I understand. This new Parisian ballerina is very good, but not as poised or restrained as we would expect to see in an English woman. Is that correct?"

"Mm. Yes."

"Tell me, would *you* go to see this woman perform?"

A crooked grin played across his lips, yet there was no chance he would detail LeClair's erotic style to his mother. "Indeed, I would."

"And would you enjoy her dancing?"

"Very much so."

Mother snapped open and fluttered her fan. "Everyone expects a bit of sauciness from French performers. Why are you worrying?"

Because she dances like a hellcat and you will be shocked right down to the toes of your stockings. Not to mention, if she is not sensational, you will disown me. "People will be so terribly disappointed not to see Marie Taglioni, I'm afraid they will try to refund their tickets, even though I've made it clear no sales will be reimbursed until after opening night."

"Well then, it is doubly important for me to attend and show my support. Remember, the House of Ravenscar dictates fashions and trends as much or more than any other dukedom in the kingdom."

Drake nodded. The House of Ravenscar may soon become the Right Honorable Hovel. Bless his mother's heart. A fierce matriarch, she would not sit idle while gossip about her son ran rife through London—unless things grew out of hand. Then they would both flee to the country to weather the storm.

"I shall announce an after-theater soiree," she ventured, already scheming. "Invite the cast leads, especially your new ballerina. Let us reel in the buzzards before they have a chance to whisper amongst themselves."

"Perhaps your idea would be preferable to the champagne and cakes I had planned in the theater vestibule." People would be less likely to voice any condescending opinions under the watchful eye of Her Grace.

"Excellent." Mother reached across and patted his knee. "On a more serious note, a fresh contingent of young ladies has arrived in Town for the Season. Yesterday, I met Lady Blanche Boscawen, daughter of the Viscount of Falmouth and she seems quite enterprising..."

Drake turned a deaf ear to her banter. He didn't want to meet the daughter of Lord Fowl Mouth or any of the other chicken-brained debutantes his mother never ceased to parade under his nose. Yes, he had a responsibility to continue the family line, but he would do so in his own time—at least a good five years hence.

Chapter Five

Easter Monday, 8th April, 1833

"Again!" bellowed Monsieur Travere while the dancers in the *corps* moaned.

Refusing to give in to her exhaustion, Bria threw back her shoulders and moved to center stage. She would ignore the searing pain in her toes and her aching muscles no matter what. Yes, hours ago blisters had formed and by the way her toes stung, they were bleeding. She'd bled many times before, though now there would be no time to heal.

"The lot of you sound like a herd of goats! Where is your grace? You spend a week traveling and your journey wipes away years of study? Need I remind you our debut is tomorrow?" Red in the face, Travere stamped his foot. "We are already in jeopardy of losing our contract. Do you want to return to Paris in shame?"

Bria hung her head. Everything this day had gone wrong. The orchestra played all the wrong tempos, Chadwick Theater's stage was narrower and deeper than *Salle Le Peletier* and it made the choreography awkward. The side seam on her costume tore, her wings had fallen off twice. Good heavens, if the ballet opened today, they would be laughed out of England.

"No!" she shouted. "We will not consider returning to Paris."

In quick succession, Monsieur Travere rapped his baton on the edge of the stage. "You say that, Mademoiselle LeClair, and yet your performance today has been abysmal. Just like everyone else's."

She gripped her arms across her midriff, internally berating herself. The dance master was right. She'd been awful. If she didn't pull herself together, she would let everyone down—the troupe, the duke, and, most of all, herself. If she danced like this during the performance, she might as well go throw herself in the Thames. She would be worthless, a fallen woman with nowhere to turn, as helpless as she'd been when she'd been cast out of her home by her assumed uncle. This was her chance. If she failed, Monsieur Marchand would never allow her to set foot in *Salle Le Peletier* again.

"Pardon me, Monsieur Travere," said the conductor. "But the orchestra is done for the day. We've already exceeded our contract by an hour."

"Are you out of your minds?" the dance master shouted, throwing his baton out to the parterre. "Your performance has been the worst of the lot. How can we open tomorrow with the rubbish you played this day?"

The conductor slammed his score closed. "You, sir, are a hothead, and I will remind you I will be standing here in front of the stage, commanding the tempo when the curtain opens tomorrow. Fear not. I am, and my musicians are virtuosos. We have taken your direction, made changes accordingly, and now we are leaving."

While the musicians walked out, Travere kicked a music stand, sending it clattering to the floor. Then he glared up at the stage. "At whom are you staring?"

Bria glanced at the others over her shoulder. They all looked as haggard as she felt. "We go again," she said, assuming her position. "That is what you asked."

He swept his arm through the air. "*One*, two, three, *four*, five, six…"

Spinning across the stage, she steeled her mind to the pain. Her blisters had bled before, and it would happen again. Later she'd soak her toes in brine and tomorrow night she'd wrap them, but right now she would endure the pain and show the Duke of Ravenscar exactly how much she wanted, needed, desired to play the role of the Sylph. No one would smite her opportunity. Bria's toes could bleed through her slippers and she would not utter a word of complaint. *Grand jeté, fouetté* and pose in *attitude*. On and on she danced, willing herself to be strong. After a simple *pas de bourrée*, she stumbled, her toes torturing her efforts. Recovering quickly, Bria didn't stop. She didn't grimace. She endured through to end of the finale. Only then did she dare to glance at the dance master.

Travere pursed his lips, disappointment broadcast in his stance, his frown, his sullenness. "Enough!"

Everyone exited the stage while Bria dropped to the floor and removed her slippers. Good heavens, six of ten toes were bloodied. *I cannot allow a few tiny blisters make me founder. Not again. Tomorrow must be perfect!*

"Do you have a salve for those?" She looked up to find Mr. Perkins offering her a stoppered jar. "Put this on after you soak your toes tonight, and then ensure you apply a healthy dollop before you wrap them for tomorrow's performance."

Accepting the gift, she stood. "Are you familiar with toe dancing?"

"No, but I am familiar with blisters."

"Thank you." She assumed the position to rehearse the scene yet again.

"What are you doing?"

"Practicing. I cannot go home this night until I am satisfied."

"You've practiced enough." He offered his elbow. "Let us take a walk."

"But—"

"Just a brief stroll through the theater. In my experience, an artiste who has been working all day will only see her performance decline until she has rested."

"Your experience?"

"I've been involved with theater management all my life. Though, as I'm sure you are aware, this is the first time toe dancing has been performed in Britain." When she took his arm, he strolled down to the parterre. "Why are you a dancer?" he asked.

Bria almost laughed aloud. "I love ballet with my whole being. I cannot imagine doing anything else."

"I can tell you're passionate about it by the way you dance from your soul. I'll wager you want to be successful so badly you ignore your own needs."

She nodded, deciding not to tell him about swooning into the Duke of Ravenscar's arms.

"How long has it been since you've eaten?"

Had His Grace told Mr. Perkins about the swooning incident? She hoped not. "I ate a good breakfast."

"So, you're tired, you're hungry, and your feet hurt like they've been branded by a red-hot poker. Am I right?"

"Yes," she whispered, scraping her teeth across her bottom lip.

He took her by the shoulders. "I've been watching you rehearse all day. Believe me when I say the conductor has noted the musical issues, you are the most excellent ballerina London has ever seen, and if you do not go home and take care of your feet, Chadwick's patrons will not witness what I have seen. Do you understand?"

No matter how much she wanted to object, she let out a long breath and nodded. As they turned back toward the stage, she asked, "Of all the operas, plays and ballets, why did Chadwick Theater choose to open with *La Sylphide*?"

"Ravenscar wanted a spectacle that would be unmatched for the Season. He saw the opening debut of the ballet last year in France and knew then he had to have it. I must say, however, I do not think he would have chosen *La Sylphide* if Monsieur Marchand had told him Marie Taglioni's understudy would be taking her place."

A lump the size of her fist expanded in Bria's throat. If the ballet failed, only she would be to blame. "And I have disappointed him royally."

"Not you, my dear. If the blame lies with anyone, it is Marchand." When they arrived back at the stage, Mr. Perkins patted her hand. "Now take my salve, have a good rest, and give us a stellar performance tomorrow night. Promise?"

"I promise to do my very best. I give you my oath I will not disappoint you or the duke or the patrons of this theater." She curtsied while her heartbeat rushed in her ears—her entire body tense with nerves. On the morrow she must face the most important day of her life. "Thank you, sir."

Chapter Six

Chadwick Theater, Tuesday, 9th April, 1833

Drake had spent the better part of the day avoiding the uproar that came with the first *Morning Post* released after the holidays. Well aware there was a five-minute overture, he arrived at the theater two minutes after the performance began, looked no one in the eye and hastened straight for his box. Mother was already seated with her usual friends: widows, Lady Anabelle and Lady Eloise, and Mr. Edwin Peters, a well-to-do gunsmith who kept company with Drake's mother far too frequently.

He kissed her on the cheek. "You look lovely this evening."

Mother rapped his arm with her fan. "I was about to think you had decided not to come. It's not like you to move to the rear of the guard in battle."

"Only avoiding being mobbed by hundreds of livid patrons." Regardless of his attempt to smooth things with the papers. The dashed headlines had read, *"Ravenscar's Fortune in the Hands of a Foundling"*. He'd strangle Maxwell if the man ever again dared to show his face. Drake greeted the other guests and took his seat, opening his program for the first time.

Britannia LeClair.

Fancy that. The Sylph was named for his beloved Britain. That was one which hadn't crossed his mind. *Britannia*? For a French lass? But he liked it. The name suited her tenacity.

He sat back and focused on the curtain while angry stares from boxes across the theater fixated on him. No, Drake didn't need to look to see people staring. Some dared to boo, while the hiss of whispers singed his ears, as did the rumbling murmurs from the gallery. Above the orchestra, the tension in the air was as charged as a courtroom trying a murder case.

When the curtain opened to a danseur dressed like a Scotsman sleeping in an armchair, the tension eased a bit. But everyone in the theater gasped when Britannia LeClair danced onto the stage with a pair of graceful leaps. Though flawlessly executed and extraordinarily lofty, her *grands jetés* mightn't be the reason for the audience's reaction. The hem of her winged costume was so short, it almost revealed the ballerina's knees. Yes, in France, Taglioni had shortened her skirts a bit, but LeClair's gossamer gown, in and of itself, was scandalous.

Along with Drake, everyone in the theater leaned forward, their jaws dropping while the Sylph flitted about the sleeping Scotsman on the tips of her toes, barely skimming the floor. Her leaps were like watching a feather sail on the breeze, her feet only to brush the stage before flowing into twirls and arabesques—a nymph with wings.

A London crowd had never seen such precision, such effortless grace. Drake gulped. Neither had they seen a woman's skirts so short. His mouth grew dry—such shapely and muscular legs. What would such sleek calves feel like wrapped around him? He glanced to the faces he could see. Every man in the theater was thinking the same, and every woman looked thunderstruck, including Ladies Anabelle and Eloise. Only Her Grace smiled, her hands folded, poised like a queen.

The reactions were expected, though Drake's trepidation didn't ease. He wanted to strangle every last man for their lewd thoughts. How dare they? Miss LeClair was an innocent, performing only to delight Chadwick's patrons with her grace. Fortunately for the women in the audience, the danseur in his kilt showed more of his legs than did Miss LeClair. His leaps were high and exciting, though his candle was but a flicker compared to the torch that shone when Britannia commanded the stage.

By intermission, he'd heard everything from tepid applause to gasps to cheers. Miss LeClair's dancing thus far had been vigorous, though somewhat more reserved than a few days prior. Then again, the scene with the sylphs which Drake had viewed at rehearsal was in the second act. He rubbed his fingers, anxious to see her dance it again. Was she as stupendous as he'd remembered?

Britannia. The name does suit her.

As the curtain closed for intermission, the theater erupted in an uproar. Drake couldn't make out a single conversation from down below because everyone was talking and shouting. The gallery was louder than a boxing match.

Mother leaned in. "I see what you mean. The young lady certainly is no Englishwoman." She patted her chest. "Heaven forbid."

"She is quite talented," said Mr. Peters, his eyes glazed.

Both Lady Anabelle and Lady Eloise looked on as if they were tongue-tied. Most unusual for the pair of chatterboxes.

Drake stood. "If you'd care to join me, I will venture down to the vestibule and brave the critics."

No sooner had he offered his hand to his mother when the Earl of Fordham and Viscount Saye filed into the box. Her Grace remained seated.

"Ravenscar, you dog!" piped Fordham. "When I read this morning's paper, I was certain the theater would be empty and the only good use for it would be firewood."

"What happened to Taglioni?" someone hollered from the corridor.

"Is it true you only found out she wouldn't be honoring her contract when the ship moored?" asked Saye.

"It is true." Drake raised his voice while the box was mobbed. "Our only option was to carry on with Miss LeClair. I say from experience, she is as talented as Taglioni."

"The same?" Saye asked. "I may need to book passage to France."

"As good, but different. Livelier and more graceful in my estimation." Drake grabbed his friends by the elbows and whispered, "What is your opinion? Will I be crucified come morning?"

"I like her," said Fordham.

"But will polite society?" cautioned Saye.

Drake gave them each an exasperated look. "We *are* polite society."

"Monsieur Bonin is quite good," said Lady Annabel from her chair.

"I agree, he is very dynamic." Drake returned his attention to his friends. "Perhaps the male lead is proficient enough to interest the fairer sex."

"Then I feel sorry for the ladies," said Fordham with a lecherous grin. "Will you introduce me to Miss LeClair after the finale?"

Splaying his fingers, Drake regarded the earl with a furrowed brow. "You're coming to my mother's soiree are you not? Did you receive my missive?"

"Saye and I will be there...and Miss LeClair?"

"She has been invited along with the other principals."

Fordham grinned and thwacked Drake on the shoulder. "Perhaps it is time for me to acquire a new mistress," he whispered.

Clenching his fist, Drake considered how the earl might look with a swollen nose. Thankfully, Mother and the ladies were engaged in conversation. "What happened to Mrs. Walpole?" Drake asked, his whisper straining through his teeth.

"A man can have two mistresses." Fordham smirked like a lecherous cur. Regardless if he'd been Drake's roommate at Eton, the man could be as shallow as a mudpuddle. "Where is it written we must keep only one?"

"Agreed," said Saye, who was between mistresses, and also a miserable rake.

A blast of heat spread across the back of Drake's neck. "Give it a rest, gentlemen," he said, raising the tone for all hear. "Chadwick's ballerina has only just arrived in London. Let the poor dancer have a chance to settle before you wolves start chasing after her skirts." He started for the box's exit, but the corridor was still mobbed with people voicing their opinions quite openly:

"I didn't know a woman was capable of leaping so high."

"It is remarkable."

"It is scandalous!"

"It is obscene," said a lady.

"You're only saying that because you are a prude."

"Well, I've never!"

"Ravenscar," someone hollered, Drake had no idea who. "Are you sending them back to France?"

"No!" yelled a man. "I'll be back on the morrow. You cannot see this ballet just once."

"I'm cancelling my box," complained a man with a gravelly voice.

"I'll take it!"

Drake scratched his head and sank back into the chair beside his mother.

She patted his arm. "I venture to guess you have a success on your hands."

"Good God, I hope so."

***

Mr. Perkins' salve had worked wonders. With her toes wrapped, Bria focused on the dance, her breathing, the music. This was her chance—possibly her only chance—and she would do her best to show all of London she was worthy of being the Sylph just as much as Marie Taglioni who was preforming this very night in Paris. Pulling from the depths of her soul, she danced as a woman possessed. Nothing else mattered, not the other dancers, not the crowd, nothing but doing her best to please and, as the second act progressed, so did her effort.

Bria's only distraction was the presence of His Grace in the grand-tier center box. The intensity of his stare cut through the darkness of the gallery. And every time she stepped on stage, she heard the power of his voice:

"*You are not the only one who will be ruined if La Sylphide is a failure.*"

"*Your opening performance must be flawless…*"

"*The nobility are like dogs to a bone when it comes to gossip. And they will be gnashing their teeth to see me fail.*"

She couldn't fail. On stage this night, she wasn't dancing for the love of ballet, she was dancing for her very breath.

Dancing for *him*.

Dancing because he had made her see the grave importance of this single night.

Monsieur Marchand had repeatedly told her to build her performance and save the crescendo for the end. Bria had learned that lesson well, and by the final scenes, her leaps had grown higher. Her arabesques were perpendicular with the floor rather than horizontal. Yes, all of society expected an arabesque lower than the hips, but she could go higher— craved to stretch the boundaries of her abilities. That is why Marchand and Travere had chosen her for the lead. That is why she was on stage in a fabulous new theater in London. Marie Taglioni had shocked Paris by dancing on her toes and shortening her skirts. Well, Bria did the same and more. On the road to success, a woman must prove herself to be exemplary. To push margins and deliver a performance from the depths of her soul.

When she pirouetted and dipped into her final curtsy, Bria's breath rushed in her ears. The strings played their final note. Listening for applause, the air in the theater grew heavy with silence.

Silence.

Bria's heart sank to her toes as she dared to glance up.

Straight ahead, Ravenscar stood in his box. "Bravo!" he bellowed, clapping his hands.

As if his acceptance was what the patrons needed, they followed his lead. Suddenly, with a raucous cheer, the entire theater erupted in applause. Her eyes stung as she straightened. Smiling at His Grace, she blew him a kiss, praying all she had given was good enough. Praying he would not send them home in shame.

Gérard Bonin, lead danseur, grasped her hand and pulled her off the stage for the curtain call. "You were fabulous, *ma chérie.*"

"You as well," she said, catching her breath.

After the *corps*, Bria followed Gérard on stage to take her final bow and the applause grew louder. Even people in the boxes were on their feet. Five curtain calls were made before the applause faded. And when it was over, Gérard wrapped her in a smothering embrace. "After that performance, I doubt Ravenscar will be shipping us back to France before our contract ends."

Monsieur Travere hastened on stage from the wings. "Bravo, both of you. Change quickly. The principals have been invited to a soiree at the duke's home."

Bria glanced to Pauline. "Only the principals?"

"*Oui*, you, Gérard, Florrie, Nanci and Claudio."

Pauline shrugged and turned away. The rest of the cast was heading to the Welcome Inn to celebrate the opening.

Dashing to catch up with her friend, Bria grasped Pauline's hand and pulled her toward the dressing room. "I'm sorry."

"I feel sorrier for you." A sad smile turned up the dancer's lips. "You have to endure Florrie and Gérard for the night."

"Not to mention the nobility. They make me feel so…so *inadequate*."

"Do not even say it." Pauline thrust her finger in the direction of the stage. "You just gave the most sensational performance of your life. Don't let those dragons make you feel any less than a queen *ce soir*. You may not realize it now, but you are already a diva."

"And your head is full of stars." Bria slipped the costume from her shoulders and held up her best gown. The India muslin looked like a rag compared to some of the finery worn by the women in the audience, though she had added pink ribbons for flourish. "I wish I had something more suitable to wear."

"Perhaps we should pay a visit to the modiste."

Bria stepped into the frock and slipped in her arms. It had been difficult to make ends meet when living on *corps* wages. Others had parents to help them gain a start. *No one had helped me*. "Perhaps after we receive our wages."

Dutifully, Pauline began tying the back laces. "Just smile. One smile from you is worth more than silk."

"But not more than diamonds."

"Stop. You've been invited to a soiree in the home of a duchess. Enjoy yourself."

"Britannia!" Monsieur Travere's voice rumbled through the door.

"A moment," she replied then glanced over her shoulder. "Nearly done?"

"Just finished the bow." Pauline gave her a pat. "Rouge your lips and primp your curls. The task master can wait."

Chapter Seven

A string quartet played Mozart while Drake stood in the entry of the reception hall where he could keep an eye out for Britannia's arrival. Beside him stood his boyhood friend from Alnwick to the north of Peak Castle, and Drake's favorite sparring partner. Hugh Percy, heir to a dukedom and Drake's closest ally. "The success of Chadwick Theater must last throughout the duration of the Season. One night of perceived success in no way validates our wager."

"Those were the terms," Drake agreed. Though he hadn't lost his fortune this night, the coming weeks would prove him a king or a pauper. He had made his wager with Percy when Chadwick Theater was only a whim of an idea, though after he'd returned from Paris he'd been convinced he was bringing a sensation to his new theater. Perhaps Percy was the one person who wouldn't throw him to the wolves if his venture failed—though he would insist Drake make good on their wager. "What is your opinion? Do you think sales will sustain?"

"My guess is they will. The men will come for the spectacle, and the women will come to keep an eye on the men."

Drake took a hearty sip of his champagne, wishing it were something stronger. "I think Miss LeClair gave an exemplary performance."

"Remarkable for a foundling. I never would have guessed her beginnings were so crude unless I'd seen it in the papers."

"She could be the daughter of a chimney sweep," said Lady Eloise, glass of champagne in hand.

"Or the daughter of Tsar Alexander," Drake countered. "The point is we have no way of knowing."

"That is correct," said the Duke of Beaufort, who at the age of seven and sixty had purchased two boxes at Chadwicks for the Season. He was both wealthy and proliferous which was financially beneficial for London as a whole. "Tell me, Ravenscar, where—"

Beaufort's words were swallowed by the steward's announcement: "The esteemed Monsieur Travere, Mademoiselle LeClair, Monsieur Bonin, Mademoiselle Bisset, Mademoiselle Caron, and Monsieur Gagné."

The crowd applauded politely. Drake stepped forward, took Britannia's hand and applied a brief peck. As he straightened, a bouquet as wild as an enchanted forest draped with wisteria washed over him. Good God, now the woman had been rested and fed, up close she looked stunning— gorgeous. In fact, there weren't words. Where had his dormouse gone? It was far easier to resist a plain, half-starved foundling. "Welcome," he croaked, gesturing to all the artistes. "May I offer you congratulations on a splendid opening performance."

She turned cherry red. Was there a hint of unease in the lioness' eyes? But before he could offer assurance, Miss Florrie Bisset who played the supporting female lead, painted on a faux smile and wrapped her fingers around Drake's arm. The woman's gesture was inordinately brash, adding credence to the promiscuous reputation of professional women dancers. "We are delighted to be here, Your Grace."

Drawing his arm away, he led the party inside where a footman offered them their choice of champagne or port wine.

As expected, Britannia chose the champagne, giving a soft thank you to the footman. She sipped while turning full circle, taking in the reception hall painted in ivory and trimmed with gold. Above, mirrored chandeliers were all alight with wax candles, making the room nearly as bright as a summer's day.

"This is the mansion you mentioned?" she whispered.

"Yes, but Ravenscar Hall has nothing on Peak Castle."

"And where might that be?" asked Gérard Bonin, strutting forward as if he'd been responsible for the five curtain calls. He sipped his port and blast it if the Frenchman didn't flutter his damned eyelashes.

"Northeast of York," Drake explained. "On the coast in a remote area known as The Peak, not to be confused with the Peak District near Sheffield."

"Ah." Bonin clapped a hand to his chest and sighed, acting flippant even for a Frenchman. "*Je suis en amour.*"

Fordham elbowed his way in front of the danseur. "I was wondering when the artiste of the hour would arrive. Thomas Newport, Earl of Fordham at your service, but I like my lady friends to call me Tom." He grasped Britannia's hand and planted a lingering kiss, then drew her fingers over his scheming heart. "Mademoiselle, your dancing was stupendous."

Grumbling under his breath, Drake followed as Fordham led Miss LeClair toward the doors to the orangery where, if left unattended, the fox would be able to make a quick exit.

"I am positively dying to know how you manage to extend your leg so high." Fordham continued with his flattery, which Drake knew all too well was intended to endear himself to the poor innocent in order to make her think he was smitten.

"Yes, I've never seen such a thing." Saye muscled in, taking Britannia's other hand and introducing himself with much the same flourish as his partner in crime.

"Perhaps we can engage you for a private demonstration," Fordham said.

Britannia glanced between the two lords. "I think—"

"Absolutely not." Drake squeezed Fordham's wrist, forcing the earl to release Miss LeClair's hand, then stepped between them with a genteel smile. "What I find astonishing is the toe dancing. Does it not hurt?"

Britannia nodded, looking back at Drake, as if pleading with him to stay nearby. He followed, admiring the way her curls bounced and shimmered like copper in the candlelight. "It does, but my toes have grown calluses."

"Truly?" Fordham again pushed his big nose between them.

"Yes, and in the past year, the company's cobbler has improved on Mademoiselle Taglioni's design by reinforcing the slippers with glue and wood. And I use lamb's wool for padding."

"There she is, the woman who dazzled us all." Bless Mother, she approached Britannia with a radiant smile, her hands outstretched. "Welcome to Ravenscar Hall. My son told me about your interesting dance style, and I must say tonight's performance did not disappoint."

"Thank you. You are too kind, Your Grace." Britannia curtsied deeply, keeping her chin lowered and looking uncomfortable. "And thank you for inviting us to your immaculate home this evening."

Lady Calthorpe, a petite woman, peeked around Mother's shoulder. "Your dancing was astonishing, Miss LeClair. I for one am an instant admirer. I adored your vitality." One of the Duke of Beaufort's seventeen children, Drake had always looked fondly upon the baroness, aging well and in her late thirties. "My, your English is impeccable, my dear."

"How nice of you to say so." Britannia's gaze seemed to linger on the woman's face. She leaned forward as if a question danced on the tip of her tongue.

Lady Calthorpe appeared unperturbed by the ballerina's staring. "Before you arrived, His Grace told us about your unfortunate beginnings."

Again blushing, Britannia ran the ends of the pink ribbon at her waist through her fingers. "Yes. 'Tis embarrassing to admit, but I am a foundling."

"No one ought to feel poorly about their beginnings. Did you have a guardian?" asked Her Ladyship.

"I was taken in by a wonderful couple in Bayeux."

Opposed to the ballerina, the baroness' coloring paled. "Pray tell, what is your age?"

"Ah—" Flustered, Britannia glanced to Drake.

"My word, Charlotte." Beaufort stepped beside his daughter and grasped her elbow, his port sloshing over the rim of his glass. "Give the poor artiste a bit of room to breathe."

"A moment. I have another question or two to ask." The baroness tugged her arm free with enough force to make Beaufort's port spill. To everyone's horror, the ruby liquid splattered straight down the front of Miss LeClair's gown.

"Oh no!" chirped Her Ladyship. "Please forgive my clumsiness."

"Well done," Beaufort mumbled in a barely audible tone, though Drake didn't miss the dissention from one of Chadwick Theater's greatest benefactors. Were the gossips making a mockery of tonight's performance behind his back? Unfortunately, now was no time to confront the man.

Britannia gasped, gaping at her dress. She looked to Drake, her eyes filled with panic.

The Earl of Fordham offered his kerchief.

She took it. "Is there a withdrawing room where I can compose my person?"

"Straightaway. Come with me, dear." Mother grasped Britannia's hand.

Drake followed them to the grand staircase until Her Grace turned and thrust out her palm. "I shall call my lady's maid and she'll find Miss LeClair something to wear. There's no need for you to leave our guests."

"Of course. My thanks, Your Grace." Drake bowed his head, then shifted his gaze to Britannia. If only they could have a moment alone where he could truly tell her how much he'd enjoyed her performance this evening. Duty bound to accompany his mother home, there had been no time to venture backstage and congratulate the ballerina. "You are in good hands, mark me. And I will ensure your gown is replaced."

"Thank you. I haven't quite saved enough coin for a new one as of yet."

Drake watched as they ascended the stairs, frustrated as hell not to be the one escorting Britannia upstairs. She threw a forlorn look over her shoulder before they rounded the landing. Bless it, she was new to this country and ever so fragile, and it didn't help to have every man in the hall slavering over her. He'd only been acquainted with the nymph for a short time, but he already knew she wasn't like the others. She was virtuous and talented and...and vulnerable.

"Well, that put a damper on the evening," said Fordham.

"Indeed," Saye agreed. "Your ballerina has us all mesmerized. Did you see her eyes? They're as spellbinding as a doe's."

Clenching his fists at his sides, Drake faced them. "Both of you had best find someone else upon whom to project your affections. That young lady is not to be trifled with."

Fordham's jaw dropped as he exchanged glances with Saye. "Do not tell me you have eyes for her?"

"Pull your mind out of the gutter. Miss LeClair is my responsibility, not to mention she potentially is the biggest draw for Chadwick Theater this Season and I will abide no man who puts my venture in jeopardy, especially one of you."

***

Bria wiped the stain with Fordham's handkerchief and followed the maid down the corridor.

The woman spoke over her shoulder. "I'll take you to Lady Ada's chamber. We might find something suitable for you to wear in there, though I daresay, not even our scullery maids are a small as you, miss."

"I'm sorry to be a bother." She dabbed again. "I doubt I'll ever be able to remove this stain."

"Wine is difficult, but if anyone can do it, our laundress can." The maid opened a door and gestured inside. "She always manages to clean every spill from His Grace's clothing."

"His Grace? Are you referring to the current duke or his father?" Bria stepped inside a bedchamber that was four times the size of the room she shared with Pauline. Colors of periwinkle and cream made the chamber a happy room with a fourposter festooned with satin bedcurtains.

"The son. His father has been gone near ten years now. Drake Chadwick grew up in this house during the Season, of course, though I think His Grace prefers to be up north."

"Have you been there?"

"Peak Castle?" the maid asked over her shoulder as she stepped through an archway and opened a trunk.

"Yes." Bria tapped a rocking chair and watched it sway, sparking memories of a similar chair from her childhood. She'd lived in a manor once. Not a palatial residence like this one, but a home with many comforts.

"Heavens, no. The family employs a full staff of locals from The Peak."

"Of course." Bria shook her head. This was a world as foreign to her as the depths of the sea. No wonder His Grace preferred his Half Moon Street town house. At least a person could find the exit when they wanted to venture outside.

"Ah." The maid pulled out a blue redingote and shook it. "This ought to suffice. It might be a tad long, but it opens in the front and you shouldn't trip."

"'Tis beautiful." Bria slipped it on, but the overdress dwarfed her.

Tsking her tongue, the maid stood back. "This will not do at all."

"Honestly it should be fine to see me home. I can roll up the sleeves."

"No, I'll tack them up and while I'm at it I can move the buttons for a better fit. It shan't take me but a moment."

Before Bria could object, the lady's maid swept out the door and left her alone in Ravenscar's sister's bedchamber. The tapping of raindrops sounded at the window. She rubbed her outer arms, wishing she was back in the tiny attic room with Pauline. How humorous for everyone to watch the poor foundling being drenched in red wine. Her only evening gown ruined.

Well, at least she would have an excuse not to attend any more soirees for a time. All those wealthy people. No wonder the duke thought she was a shrinking violet. She was completely, utterly out of her element in every way.

Bria strolled to the bed and ran her fingers over the silky coverlet. *What would it be like to be raised in such opulence?*

When the door clicked, she looked up expectantly. "My heavens, you couldn't have altered the redingote that quickly."

"I beg your pardon?" Ravenscar replied in his deep bass as he stepped into the chamber.

Snapping her fingers behind her back, Bria's stomach leaped. She oughtn't be touching the coverlet. What if she marked it? "Your Grace, should you not be with your guests?"

"They are my mother's guests." He moved inside, one corner of his mouth turned up in a lopsided grin, seeming as if he wasn't sure if he'd found the right room. Despite his expression, his elegant and polished theater attire suited the chamber's opulence, while Bria felt discordant and ill at ease.

"Though," he continued, "I do appreciate Her Grace's efforts to support Chadwick's grand opening." Stopping in front of her, the duke reached out, then closed his fist and drew it over his heart, his teeth catching his bottom lip. Good Lord, could a man look more beautiful?

"S-she's a very gracious woman. You are fortunate to have her." Bria toyed with the long pink ribbon tied around the waist of her dress.

With one more step in, he grasped the silk from her fingertips and together they watched it run across his palm. Bria backed away, her stomach performing involuntary *entrechats*.

"She is and I am." His gaze grew dark, meandering down her stained dress. "Ah…where is Mother's lady's maid?"

"Stepped out for a moment to make a few alterations of your sister's redingote."

"Right," He grinned again, bigger this time. "I imagine there's nothing in this house that would fit you."

"Is she here? I wasn't introduced."

Azure eyes met hers—mysterious eyes reflecting intelligence, vitality, and, *oh heavens*, hunger. "Who?"

Bria licked her lips. "Your sister."

He chuckled as if at his own absentmindedness. "Ada is expecting her second child. She's now Viscountess Bindon, living in Dorset."

"Oh my." Turning her back so she wouldn't have to endure his disarming gaze, Bria smoothed her hands over her hair. Had any pins come loose in the mayhem? And why had she suddenly become so self-aware? "Honestly, I would be fine to don my cloak and return to the boarding house."

"That wouldn't do. You still have admiring fans waiting in the reception hall."

She sensed him move closer, shivering as his warm breath skimmed the back of her neck. "I wanted a moment alone to tell you myself, your performance this evening was nothing short of magnificent. There were times when my heart stopped and I was unable to breathe. If half the patrons in the audience reacted as I, Chadwick Theater will be sold out for the duration of the Season."

Sighing, Bria reflected on the ballet. She hadn't been the only one who'd given her all. "Monsieur Bonin was fabulous."

"His performance was but a shadow to your brilliance."

Her thundering heart beat so wildly, she clasped her hands to quell it. "Surely you exaggerate, Your Grace."

"Not at all." Another whisper of warm breath washed over her. "You were every bit as good as Mademoiselle Taglioni. More so. And…and I'm irritated by the way my friends fawned over you."

"They were gentlemanly enough. I'm sorry I behaved awkwardly."

"No. You were delightful." Though the duke's voice was soft, it was intense and sure. "They were imposing and overbearing."

Bria turned her head, glancing over her shoulder. "I'll improve when in the public eye. I'm not accustomed to being among so many important people."

A large, masculine hand touched her arm. "You felt beneath them?"

"Yes. Why would I not? I am a foundling."

"Sometimes people rise above their birth and accomplish amazing things." His hand smoothed down the length of her arm and he gently squeezed his fingers. "Face me, Miss LeClair."

If she turned around now, there was every chance she might swoon into his embrace again. No one had ever spoken to her thusly. It was as if he understood her deepest thoughts. As a duke, Ravenscar could never think of her as his equal. But in private, he seemed to be more at ease—more human. With the coaxing of his fingers, she relented and turned.

Still smiling, his eyes searched her face while he cupped her cheek. "You are an astounding talent on the stage—enchanting like nothing I have ever seen."

She sighed into the delight of his touch. "Truly?" Bria didn't recognize the breathlessness in her reply.

"I never pay a compliment unless it is warranted." Those smoldering eyes fanned by long black lashes, shifted to her mouth. His breath caught. So did hers.

"If I could grant you one wish-come-true, Miss LeClair, a boon freely given for tonight's performance, what would it be?"

She instantly thought of the Sylph, a creature not of the earthly realm, who'd longed for the love of a simple Scottish farmer. A love not meant to be. Bria knew better than to wish for the impossible. And yet…

"I would like one kiss," she said, her limbs growing numb as she uttered the words. "Do not misunderstand. Maintaining my virtue is of utmost importance to me. I do not go about demanding or even permitting kisses, Your Grace. I do, however, dance the role of the Sylph. And just once I'd to know what she longs for without risking the heartache she endured."

Ravenscar twisted a gold signet ring around his smallest finger. The ring was crested with a unicorn rampant. How fitting that his crest should be a mythical creature.

"I once aspired to the stage."

Of all reactions, Bria did not anticipate his admission and His Grace's expression suggested he hadn't planned to offer it.

"Dukes do not tread the boards," he went on. "I know what it is to yearn for that which cannot be. If it is a mere kiss you wish for, I would be honored to be the man to give it."

He didn't offer a rakish grin as she might have expected. He looked curiously serious, which Bria found more alluring. She suspected few saw this side of him, and even fewer knew he'd once wished to be a performer.

New sensations curled through her body. She wanted to kiss him, to taste his lips. Alone and standing with a duke in a fairytale chamber, suddenly all Bria wanted was to know what it was like to let him stoop down, to draw near, to meet his lips.

"Thank you," she whispered, taking a step nearer.

He closed the gap and in a rush of tingling, he brushed his mouth across hers. Sighing, her knees turned boneless while his gaze met hers.

One kiss on the most important night of my life. Why should I not?

Her trembling fingers slid to his waist while she took one last step into him, drawn by the magic of the night. Those powerful hands shifted to her cheeks as he closed his eyes and kissed. His tongue skimmed across her lips. Bria stiffened for a heartbeat, but he persisted. Light, gentle sweeps politely asked to enter her mouth. Timidly, she opened for him and, for the briefest of moments, his tongue caressed the tip of hers.

As if she'd grown wings and began floating, she followed his lead as his kiss grew more impassioned, more demanding, more—

"Beg your pardon."

With the lady's maid's three words, Bria jumped away, clapping her fingers to her face. "I-I-I—"

"I was just congratulating Miss LeClair on her debut."
His Grace bowed. Twice. "Forgive me for my overt display
of enthusiasm. I will leave you to change."

Completely flummoxed, Bria stood dumbfounded while
she watched the duke stride out the door. The man could
make butter melt with the heat of the fire in his eyes. Slowly,
she brushed a finger across her lips, the sensation of his kiss
lingering. It may have merely been an act of enthusiasm to
him, but she would cherish this moment for the rest of her
days. Didn't all girls remember the thrill of their first kiss?

Her dilemma? She must never let it happen again.
Dancing was her life, her love, her master. Being alone with
the Duke of Ravenscar was dangerous. And kissing him
would lead to nothing but heartache.

Chapter Eight

Drake jabbed with the right then danced to the left. With Percy's block, he saw his opening and threw a hook, landing a facer exactly where he'd aimed.

Grunting, Percy staggered backward. "God's stones, Ravenscar. What has your bristles up this morn?"

"Bugger all. You're just slow, you maggot." Drake danced in place and beckoned with his boxing gloves. "Come. Another round."

The future Duke of Northumberland stepped out of the sparring ring. "I think not. You've got something in your craw and I know better than to play the stand in for a whipping boy whilst you take out your ire."

"What do I have to be angry about?" Drake asked, growling a little too much. "Ticket sales are rife."

Percy tugged open the laces on his gloves. "That's exactly what I was thinking."

Drake threw a half-dozen jabs through the air. Percy had no idea how close to the mark he was. Damnation, Drake was a bloody gentleman and the only thing he could think about was kissing Britannia LeClair last eve—and how much he wanted more. Why the devil did he have to kiss her?

Oh yes, Miss LeClair if you want to kiss a duke, by all means use me as your dupe.

For the love of God, he wasn't supposed to enjoy it. She'd enchanted him, the minx. He was a bloody man, not a mannequin. Contrary to what people believed, blood pulsed beneath his skin.

Now, every time he looked at the woman he would be reminded of the wildness of her taste, her eagerness, of being washed in the scent of wisteria while experiencing the sensation of floating. Merciful mercy, the damned floating. No mere kiss had ever made his knees go weak. Not like last night. Ravenscar was supposed to be in control, supposed to be chivalrous. Who knew what had come over him when he'd dipped his head and brushed his lips across hers?

She wasn't just the Sylph on stage, she embodied the nymph off stage as well.

Snarling, Drake threw six more jabs.

"See?" said Percy. "You have something in your craw."

"I have no idea to what you are referring."

"Right. And I'm Saint Christopher."

Drake shot him a look. "Just leave it alone."

Percy tugged off his gloves. "If she's going to be out in society, you ought to at least ensure the woman is properly attired."

"I beg your pardon?"

"Your new diva. And do not try to deny it. I saw how every man in the hall slavered over Miss LeClair last eve including you, Ravenscar."

Drake grumbled under his breath. "She's a quandary...and too lovely for her own good."

"She's a novelty. And you'll have your hands full if you intend to keep the wolves at bay."

Drake scowled. Again. Bloody Christmas, he already had his miserable hands full.

***

"*Alors*," said Pauline, sitting beside Bria on the bed and pulling the parcel from her grasp. "This one is from the Earl of Fordham, did you say?"

Bria leaned in and watched her friend open the gift. "I met him last night. He was a bit forward."

"*Eau de parfum*." Pauline dabbed a bit behind her ears. "Mm. At least he has good taste."

Inhaling deeply, Bria sampled the scent while she reached for the earl's missive. "*Oui*, it is nice."

"What did he write?"

"'*Please do me the honor of sharing my phaeton for a jaunt through Hyde Park this afternoon…*'"

"This afternoon? Does he not realize you have a rehearsal?"

"Evidently not." She set the letter aside. "I'll send my regrets."

"And thank him for the perfume."

"That, too." Bria watched Pauline place the bottle atop the small table between their beds, wishing Fordham hadn't sent the gift. And the others as well, for that matter.

Pauline plopped back down and grasped Bria's arm. "I sense your unease."

"I do not want to be indebted to anyone." She gestured to the gifts strewn across the bed. "It doesn't feel right to accept all these things."

"Where is it written a ballerina cannot receive a gift of appreciation from an admirer? Marie is showered with flowers and the like every night. Goodness, if you want to be a wallflower, you should have stayed in the *corps* with me."

"You're Florrie's understudy now. It won't be long until you're a principal as well. I cannot wait to be there to see all the gifts you receive after your debut." Guilt. That was why Bria didn't want these things. It wasn't right for her to receive so many gifts while the person who had been her best friend through thick and thin had not.

She selected the next missive, stamped with a blank. "Odd, this one bears only my name."

"No sender?"

"*Non.*" She broke the seal and unfolded it. As she read, a sickly chill churned her stomach. "Not everyone enjoyed last night's debut."

"*Mon Dieu*, you look as if a ghost just crossed your path. Quickly, read it aloud."

The parchment trembled between Bria's fingers as she translated the English into French, "*Miss LeClair, your dancing is disgraceful and unfitting for Britons. Take your immoral conduct and return to France. You are not welcome here.*"

"Gah!" Bria crumpled the missive against her roiling stomach. "This invalidates every last complimentary letter I've received."

"It most certainly does not." Pauline snatched the parchment and crumpled it even more. "Who would write such a thing?"

In an instant, Bria went from sailing on a cloud to crashing into a stone wall. A letter like that was enough to drive a girl crawling under her bed to hide throughout the duration of the Season. No, not everyone would appreciate her dancing, but she didn't expect to receive such a scathing personal strike. She dared lean over and peek at the missive again. "It isn't signed."

"Unbelievable." Pauline scanned it as if she could read English. "Whoever wrote this is a coward. I'm throwing it out."

Bria curled over, covering her face with her hands. Why did people feel the need to be so callous? Ever since the LeClairs died in Bayeux she had encountered bullies and browbeaters at every turn. There was no reason for it. What had she done that was so disgraceful? Shortened her skirts an inch? Dance with passion? Tears blurred her vision as she glanced to the complimentary missives and gifts she'd already opened. Why must one evil naysayer ruin the joy?

Pauline tore the letter, tossed it in the rubbish, then brushed off her hands. "We shall put those words of bitterness out of our minds and not think on them again." Picking up the next missive, she resumed her seat on the bed. "Only a few more to go. Open this one. Providence tells me it will be far more pleasant than the last."

Bria didn't take it. "I think I'd rather wait."

"Truly?"

"*Oui.*"

"I see." Pauline tapped the missive on her palm. "You receive one bad apple and you'd prefer to brood for the rest of the day?"

"I certainly cannot make emotions rise and fall like a lantern wick."

"Perhaps, but you can choose to look at the odds."

Out of the corner of her eye, Bria regarded her friend, waggling her eyebrows, blast her.

"You have received a dozen or so glowing missives, some with lavish gifts, and you are choosing to allow a solitary curmudgeon to ruin your entire morning. Not everyone is going to love you."

"I know."

Pauline shook the letter. "Then open this blessed missive or I'll do it for you."

Sighing, Bria took it. Perhaps she was being overly sensitive. But how did one shrug off such slander to one's character and pretend to be unaffected? She examined the seal. "Oh my goodness."

"What is it?"

"This one's from Baroness Calthorpe. She's the lady who spilled wine on my dress."

Pauline clapped a bereft hand over her heart. "Someone spilled wine on you? And you didn't tell me about it?"

Bria cringed, glancing at the soiled dress now draped over her trunk with the stain hidden. "Forgive me. You were asleep when I arrived home last eve."

"Good heavens, what happened?"

"Nothing untoward aside from the wine…" *And I kissed the Duke of Ravenscar*. Avoiding Pauline's eyes, Bria read the missive, which, thanks to Pauline's insistence, did help raise her spirits.

"Did the baroness soil your gown on purpose?"

"Heavens no. She accidently bumped her father's glass." Bria shook the parchment. "Listen to this:"

"Dear Miss LeClair,

Please allow me to say how much I enjoyed La Sylphide. Your performance was brilliant. I have never seen a ballerina dance with more grace, style, and passion. Once more, I must apologize for ruining your gown at the soiree. In recompense I have established a credit of twenty pounds in your name at Harding, Howell and Company on Pall Mall. They carry all the best ladies' accoutrements in London with fans, gloves, ornamental items, and haberdashery of every description, including silk, muslins, laces and the like. They even have a line of perfumery.

I trust you will find something to suit your fancy.

Sincerely,

Charlotte Calthorpe"

"Twenty pounds?" Pauline plucked the missive from Bria's fingers and waved it like a flag. "That's more than my entire year's pin money."

"Mine as well, but I'm guessing it won't go far at a fancy shop on Pall Mall. Isn't that where all the wealthy buy their things?"

"It is and, moreover, I think you might need to be a member of the gentry to venture into that part of London."

"Nonsense." Pulling the letter from her friend's fingers, Bria refolded it, wondering if there was any truth to Pauline's claim. She wouldn't want to visit a high-end shop only to be turned away. How dreadful would that be? It would embarrass her to her toes. Had Lady Calthorpe considered such a thing?

Last night, the baroness had been pleasant and inquisitive. For a moment, Bria thought she might have met Her Ladyship before, but how could she have? She'd never been to England, and certainly wasn't familiar with the woman's name...and the baroness' father was a duke. Aside from Ravenscar, Bria had never encountered anyone as important as a duke. In fact, she knew little of and, after last night, was decidedly ill at ease among nobility. *Which is another reason why I am averse to Lord Fordham's invitation to ride through Hyde Park.*

"Well, you certainly won a great many admirers with your debut." Pauline picked up a pair of exquisite doe leather gloves. "Do you mind if I borrow these?"

"Why not? Take them. You deserve them more than I do." How could Bria say no? If it weren't for Pauline, she would have withered on the vine living among so many thorny and competitive dancers. And this morning, she had been given so much while her dearest friend, the nicest person she knew, received nothing. All the gifts had been unexpected—a reticule, a bonnet, posies of flowers, three gold sovereigns, not to mention the perfume from Lord Fordham. Moreover, she'd been invited to balls, soirees, and teas. In all, it was overwhelming.

"Miss LeClair?" a knock came, though by now she recognized the delivery boy's voice.

Pauline sniggered. "He's climbed the stairs so many times, the poor lad is going to be sore on the morrow."

"Perhaps we should have taken a room on a lower floor." Bria hastened to open the door.

The boy looked up at her with enormous blue eyes. "The Duke of Ravenscar is waiting, miss. And he has a carriage outside."

At the mention of the man who hadn't left her thoughts since she'd practically begged him to kiss her, Bria's stomach fluttered. Trying not to blush in front of Pauline, she knit her brows. "Did His Grace say why he is here?"

Squirming, the lad turned one foot inward. "Said something about a modiste, and he gave me a coin to make you come quickly."

"Oh, did he now?"

"Yes, now come." The lad beckoned with a wave of his hand.

"Give me a moment."

"But—"

Bria shut the door and dashed to the dressing table. "My hair is a disaster."

Pauline picked up the brush. "No one's mistress, did you say?"

"Hold your tongue!" Her hackles bristling, Bria stamped her foot. "Absolutely not. The duke promised to replace my gown and now that I have the credit at Harding, Howell and Company, I will not need his help."

"Mm hmm." Pauline sniggered. "So, why am I putting up your hair?"

"Because I cannot go downstairs looking like an alehouse wench."

Twisting Bria's long rope of tresses into a chignon, Pauline reached for a hairpin. "Do you want to know what I think?"

"No."

"Well, I'm going to tell you anyway. You dined with him. His mother invited you to her mansion."

Bria held up her finger. "She invited all the principals."

"That's because it wouldn't have looked proper for her to have only invited you."

"Oh, please."

"And now he's downstairs waiting to take you to the modiste? He's a duke—an important man with many responsibilities. Not to mention the magnate who built our theater. Something is afoot with him. Mark me."

Bria clapped her hands to her face to hide her flushing cheeks. Goodness, she couldn't say a word about the kiss. He didn't care about it. She had asked him to humor her. That was all. Nothing more. She must stop thinking about accursed kissing.

His Grace had told the lady's maid he was merely congratulating me. Even if it was a lovely, unforgettable kiss. Impassioned, bone melting...

She glared at herself in the mirror.

It meant nothing to him.

How could she think it could possibly have meant more than the granting of one wish—at most, an expression of appreciation? Dance was her master. Nothing else.

"I'm going thank him for his generosity and tell him to go away." After rouging her lips, Bria headed for the door.

"Don't forget your cloak," said Pauline, "or your gloves...or your bonnet."

"I do not need them."

"Yes, you do."

Not listening, Bria followed the boy down to the entry. Not surprisingly, Florrie was making a nuisance of herself, batting her eyelashes at Ravenscar. As usual, the dancer wore a low-cut gown, stood with her shoulders back, displaying what cleavage she could. Obviously, she was wasting no time laying claim to her targeted duke.

Pocket watch in hand and tapping his foot, His Grace looked anything but amused.

As soon as he looked up, he grinned, blast him. The man must stand in front of the mirror and practice his smile. Such a mien was too irresistible for anyone of the female variety. "Ah, Miss LeClair. It is lovely to see you this morn." He grasped her elbow and brushed past Florrie who stood gaping like a jealous lover snubbed.

Bria shot an apologetic grimace to the dancer while trying to tug her arm away. "Thank you for your concern, Your Grace, but I am perfectly able to purchase my own clothing."

"Nonsense," he said, squeezing his fingers and practically dragging her outside. "We are going to the modiste. It is all arranged."

The coachman opened the door to a shiny post chaise.

Before stepping on the stool, Bria was finally able to draw her arm away. "But I need—"

"Your cloak and gloves, my lady," said Pauline with a teasing curtsy. Bless her, she knew there'd be no stopping Ravenscar, especially with his determined grinning.

"Thank you." Bria blew her a kiss. "You are so dear to me, my friend."

After tipping his hat, His Grace offered his hand and helped her inside where he then sat opposite. "I never care to be alone in the presence of that woman again."

"Florrie?"

"The one who played Effie in the ballet."

"I see. But she has the pedigree you were so interested in. Her father is a choreographer for the Paris Opera and her mother a famous soprano."

"I don't care if she's the daughter of King William."

Bria ran the curtain tie-back through her fingers— heavens, it was made of gold silk. "That's quite a shame, she will be disappointed."

"Does she make a habit of engaging noblemen in conversation?"

"Only those who might be interested in…" Bria couldn't say it.

"Ah, yes." He cleared his throat. "Did you see this morning's headlines?"

"I haven't."

He picked up a paper beside him on the bench and smiled. Again. Were young ladies permitted to tell dukes not to smile? Before she could ask, he cleared his throat. "The *Times* says, '*LeClair dazzles and shocks in the most acclaimed ballet of the century*'." He traded one paper for another. "And the *Gazette* says, '*Exotic romp through Scotland, LeClair's dancing is nothing shy of scandalous*'."

A stone sank to the pit of Bria's stomach. "The *Gazette* didn't sound complimentary."

"On the contrary. People will be queuing around the theater for tickets to see something exotic, bordering on scandalous."

"I hope you are right."

"I am." He stared at her as if there were nothing else in the carriage at which to look. Why not read the next article from the paper still in his grasp—anything but staring directly at her with those shocking blue eyes? But it seemed he'd done his reading for the day and was more intent on smiling and looking far too tempting. His lips glimmered with moisture, pursed in a very self-assured expression, and every bit as kissable as they had been last eve.

Bria glanced away. "I don't like being referred to as scandalous. My dancing is art. There is nothing shameful about it."

He set the paper aside. "I agree."

Perhaps she ought to change the subject. "So, as I tried to say before you all but abducted me, I am perfectly able to purchase my own clothing."

"Last eve, you said you had no money for a new gown."

Not ready to tell him about the twenty pounds from Lady Calthorpe, Bria thought up her next best excuse. "Once I receive my wages—"

Ravenscar held up his palm, stopping her mid-sentence. "I said I would replace your gown and I am a man of my word. Please allow me to fulfill my promise." He pinched a bit of her skirt between his fingers. "It hasn't escaped my notice that I have now seen you in three different dresses, each of which is…" He waved the cloth like a flag, his lips twisting as if he'd stopped himself from saying something crass. "Dash it, my servants are better clothed."

She batted his hand away. "I beg your pardon. This dress is nearly new." It wasn't. After paying an investigator in Paris, Bria hadn't enough coin to buy any dresses in the past year, but she wasn't about to own to it. "We wouldn't, by chance, be venturing past Harding, Howell and Company, would we?"

One black eyebrow shot up. "Our first stop—to purchase material, then on to my mother's modiste."

Bria smoothed her skirts where he'd pinched the fabric. Perhaps she would be allowed in the shop after all. "It is very thoughtful for you to be concerned about my wardrobe."

"That's better." He sat back with a discerning eye.

"Though it isn't necessary."

"I deem it is. It is in my interest to see that you present favorably to society."

"Do you think if I go about town in pretty dresses people will like me better?"

"It has nothing to do with what other people like. Well…not exactly. Polite society expects a certain decorum. There are rules. Boundaries which mustn't be crossed. I'm sure my mother's soiree last eve is only one of many parties to which you will be invited and you, as the theater's diva, must play the part both on and off stage."

"I suppose you're right. Only this morning I received a number of invitations. So many I couldn't possibly attend them all."

"To where, may I ask, have you been invited?"

"Ah…" Perhaps she shouldn't have been so hasty to boast about the pile of missives she left on her bed. "I haven't even opened all the letters yet." Bria drummed her fingers, trying to recall. "There's a luncheon at Vauxhall, a tea hosted by Lady Eloise, and Lord Fordham asked me to go riding in Hyde Park with him this afternoon—"

"Fordham?" The duke pounded his fist on the bench. "That brigand."

"I thought he was your friend."

"Of late I wonder. I would steer clear of the earl if I were you. He has a reputation as a rake."

"I see." Bria sniggered. "Perhaps he should ask Florrie to go riding."

The duke chuckled. "Your sense of humor is delightful, Miss LeClair. I shall suggest Miss Bisset to him right after I tell him to stop badgering you."

"I hardly call an invitation to go for a ride in the man's phaeton badgering."

"You don't know Thomas Newport. His invitation was only a precursor to spirit you alone so that he can take liberties." Ravenscar tugged down his cuffs. "You'll find propriety in England is far more rigid than it is in France."

"Oh? Can you give me an example?"

"First of all, riding in Fordham's phaeton would draw a great deal of—ah—attention."

Bria spread her arms wide, gesturing from one wall of the carriage to the other. "Am I not riding in your carriage? Surely that is more scandalous in England than riding in an open carriage like a phaeton?"

"Our situation is completely different. You are in my employ."

"So, in London society, such an arrangement is permissible because of our master-servant status?"

"I deem it is."

"Then I venture to guess it was completely proper for you to come to your sister's chamber last eve."

"No." His eyes shifted aside, as if he harbored regret for his actions. "I must ask your forgiveness for last night. That was a mistake."

Her stomach churned. Bria couldn't look at him. Of course, he'd only kissed her because she'd asked him to. And she had no reason to believe the gesture had meant anything to him. "I thought as much," she forced herself to say, trying to sound unaffected.

"Nonetheless, I suggest that until you are familiar with London society, you discuss your engagements with me prior to accepting them."

She considered his request for a moment. On one hand it made sense because she wasn't completely familiar with England and all their societal rules—in France, with the Revolution and the Napoleon Wars, too many of the nobility had been lost, too many men as well, making it impossible for women of Bria's class to worry about having an escort for everything. On the other hand, reporting her engagements to Ravenscar was downright awkward and imposing. She would be in London for months and the last thing she needed was His Grace overseeing her affairs.

She crossed her ankles, the gesture making her toes brush the tips of his boots—contact that sent gooseflesh rising across her skin. "I'm sure you are far too busy to concern yourself with something as trivial as my engagements," she said, trying to sound in control, giving no indication of the queasy *grands jetés* performing in her insides.

"Hmm." His gaze met hers, but it wasn't blasé or impassive. His eyes were as dark and intense as they had been last eve. "Perhaps you're right. But do not hesitate to ask if you have any doubt about an invitation. Case in point, Fordham's request to go riding—or any man's invitation for that matter."

Perhaps she'd misread his expression. Did he look at every woman with such intensity and then carry on with the conversation as if his gazes were passionless and reticent?

"Thank heavens I'll be in rehearsal this afternoon." Bria looked out the window just as the carriage passed a sign that read, *"Private Inquiry Office"*. "What street is this?" she asked.

Leaning forward, His Grace glanced out. "Regent."

She made a mental note. There were definitely a few things she wanted to accomplish herself without her employer's watchful eye. What if she turned up something about her past she'd rather keep under wraps? Thus far, the only person who knew about Bria's keepsakes was Pauline. Now definitely was no time to reveal her secret. With the papers distorting the truth, who knew what they might report if her inquiries became common knowledge?

Chapter Nine

"Ah, Miss LeClair, we've been expecting you," said Mr. Harding, coming out from behind the counter of his haberdashery.

A tad confused, Drake looked from the shop owner to Britannia. Had his mother sent word ahead? "They were expecting you?"

She shrugged, giving nothing away. "Was the incident with the glass of wine in the newspapers as well?"

"It was not."

Two ladies stared in disbelief while Mr. Harding pulled Britannia deeper into the shop. "I attended the ballet last night and your performance was nothing short of extraordinary."

Drake rubbed his thumbs under his lapels and gave the women a tepid bow, right before they sidled out the door.

"This is abominable. I cannot believe the clientele they have stooped to entertain, and on Pall Mall," said a pretentious, elderly woman. She and her accomplice moved to the perfumery rather than the exit.

Drake recognized the woman as the wife of Mr. Wainthorpe. New money, and obviously inflated with her own self-importance. He moved near enough to speak quietly. "Perhaps you'll find the patrons more to your liking at Leicester Square. After all, I have never been in the company of others when my rank was not lofty enough for my peers."

Mrs. Wainthorpe huffed. "I was not referring to you, Your Grace."

He gave a cursory bow of his head. "Did you attend last night's opening at Chadwick Theater?"

Her arrogant nose turned up with her sniff. "I most certainly did not."

"I see. Then might I suggest you refrain from being so generous with your opinions until you actually have an idea regarding the subject upon which you are speaking."

"Ah." Turning a shade of chartreuse, the woman practically gagged on her own indignation. "I have never been thus insulted in my life...and by a duke of all people. Wait until my husband hears about this." She snatched her companion's elbow and started for the door.

Drake followed. "Please do give Mr. Wainthorpe my regards. And let him know he is welcome to join me in my box for tonight's performance of *La Sylphide*."

Once Mrs. Wainthorpe fled out the door, Drake took a good look around the shop for any other snobbish prudes who might be lurking. Fortunately, the remainder of the patrons were tending to their own affairs.

Mr. Harding had taken Britannia to the rear of the shop where they were looking at fabric. Drake hastened toward them. "To begin with, Miss LeClair will need a ball gown, an evening gown, two day gowns, matching trimmings, and a cloak."

"*Mais non.*" Shaking her head, Britannia slashed a parasol through the air as if it were a foil. "One evening gown. At these prices, I can afford no more—and I've yet to pay a modiste."

"What makes you think you're paying?" Drake asked. "As I said earlier, it is in the interest of Chadwick Theater for you to present well in public as our premier ballerina. You are a diva—one of England's most acclaimed guests and must be attired accordingly." Drake snapped his fingers at Mr. Harding. "Miss LeClair's expenses shall be invoiced to me."

Britannia reached inside her reticule and pulled out a missive. "But I have—"

"I'll hear no argument."

"Very well." She replaced the document. "I'll allow Chadwick Theater to intervene this once only."

Mr. Harding licked his lips, all too anxious to show them the latest fabrics and matching fans, gloves, hats and reticules. After a good two hours of selecting the finest of everything Harding, Howell and Company had to offer, Drake escorted Britannia a few blocks to the modiste for measurements.

"I do appreciate your generosity, but last night you said you would replace one gown. That would have been enough. What are people going to think? You purchased an entire new wardrobe on my behalf, not to mention all the accessories to go with them. They will assume the worst."

The same thought had passed through Drake's mind, though he'd discounted it. Besides, let the vultures think what they like. Perhaps if Fordham believed Britannia to be Ravenscar's mistress, the rake would set his sights on Miss Bisset or one of the other dancers. "People will assume what they will. I care not. Ours is a professional relationship and that's what matters."

"To you." She walked on at a ferocious pace. "I'm not enamored with the idea of people thinking I am your mistress when I am not."

Drake lengthened his stride. "Would you like to be? Rhetorically speaking, of course." Damnation, the words passed his lips before he had a chance to swallow them. *What a nonsensical thing to ask.*

She stopped, thrusting her fists downward. "Absolutely *not!* Aside from the fact that I hardly know you, I have no intention of becoming anyone's mistress. Ever!"

Drake grinned. Had they not been standing on a busy footpath, he might hug her and whirl her around in circles. Fordham be damned. Perhaps his question wasn't as shortsighted as he'd thought. Her conviction gave him a great deal of ease. He would stand beside his commitment to avoid becoming involved with anyone at Chadwick Theater, and he needn't worry about his lecherous friends…for the most part. Though he would be keeping a very close eye on their activities where Miss LeClair was concerned.

It was unfortunate his mother hadn't introduced him to any ladies with Britannia's fortitude, however. When he did decide to marry, he sincerely hoped to find someone with her pluck, her spirit, her stamina. Confident, virtuous, hard-working and determined to succeed—he barely knew the woman yet had uncovered many redeeming qualities. She was certainly an inspiration for other young ladies eager for a profession in the performing arts.

***

After arriving at the boarding house much later than she'd intended, Pauline met Bria in the entry. "Have you been with the duke all along? 'Tis almost time for rehearsal."

Bria glanced at the floor clock at the end of the corridor. "If I'd known it was going to take so much time, I would have insisted on going on one of our rest days."

"We haven't a moment to lose or we'll miss our warm up."

"Heaven forbid. Monsieur Travere will start recruiting replacements for us both."

Bria gave her parcels to the houseboy and paid him a halfpenny to take them up to her room.

Pauline tugged her out the door. "Did you hear? The entire troupe has been invited to a private ball to be held by

Edward Hughes—word is his estate is magnificent. He inherited a vast fortune from his stepfather who was an admiral of all things."

"Truly?"

"*Oui*, a fortnight hence on a Monday when the theater is dark." Pauline leaped with a little *jeté*. "I am so looking forward to it!"

Bria looped her arm through her friend's elbow. "And we'll have a whole day to prepare. *C'est manifique!*"

Florrie met them at the stage door. "Here's the prima donna come from her trip to the elite modiste. What was it like to rub elbows with England's nobility? Did the duke give you a French kiss?"

Bria gulped. To what was Florrie alluding? She couldn't possibly know what had happened in the bedchamber at the soiree. Could she? Nonetheless, Bria feigned utter innocence. "You know I am not interested in an affair with Ravenscar or anyone else."

"That's right." Florrie followed them inside like an irritating horsefly. "The Sylph is so much better than the rest of us. One successful performance and you think you're as good as Marie."

"Stop it." Pauline shouldered between them. "You were there when Bria told Ravenscar she didn't want to go shopping with him."

"But she went, didn't she? And after I told both of you he was mine."

"You can have him, or perhaps Lord Fordham. Evidently, the earl is looking for a mistress to keep his lust at bay. Though Ravenscar mentioned no such thing." Bria stormed into the dressing room.

In the blink of an eye, her blood ran cold. All of her makeup powders were opened, turned over and spilled in a heap. Her hairpins were strewn across the floor, as was an entire parcel of lamb's wool.

"Florrieeeeee!" she yelled as she faced the devious shrew. "How dare you ruin my things? I know you wanted to dance the Sylph. You've always thought yourself superior, but this is taking things too far."

Florrie stood with her mouth open as if she had only just seen the havoc she'd wreaked. "I didn't touch your—"

"To the *barre*, ladies!" bellowed Monsieur Travere. "You've had the entire day to chatter. When I make a call for a four o'clock rehearsal, I expect you to be a quarter of an hour early. How many times must I repeat myself?"

"*Pardon*, monsieur," Bria said, while she shoved her feet into her slippers.

"Look at this pig sty!" he bellowed, growing red in the face. "Britannia, I am shocked. I expect your toilette to be clean before you leave tonight. You may be dancing the lead, but you have not yet earned fame and fortune. Until you can afford to pay a maid, I expect you to keep your things tidy."

"*Oui*, monsieur," Bria replied while fury thrummed through her blood.

"She didn't do this," Pauline said as she started for the stage.

"I do not care." Travere glared as if he could blow fire through his nostrils. "Britannia will be the one to clean it up."

Florrie sniggered from behind while they took their places at the *barre*.

Bria touched her toes where she could give the wretch an evil eye. "Not only did you lay waste to my toilette, you choose to laugh?"

"Oh, yes, I'll laugh, but do not blame me for the mess. I had no hand in it."

Now she denies her actions as well.

Toward the end of rehearsal, the boy from the boarding house dashed from the stage door. "Miss LeClair! Someone has ransacked your chamber!"

Chapter Ten

On Saturdays, Drake regularly paid a visit to his mother for tea and cakes. It had become their ritual for sharing their news and planning the weeks ahead.

Mother pulled her shawl about her shoulders. "The days are growing warmer at last."

"And longer." The conversation always started with a mention of the weather before Her Grace poured. "I'll be glad when the rain slows a bit, however."

"But the rain ensures a healthy harvest come autumn." She picked up the teapot.

Drake held out his cup. "That it does."

"And how is your theater venture? It has been nearly two weeks. Are ticket sales what you'd hoped?"

"They are. We've been sold out every night, and advance sales for the next two months are strong I'm thrilled to say."

After his trip with Britannia to Harding, Howell and Company, he'd taken great pains to keep his distance, especially since she was so emphatic about keeping the wolves at bay. Not that he was one of the proverbial wolves. But restraint on his part was certainly necessary. It wouldn't suit to be caught kissing an employee in his theater—to give her the slightest hint as to how much she consumed his thoughts.

"And your investment?" Mother asked. "Do you think it will be worthwhile in the long term?"

"It should pay dividends tenfold, though I do not expect full recompense for at least two years. After that, I daresay the House of Ravenscar will be wealthier than the crown." His lenders were content for the most part. And Monsieur Marchand had accepted a renegotiation of the terms. It seemed Drake had dodged financial ruination at least for the time being.

The saucer clinked when Mother set down her cup. "With the way the king spends money, I'd say such a feat is not terribly remarkable."

"You may be right." Drake sipped his tea. "And how are things with the patronesses at Almacks?"

"Hectic this time of year as usual." Mother pinched a tiny cake between two delicate fingers. "I expect to see you there on Monday next. I'm billeted as the hostess. By the way, I sent you an invitation a month ago and you haven't responded."

"Forgive me. I didn't realize I needed to send a response, since you know I'll endeavor to attend." Frowning, Drake reached for one of three cakes that looked as if the pastry chef had spent hours applying tiny baubles. It took seconds to pop the morsel into his mouth. "But Monday next? Hughes is having a ball that same evening. He's invited the entire cast of *La Sylphide*. Such a conflict is inexcusable. Surely he knew about Almacks' event."

"Most likely he did, but he's not one of us, dear. He's new money."

"That may be so but, with his fortune, I would think many in polite society would be anxious to befriend him— introduce their daughters and inject some of that newly-earned coin into old and mismanaged coffers."

"Mr. Hughes is gluttonous and loud."

"And I venture to guess he did not receive an invitation to the first ball hosted by the esteemed Dowager Duchess of Ravenscar?"

Mother pursed her lips, a telling sign.

"Well, therein lies the problem. I daresay if the dancers from *La Sylphide* will be attending his ball, so will most of the *ton's* single gentlemen."

"How can you say such a thing? Almacks is the pinnacle of the social elite. It is the place to be seen."

"Unless the most talented dancers in Europe will be elsewhere with the promise of a more entertaining evening."

Mother regarded him as if shrewdly aghast, an expression polished by years of being a duchess. "Do not tell me you are planning to attend Mr. Hughes' ball."

"I'd planned to." Suddenly overwarm, Drake stretched his collar. "After all, I am the man who invited the troupe to come to London. I ought to be there."

"But you have no responsibility to associate with those people outside the theater. You have seen to it they are paid a fair wage, properly housed and fed. Your relationship should be no more than master and servant."

And Lord High Protector. Drake looked to the portrait of his father above the mantel dressed in military uniform. It seemed the Dukes of Ravenscar were destined to protect something, be it country or damsels. Nonetheless, Mother was right. He'd been reminding himself of her very words every other thought. Still, Miss LeClair was going to Hughes' event and so were Fordham and Saye, and a number of other dandies who could manipulate themselves under the poor ballerina's skirts so fast, she wouldn't know she'd been ravished until it was over.

"Besides," Mother continued, "Lady Blanche will be at Almacks, and I've been ever so anxious for you to meet her."

"Lady Blanche?"

"Daughter of the Viscount of Falmouth."

Fowl Mouth. "Ah yes, I recall." Drake hid his frown behind his cup.

"Do not affect your silent sullenness with me. I expect you to be there and dance with Her Ladyship. I am withering where I sit awaiting grandchildren."

"Ada has been quite adept at fulfilling your wishes."

"You know to what I am referring, and you need an heir. This is the Season, Drake. You are not growing younger."

He sighed, pouring for himself. "If it will please Your Grace, I will call into Almacks and dance with Lady Blanche."

"That's all I ask."

***

In the following fortnight there had been no more incidences of someone rifling through Bria's things, though the intrusion had made her uneasy. Thank heavens nothing had been stolen—but that made the incidences all the more confounding. Florrie continued to purport her innocence, but Bria didn't believe her. Aside from Pauline, Florrie had been the only one to see her leave the boarding house with Ravenscar. To add to her guilt, she had clearly been hostile when Bria met her at the theater.

Still, there had been no irrefutable proof and Bria let it pass.

Today, she finally got a chance to venture out alone. Bria rubbed her fingers over the miniature hidden beneath her gown, standing on the footpath in front of the door that read *Private Inquiry Office*. In small letters beneath read the name Mr. Walter Gibbs, Investigator. Taking a deep breath, Bria clutched her reticule and prayed her two pounds and four pence would be enough.

Inside, a flight of stairs took her directly to the second level and another, rather unpretentious door. She knocked.

A man who looked like a clerk opened the door and looked out over her head. After Bria cleared her throat, he dropped his gaze and frowned. "Hello, miss. Do you have an appointment?"

"Do I need one?"

"What is the nature of your call?"

"I have a missing persons inquiry. My name is Miss LeClair from France."

"I'll see if Mr. Gibbs can squeeze you into his schedule." The man gestured to a bench just inside the door. "Please have a seat."

Bria glanced about the small entry with a pastoral painting askew on the wall. The Inquiry Office didn't seem busy at all. In fact, it was a bit too quiet.

Before she took a seat, the man returned. "You're in luck, Miss LeClair. Please follow me."

She forced a smile, though the man's harsh mien gave no pretense of friendliness.

Ushered into offices lined with books, the investigator stood from his place at a writing table and was introduced as Mr. Gibbs. "Miss LeClair, I understand you have a missing persons inquiry from France?" He was tallish, clean shaven, with brown hair and a long nose to match his gaunt face—a face that made her feel about as welcome as a moray eel. He gestured for her to sit in a chair across from his and resumed his seat behind the table.

Bria clutched her reticule tighter as she contemplated a hasty exit. If Mr. Gibbs wanted patrons, he might at least try to appear pleasant—and that went for his clerk as well. "Ah, my inquiry is not exactly missing persons…I suppose it is, but the person is missing to me, and most likely not missing to themselves."

The man snorted with an air of arrogance. "That is usually the case when someone goes astray. Perhaps if you explain your situation, I'll be better able to discern if I can be of assistance."

Taking a deep breath, she removed the miniature from around her neck and produced the handkerchief from her reticule. "Pauline and I—"

"Pauline?"

"My dearest friend. If I could call her a sister, I would."

He leaned forward, eyeing the portrait in her hands, his gaze narrowing. "Go on."

"Very well. We have already ascertained that the kerchief bears the emblem of the Prince Regent."

"Mm hmm." Gibbs reached for the handkerchief then used a quizzing glass to examine the coat of arms. "The prince ascended to the throne in 1820 and passed away three years ago. When did you acquire this?"

"I'm not completely certain, but upon the death of my *guardians*, if you will, I found it in a box with my name engraved atop." While the man stroked his chin and looked on with a judgmental glare, Bria continued to explain about her past. She handed Mr. Gibbs the miniature. His eyes popped a bit—not unusual because the woman in the portrait was quite comely.

When she was finished, the man tapped the portrait's tiny frame. "So, in truth, you have no idea if this woman has any relation to you whatsoever?"

"I do not. Though she might be my mother."

"And she might not be."

"True." Bria's resolve strengthened with her smile. "But we do have a familial likeness."

"Hmm." He picked up the kerchief and rubbed it between his fingers. "When George the Fourth was Prince Regent he had quite a reputation for being a philanderer—there are a great many of his by-blows about."

She nodded, heat burning her cheeks, fully aware that discovering the identity of the woman in the portrait might end up labeling her as a bastard. Though Bria didn't know what would be worse, being a bastard and knowing about one's family, or being a foundling and completely alone.

He pushed the items across the table with a pronounced frown. "Do you truly want to churn up an old scandal which might have brought shame to this woman, and possibly her entire family?"

Bria slipped them into her reticule. "I wouldn't want the *Grande-Duchesse* to suffer. Absolutely not. I only would like to know something about my parentage, who I am, where I'm from. If it would be detrimental for her or her family, I would not reveal myself."

"Your mother may well still be in France, *if* she is even alive."

Bria gulped. The man could be brutally blunt. "She could be anywhere."

"And what about my fee?" Mr. Gibbs picked up a small dagger and started cleaning his nails. "What can you pay?"

"I have two pounds."

His knife stilled. "Two pounds will merely buy you an inquiry or two and, honestly, this case is so old I doubt it will be worth your coin."

"If there is anything you can do, anything at all, I would be in your debt."

"Very well. Since you seem to be eager. I wouldn't want you throwing your coin away on someone less qualified." He set the dagger aside then reached a slip of parchment. "You were christened in Bayeux did you say?"

"Yes."

He dipped his quill in the inkpot. "In what year were you born?"

"1814."

He wrote her name and birth year on a slip of parchment. "An interesting time in history."

"Indeed. The Bourbon monarchy was restored for a brief period and it seemed as if Napoleon's war had ended."

"If only he hadn't escaped prison we would have avoided Waterloo."

"Yes."

"Is there any other pertinent information you can add? Monsieur LeClair was a successful merchant, did you say?"

"Yes."

Mr. Gibbs' quill oscillated through the air as he wrote. "And Madame LeClair provided your inspiration to the ballet?"

"*Oui.* She was English and gently born. Her father was a vicar from Gloucestershire."

Again, he dipped the quill in the inkwell. "Interesting. I take it that is why your English is so precise."

"Since I discovered the keepsakes, especially the kerchief, I've always wondered if there was a reason I was placed in a home with a British subject."

Mr. Gibbs winced, his quill stilling for a moment before he looked up with an insincere smile. "This information is so scant I doubt I'll be able to churn up a thing. Nonetheless, I will be in touch."

***

Bria exited the private inquiry office, anxious to join the troupe for a luncheon and day out in Hyde Park, which was a long walk west along Grosvenor Street, according to the mistress at the boarding house. Mr. Perkins had said the Duke of Ravenscar arranged the affair, though Britannia doubted the duke would be present. Since the opening of *La Sylphide*, he had been rather scarce aside from his ever-present and commanding presence in his box during performances.

She didn't blame him for keeping his distance. What must he think of her begging a kiss on opening night? Goodness, she could be daft and ought to be mortified by her behavior. But she wasn't. Their wee tryst was her secret. A moment in time she would remember always.

In fact, she replayed the kiss in her mind over and over each night before she fell asleep. What would have happened if the maid hadn't come in? It was impossible to forget the strength of his arms, the way her blood had rushed as if champagne were bubbling through her veins.

She knew why Ravenscar was staying away and she didn't blame him. He may have pretended to be aloof after the maid caught them, but the tenderness he'd imparted when he had kissed her had to be genuine.

Wasn't it?

At the corner, she stepped off the curb just as a flower cart pushed past. "Watch where you're going, miss," hollered the vendor.

"Sorry." Picking up her skirts, Bria looked both ways. The traffic was horrendous with carts and carriages all wheeling past at different speeds. When she saw a break, she dashed across.

At least she tried.

A black shiny phaeton sped from behind a hay wagon—straight for her.

Her legs taking over, Bria took a flying leap toward the curb, her toes just catching the edge. With a sweep of her left leg, she cheated death by a fraction. Behind her, the carriage's wheels screeched as the driver pulled two chestnut horses to a halt. "Madam, are you trying to commit suicide?" A deep voice boomed.

She cringed. Indeed, Bria would recognize that voice anywhere. Slowly, she turned and faced Ravenscar, the figure of masculine perfection, the ribbons held firmly in his gloved hands, looking like king of the courts, ready to send her to the bowels of the Tower to face the executioner for making a frantic dash in front of his carriage.

Until those icy blue eyes opened wide with recognition and something intense. Something she couldn't quite put her finger on. "Britann—ah, Miss LeClair, I am astonished to see you here. What on earth are you doing dashing across the busiest street in London?"

She glanced back to the inquiry office, thanking the stars she wasn't standing in its doorway. "I'm heading for your luncheon at Hyde Park."

"You're walking all that way? Mr. Peters was supposed to arrange carriages."

"He did. Ah…the day is so lovely I thought I would walk instead."

The duke leaned toward her and offered his hand. "Well, you may as well ride the rest of the way. Come, I'll give you a lift."

His hand completely covered hers as, with one arm, he hoisted her up, her feet hardly skimming the steps. She slid onto the bench and folded her hands atop her reticule, all too aware of the man beside her. "Thank you for your kindness, Your Grace."

"I'm not sure how kind I'm being. After seeing you fly in front of my team, I was certain I'd be scraping your bones off the cobblestones."

"Forgive me. I didn't see your carriage behind the hay wagon."

"We're fortunate you are so nimble, else my theater would be without its Sylph." He cued the horses for a walk, then grinned down at her. "Other than running out in front of carriages, have you been well?"

"Yes, thank you. Though…" She stopped. What should she say? *I've missed seeing you backstage? I wonder if you would mind kissing me again since last time we were interrupted, and I have the strongest feeling there would have been more?*

He regarded her out of the corner of his eye. "Yes?"

"It is always comforting to see you in your box every night."

"I wouldn't miss a single performance."

"I'm glad. I like having you there. I feel as if we are…"

Good heavens, it would be nice if she held her tongue.

"You were saying?"

"Friends."

"Ah, yes. I suppose we are. Though I've never…"

Now His Grace wasn't finishing *his* sentences. That simply wouldn't do. If he didn't finish, Bria mightn't sleep at night for trying to figure out what he was about to say. "You've never what?"

"Well, all of my friends are men."

She wound her finger around her reticule's drawstring. "Most of mine are women, aside from the men in the *corps*, of course."

As they turned into Hyde Park and approached the white tents set up for the luncheon, Pauline and Florrie stood side by side and gaped. Bria put her finger to her lips to shush them.

"Ladies," said Ravenscar as he pulled the horses to a halt. "My team nearly trampled our Sylph when she dashed across Regent Street."

"*Alors*," said Pauline, clapping her hand over her heart.

Of course, Florrie showed no sympathy. "Always out to attract attention are you not, Bria?"

She didn't wait for Ravenscar to walk around and help her down. "Not that kind of attention."

As soon as Bria's feet hit the ground, Pauline pulled her aside. "I thought you were going to see the investigator," she whispered.

Bria checked behind to ensure no one was eavesdropping. "And that's exactly what I did."

"And His Grace just happened past?"

"His phaeton nearly ran me over, mind you."

Pauline giggled. "Imagine if you'd been injured. He'd be irate and have no one to blame but himself."

Bria looked his way. Ravenscar stood beside Mr. Perkins looking directly at her. She quickly turned her back. "He was furious with me, but I didn't see his carriage from where I was standing."

"I imagine you frightened him something awful."

"He frightened me, that's for certain."

Pauline tweaked the bow on Bria's bonnet. "He's still watching you."

She didn't need to glance over her shoulder to know Ravenscar was staring. The heat of his attention seared her spine with the intensity of blue flame. "He's probably just ensuring no one else tries to run me down."

"I think he likes you."

Smacking Pauline with her reticule, Bria shook her head. "Stop. He likes all of us. That is why he's sponsoring today's luncheon. Speaking of which, let us find a place to sit." *As far away from His Grace as possible.*

Chapter Eleven

Preparing for the Hughes ball, Bria turned in front of the mirror, making the pink organza skirts of her new ballgown billow. "I think I like the latest style, not quite off the shoulder," she mused, adjusting her stays so her bosoms showed a hint of cleavage.

"And those gigot sleeves are a work of art." Pauline nudged beside her, smiling in the mirror. She brandished a white ostrich feather and pinned it in Bria's hair. "And I do believe this is the first time you are wearing a prettier dress than me."

Biting her lip, Bria looked to the worn floorboards. Her friend was right. Pauline wasn't wealthy, but her father always ensured his daughter was stylishly clothed—and her gown was darling. "The blue makes your eyes stand out like stars."

"At least it's my favorite color." Pauline handed Bria a blue feather which she in turn pinned so it dangled just above her friend's eye.

"The feather adds a saucy touch." She gave her work a pat. "And this will stay in all night."

"I believe you. Those pins have teeth."

Bria stepped back and admired her work. "You do not want the plumes to fall in your eyes whilst you're dancing, do you?"

"*Non.*" Pauline picked up both pairs of elbow-length gloves and handed the pink to Bria. "It is a shame there is a ball at Almacks tonight. I'm afraid there won't be many people at the Hughes private event. What say you?"

"I have no idea. Regardless, I intend to have a lovely respite. What with the traveling, the rehearsals and performances, both of us need a night out."

"And we shall have it."

Bria pulled their cloaks off the hooks. "'Tis time to head downstairs. The carriage should be waiting."

The pair had decided to pay a little extra and hire a hack between themselves. Too many times Bria had shared rides with six others and they always managed to be the last to leave, which meant feeling like a wet rag the next day.

Once they arrived, it took about a half-hour before the carriage processed through the queue on Mr. Hughes' oak-lined drive. Against the dusky sky the sprawling mansion posed a picture on a well-manicured estate in Kensington.

Bria and Pauline both sat forward, eagerly watching out the window. "Did you know there is a royal palace not far from here?" Pauline asked.

"I did not."

"Imagine, your ancestors may have built it."

Bria gave her a nudge. "Stop. My ancestors were more likely to have spent time in the Tower of London's dungeons than a royal palace."

When the carriage finally stopped in the circular drive, they were met by footmen who escorted them up a marble staircase. After checking their cloaks, they received their dance cards and were announced as Miss LeClair and Miss Renaud.

Not unlike balls in Paris, a number of important people queued in a welcoming line and greeted guests, with Mr. Hughes at the end. He had thick sideburns and a moustache, spoke with a pronounced lisp and smiled warmly at his guests. Moreover, he was the first to sign both Bria and Pauline's cards.

"I think he's genuinely happy to have us here," Bria whispered as they moved into an enormous ballroom painted in white. The chandeliers overhead glowed with hundreds of candles made brighter by squares of mirrors. It wasn't quite as opulent as Ravenscar Hall but, still, the room oozed wealth.

"Oh, I daresay he is thrilled to invite an entire troupe of dancers to his ball. We are professionals. There's no one better with whom to enjoy a waltz." Pauline spread her arms wide. "Look at all the coattails. I'm guessing there are far more gentlemen in attendance than at Almacks."

Bria admired an entire line of men in pristine black tailcoats. "I pity those poor debutantes who are anxious to find husbands."

Pauline chuckled. "I doubt pity is the right word."

Thomas Newport stopped and bowed. "Miss LeClair, Miss ah…"

"Renaud," Bria finished, curtsying before turning to her friend. "Pauline, have you had the pleasure of meeting the Earl of Fordham?"

"And Viscount Saye?" added Richard Fiennes who always seemed to be in Fordham's shadow.

Pauline flushed, giving a graceful curtsy. "It is my pleasure to make your acquaintance," she said in heavily-accented English.

Fordham slipped the dance card from Bria's fingers and held up a sharp pencil. "I was disappointed when you missed our ride through Hyde Park." He signed right below Mr. Hughes and returned the card.

"Forgive me," she replied. "But I do have a duty to Chadwick Theater and cannot miss a rehearsal when one is called."

The earl's gaze slipped downward and paused a bit too long on Britannia's bosom. "No apology is necessary. I should have thought you would be engaged, especially the day after the ballet opened."

"Are you settling in now?" Lord Saye asked.

Pauline nodded. "We are, thank you."

He pointed to her dance card. "May I?"

"Certainly." She giggled. "It would be awkward for a troupe of dancers to attend a ball without dancing."

"It would, indeed." Lord Fordham signed Pauline's card as well.

"Have you had the pleasure of chatting with Miss Bisset?" Bria gestured to Florrie who was standing beside Mr. Hughes.

"Ah, yes. She was at the Dowager Duchess of Ravenscar's soiree. I found her quite chatty. We spoke for..."

Bria tuned out the earl while she scanned the room for a tall man with black hair and coattails, no doubt.

"He's not here." Fordham tapped Bria's shoulder, giving her a knowing look. "Ravenscar's mother is a patroness at Almacks."

"Ravenscar?" Bria asked as if she hadn't been searching for the man. "It is only right for the duke to attend his mother's exclusive ball though invitations only went out to members of polite society."

"Which is why we are here, what say you, Saye? I'd reckon the lion's share of the gentry would rather be in Kensington this night."

"And they are." The viscount swept his upward palm across the scene. "My guess is news of the success of *La Sylphide* has brought them to Hughes' mansion in droves."

Bria gave Pauline a wink. They had worked so hard, it was uplifting to have Londoners accept them. Of course, there were critics, but naysayers lurked everywhere, even in Paris.

And as the evening progressed, it didn't escape Bria's notice that Lord Saye danced with Pauline twice. She flirted unabashedly. In fact, she seemed captivated by the nice-looking nobleman, slender and of average height with blue eyes and fair hair. He carried himself with an unpretentious air and didn't seem as much of a predator as Lord Fordham. Even without Ravenscar's warning, Bria found the earl to be brash—definitely more suitable for someone like Florrie.

Both she and Pauline danced every set until intermission was called and they were ushered into the dining hall for the evening meal. Three courses all served with wine, the first with soup and bread, the second with five different meat and vegetable dishes and the third with irresistible cakes and ices along with port. But by the end of the meal, Bria was ready to head for the boarding house. It seemed as if London parties were never as fun without the Duke of Ravenscar.

***

Just as Drake had imagined, Almacks wasn't quite the bustling hub of activity usual for a ball early in the Season. The ballroom glimmered in a sea of taffeta and lace and smelled as fragrant as a field of lilies. He stood with a glass of champagne in hand, chatting with Baron and Baroness of Calthorpe, which was much preferable to striking up a conversation with a nervous debutante attending her first ball of her first Season.

Mother slipped beside him, her lips in a white line—a sure sign she was madder than a hornet. "I hope Mr. Hughes is happy with his den of debauchery this evening. It has drawn too many eligible gentlemen away from what should be the ball of the year."

"Perhaps it isn't such a bad thing for the Season to begin slowly," said Lady Calthorpe. "I recall during my debut, I attended a masque and was absolutely overwhelmed. I'd been raised in Gloucester and despite being the daughter of a duke, I truly had no idea how to handle myself among gentlemen. Mind you, though they possessed rank and titles, some behaved like absolute scoundrels."

"Well said, my dear." The Baron of Calthorpe looked a bit awkward in his coattails and Drake imagined him much more comfortable wearing tweed, hunting on his country estate with a pair of Gordon Setters. "Young ladies need time to adjust to the London scene."

"Well, I hope this is not the commencement of the downfall of polite society," Mother said.

Drake held his tongue. With the fortunes being made by entrepreneurs, the downfall of the *ton* and exclusivity owed only to the nobly born had already begun.

"There's a sizeable crowd, and next week there will be no conflict with Almacks." Lady Calthorpe gave a polite curtsy. "If you will excuse us, Your Graces, Calthorpe and I are expected in the card room."

"Of course." Mother grasped Drake by the elbow. "Come, dear. There's a young lady I'd like you to meet."

Resolutely, Drake allowed Her Grace to pull him through the sea of bright-eyed debutantes, all giggling behind their fans, no doubt longing for a chance to dazzle a duke. He'd grown accustomed to the stares, though would always rather be anywhere than a ballroom this time of year.

Mother introduced Lady Blanche whose coloring was a likeness to her name. As expected, Drake engaged the daughter of Viscount Falmouth in conversation, finding her to be the epitome of good manners and excellent breeding—not at all what he wanted in a wife and everything his mother expected. Of course, manners and breeding were necessary, but a sense of humor and expression of passion were descriptors he might envision for his future bride. Unfortunately, overt passion was discouraged by *The Mirror of the Graces*. Drake knew why. Young ladies who were flippant and predisposed to temper tantrums oft disgraced themselves and, as a result, society had labeled passion akin to the fervor Miss LeClair demonstrated on stage as being vulgar.

Playing the dutiful son, he danced with Lady Blanche and a number of other young ladies, but at intermission, he slipped away and instructed his coachman to take him to Mr. Hughes' residence. His plan? After he checked to ensure Britannia and the others were well, he'd return to Almacks with his mother none the wiser.

When he arrived, the musicians were taking a recess and Miss LeClair stood in the ballroom with her back to him. He accepted a glass of champagne from a footman and stood behind a pillar where he could observe without notice. No matter where she was or what she wore, Britannia served as a shining beacon in any room she graced.

Tonight, her cinnamon hair was elaborately knotted atop her head, exposing her long, slender neck. The modiste had captured perfection with an elegant cut of the nape. Starting at her shoulders, the gown plunged into a wide V. With Britannia's subtle movement, the silkiness of her skin enticed. How much would any man present pay just for one chance to brush his fingertips across her statuesque perfection?

Drake sipped. *I'd kill anyone for the mere suggestion.* Two more men joined the ever-growing circle with Britannia in the center. Perhaps her gown was too damned revealing.

Blast it all, for the past fortnight, Drake had thought of little else than the ballerina, but he'd kept his distance on purpose. No use giving the gossip columns something more to write about. He had vowed to protect Miss LeClair, not debauch her. Unfortunately, he doubted any other female in the British Isles had a chance of tempting him while the ballerina was in London. His mother would simply have to wait another Season or two before her wish came true.

A young lady who'd been chatting with Britannia spotted him and pointed.

Drake wasn't ready for the melting of his knees when the diva turned. God's bones, how had he ever considered her anything but exceptional?

"Your Grace. I'm surprised to see you here." As hypnotic as the Sylph, she smiled while they moved together and joined hands as if they were old friends.

"I cannot stay long." Bowing, he gave the back of her hand a kiss. "Are you having a good time?"

"We are dancing, how could we not enjoy ourselves?"

"Well put." He looked to the young lady from the *corps* and bowed. "I do not believe we have been properly introduced, madam."

"This is Miss Pauline Renaud, my dearest friend. Though you know of her, I do not think you have been formally introduced." Britannia gestured to the woman—one of the *corps* dancers. "Allow me to introduce the Duke of Ravenscar."

Pauline curtsied. "'Tis my pleasure to meet you, monsieur."

"You Grace," Miss LeClair corrected.

"*Pardonnez-moi*, Your Grace."

He chuckled at Pauline's heavily-accented English, which he'd first expected from Britannia. "You both look lovely this evening. And Miss LeClair, your gown turned out splendidly."

"Thank you, and especially your mother's modiste."

He'd paid extra to have the sewing expedited, and the additional coin had been well worthwhile. Britannia glowed like a ray of sunshine bursting through a forest's canopy.

Viscount Saye joined them. "Ravenscar, I didn't expect to see you this evening. Cut mummie's apron strings, did you?"

He shot the man who'd once been his partner in crime at Eton a leer. "Hold your tongue. And why are you not making an appearance at Almacks? Hasn't the dowager viscountess come to London as of yet?"

"My mother has no say in my affairs." Saye directed his attention to Miss Renaud. "The next dance is a waltz. Is your card full?"

"I believe I have reserved the next dance for you, my lord."

While Saye offered his elbow, Drake glanced to Britannia. "A waltz, did he say?"

"Yes."

He leaned in. "Is your card full?"

"Pauline and I both purposely kept our cards open for the second half of the evening."

"Why? Were you looking to monopolize some poor man's time?"

"Possibly."

"Scandalous."

She placed her hand in the crook of his arm. "Though Fordham told me you weren't coming, I didn't relinquish hope, Your Grace."

His tongue went completely dry. He glanced at her out of the corner of his eye while his heartbeat sped. No, not a single well-bred debutante at Almacks this evening had come remotely close to soliciting any sort of romantic inclination, yet after exchanging a few words with Miss LeClair, he was ready to spirit her to a side room and steal another kiss. Something which he definitely intended on not doing, which was exactly why he had kept his distance the past fortnight. Britannia had been waiting for him to come to Hughes' ball? That, in and of itself, was a warning he should heed.

The introduction to the waltz began as they stepped onto the floor and assumed their positions. "Do you enjoy dancing?" she asked.

"Very much."

Those whisky eyes widened. "Surprising."

How did she make his heart melt merely with a look? "Why?"

With the count of three, Drake pressed his palm into the small of Britannia's back and together they began the waltz.

Not surprisingly, the woman followed his every nuance, not afraid to take gliding steps for the downbeat.

"I don't know." Her gaze meandered to his chest. "You seem so *worldly*…and…ah…*strapping*."

Drake nearly tripped over his own feet. Was it her perfume? Or was the lady flirting?

"What other pursuits do you engage in to maintain such a physique?" she asked, her eyes wide, staring at him as if she performed the waltz without giving the steps a thought.

For a moment he couldn't breathe. Did she know how much she was tempting him? And good God, she followed his lead like water in a brook. Together they moved and flowed without effort, and she thought he was fit? "I-I spar—boxing most mornings with Lord Percy."

"A sport which demands a high level of skill."

"I daresay not as much as ballet."

"Perhaps, but you need a good foundation to win."

"True."

Britannia slid her fingers to the top of Drake's arm and squeezed. "And my guess is your training has been superb."

If only he could roar. Not only had she drawn him in with her loveliness, with only a few words, she'd made him feel like a king.

Unable to help himself, he tugged her closer—too close for Almacks, but not bloody close enough for him. Her silky skirts brushed his calves as she lost herself in the dance, smiling, laughing softly, her head swaying in time with every step as if she were one with the music. Britannia was more fairy than human, more endearing than a rose, and more tempting than any imaginable fancy known to man.

Seemingly unaware she'd captured him in her spell, she clapped and chuckled when the waltz came to an end. A sultry chuckle. One that stirred him right where he shouldn't be stirred. "The first time I saw you, I thought you would look magnificent on stage, and I wasn't wrong. You are a wonderful dancer."

She? The nymph who could make grown men swoon and lose their ability to speak considered him anything but passible at waltzing? "Thank you. From you, that is quite a compliment." He offered his elbow and led her off the floor before his ego inflated the entire room.

"Where did you learn to dance?" she asked.

"At Eton mostly. Schoolboys are not allowed to move on to Oxford without showing some finesse in the social arts. And my mother insisted on private lessons in the summers. She firmly believed that a future duke should never be embarrassed in public."

"Well, she was successful at ensuring quality dance instruction. But being an efficient dancer is only a small piece of living in the public eye, surely."

"Very true." One corner of his mouth twitched. "I've also mastered the art of acting."

"Stage acting?"

"Only when I was a lad. Of course, dukes do not act in plays. Do not tell anyone, but my acting is mainly in the public eye. It is very English to be in constant control of one's emotions." He snatched a lone glass of champagne from a footman's tray as they strolled past a sea of smiling faces.

"Where are we going?"

Taking a drink of champagne, Drake spied an exit. "Do you mind taking in a bit of air? Dancing made me overwarm."

"Wouldn't that provide fodder for the gossips?"

"I imagine there are others taking a turn on the terrace." He handed the glass to her. "Apologies. There was only one."

"Thank you, I'm parched." She sipped. "Mm, this is quite good."

"You like champagne?"

"I like this."

Drake peered through the French glass doors. "As I thought, there are several others outside. I suppose the journalists will have to find someone else to throw to the wolves tonight."

He opened the door and ushered her out while couples nodded and said hello. Spotting an unoccupied corner, he pressed his palm into the small of Britannia's back and steered her toward it. Even better, a canopy of trees hung over the rail, giving them privacy.

He toyed with one of her lazy curls. "I haven't yet told you how beautiful you look tonight."

"Ah, but you have." After taking another sip, she handed him the glass.

"I was just being polite." He drank again allowing the bubbles to tickle his tongue before swallowing. "Your dress is spectacular. Everyone else in both ballrooms here and at Almacks pales in comparison."

"Thank you for the compliment. I gather you must have received top marks in charming ladies at Eton...or was that Oxford?"

Chuckling, he set the glass on the rail and backed her further into the tree's shadows. "How did you guess?"

Britannia swayed as if a tad tipsy—or happy. "Oh, please do not make me divulge my deepest secrets."

He caught her fingers and drew them to his lips, brushing an airy kiss across her knuckles. "But I want to know."

She met his gaze before her eyes shifted aside. "You have a way of setting my insides aflutter."

He dipped his chin and breathed in the floral scent of her hair. Orange blossoms tonight. *Lord save me.* "I think..."

With his hesitation, Britannia's tongue slipped to the corner of her mouth as if tasting something sweet there. Suddenly, Drake had no idea what he was about to say. The need to sample her lips consumed his mind. He craved to have that delicate, pink tongue dance with his at this very moment.

It took less than a heartbeat to bury her in his arms and lay claim her mouth. As their lips joined, he was lost in the searing heat stretching through his body. She tasted so damned sweet, her lithe body molding to his hard like a perfectly matched pair. Never in his life had he wanted a woman as much as he wanted Britannia. Here. Now. Without hesitation. He wanted her naked and beneath him. For weeks she had driven him to the brink of insanity every time he saw her dance, and now he craved to satisfy his wildest dreams.

And when she moaned, his knees buckled. His fingers pillaged from her hair to her back to…oh yes…her tight derriere.

His cock lengthened with every stroke of his tongue. God save him, if he didn't take control of himself, he'd hoist her onto the rail with her skirts hiked up over her slender thighs. Long legs, he'd itched to caress with her every *arabesque*.

He opened his eyes wide enough to check to see if any of the others were nearby.

As his attention drew away, Britannia slid her palm to the middle of his chest. "We mustn't."

His gaze snapped to her face. Her eyes glazed, her lips swollen from the intensity of his kiss. But still she shook her head.

Realization of his err washed over him. Good God, he'd nearly acted on his base desires. This was his dancer. A woman in his care. What the hell had he been thinking? If he kept her in his arms one moment longer he might just act on his inappropriate desires. Abruptly, he released his hands. "Forgive me."

"I think we should go back inside." She took a step away. "The romantic feelings coursing through me whenever I am in your presence are wrong—and kissing only serves to make it worse. You mustn't tease me, else I'll begin to fantasize that the dizzy and passionate flutter in my breast might lead to something beyond master and servant. Especially with...*you*." Her final word was whispered—albeit a pained whisper.

Drake watched as she started away, knowing she was right while longing burned a hole in his heart. Had he teased her? No. He'd simply complimented her gown...and generally told her she was the most beautiful woman in London...and then kissed her senseless.

He groaned.

Dash it, if he didn't come across like a rake, he didn't know what would.

How daft could he be? What was he doing out on the terrace with one of Chadwick Theater's principals, albeit a lovely, stunning, tantalizing creature? And with so many others present?

Damnation, she's bloody right.

Chapter Twelve

Her mind muddled by a myriad of emotions, Bria rushed through the ballroom, searching for Pauline. How dimwitted could she have been? Of course, everyone knew she'd hoped to see the duke when she arrived at the ball. Were all her secrets so transparent? It had caught her off guard when Lord Fordham said Ravenscar was attending the ball at Almacks. Later, when she'd turned around to find him staring at her, the hard shell she'd wrapped around her heart crumbled. Her stomach grew as effervescent as champagne. She'd batted her eyelashes and fawned upon him as if they were—God forbid—lovers. Over and over she'd told herself he was untouchable by anyone in her class. Untouchable!

Bria's mind knew it. Why was it so difficult to convince her heart?

Unable to find Pauline on the dance floor, she dashed through the parlor, the card room, finally opening the door to…

"Pardon me!" Covering her mouth, Bria backed away. Pauline was wrapped in Lord Saye's arms and in the midst of a passionate kiss.

The couple drew apart, but not as if they'd been caught in the same way Bria had jumped from Ravenscar's arms when the lady's maid had entered the bed chamber. Pauline and

Lord Saye turned their heads, apparently quite reluctant to release each other.

"Is all well?" asked Pauline.

Bria glanced down the passageway, catching Ravenscar searching over the tops of people's heads before he looked directly her way. "I-I was hoping you would be ready to leave."

Pauline exchanged glances with Lord Saye. "Now?"

The viscount took the girl's hand. "If you're not ready to go, Miss Renaud, I'd be delighted if you would allow me to escort you home."

The hopefulness in Pauline's eyes spoke loudly enough to melt a shrew's heart. "Would you mind to terribly, *ma chérie*?"

Blast my everlasting luck.

"No. Enjoy your evening." Bria closed the door just as Ravenscar stepped beside her.

"Britan—ah—Miss LeClair, I want you to know that I meant no disrespect. I did not intend for our stroll outside to be demeaning for you in any way."

"I followed you out those doors willfully. Anyone with half their wits would have known what it would lead to," she whispered, starting for the cloakroom. "I am not to be trusted alone with you."

"Nor am I with you, it seems. Where you are concerned, I tend to forget myself."

He forgot himself? Good heavens, she'd melted in his arms, ready to bear his children. Which she would *never* consider. If she ever got with child, she would be married to the father.

The truth? Her emotions were impossible to control when the duke looked at her with those disarming blue eyes. "Is that so?"

"It is."

Bria presented her ticket to the attendant. "My cloak, please."

"You're leaving?" Ravenscar asked.

"I'm tired."

"But the evening is still young. And do not tell me you plan to set out alone."

"I've hired a coach and driver. I will hardly be alone."

"This will not do."

He may have wound his talons around her heart, but she'd allow no more. "Why must you continue to tell me what I should and shouldn't do, or wear, or eat? You might be a duke, but I am not yours to command."

He produced his ticket and gave it to a second attendant. "That may be so, but I would be no kind of gentleman if I didn't follow your coach to ensure you arrive safely home. 'Tis the least I can do."

The attendant appeared with her cloak, which Ravenscar plucked from his hands and held up. "Miss."

"Thank you." What else could she say? At least he wouldn't be sitting in the carriage beside her…in the dark…with those blasted tempting lips.

***

"Back to Almacks, Your Grace?" asked his coachman.

"We're taking a detour. Follow that hack." Drake climbed up to the driver's seat of his town coach. "Scoot over."

"You're riding up here?" the coachman asked, his voice cracking. In the lamplight, the man's eyes grew as wide as sovereigns.

"Mind your driving, I'll keep an eye on the carriage." Drake flicked his gloved hand. "Haste."

"Straightaway." He slapped the reins "Are we heading for Orange Street?"

"We are—then back to Almacks."

"You're taking Miss LeClair to Almacks?"

"That is none of your concern, but no. I am ensuring my star performer returns to her quarters safely."

"Do you think she will not?"

"The lady is young, beautiful and alone, not to mention petite. All it would take is one dastardly passerby to overtake her. Do you know the hackney driver she's hired? Is he trustworthy?"

The coachman cracked his whip, requesting the matched pair to step up their pace to a fast trot. "I cannot say I do."

"Then that is precisely why we are following."

"Yes, Your Grace."

Drake leaned to the side, watching Britannia's coach take the corner, not wide enough in his estimation. The hackney teetered as if poorly sprung. And then it didn't right itself as it should. With a loud scrape of metal, the left rear wheel came clean off.

Drake's heart lurched to his throat as he reached out in vain to steady the teetering hack. "Good God!"

A shrill scream came from inside while the coach plunged to the cobblestones.

"Miss LeClair!" Drake shouted, leaping from the carriage before his coachman pulled it to a halt.

He sprinted to the hackney and yanked open the door. "Britannia?" He peered inside the darkness, seeing nothing but a heap. "Fetch the lamp!" he ordered while he climbed inside, his hands outstretched, feeling for her.

The hack rocked under his weight. His fingers met with softness. The driver came from behind with the light, illuminating her face. Her eyes closed, red blood trickled at her temple. "Britannia?" he asked gently.

"Mm," she moaned, opening her eyes. "W-what happened?"

"Your hack threw a wheel. You're bleeding." He pressed a clean kerchief to her head.

She drew away. "Sss."

"Sorry. I do not want to hurt you."

Nodding, she started to move.

"Wait," he said, gathering her into his arms. "Allow me to assist you."

"I am able to—"

"No, you are not. Not until we've had a good look at your injuries. Does anything else hurt?"

"I don't think so."

Carefully, he backed out of the coach, ever so attentive not to bump the precious woman in his arms.

"I dunno what 'appened," said the driver still holding up the lantern. "I checked 'er all around afore we set out this very eve."

"Well, you didn't check closely enough," Drake growled, heading for his town coach.

The hack driver followed. "There is no chance that wheel could 'ave come off without someone tinkering with it."

He stopped. "What is this you say? You suspect someone tampered with the wheel?"

The man removed his cap and scratched his head. "I checked the axel, shaft and bolts, and all was sound."

Clutching Britannia tighter to his chest, Drake eyed the driver. "Ravenscar here. I want a full report at my town house in the morning. You, sir, are providing a service and it is your responsibility to ensure your equipment is in good order at all times."

The man glanced to his toes. "Aye, Yer Grace. I 'ave a wife and five children to feed. And I can't make a farthing if me 'ack is done in."

"Very well, then." With Britannia secure, he started up the steps of his carriage and nodded to his coachman. "Take us to Half Moon Street."

***

Swathed in the essence of maleness, Bria curled into Drake's warmth. What soap did he use to smell so delicious? It reminded her of spice cake or a Christmas ball scented with clove. Whatever the fragrance, she couldn't breathe in enough of it. And why must it feel so wonderful to be cradled in his arms while the gentle sway of the carriage lulled her sore head?

She'd received a good wallop when the hackney coach threw its wheel. Raising her fingers to her temple, she brushed them over a lump, careful not to hiss and alert His Grace. What were the instructions he'd given to the driver? She wasn't sure.

"You are taking me to the boarding house, are you not?" she asked, the effort making her head throb.

"In a roundabout way."

Bria closed her eyes against the pain. Why did things always go awry whenever she was in the presence of the duke? He must think her a walking liability. "You needn't worry about me. I'll be fine, truly."

"I am worried whether I ought to be or not." He rubbed a soothing hand along her arm. "I must ensure you make a full recovery."

"It was just a little bump to the head."

"It was a severe blow to the head which made you bleed and rendered you unconscious for a moment." He leaned over her, his breath skimming her cheek as he examined her wound. "I cannot see a thing in this light."

"The pain is nearly gone," she said, her gaze drifting along the blue shadow of his jawline until she stopped at his lips. The memory of the kiss they'd shared in the garden was fresh in her mind. For a moment the world faded into oblivion as she melted in his arms. Why had she stopped him?

"The pain easing is a good sign but, still, you are not going anywhere until my physician has given you a thorough examination."

"Physician?" She started to push from Drake's arms, but the movement made her temple throb. "All I need is a good night's rest and I'll be snapping *piqués* turns across the stage."

"I say 'tis a good thing the theater will be shuttered on the morrow as well. You need a full day's rest."

"An entire day? I'd go mad."

"When was the last time you took to your bed due to illness?"

Bria closed her eyes. "Never."

"Oh, I see. You are immune to all ailments afflicting mere mortals—not even smallpox can penetrate your iron heart."

"You are unkind to ridicule me in such a way. I've been ill before. I just have not had the luxury of lying abed and succumbing to my misery."

He took in a sharp breath as if she'd said something unexpected. "Forgive my sarcasm. Please indulge me this once. I do not think it is a good idea to make a habit of swooning and I insist on ensuring you haven't suffered anything more severe than a mere bump."

Bria gave his shoulder a thwack. "Contrary to your belief, I do not make a habit of swooning. How dare you insinuate tonight's incident with the hackney coach was my doing?"

"I didn't mean to suggest—"

"You've only seen me swoon once, and that was due to fatigue and hunger. Moreover, it was the first time in all my days such a thing has happened. I was famished and tired beyond all reason."

"Yes, miss." His arms tightened around her as the coach rolled to a stop. "Nonetheless, I will not be dissuaded on this."

Before she could argue further, the coachman opened the door and Ravenscar whisked her out of the carriage and up the stairs to his town house. As the door opened, the duke bounded through the entry. "Pennyworth, send for my physician! Miss LeClair has received a bump to the head. She'll be resting in the east bedchamber."

"Straightaway, Your Grace."

"I am able to walk," Bria said as he headed for the stairs.

"I'm sure you are," he said, though he didn't stop to set her on her feet. No, the dancing, boxing, fencing duke carried her up two flights of stairs as if she weighed no more than a bushel of potatoes.

After exiting on the second-floor landing, he pushed inside a bedchamber. Ivory wallpaper lined the walls, decorated with a filigree of pink roses, blue ribbons and gold accents. He rested her on a small bed covered in ivory satin with a French canopy. As soon as Bria's head hit the feather-down pillow she sighed with the pleasure of it.

"Allow me to remove your slippers," Drake said while a footman came in, lit the candles and attended to starting a fire in the hearth.

Bria moved her toes over the side of the bed.

The duke knelt as he pulled them off. "Your feet are so small."

"Right sized for me, I suppose."

"I'm happy to see your sauciness has been unaffected by your tumble." He grinned. "Let us tuck you under the bedclothes before you catch a chill."

Giving in, she let him help. "Isn't your mother expecting you to return to Almacks?"

"I made no promises." He smoothed his hand over the coverlet. "Besides, you are far more important."

"Than your mother?"

"Than Almacks," he clarified, taking a candle and leaning over her. "Now, let's have a look at your head."

She cringed. "Is it awful? I felt a knot."

"Hmm. There's some bruising and a gash, about a half-inch."

"That doesn't sound bad."

He pressed his fingers around the sore spot. "I don't feel other signs of swelling, but I'm no healer."

She clasped his hand, drew it to her lips and kissed his fingers. "You are very kind to concern yourself with me."

He held her gaze for a moment while a current of energy passed between them. As if their souls kissed. But the connection waned as he glanced away.

"Kindness has nothing to do with it. When I saw the carriage throw the wheel, I could have died. I should have been the person in the hack, not you. I'll have the driver's hide for his negligence."

"Do not be too hard on the man. He said he checked the soundness of the carriage and, on top of that, he has a family to support."

Shaking his head, His Grace cupped her cheek with a large, yet gentle palm. "There you are, the one who suffered the most from this night's incident and you're worrying about everyone except yourself."

"It is ever so dreary to fret over oneself."

He looked into her eyes, the intensity again growing between them. "If only…"

Smiling, Bria glanced downward, being the one to break the bond this time. Whatever he was about to say, it was best left unuttered. She could think of a hundred things—if only they were in the same class, if only she weren't a foundling, if only he wasn't a duke, if only she weren't a fallen woman in society's eyes. The list went on ad infinitum.

Rather than draw away, he leaned over and kissed her on the forehead. His lips caressed her flesh as if in silent desire while he kissed a torturous trail to her ear and along her jaw. When he reached her mouth, every ounce of Bria's restraint shed from her iron will like water off an eider duck's back. Hungry for him, she sighed while his lips opened against hers, asking permission to take more.

Bria melted into the bed as she slid her arms around his neck and lost herself in the overwhelming sensation of kissing the one man who commanded her thoughts. Yes, she admitted she had desperately wanted to see him at the Hughes ball. She wanted him to take her in his arms and reserve every set for her. She craved for him to kiss her on the terrace, though she'd goaded and tried to turn him away.

They both drew in ragged breaths when he pulled back, his face serious, troubled.

"What is it between us, Duke?" she whispered, terrified to hear the answer.

"I wish I knew." He traced the pad of his finger over the sensitive lips he'd just kissed. "I have an overwhelming need to protect you."

She tried to smile as if his words were a trifle. How long had it been since anyone cared enough to look after her? Her heart stretched. "I've been taking care of myself for a very long time," she whispered, both elated and afraid.

"I know you have, and I admire your courage. Though it doesn't hurt to have a guardian angel at your back."

"I like that you look out for me, but…" A myriad of thoughts warred in her mind. Dance was her master. *I need to tell him.*

"But?"

"I do not want to be any man's mistress."

Black brows drew together while a storm passed behind his eyes. "Who said anything about mistresses?"

Isn't that what men like you want from women like me? Bria looked away. "I thought it best for you to know…ah…before things grew out of hand."

"Your Grace," said Pennyworth, opening the door. "The physician is here."

Chapter Thirteen

The doctor ordered a day of bedrest which Britannia tried to refuse. But as the theater owner, Drake insisted she obey. Not to mention he was delighted to have a houseguest. He busied her time reading aloud and making himself refrain from stealing another kiss.

She wasn't wrong to inquire about what was happening between them. Quite frankly, he didn't know, and he didn't want to think on what the future might bring. Presently, he enjoyed Miss LeClair, full stop. He intended to respect her virtue—to put her on a pedestal and worship her for the talented woman she was. Why did there need to be an ulterior motive? Though he couldn't deny he'd considered exploring a relationship of a more intimate nature, he certainly would not insult her by asking the woman to be his mistress.

Especially not while *La Sylphide* was still playing at Chadwick Theater.

This morning, upon Britannia's insistence, Drake had sent a missive to Miss Renaud explaining what had happened and that the doctor expected Britannia to be able to perform as scheduled the following night.

Drake closed the book of Shakespeare's *Macbeth*. "Which do you prefer, tragedy or comedy?"

She narrowed her gaze thoughtfully. "I think comedy, because I enjoy laughing. There's always plenty of tragedy about, so who needs more of it?"

"Well put."

A clatter came from the staircase. "No, I will not wait in the parlor!"

Drake set the book aside. "My mother sounds rather upset."

Britannia tugged the bedclothes up to her chin. "You should have returned to Almacks last eve."

"I did exactly what I should have done, and she will simply have to accept it. Sometimes dearest Mother forgets I am duke now." He stood, intending to meet Her Grace on the stairs, but the door to the bedchamber burst open.

"There you are." The dowager duchess' gaze shot from Drake to the bed and back, her eyes filling with shock. "I must speak with you in the parlor at once."

"Excuse me," Drake said, bowing to Britannia before ushering his mother to the corridor and downstairs. He waited until they reached the ground floor, well out of the dancer's hearing range before he said a word. "It is not what you think," he whispered, opening the door to the parlor. "Miss LeClair was injured last eve when her hack threw a wheel."

"And why are you the poor chap who came to her rescue? Why not appoint your coachman, or a footman or Pennyworth? You are a duke, not a nursemaid." Mother swept inside and onto a chair. "That woman has no business in this house."

Drake strode toward the hearth, intent on refraining from engaging in a war of words, but he would make his position clear in a low, intense tone. "I daresay, it is up to my discretion whom I entertain, and you have absolutely no say in the matter."

"You think not? In light of your carelessness, I believe I should be more involved in your activities. And what about the French dancer's reputation? What will people think when they discover she's staying under your roof." Mother rapped her palm with her fan. "Whether or not you have acted respectfully, the prattle baskets will run rampant with this news."

His blood simmering to a low boil, Drake threw out his arms. "Bloody hell, she needed my help. She's not a member of the nobility, and who gives a rat's arse if the blatherskites out there think she's my mistress?"

"Mistress? For once in your life would you be serious about taking a wife, and leave the whoremongering to less respectable members of the nobility? For heaven's sake, I have worked my fingers to the bone for the past few Seasons, taking it upon myself to parade an endless number of debutantes under your nose. And you have yet to look twice at a single candidate. What are you waiting for? A goddess to come down from Mount Olympus?"

"I have never asked you to play matchmaker." Drake grabbed the back of a chair and dug his fingers into the upholstery. "Mind you, I have plenty of time to find a duchess and I will do so on my own schedule."

"You are five and twenty. You are a duke who can trace his lineage back nineteen generations!" Mother thrust her fan upward. "The woman above stairs cannot even tell you who her parents were, let alone if they were married. Your father was only six and thirty when he passed. None of us can afford to idle away time, wasting it on women of easy virtue."

His fingers drilled into the upholstery with such force, the fabric stretched to the point of tearing. "Miss LeClair is not a woman of easy virtue and I resent your referring to her as such. It isn't like you to be discourteous toward those of the working class."

"Well," Mother huffed. "I am at the end of my tether. I, a matriarch of the *ton*, hosted what should have been the best attended ball of the Season and not even halfway through, you disappeared—along with a quarter of the eligible men in London. I could not believe how you usurped me so!"

Ah, now she reveals the true source of her ire. "I apologize on that account. I had intended only to stop in to pay my respects. I fully expected to return until Miss LeClair's carriage threw a wheel."

Mother threw up her hands. "Why were you watching her carriage and not some hired man?"

"She was ready to go home and her companion was not. As her employer, before I rejoined you at Almacks, I felt the necessity to follow her hack to the boarding house to ensure she made it safely."

"Which she did not."

"Alas, no."

Mother opened her fan. Flicking it passionately, the plume atop her hat flipped about while she looked up at the picture of the thirteenth duke hanging above the mantel. "Why must Chadwick men be so difficult? All I ask is that you take my recommendations seriously. I do not maintain a hectic social calendar for my health."

"I thought you enjoyed being an engaging *grande dame*."

"In truth, I do it for you. All of it."

Drake unclamped his fingers from the chair. "Next you'll be telling me you wish to retire to the dowager house at Peak Castle and idle away your remaining years painting landscapes of the shore."

"The idea has its merits." Mother snapped her fan closed. "That is if you were properly situated, spending the Season in Ravenscar Hall with a new bride and my grandchildren."

Though his lenders were satisfied for the moment, at some time he needed to tell his mother about the Pall Mall mansion and how close she came to residing in the country permanently. However, today was not the day. Not when she was already riled. He dropped to his knee and took her hand. "You have nothing to worry about from me. I will marry. But I must find someone who takes my fancy. Someone with whom I can be allies."

"I daresay familiarity comes in time." She smacked him on the shoulder with her damnable fan. "Though not when you are entertaining the bit of muslin upstairs. There is nary a distinguished prospect out there who will bide her time while a potential suitor dallies about with mistresses. And all the diamonds of the *ton* are courted early in the Season so their weddings can be announced by the end. You must act swiftly. Lady Blanche, in particular, will not have a second Season, not a woman of quality like the daughter of Viscount Falmouth."

Drake stood. "What do you find so alluring in Her Ladyship?"

"She's well-mannered, has an impeccable family, and she's quite handsome if I may add."

"I found her rather plain. Rather guileless and sheltered."

"She is young, my dear boy. A canvas upon which you can build."

"I understand your anxiousness for me to marry, but I do not want you to feel as if it is your responsibility to find my bride. I will know the right woman as soon as I set eyes on her. Next Season the theater will be fully in Mr. Perkins' control and I will not have as much with which to concern myself. Perhaps then I'll find my duchess."

"Next Season?" Mother drew a hand over her heart. "I could be a withered prune by then."

"You will not be." He kissed her hand. "Now, if you will excuse me, I must return to Miss LeClair's bedside. We are reading *A Comedy of Errors* next."

"If you must." Mother gave a wee snort. "At least spirit her out the mews and have her taken home in a hackney.

There's no point in making a grandiose display of your escapades. Polite society will not understand."

He placed his palm in the small of her back and started for the door. "Very well. I will be more discrete."

"You care for her, do you not?"

"Let us say I admire her," he said over his shoulder. "Miss LeClair has inner strength that I haven't encountered in many women."

"Well, perhaps once she returns to France, you'll be more amenable to the idea of marriage."

"Perhaps."

After Drake escorted his mother out, he looked at the stairs with a sense of foreboding. The woman occupying his guest chamber was more tempting than lemon cream. More desirable than any debutante in London—any female in London for that matter.

But she was in his employ.

Britannia was not his to kiss. She was not his to caress or fondle or for him to do any of the other things he'd lain awake at night trying not to think about.

Mother had been right on a number of counts. The one he remembered most? There was no chance he would be able to choose a bride while Britannia LeClair remained in England.

***

A few weeks later, the stage manager popped his head in Bria's dressing room as the dancers were preparing for the night's performance. "Miss LeClair, there's a Mr. Gibbs at the stage door asking to see you."

Her heart skipped a beat as she clasped Pauline's hands. "He's the investigator I went to see," she whispered.

"Oh, yes. I hope he has some news."

"Come with me—he's a little chilly."

Mr. Gibbs stood outside, smoking a pipe. He pushed off from the wall as the dancers approached, the moonlit alley doing nothing to make him more amiable.

Bria introduced Pauline. "Please tell me you've found something."

"I have news, though I doubt you'll like it." Gibbs tapped his pipe on the brick wall. "The Prince Regent's only known mistress in 1814 was Isabella Ingram, now the Dowager Marchioness of Hertford. Presently, she is still living, though she has attained the ripe age of four and seventy. Might I add that it is highly improbable Her Ladyship is your mother. No woman could possibly survive confinement at the age of three and fifty."

"I see." Bria pressed her hands to her abdomen. "That is disappointing."

"As I said before, it will be highly unlikely to discover the identity of your mother after nineteen years. The kerchief could have come from anywhere—even purchased as a keepsake by some passerby—most likely a Frenchman."

Bria shifted her fingers to the miniature, secure beneath her costume. "Does the dowager marchioness reside in London?"

"She does, though it would be an impertinence to request an audience with the woman and show Her Ladyship your portrait. I daresay exposing her past indiscretions at her advanced age may lead the poor marchioness to her grave."

Bria's shoulders fell. "Thank you for your assistance."

He gave a clipped bow of his head and tucked his pipe into his waistcoat pocket. "I wish you well, miss. And heed me when I say you are better off not pursuing this further. Sometimes it is best to let sleeping dogs lie."

Pauline grasped Bria's hand while Mr. Gibbs strode away. "So that's the end of it?"

"He's given me what my two pounds paid for."

"But we'll each be receiving ten pounds for the private recital requested by Baroness Calthorpe. Perhaps he can dig deeper?"

Bria opened the door and pulled her friend inside. The baroness had been gracious to request a recital, scheduled for Monday next. "As he said, Mr. Gibbs is not eager to pursue the matter further. I suppose the man is fearful of ruffling aristocratic feathers."

Pauline shuddered as they returned to the dressing room. "He doesn't look as if ruffling anyone would bother him in the least. I think he's just uninterested. 'Tisn't easy digging up the past."

"Well, it was worth a try." Bria slid into her seat and picked up her pot of rouge. "At least we can discount King George as a candidate for my father."

"I wouldn't discount anything."

Chapter Fourteen

At the gracious invitation of Baroness Calthorpe, Bria, Charlotte and Florrie arrived at the Mayfair town house wearing long tulle costume skirts beneath their cloaks.

"The recital will be in the ballroom," said the housekeeper, leading them through the ground-floor corridor with high ceilings and gilt wainscoting. "The orchestra has already arrived and is preparing for your rehearsal."

"We still have an hour before the performance, correct?" asked Bria.

"Yes. Her Ladyship will bring in her guests at half-past two. Afterward, you are welcome to remain for tea and biscuits—but only for twenty minutes, and I will be watching the clock."

"We've been asked to have tea with the baroness?" asked Florrie.

The housekeeper pursed her lips as if she didn't approve of the gentry rubbing elbows with entertainers. "Her Ladyship thought her guests might want to ask questions."

Passing a portrait of the baroness, Bria stopped and gasped. As a younger woman, Lady Calthorpe had been as lovely as the woman in the miniature. If only she could ask the housekeeper in what year had it been painted. She chewed her lip and finally relented. "Do you know how long ago Her Ladyship sat for this portrait?"

"Please hurry along," the woman said without answering the question.

Bria hastened to catch up. "It is very kind of the baroness to invite us. We shall do our best to answer any queries that come our way."

"It must be amusing to be a performer." Not sounding terribly sincere, the woman opened a pair of double doors and gestured inside.

"Being a dancer is very diverting," said Florrie, waggling her shoulders, the tart. Always count on Miss Bisset to lower the standards of any event. Bria had thought twice about asking Florrie to be the third in the trio, but she knew the dance and it had taken little effort to revive the opening scene from *Ballet of the Nuns*. It premiered at *Salle Le Peletier* in 1831. All three of them had danced the number with Marie Taglioni in the lead.

"Behave yourself," Bria whispered, pulling her slippers out of her satchel.

"I always do."

"Keep in mind we are the hired entertainment, not the guests," Pauline added, carrying her slippers to a padded gilt chair. Up near the orchestra, five rows of like gilt chairs were neatly arranged facing the lion's share of the ballroom floor.

Britannia discussed the music and tempo with the conductor and by the time the guests entered the hall, the dancers were ready for their performance. A privacy screen and three additional chairs had been placed at the rear where the dancers stowed their things and waited out of sight from Her Ladyship's guests. Florrie peeked through a gap made by the hinges. "Lord Fordham is here," she said, not even trying to hide the excitement in her voice.

Pauline joined her. "There's Lord Saye. He mentioned he might come." Pauline had been spending a great deal of time with the viscount—often out all night.

"Have only gentlemen come to the recital?" asked Bria.

"No. There are more ladies than men." Pauline straightened. "Though it might interest you that the Duke of Ravenscar just took a seat at the back."

Bria clamped her fingers around the base of her seat, willing herself not to dash to the screen and peek out like an eager child. Aside from seeing his chiseled silhouette in his box at Chadwick Theater, she hadn't spoken to him since the wheel incident. "Well, at least there are a few familiar faces."

The baroness gave a brief welcome to her guests after which the orchestra played an introduction while the dancers took their places. Bria could have performed the sequence in her sleep which was a very good thing. Without the gaslights to dim the view of the audience, at every turn, she managed to end up looking directly at Ravenscar.

He was a head taller than everyone in the audience, and he watched with the same intensity Bria always sensed in Chadwick Theater. No, she didn't stop and look at him—check to see if he was watching only her, but the tingles twitting about her skin insisted his mesmerizing blue eyes missed nothing.

She liked his attention. Craved it. The potency of his gaze enlivened her. As if rays of sunshine flowed through her limbs, Bria gave her all to the piece as if floating on air.

By the time the trio curtsied to the sound of polite applause, she couldn't keep her gaze from the duke. Moreover, the man didn't bother looking away. Did he know how rapidly he was making her heart pound?

To her surprise, Ravenscar stood, strode forward and took the stage with the dancers as if he belonged in the scene. "Ladies and gentlemen, as you may be aware, Miss LeClair, Miss Bisset and Miss Renaud are presently performing

Chadwick Theater's own *La Sylphide*. As Baroness Calthorpe's esteemed guests, I have complementary box tickets for Thursday night's performance if you should desire."

"May we invite our husbands?" asked a woman in the front.

"Of course you may." Ravenscar gestured with his palm. "The baron and baroness would like you to join them for tea and cakes across the corridor in the drawing room, and our ballerinas will be on hand to answer any questions you may have for them.

"Are you taking bookings for more recitals?" asked a woman dressed in lavender.

Bria stepped forward before the duke could reply on her behalf. "We are."

"Please, everyone to the drawing room," he said. "We'll chat more there."

Bria moved beside Ravenscar as they waited for the guests to exit. "Is the Dowager Marchioness of Hertford in attendance?" she whispered.

"Indeed. She was sitting in the invalid chair in the front row." The duke offered his elbow. "May I inquire as to your association with her?"

"I read something about Her Ladyship not long ago—the article mentioned that she'd once been a great beauty and…" Bria hadn't thought her answer through and stopped before she blurted the woman had been the Prince Regent's mistress.

"I see." Ravenscar cleared his throat, stopping in the doorway. "George had quite a taste for the ladies." Drat it all, he'd guessed.

Bria chewed her lip. "I'd heard the same."

"And you are blushing to your toes, miss."

With a devilish wink, he ushered her to the drawing room. To Bria's delight, she spotted a tray filled with glasses of raspberry cordial. As Ravenscar was pulled away into the throng, she helped herself to the libation—tart, sweet and delicious.

"My dear, Britannia." Lady Calthorpe approached with open arms. "Your recital was stupendous. Everyone thinks so."

"How do you dance on your toes?" asked a lady with a purple bonnet.

"We've reinforced our slippers," said Florrie who did not once rise up on her toes during the entire piece.

"But it takes strength and a great deal of practice," added Pauline.

Lady Calthorpe moved a bit closer. "I've been meaning to ask—"

"Do you have any brandy, Charlotte?" the Duke of Beaufort interrupted, turning his shoulder to Bria.

"Always for you, Papa." Her Ladyship signaled the butler. "Branson…"

Another woman tugged Britannia's arm. "You outshine everyone, dear. I've been to see *La Sylphide* five times."

"Five?"

"Oh yes, and I'll go again."

"Thank you ever so much. Your patronage means the world to us."

With every conversation, Bria moved a little closer to the dowager marchioness until she was standing right beside the woman's invalid chair, taking quick glimpses, trying to determine if the elderly noblewoman had any likeness to the miniature. Bless it, without pulling the piece out and asking Lady Hertford, there was no way of knowing for certain.

Out of the blue, the dowager marchioness grasped Bria's hand. "I quite enjoyed your dancing, my dear."

Bria smiled, placing her other hand atop the lady's icy fingers. "Why, thank you. It is a delight to be here."

The dowager marchioness blinked, looking a tad ruffled. "I thought everyone in *La Sylphide* was French."

"Indeed, we are."

"You don't sound French."

"No, you do not, Miss LeClair," said Lady Calthorpe, returning with a cup and saucer in hand.

"Charlotte, you're needed at once," said the Duke of Beaufort quite sternly.

"If you'll excuse me." The baroness rolled her eyes with an exasperated sniff.

Bria curtsied, then returned her attention to the dowager marchioness. "I had an English…ah…*governess*. In Bayeux. Have you been there?" It was a lot easier to refer to *Maman* as a governess than try to explain the past.

The Lady Hertford drummed her fingers on her chair's wooden armrest. "No, I cannot say I have. When I was younger it wasn't en vogue to travel to France." She opened her fan and leaned in as if she had a secret. "I'm sure you're far too young to remember, but the revolution happened with that dreadful guillotine and, afterward, Napoleon's vile exploits made such an adventure out of the question as well."

"I can understand why. Except perhaps in 1814 while the emperor was imprisoned."

Across the room, the Duke of Beaufort entered with the housekeeper who headed directly toward them.

"Ah yes." The dowager marchioness smiled, her eyes affecting a faraway expression. "1814 was a memorable year."

Sensing her time had about run its course, Bria grasped the chain around her neck and pulled out the miniature. "Have you ever seen—"

"'Tis time to go, miss." The housekeeper clutched her fingers around Bria's arm and forcibly tugged her away from the elderly woman.

Bria signaled to Florrie and Pauline. "But—"

"I'm sorry. His Grace is rather insistent."

Ravenscar moved toward them, holding a bit of cake between his fingertips. "You're leaving? So soon?"

"Evidently, our time is up." Bria glanced to the floor clock before the woman had completely escorted her out of the room. They had five more minutes before twenty had passed. While footmen handed the dancers their satchels and cloaks, Beaufort looked on from the far end of the corridor, supervising the whole of their eviction. Did the duke think they would steal something?

I cannot believe that overbearing curmudgeon.

"What did you do wrong?" asked Pauline.

"This was Britannia's doing?" Florrie whispered as they were shown out the front door. "Did you insult the hostess?"

"I did no such thing. One moment I was speaking to the Dowager Marchioness of Hertford and the next I was being escorted out of the drawing room."

The door again opened, but this time Ravenscar, Saye and Fordham stepped outside.

"Fresh air!" said Lord Saye, donning his top hat.

Lord Fordham tugged on his gloves. "I daresay the overpowering essence of perfume was as intoxicating as a bottle of gin."

"Gin? I do like the ring of that." Saye turned to the ladies. "Would you care to accompany us to the Royal Saloon?"

Bria tossed her satchel over her shoulder. "No, thank you, my lord."

"Speak for yourself." Florrie looped her arm around Lord Fordham's elbow. "Pauline and I would be delighted."

Ravenscar inched the satchel from Bria's shoulder. "If you aren't up to a tot at the saloon, please allow me to escort you to the boarding house."

Bria caught the leather strap. "I assure you, that isn't necessary."

Ravenscar tugged harder. "I'd be no gentleman if I didn't insist."

She relented. "Have you no carriage, Your Grace?"

"I didn't need one."

"Oh, that's right, you like to walk."

He offered his arm. "I do."

"I do as well." Her palm felt nice in the crook of his elbow, almost as if it belonged there. Almost. But if anything showed Britannia her place in the world, it was being tossed out of Lady Calthorpe's town home as if she were about to steal the silver.

"How is your head? All healed?" he asked.

"For the most part. There's still a tad of bruising, but I covered it with pearl powder."

"Do not say that too loudly. In England the use of products to enhance one's appearance is strictly frowned upon."

"Unless you're a stage dancer." As they strolled further from the town house, the hotter Bria's nape grew. "I do not know what happened back there, but I think the Duke of Beaufort decidedly doesn't like me."

"Why do you say that?"

"Initially the housekeeper told us we would be given twenty minutes to answer questions at the tea. I was discussing France with the Dowager Marchioness of Hertford when Lady Calthorpe joined the conversation. No sooner had she asked me a question when the duke demanded her immediate attention. And the next thing I knew, we were escorted out the door."

"Hmm, that does seem rather odd. Perhaps Beaufort was involved in the Napoleonic wars and rues any discussion of France."

"If so, then why did the baroness invite him? Further, why did he come to the recital? He knows all of us are from Paris."

"True." The silver tip of Drake's cane tapped the footpath. "Though I don't think he's an admirer. He canceled his box after opening night."

"Oh dear, I am sorry."

"Not to worry, it was snatched up the same day."

On the opposite side of the street, Bria spotted Mr. Gibbs watching them. She gave a wave and the detective tipped his hat before heading off in the opposite direction.

"You know that man?" asked Ravenscar.

"I do. He's an investigator."

"Why on earth would you need to be acquainted with an investigator?"

Bria could have bit her tongue. If she had thought, she might have ignored Mr. Gibbs altogether. "He has an office on Regent Street. I asked him to look into a personal matter."

He cast a dark look out of the corner of his eye. "What personal matters could a Parisian ballerina possibly have in London?"

"Believe it or not, my life didn't begin the day I stepped on Chadwick Theater's stage."

He stopped and faced her. "That is not an answer."

She looked up at a lamp post—anywhere so she didn't have to meet the intensity of his gaze. "It is a private matter. One I'd rather keep under wraps."

Crossing his arms, his black eyebrows drew together. "One you do not care to share with me? Do you feel you cannot trust me—after everything?"

"It has nothing to do with trust. I must pursue this alone. And after five years, I've discovered no one can help me. Not even, as I have discovered, Mr. Gibbs."

They walked in silence until stopping outside the boarding house. Drake released Bria's arm and smoothed his hand along her shoulder. "I'm sorry I questioned you. All of us have business to attend. It was shortsighted of me to assume you would not."

"Thank you."

"But I want you to know I am a resource for you. Whatever you should need." He brushed a curl from her face. "You do know that, do you not?"

Her heart melted at his simple gesture. If only he weren't a duke. "Yes, and I appreciate everything you have done for me."

He grinned. "I've missed having you in the guest chamber."

"I've missed being there as well. You spoiled me far too much."

He brushed her cloak with the tip of his finger. "Britannia...I can't...because you are a...it wouldn't be..."

"I know." She rose up and kissed his cheek. "Thank you for being a gentleman."

Before she wrapped her arms around him and completely humiliated herself by declaring her undying love, Bria turned and dashed inside.

Chapter Fifteen

En arabesque, the Sylph kissed the sleeping James in the first scene of Act One as she did every night. And when he awoke, the mythical creature dashed to the wings.

"That was lovely, *ma chérie*," said Pauline, kissing Bria on both cheeks. "How do you make it better every time?"

"You are full of nonsense." Raising her skirts, she pointed her toes. "My right ribbons have come loose. 'Tis a miracle I didn't fall on my face."

"You'd best hasten to fix them…that's my cue," Pauline said as the music changed.

"*Bonne chance, mon amie.* Dance well."

Bria hastened to the dressing room while the rest of the cast danced onto the stage for the second scene. Not only had Bria's ribbons come loose, the stitching had worked free yet again and was holding by two tacks. Quickly removing the slipper, she plucked a threaded needle from the pincushion where she kept it at the ready.

It only took a few minutes to whip a half-dozen stitches. She pushed her foot back into the slipper and pulled the ribbons tightly across the arch of her foot. Taking extra care, she wound the shiny satin around her ankle, ensuring the laces were tied snugly, and the knot tucked inside. Rising onto her toe, she tested her repair.

It will hold.

The music indicated she still had a time to spare. She moved to her toilette to freshen her lip rouge and looked in the mirror.

Then she froze.

Mon Dieu!

It wasn't her reflection that stopped Bria's breath, it was the fire blocking the doorway.

A spark popped and sailed toward her legs while the flames leaped higher. Spinning in a circle, she frantically searched for something, anything to staunch it. With no other option, she grabbed her cloak from the peg.

"Help!" she shouted, thrashing the woolen garment atop the fire. Heat from the flames burned Bria's face as she gritted her teeth, furiously working to snuff it. The stench of sizzling wool stung her nostrils. "Help!"

Screams and shouts came from the stage, but Bria didn't stop. The smoke grew thicker as she worked, her eyes burning.

She gasped for breath, her arms beginning to shake from her effort.

"Stand back!" On the other side of the doorway, a prop laborer wielded two pails of water.

Bria scooted away while the man doused the flames. The timbers hissed and crackled as black water washed over her slippers.

"My God, what happened?" Ravenscar asked, barreling into the dressing room with Mr. Perkins on his heels.

All eyes shifted to Bria while the duke reached for her shoulders, stopping before he touched her. "Miss LeClair, are you injured?" His tone was stately and official, as if they had never shared a kiss or stolen moments alone in his town home. But then the entire cast had congregated just beyond the door.

Bria smoothed her hands down her tulle skirts and felt no pain. "I think not."

"Nonetheless, we will close the theater for the night." The duke turned to Mr. Perkins. "Make the announcement. Refund all tickets."

"No!" Bria caught Mr. Perkins' wrist before he started off. "Is anyone else injured? I heard screaming."

"That's because we saw the fire," said Florrie.

Turning to the duke, she stretched to her full height. "If it was just me who was in danger, then I assure you I am well enough to continue."

Ravenscar pulled the singed cloak from her hand. "Are you certain? You've had a terrible scare. No one expects you to carry on."

"*I* expect to finish the performance, and I am perfectly able." She stepped over the charred threshold, beckoning Mr. Perkins. "Come with me, sir. I will help you explain to the audience."

On stage, the theater manager held up his hands, requesting silence. "Ladies and gentlemen, we suffered a small fire outside Miss LeClair's dressing room. She assures me she is unharmed and intends to continue with the performance."

Bria threw kisses to the audience. "*Mes amis*, thank you for coming tonight. Please forgive the interruption. The fire has been doused with no harm done. Please resume your seats." She gave a nod to the conductor while Monsieur Travere called for places.

***

Though he lauded Britannia's heroics, Drake sat through the remainder of the performance with every muscle in his body clenched. Britannia could have been badly burned. Christ, she could have died. Who gave a rat's arse about his theater? The woman he'd come to admire and adore above all other performers had been in frightful peril.

Before the curtain call, he found Perkins. "Bring Miss LeClair to my rooms. I need to have a word."

"Yes, Your Grace. If it's about the fire, I assure you I will have an investigator here first thing in the morning."

"Good man. And we'd best step up the security. Something is afoot. I feel it in my bones and we will not sit idle whilst some dastard plays us for fools."

Chadwick Theater had a small suite of offices behind the fourth tier of boxes where Drake paced until Perkins showed Britannia in. He gave the stage manager a nod. "Please leave us."

"As you wish."

Still in costume, Bria waited until the door closed. "Your Grace, I assure you I am unharmed."

Releasing a pent up breath he hadn't realized he'd been holding, he took two steps and pulled her into his arms. "Dash it all, my heart nearly burst to smithereens seeing you there, charred with smoke, a half-burned cloak in your grasp."

Her hands slipped around his waist as she rested her head against his chest. He cradled her to him. It drove him mad not to be able to hold her like this whenever he pleased. "I'm sorry I frightened you."

"You? The fire frightened me, not you...and whoever lit it. My oath, the thought of losing you scares me to my bones." He strengthened his grip around her, wishing never to let her go. "You must know how dear you are to me."

"I am?"

"Yes. Oh, yes." It took all his self-control to keep from saying he hadn't looked at another woman since Britannia had stepped into the theater in April. To stop himself from declaring he wanted to be the man to protect her for the rest of her days, he buried his nose in the curls piled atop her head. Now was no time to turn into a lovesick fool. It was his duty to see to her safety, and he'd just failed miserably.

Drake squeezed his eyes shut and kissed her forehead, not yet ready to release his embrace. "Is there a reason someone might be trying to hurt you? Did you have a bad experience in France you haven't told me about?"

She turned her face up and looked at him directly without a hint of fear. "Nothing like this ever happened to me in France."

Yes, those whisky eyes were pure and honest. Britannia's gaze mesmerized him. Staring at her lovely face made a fire rage in his breast and a tempest swirl in his loins. He had no business holding her in his arms. But for once in his life, he threw propriety out the window. Without another word he shifted his gaze to Britannia's lips—the color of roses, pert and perfect. Slowly, deliberately, he lowered his head and met those delicious lips. He'd only intended it to be a light kiss, but the womanly sigh of desire rumbling from her throat drove him straight to the brink of insanity.

In a rush of passion, his mouth opened against her, begging for more. As if consumed by madness, he rubbed his hands up her back, threaded his fingers through her curls, and dove deeper into heaven. His balls were on fire. His cock harder than it had ever been in his life.

And God save him, she turned to sweet, warm cream in his arms. A valiant foe, she matched him swirl for swirl, caress for caress, moan for moan.

It wasn't until he backed her against the wall that he realized how far he'd gone—how close he was to raising her skirts and taking her where he stood.

A lead ball sank in his gut.

Britannia LeClair was not his to love. And he could not ever break her heart.

With his next breath, he pulled away. "Please forgive me."

***

That night Drake didn't sleep and as dawn rose, he didn't bother ringing for his valet. He donned a pair of buckskins, top boots, and a morning coat. Downstairs, he found Pennyworth in his chamber, preparing for the day's work.

The butler immediately rose to his feet. "Your Grace. I didn't expect you so early."

"I need a favor."

"Of course, I am at your service."

"There was a fire at the theater last eve."

"My word. Was anyone injured?"

"No, by the grace of God. However, too many things have happened to Miss LeClair to be coincidence."

"Do you think the young lady is in danger?"

"I do not know yet, but I will no longer sit idle while there is the possibility that someone is, indeed, trifling with her."

"What do you require of me?"

"I want you to find her a secure apartment. West End, of course. She'll need a cook, a housekeeper with experience as a lady's maid, and a butler—I envision the butler to be an ox— someone skilled at boxing. I'd like the arrangements to be made in confidence."

"With a private exit as before?"

"A private exit, yes. But let me make it clear I am not taking Miss LeClair as a mistress, I am merely taking steps to ensure her safety."

"Rooms will be difficult to find at short notice, but I have my sources."

"Thank you."

"When will she move in?"

"Today."

"Today?" Pennyworth's voice cracked.

"Make it happen." Drake tugged on his gloves and headed for the mews. There, he took his horse and paid a visit to the hackney driver. It only took a few inquiries to find the coachman at a rundown public stable in St. Giles, bent over and picking his horse's hooves.

Drake stood for a moment, his arms crossed, debating whether or not to kick the lout in the arse. Deciding to take the high road, he spoke in a low growl, "I asked you to report your findings after your hack threw a wheel."

Like lightning, the man dropped the horse's leg and straightened. "Yer G-grace. I didn't expect to see ye 'ere."

"Obviously. But when I ask a man to do something, I expect it to be done." Drake placed his palm on the hindquarter of the gelding to ensure the horse knew where he stood.

"I stayed away 'cause I thought ye'd be angry."

"You thought correctly. And now I'm doubly angry because I had to go to the effort of finding you."

"I didn't do nothing."

"That's right. You sat on your laurels and did nothing. You owe me a report on what happened that night. You told me you checked your hack before taking Miss LeClair and Miss Renaud to the ball. What were your findings the next morning?"

"I tell ye true, I 'aven't a lick of proof, but the linchpin was missing. It was snug when I set out. I check my gear thoroughly every morn, I do."

"So you're saying the pin was tampered with?"

"I reckon so, Yer Grace."

"You knew this, but you did not come forward?"

"I cannot prove it, I just know. What would ye 'ave done to me if I'd come claiming the linchpin was missing and I suspected tampering?"

Before he answered, Drake took note of the poor state of the stable. Not only was the building in shabby repair, manure covered the floor. Bloody hell, anyone could pick up a shovel and keep the place tidy. "I might have paid you a healthy reward, but now you will receive nothing. Because you did nothing."

Drake mounted his horse and rode away without a backward glance. No wonder the driver was having difficulty making ends meet. He was his own worst enemy and thicker than ox hide.

After arriving at the theater, he used the stage door. Carpenters were busy making repairs to the fire-damaged timbers.

"Ravenscar." Perkins stepped around the laborers. "I suspected I'd see you here this morn."

"What have you found?"

"This." He held up a burnt cinder and sniffed it. "It has a potent odor of fish."

"Whale oil?"

"It is."

"So you have proof then, someone tried to kill Miss LeClair."

"Or give her a good scare. I reckon the culprit would have lit a bigger fire if he was serious."

"I want to know who was back here, how did he…or she get in? I want a guard on Miss LeClair's door whenever she's in the theater."

"Already arranged. I hired two men-at-arms. One for the stage door, and one to keep an eye on our ballerina. They start tonight."

"Good work. And the culprit?"

"I'm still digging into his identity. If the bastard was seen, I'll know about it by the day's end."

"Send word as soon as you learn anything."

"Straightaway, Your Grace."

***

By midafternoon, Pennyworth had made the arrangements for Britannia's new accommodations. For discretion, Drake reversed the doors of his town coach from displaying his family crest to solid black. He wanted no one to know what he was up to or where he was going.

He asked the coachman to drive up in the alley behind the boarding house. Wearing an unpretentious Benjamin top coat, Drake slipped in through the kitchens, tipping a lad a half crown to escort him to Miss LeClair's quarters.

He had to stoop as the boy led him up four flights of rickety stairs.

"This is it here."

After Drake gave a nod, the lad knocked on the door. "Miss LeClair, you have a visitor."

"A moment," she called through the timbers and, after much rustling, she opened the door. "Goodness me, Your Grace. Should you be up here?"

Why on earth did she always make him affect a lopsided grin like a schoolboy? He ran a hand across his mouth. "I am standing here, am I not?"

She popped her head out to the corridor. "Did anyone see you?"

"No, miss," the lad replied. "I brought him up the servants' stairs."

"You did what?"

Drake pointed to his temple. "I only knocked my head once."

"But why are you here?"

He glanced to the lad. "Thank you, I can manage from here." He leaned to the side and looked around Britannia. "Where is Miss Renaud?"

Looking sheepish, a red blush spread across her face. "Keeping company with Lord Saye…ah…yes. She is."

"I see." He saw only too well. "How long has she been away?"

"Not long."

"He's putting her up, is he not?"

Britannia gave a defeated nod.

"That just serves to cement my decision all the more. May I come inside?"

"Must you?"

Drake understood her reluctance. The last time they were together behind closed doors he'd scarcely been able control himself—pulling her into his arms and devouring her with kisses. Well, this time he was in complete control as a duke should be. "I could say what needs to be said out here in the passageway, though I deem a certain amount of confidentiality is necessary."

She stepped aside and ushered him in. "Very well."

With no more than two steps, he was in the center of the room with nowhere to go without bumping his head. "Good Lord, you've been staying in this hovel? It is smaller than Ravenscar Hall's china closet."

"It suits me fine. At least up here Pauline and I have a modicum of privacy."

"Had I known you were relegated to the servant's quarters, I would have made other arrangements sooner."

"Sooner?" Bria scooted backward, managing not to thump her head on the eaves. "What arrangements?"

"I've done some investigating. The fire at the theater was not an accident."

"No?" Gasping, she clapped her hands over her mouth. "Who would do such a thing?"

"My very thoughts as well." He spotted a portmanteau under the bed and tugged it out. "I also found your hackney coach driver this morning—the miscreant from the Hughes ball. The thrown wheel was no accident. He thinks someone tampered with the linchpin."

"Heavenly stars! Someone is trying to scare me?"

"Or kill you." Drake tossed the case on the bed and unbuckled it. "I am taking immediate action. I will not sit idle while there's a madman out there threatening your life."

"This is terrible."

"And that is exactly why we must act swiftly, alerting as few people as possible." The only place he could stand straight in the damned attic chamber was between the beds, but he did so with command. "Now tell me, is there anyone in the troupe who could be responsible for these crimes?"

Wide eyed, Britannia clutched her fists beneath her chin. "I cannot think of a soul. True, some of the dancers in the *corps* are jealous, but they wouldn't resort to attempting murder."

"What about your understudy?"

"Florrie? I thought she—" Shoving the heels of her hands against her temples, she shook her head emphatically. "No! She was on stage when the fire was lit—so was the rest of the cast."

"Blast." He gestured to the open portmanteau. "I have secured private rooms for you where you shall be under my protection at all times. You'll have a housekeeper, a cook, and a butler who is also able to act as a bodyguard. There will be an unmarked coach available for your personal use at all times."

Still holding her head, she craned her neck, those whisky eyes filled with shock. "How am I expected to pay for all of this?"

"Chadwick Theater will assume all of your expenses. It is only fitting."

Without lifting a finger to pack her things, Britannia sat on the bed opposite. "The theater will foot the bill for me to live like a queen?"

"Hardly a queen. A princess, perhaps." Drake turned full circle, scarcely able to move. "And had I been aware that you were living in hovel too small to be called a room, we would have done so two months ago." He'd have words with Mr. Perkins about this arrangement—or was it Travere who thought so little of his protégé? Whomever was responsible, Drake would ensure the theater didn't commit such errors in the future.

"At least I will not be a burden for long." Bria sat on the bed. "As soon as *La Sylphide's* Season is over I will return to Paris. Good heavens, why is this happening?"

Drake's mouth grew dry. He hadn't allowed himself to think about the end of the ballet and Britannia's return to Paris. But as the words escaped her mouth, his heart twisted. How could he protect her if she was on the Continent? But on the other hand, how could he keep her in London when there was a madman on the loose?

"Are you afraid?" he asked, keeping his voice steady to mask his emotions.

"Who wouldn't be? You've just informed me I am being stalked. With the scoundrel's every act, things grow more perilous. I-I'm terrified!" Curling over, Britannia grabbed a pillow and buried her face. "I try so hard. Why does someone want to do me harm?"

As her shoulders shook, Drake slid beside her. "This shouldn't be happening to you. It should never be you." He pulled her onto his lap and rocked, clutching her to his chest for dear life. "Believe me, I want to find this scoundrel more than anyone."

She nestled against him, a tear spilling onto his coat. "But until then, I will be forced to live in fear. M-my freedoms stifled."

"Not stifled but protected." He smoothed his hand over her hair. God, she was more precious than any passion or any human being he'd ever met. "Please, Britannia. Let me do this for you."

An anguished sob caught in her throat while he continued to hold her. "I hate this."

"I know, my dearest," he whispered into her hair. "It is not fair that you should suffer. You are the kindest, most selfless person I know."

Closing his eyes, Drake pressed his lips to her temple—merely her forehead and not her lips. "The devil be damned if I allow one more malfeasance to befall you."

"No, none of this is your doing." She slipped her arms around his waist.

"Nor is it yours." He captured her face between his palms. "Allow me to take care of you—to put an end to this madness."

"But people will think the worst."

"Does it matter?"

"Yes, to me it does."

"You are a woman of great conviction and I respect that. Wear a veil. My carriage doors have been turned to hide my crest. We shall slip out through the rear entry to the mews."

As she raised her tawny eyelashes, her hypnotic gaze made Drake's good intentions fade into oblivion. It took every ounce of strength in his body to resist her pert lips, the lithe, feminine form perfectly molding to his lap. He lost himself in whisky and woman. With an unexpected wildness, Britannia closed the gap and kissed him. Drake's low growl rumbled through his soul as his heart raced, consuming her with the pent-up desire he'd been suppressing for weeks.

Just one kiss, one bone-melting, savoring kiss and then I'll apologize and take her away from here.

Chapter Sixteen

"One thing I'll say about Ravenscar is he has very good taste," said Pauline, twirling through Bria's new drawing room. "And you deserve to be pampered more than any member of the cast."

"I don't know about that." Bria patted the red velvet settee beside her. "Come and sit before the tea cools."

Executing pirouette, Pauline gracefully landed on the seat. "But isn't it wonderful to have your own suite of rooms with your own servants?"

"Wonderful and daunting." Even the silver tea service engraved with ornate filigree wasn't hers. Yes, the suite of rooms lavishly exuded wealth from the matching settee and chairs to the mahogany table, to the marble hearth—wealth she didn't have. When she left for Paris, Bria would leave it all behind.

"Why do you say daunting?"

Over the past few weeks, Ravenscar's generosity had been nothing short of knightly. But the whirlwind of changes had been overwhelming as well. Now situated in secret rooms where Pauline was the only guest aside from the duke, she felt as if she'd been placed inside a gilded box. And no one was at fault. Someone had tried to kill her more than once, and His Grace had pulled out every stop to ensure her safety.

Shrugging a shoulder, Bria poured. "You and I managed just fine without servants, and now I have a butler, a cook and a housekeeper—"

"Who also acts as your lady's maid."

"Even though I'm not a lady."

"Who says you are not?"

"Oh please, you have brighter stars in your eyes than I do." Bria set the teapot down and removed the top of the sugar bowl. "Would you like one spoon or two?"

Holding up her palm, Pauline shook her head. "None. If I start sweetening my beverages, I'll never be able to tie my stays."

"Me as well." Often there had been no sugar available to add to her tea. Why start using it now? "You haven't told me. How is Lord Saye?" His Lordship had made arrangements to be Pauline's benefactor shortly after the Hughes ball.

A blush sprang on her friend's cheeks. "Marvelous, though I daresay the rooms he has given me are not as nice as these by half."

"My, how we live in the moment." Smiling, Bria leaned nearer. "Are you comfortable?"

"I am."

"Are you happy?"

"Very much." Pauline set her cup down and looked toward the hearth, not being very convincing.

Bria clasped her hand. "I hope His Lordship is being kind."

"He is."

"Truly?"

"He comes and goes. He's pleasant, but keeps me at arm's length, so to speak." On a sigh, Pauline reclined into the cushions. "Given our arrangement, I didn't expect to fall in love. Though he has asked me to remain in London after the Season."

"Surprising."

"*Oui.*"

"How do you feel about staying here while the rest of us return to Paris?"

"He only mentioned the idea last night. He is gentlemanly, and our arrangement is nice." Pauline traced her finger along the settee's golden cording. "But if you decided to stay here with Ravenscar—"

"No, no, no." Bria moved the tea service aside and stood. "I am not the duke's mistress. I cannot expect him to maintain these rooms once *La Sylphide* closes."

"But imagine the expense. Surely you know he expects something more from you now—"

"Stop right there! Do you think dancing the Sylph means nothing to him? Our ballet is bringing in revenues to his theater and after the fire and the thrown wheel, he decided the boarding house wasn't safe enough."

"Though it seems to be fine for the rest of us."

"The rest of you are not being stalked by some lunatic. Besides, since you started keeping company with Lord Saye, I was staying in that attic room alone."

"Right, and Ravenscar is the perfect gentleman," Pauline said, with an exaggerated roll of her eyes.

"He is our *employer*. He cannot take advantage of the master-servant relationship. It wouldn't be proper."

"And no man has used such power to his advantage."

"Not the Duke of Ravenscar." Unless kissing counted.

Waggling her eyebrows, Pauline tossed the pillow into Bria's hands. "But you like him."

Collapsing back onto the settee, Bria buried her face in a red velvet pillow. She had never discussed their kisses with anyone and now was no time to confess to Pauline. Besides, every kiss with the duke ended with an apology. Though she couldn't deny the passion. Even she was beginning to realize the magnetism between them was as difficult for His Grace to feign indifference to as it was for her. Nonetheless, they had managed to maintain a professional relationship with only a few slips now and again.

Thank heavens the Season would be over soon and she'd return to France. Putting the channel between her and Ravenscar was the only surefire way to ensure their fondness was snuffed once and for all.

"You cannot hide your feelings from me," Pauline said. "I'm not blind. Every time he is in the same room, it's as if everyone else fades into oblivion. He's like your very own knight in shining armor."

"Do not start putting ideas in my head." Bria peeked out from the pillow while hiding her smile. Aye, he'd saved her in more ways that she cared to admit. "He is duty bound to marry a gently-bred woman of the *ton*, and I will not have my heart broken."

"I think it is too late for that."

She threw the pillow at her friend. "Hush."

"So, you're planning to leave all this in a few weeks when *La Sylphide* closes?"

"Yes." Gulping, Bria swallowed against the thickening of her throat. Her return to Paris wasn't forever. However, she planned to return to England and when she did, Ravenscar most likely would have found his bride. Surely he would be easier to resist if he were not a single man. "Though the duke has talked about bringing us back for another Season."

"Us or you?"

"Me, but I think he means all of us."

"He could use local dancers for the *corps*." Pauline reached for a biscuit.

"If so, then possibly your idea to remain in London has merit. I'm sure you'd be one of the first dancers hired." Bria refilled their cups. "So, with that settled, have you given any thought as to what you'll wear to Ravenscar's end of Season ball?"

"There hasn't been time, but Lord Saye has opened an account for me at Harding, Howell and Company."

"That's exciting. I'm thrilled for you."

"I thought you'd be disappointed in me."

"How you choose to live your life is not for me to judge. Things are not easy for ballerinas, and I fault you for nothing." Bria held up her cup in toast. "Let's visit the haberdashers' together. I still haven't spent the twenty pounds Lady Calthorpe gave me."

"Oh, let's. It will be diverting."

***

Thanks to Pennyworth's excellent hounding skills, Drake was able to exit his mews, cross to the neighboring rear garden, walk the equivalent of a half-block, and slip into the rear entry of Britannia's suite of rooms all without setting foot on the street. In turn, she was also able to travel incognito to and from the theater in an unmarked coach, wearing a veil, the butler doubling as her henchman.

Better yet, her butler was married to Miss LeClair's housekeeper and they were both a great deal older. Indeed, Pennyworth had exceeded expectations with this arrangement.

But time was passing much too fast. It was Sunday and a fine afternoon for a ride when Drake knocked on his ballerina's door.

The butler answered.

"Is she ready?" Drake asked.

"Right on time," Britannia said, waltzing down the corridor, wearing a poke bonnet and pulling on her gloves. "I like men who adhere to schedule."

"Oh? You have established select opinions, have you?" He bowed, allowing her to pass. "What else do you like in men?"

He followed her through the labyrinth of corridors and down to his mews where the grooms had his shiny, black phaeton rigged and waiting with a perfectly matched pair.

Britannia stopped. "Do you mean to say we'll be riding in plain sight?"

"The only reason we've been hiding you is so that no one will know where you're staying. It is such a nice day, it would be shameful not to enjoy it."

When one of the geldings stamped his foot and snorted, the lady smoothed her hand along his mane. "These fellows are eager to stretch their legs. They are athletes, you know. Horses need to run just as much as I need to dance." She performed a neat *rond de jambe*. "I cannot believe there are only two more weeks until *La Sylphide* closes."

Drake's shoulders dropped. No one needed to tell him Britannia would be returning to Paris in a fortnight. The imminent end of the Season bedeviled him every waking moment. Bittersweet was the anticipation of her departure, but it had to be. He couldn't admit to falling in love with a ballerina. It simply wasn't done.

Forcing himself to take a deep breath, Drake offered his hand and helped her climb into the carriage. Her fingers were so small in his palm—delicate, yet firm and sure like the rest of her. But the smallness of them made his heart squeeze all the more. Once it became clear Chadwick Theater would be successful, he'd put the impending end of Season out of his mind. True, plans were in motion to bring Miss LeClair back to London for another Season, but the fact of the matter was he could barely imagine having her leave for Paris in the interim. How could he protect her when she was in France?

She had become a friend—damn it all, she was far more than a friend. He looked forward to seeing her dance every night, to venturing backstage and watching her smile as he complimented her performance. And Pennyworth had gone to such great lengths to arrange their secret goings-on. He referred to them thus because they were not having an affair. They had an *arrangement*. A comfortable, secret, treasured arrangement with stolen kisses here and there. Did he want more? God yes. But at least Drake loved being able to visit Britannia whenever he desired with no one the wiser.

Once he climbed up beside her, he gathered the ribbons and headed for Hyde Park at an easy walk. There was no rush. To hurry seemed only to bring the end of *La Sylphide* more quickly.

"Are you going to Peak Castle after the Season?" she asked.

"I am. I always enjoy spending the end of my summers there. Winters, too."

"But you adore London and the theater. It's difficult for me to picture you off in the country."

"If I recall, I said I once aspired to the boards. I didn't say I was a consummate carouser."

"No?"

"Truth be told, I'm a bit of a recluse."

"And what about your mother? Does she travel north with you?"

"She does. She maintains the dowager house on the shore, though I suspect she prefers Ravenscar Hall."

"She seems happy there."

"I think she is."

"And you'd rather reside in your unpretentious town house?"

"It suits my needs when I'm in London. But my favorite is Peak Castle."

"What do you like about your grand fortress?"

"First of all, it is familiar. I grew up there. In the mornings, I walk along the beach. No one is about at that time of day. I can stroll for miles discovering the treasure brought by the night's sea."

"It sounds marvelous." She leaned against his arm, smiling. He liked the familiarity of her touch. Through their layers of clothing, the contact made a thrill of gooseflesh rise all the way up to his nape.

When he inhaled, the air caught in his throat. "It is." He feigned a lazy smile—not wanting to reveal the affect she had on him, lest she draw away. "And the hunting in the North Moors is not to be surpassed in my opinion…I wish…" He held his tongue. Drake had no business stating his dreams aloud. It wouldn't be fair to Britannia.

"Yes?"

"Pay me no mind. I shouldn't have said anything."

Coy, whisky eyes drifted upward as she regarded him. "Why, because dukes are not allowed wishes?"

His muscles tightened around his lips. "They are not. Dukes are in the business of *granting* wishes."

She gave his arm a playful nudge, making those tingles frisk across his neck more erratically. "I didn't realize you could trace your lineage back to the fairy folk."

He laughed. "I do like your banter, Miss LeClair."

"You've called me Britannia many times before."

"I have. Forgive me for taking liberties."

"I like it when you call me familiar. Though my closest friends call me Bria."

He glanced at her out of the corner of his eye. Even wearing a bonnet, she was the most beautiful creature he'd ever seen. "Hmm. I think Britannia suits you better."

"Why?"

"Because you are too elegant for a Bria. You are courageous, beautiful, strong, and have more fortitude than many men I know. That definitely qualifies you as a Britannia in my eyes."

"Thank you." As he drove the team onto Hyde Park's ever-busy Rotten Row, she straightened, leaving an emptiness where her arm had been. "Now tell me, what is it you wish for? What is it a duke's breeding prevents such a man from uttering?"

"'Tis nothing. And it is no use dwelling upon that which I cannot have." He slapped the ribbons, requesting an easy trot. "So, before I say another word, there is a reason aside from the weather why I asked you to go riding."

Craning her neck, she gazed at him, eyebrows arched over those exquisite eyes, the sun turning them amber.

"I have a proposal for next Season's performances."

Her rapt interest made it difficult to focus on the subject at hand. "I'm listening."

He forced himself to look away and offer a nod, greeting a passing carriage. "Rather than one Season-long ballet, I'd like to showcase an assortment of ballets, say, three. With you in the lead, of course."

"Three will be a challenge."

"Yes, you'll need to perform one while rehearsing the next."

"That sounds like something I'd enjoy—and we're not unaccustomed to rehearsing by day and performing by night. What would you think about using local dancers?"

"If we can find them, I would prefer it."

"Perhaps we should open a ballet school."

Driving the horses off the thoroughfare, he pulled them to a stop. "You sound as if you've given some thought to the idea."

"I envisioned the concept after Pauline told me she was planning to stay on in London."

"She is? Will you not miss her when you return to Paris?"

"Very much so."

"Hmm." He rubbed the ribbons between his fingers. Could he convince her to stay as well? "In light of our new venture, you could stay on as well—you could audition dancers for the new ballets."

"Mr. Perkins ought to be able to handle the auditions. Besides, as far as I know, no one is trying to stalk me in Paris."

Drake's contacts still had no leads on the scoundrel. "Perhaps we should put more thought into your school idea. And as for your stalker, you have my word I will not sit idle while he is at large."

Britannia leaned into him as she looped her arm around his—an inordinately familiar gesture—one he would cherish always. "Why do you think it's a man?"

He leaned nearer as well, craving her touch. In a fortnight she wouldn't be there to caress. How would he survive? "The wheel," he explained. "Few women would think to loosen a linchpin and if one did, she would be very conspicuous approaching a carriage with a pair of tongs."

"Unless she has an accomplice."

"What are you saying? Do you suspect anyone?" he asked, turning his nose and inhaling the scent that was uniquely Britannia.

"Not really. I thought of Florrie at first, but she couldn't have started the fire—and I don't think she's evil enough to do something that might kill me."

"No. I just do not understand it." Unable to resist, Drake cupped her cheek and kissed her forehead.

Gossips be damned.

Chapter Seventeen

"Miss LeClair, how lovely to see you again," said Mr. Harding as Bria entered the haberdasher's shop with Pauline on her arm.

She gave him a warm smile. "Good afternoon, sir. Please allow me to introduce Miss Renaud. She dances in *La Sylphide,* as well. If I remember correctly, you had an opportunity to see the ballet."

"I did, but I have tickets for next week and I am greatly looking forward to seeing it again."

"*C'est bon,*" said Pauline. "Next week is our grand finale."

"Which is why we're here." Bria fingered a shiny, pink ribbon. "I'm looking for gloves and accessories and Pauline needs fabric."

"A new gown?"

"*Oui.*"

"Do you have a modiste secured?" asked Mr. Harding. "It will be difficult to have a dress made on such short notice. The end of the Season is the second most frantic time for seamstresses—mothers of daughters who haven't received a marriage proposal are at their wits end."

Pauline ran her finger around the tip of a frilly, white parasol. "Do you know of anyone who might be taking new clients?"

Mr. Harding snapped his fingers. "I should have thought. A seamstress left her card a few days past. Mind you, I cannot recommend her work, though she was handsomely attired."

Bria looked to Pauline. "I'll wager she does good work if she called in here."

"*Oui, oui.* I would be grateful if you would give us her information."

"Very well, I'll write her address on your parcels before you leave." Mr. Harding led them toward the back wall lined with fabrics. "Now, Miss Renaud, tell me what you are looking for. New silks arrived from the Orient. I daresay you would look lovely in a daffodil yellow."

As she passed a display of gloves, Bria stopped. "I think I'll do some browsing if you don't mind."

"Be my guest," said Mr. Harding.

She bent over a pair of white kid gloves exquisitely embroidered with a rose vine extending from the fingers all the way up to the elbow. Beneath the glass, she could only imagine how much they cost. She craned her neck for a better look at the tag, partially hidden by the little finger—*Italy*. No price showed.

Why not indulge myself for once?

Before Bria asked the attendant to bring them out, her attention was drawn to a conversation near the counter. "How about a thread waxer? The ladies say there is nothing better to crimp the ends for easy threading," said a clerk near the sales counter.

"Let me try one," replied an elderly woman, her voice reedy. "I'm not about to purchase anything until I'm confident it will work."

Unable to see the patron who was talking, Bria moved a bit closer until a woman in an invalid chair came into view. *Oh my!* Holding a quizzing glass, the Dowager Marchioness of Hertford ran the end of a string of silk across a ball of wax made to look like a strawberry with a silver cap fashioned like leaves. Her hand trembled while she bit down on the corner of her lip and attempted to thread a needle while continuing to hold the glass.

"I daresay you need more hands, my lady." Bria stepped into view. "Can your lady's maid help?"

"She can, but I'm not dead!" The woman stiffened, regarding her with enormous, rheumy eyes. "I would like to do some things myself."

Bria glanced to the clerk. "Do you have a monocle? That might be the solution for Her Ladyship. At least it would free both her hands for embroidery."

"Indeed." The man smiled broadly. "We have quite a selection of monocles. Give me a moment and I'll bring over the display."

Finally, my chance.

Pulling out her miniature, Bria snatched the opportunity to speak to the dowager marchioness before the man returned. "Good day, Your Ladyship. I do not imagine you remember me."

The woman cheeks wrinkled with the purse of her lips. "My mind isn't completely gone. You are the young lady who dances with such passion."

"Thank you." Bria held out the miniature. "I was wondering if you might help me. After the couple who fostered me passed away, I found this portrait in a box bearing my name along with a handkerchief that sported a royal monogram. I think the lady in the painting may be a relation of sorts, but I have no way of knowing. You wouldn't happen to recognize her?"

The old woman raised her quizzing glass and examined the miniature. "Lovely. She looks like you. When did you say the woman sat for the portrait?"

"It must have been around 1814, possibly a bit earlier."

The woman turned a tad green. "I must say my memory isn't what it once was."

"Thank you for humoring me. I am grateful." Bria reached for the miniature, but Her Ladyship leaned closer with her glass.

"A moment. This was painted by Adam Buck. An astounding artist, the favorite of the royals."

"Even twenty years ago?"

"Especially twenty years ago. Whoever the lady in this miniature is, I can say she is someone of importance. Of that I have no doubt."

"Is Mr. Buck still in London?" Bria had never bothered with the signature because, to her, it was illegible. Fancy it had been painted by someone famous.

"Alas, no. I attended his funeral not but two months past."

"Two months?" For the love of God, Bria had been in London nearly four. If only she'd had this information when the ship arrived, she might have gained an audience with the artist who painted the *Grande-Duchesse*. "Thank you. You have given me more information than I have been able to uncover in five years of searching."

"Hmm." The dowager marchioness tapped her quizzing glass on her armrest. "You might ask Ravenscar. After all, you are performing at his theater."

"Ravenscar, my lady?"

"His mother is a patroness of the *ton* and has been for over twenty years. If anyone can identify your mystery lady, it is she."

"Wonderful idea, I shall ask." Bria slipped the miniature back in its hiding place. Honestly, she hadn't wanted to involve the duke for a host of reasons, the first being he was her employer and she cared very much what he thought of her. When they'd first met, he had been intent on uncovering information about her past and she'd been afraid to give it. She still wasn't enamored with the idea, especially if the outcome proved her to be a bastard.

"Here we are." The clerk approached with a velvet-lined tray sporting at least a dozen delicate monocles, a few dainty enough for Her Ladyship's use.

"Do other noblewomen use these?" Lady Hertford asked.

"Yes, indeed, a great many gently-bred women have them. Might I suggest the one with the ivy leaf bale?"

"Oh, yes," Bria agreed. "That one is ever so feminine."

"May as well." The dowager marchioness nipped the monocle with her perfectly manicured pincers. "It is astonishing the crutches a lady must resort to using in her old age. Hence this chair. I loathe it."

The clerk straightened. "But an invalid's chair enables you freedoms you wouldn't otherwise have, my lady."

Her Ladyship blinked in succession, affixing the glass in place. "Which is why I am sitting in it sampling monocles and thread wax."

"I think the glass looks quite distinguished." Bria curtsied. "If you'll excuse me, I'd best join Miss Renaud."

Out of the corner of her eye, a dark shadow moved past the window. But when Bria turned for a better look, the only person she saw was a boy selling newspapers.

"Bria, I need your opinion." Pauline dragged her to the rear of the store. "Which ribbon looks best with the yellow organza, the white or the rose?"

"I think the rose is more vibrant."

"Me as well." Pauline leaned nearer. "You have the most astonishing look in your eye. What is it?"

She patted the hidden miniature. "I think I might be a bit closer to finding the *Grande-Duchesse*."

"*C'est magnifique!* Tell me what you've learned."

"Later. I'll relay all on our walk to the modiste."

***

"Pretty rose, Your Grace. Is it for our Sylph?" asked Florrie as Drake ventured backstage after the curtain call.

"It is."

The woman flicked her curls. "You spoil her."

"I daresay Miss LeClair has earned far more than a simple rose."

"Perhaps one day I'll be so lucky to receive a flower from a duke."

"Then you're in luck. I bought one for every member of the cast. Mr. Perkins will be handing them out, I believe." Drake shifted his attention to the guard posted outside the dressing room door. "Is Miss LeClair within?"

The man knocked. "She is, Your Grace."

They waited.

The man knocked again. "Miss LeClair?"

She didn't answer.

Drake's heart stopped.

"Move aside!" he ordered, barreling into the chamber.

Britannia sat in a chair holding a missive between trembling hands.

"What the devil is it?"

With a shrill gasp, she tossed the letter onto the toilette. "'Tis nothing."

"Right. Nothing makes you shake like you're frightened half out of your wits." Marching forward, he snatched the missive from the table.

"Don't."

He hesitated. "All right, if you do not want me to read your correspondence, at the least tell me what has upset you."

"I didn't ever want you to know."

"Want me to know what, exactly?" He squeezed the rose's stem so hard, the thorns dug into his palm. Damnation, he'd gone to great lengths to ensure her protection. Was this a clue to the identity of her stalker? About to jump out of his skin, he drew in a deep breath. "By now haven't you realized there is absolutely no reason to hide *anything* from me?"

"Tell him," Miss Renaud said from the doorway. "Lady Hertford said his mother might know. *Alors*, this is your only chance of discovering the truth."

"Britannia?" He yanked the damned thorn out of his skin and licked the blood. But now was no time to shower the woman with a trite gift. He needed answers.

"You're right. Leave us and close the door please," the Sylph said before picking up the missive and reading aloud:

"You've had your warning. You should have returned to Paris. We do not want your kind here. I know what you are looking for and you shan't find it. Should you pursue the matter further, you will force me to take drastic measures."

"Good God." Drake slapped the damned rose on the toilette. "Who signed that compilation of drivel?"

"'Tis unsigned of course, just like the last one."

"The last one?" His voice cracked. "How many of these letters have you received?"

"This is the second. The first came after opening night."

"Opening night? You hadn't been in London a week. To what *matter* is this phantom referring? Surely, he is mad." To avoid gripping her shoulders and shaking her senseless, he raked his fingers through his hair. "Tell me at once!"

"I didn't want to appear less in your eyes than I already am." Her shoulders sagged while she tugged the chain that she always wore around her neck until she produced a frame no greater in diameter than two of his fingers.

"Is that a miniature?" he asked.

"Yes." She held up the portrait of a young woman, one with an uncanny resemblance to Britannia. "This was in a box with a handkerchief and a small amount of money. I'd never seen it before Madame and Monsieur LeClair died, but it was clearly mine. I'll show you."

From a drawer in her toilette, she produced a small wooden box with *Britannia* etched on a brass nameplate and opened it. From within, she pulled out a yellowed handkerchief. "These are the only two clues to my parentage."

"Are you certain?"

"As sure as I can be."

Drake examined the monogram on the kerchief. "This bears the seal of the—"

"Prince Regent," she finished. "After my inquiries in Paris as to the identity of the woman in the miniature led nowhere, I thought something might come to fruition here."

"And that letter proves you've happened on to something."

"I don't know if I have or not."

"Whoever the woman in the portrait is, someone is willing to go to great lengths to ensure you do not expose her. Bless it, Britannia, why did you not tell me about this sooner?"

"I-I was afraid. A-and I'm trying to be discrete. Though I want to know who she is, I mustn't do anything to sully her reputation."

"I daresay she deserves any incrimination coming to her." His ire boiled beneath his skin, Drake hauled over a second chair and sat opposite Britannia. "Is there anything else you ought to tell me?"

She wrung her hands. "That's everything."

"Very well. Now that we have your darkest secret out in the open, start at the beginning. Is this box how you learned you were a foundling? Didn't you once say you'd thought the LeClairs were your parents?"

"I did." She wiped her eyes, looking like a half-drowned kitten. "When they contracted smallpox, no one in Bayeux would help me care for them. But they sent for Monsieur LeClair's brother once they had gone. He was a loathsome man, but *he* inherited the estate and I was at his mercy."

"Good Lord, do not tell me he ravished a child."

"No, but he did show me my baptismal record. Translated into English it read: *Britannia, no surname, a foundling.* Then he cast it into the fire, insisted he had no responsibility for my welfare, and demanded I be gone from his house by dawn the next day."

"And you were, what, fourteen years of age?"

"Yes. With the money from the box, I purchased coach fare to Paris and pleaded with Monsieur Marchand to give me a place in the Paris Opera Ballet School."

"And he did so? At the age of fourteen? Did you have any prior training?"

"Madame LeClair was in the *corps de ballet.* She's the one who tutored me in everything. English, Latin, mathematics, and, especially, dance."

Scarcely unable to believe the outpouring of her childhood with him having been none the wiser, Drake ferociously twisted his signet ring. "She must have been raised well."

"Monsieur Marchand said she was the daughter of a vicar from Gloucestershire."

"Interesting, I wonder how such a woman came to be your foster mother."

"I have no idea." Britannia picked up the rose and tapped it against her cheek. "But my birth was definitely recorded in Bayeux. I remember the town's letters in bold across the top of the document."

Drake snatched the missive, rapping it with his finger. "So, the phantom who wrote this—a reprehensible *coward*—is responsible for the carriage wheel, the fire and two threatening missives."

She tried to hide a cringe behind the flower, but her eyes betrayed her. "I believe he also rifled through my things both here and at the boarding house."

Fire burst through Drake's gut. If he ever uncovered the identity of the felon, he would strangle the life out of him with his bare hands. "When was this?"

"Not long after *La Sylphide* opened."

"And you failed to tell me?"

"At the time I thought Florrie was the culprit."

"Nonetheless, you should have said something. At least informed Mr. Perkins." Drake's mind raced. How on earth did a minister's daughter from Gloucestershire end up in the Paris ballet school...and then move on to foster an infant in Bayeux? Nothing made sense. "Allow me a closer look at the miniature."

The piece had been painted on porcelain and set in a gold frame with no markings on the back. "What was it that Miss Renaud said about Lady Hertford?"

"I saw the dowager marchioness in Harding, Hamilton and Company and asked if she might know the woman in the picture. It had to have been painted twenty years ago or so."

Drake blinked twice at Britannia's nerve. Not many would be so bold to approach a noblewoman and embark on a question and answer session. "Out of the blue, you walked up to a dowager marchioness and asked her to identify your miniature? Why her?"

"I hired Mr. Gibbs to make some inquiries and he advised me that Lady Hertford was known to have been—ah—*mistress* to the Prince Regent during the year of my birth."

"Mr. Gibbs of all questionable characters? That man is a scum-swilling snake." Drake inhaled to keep from cursing the man to holy hell. "When was this? Does the timing of the first missive coincide with your meeting?"

"*Non.* I received that letter before I visited his offices. Besides, he's the one who told me Lady Hertford was the Prince Regent's only known mistress before I was born. But the miniature clearly isn't of her." Britannia ran her finger along the chain dangling from Drake's grasp. "Oh, but she did tell me the portrait had been painted by—"

"Adam Buck." He placed the piece in her palm, relieved to hear Gibbs had acted respectably. "Her Grace used him on occasion."

"And that's about the whole of it. With Mr. Buck being English, and the monogramed handkerchief, I cannot help but conclude that my mother was from Britain."

"Has anything else happened that you haven't told me about? What about the wine incident with Lady Calthorpe?"

"Surely that was an accident. *Mon Dieu*, she invited us to her home for a recital." Britannia replaced the chain around her neck. "Though…"

"What?"

"'Tis but a feeling." She shook her head. "I'm certain I'm wrong."

"We've not much to go on. Feelings are mechanisms to tell us things that may be lurking beneath the surface. You've started down this path, you may as well tell me the rest."

"Very well." Britannia met his gaze with a deep inhalation. "At the Calthorpe town house, I saw a portrait of Her Ladyship in the corridor outside the ballroom. For a moment I thought it had a likeness to the miniature. But truly I couldn't be sure and discounted it as silliness. Of course, if the baroness knew she was my mother and wanted to keep the fact hidden, she wouldn't have been so kind."

Unless she's in the dark as well. Lady Calthorpe's father was the Duke of Beaufort, a very powerful man. He'd also been the person holding the overfull glass of port at Her Grace's soiree.

"May I borrow your miniature?" Drake asked. "I'd like to present it to my mother without her knowing it is yours."

"Do you believe she would lie about it if she knew?" As she gave it to him, her fingers lightly brushed his.

A whisper of awareness danced up his arm. "Honestly, I have no idea what to think."

As he stood, she did as well. "I'd rather go with you."

"Allow me to test the waters first." He cupped her face his between his palms. "You have come to mean so much to me, I couldn't bear to see you hurt."

While her tongue slipped to the corner of her mouth, Britannia's gaze meandered to his lips. "Thank you for the rose. 'Tis for me, is it not?"

"Yes." Pulled by an indescribable force, Drake dipped his chin. "I'd hoped to deliver it under happier circumstances."

Yes, he knew the last place he should kiss her was backstage.

Merely one stolen kiss behind a closed door?

On a relenting sigh, he lightly brushed his lips across hers. Her sweet, soft breath against his mouth hinted of unspoken promises.

Forcing himself to drop his hands to his sides, Drake backed toward the door. "Please forgive me. I shall visit my mother on the morrow."

Chapter Eighteen

Still wearing her dressing gown, Bria read the morning *Gazette* while sipping tea in her parlor. The rooms Ravenscar had provided were so comfortable, she rued the need to return to Paris. But staying in London was out of the question. As soon as the Season came to an end, she must leave. Even the idea of returning next year was dangerous. What if the scoundrel behind all these awful deeds remained at large? What if he tried to kill her? Or kill someone else? What if the fire had grown out of control? She would already be dead, moreover, she might have been the cause of other deaths as well.

"The Duke of Ravenscar, miss," said the butler.

Not waiting for her reply, His Grace stepped into the parlor, his face grim. "Mother has gone to bloody Brighton."

The saucer clinked as Bria replaced her cup. "Oh no. And I'd hoped so much for her to be able to identify my miniature. When will she return?"

"I have no idea, but I am not waiting. 'Tis just over a half-day's journey. I've asked the grooms to prepare the town car. Will you go with me?"

With the flurry of butterflies in her stomach, she almost said yes. "But I'd miss tonight's performance."

"Your understudy can cover for one night."

"Florrie?" Bria snorted. "She's awful on point."

"'Tis only this once. Let the girl have a turn. Besides, I've already sent word to Mr. Perkins."

"Without asking me first?"

"I can always advise him of a change of plans, but I need your answer forthwith. Do you want to come along or not?"

She wouldn't hesitate if anyone in the troupe besides Florrie was her understudy. Bria tapped her fingers on the teapot handle. If she did take the night off, it would give Pauline a chance to dance the part of Effie. "All right, I'll go." Bria stood. "But first I must change."

"And pack a portmanteau. We'll stay over by the sea and come back first thing in the morning."

"There are rooms enough for the both of us?" she asked.

"Yes. My town house in Brighton is every bit as big as the one on Half Moon Street."

"The mind boggles at the extent of your wealth. I simply cannot fathom it." Bria used a hand bell to ring for her maid then quickly hastened to her chamber to don a day gown and pack her necessities in her only portmanteau.

Ravenscar set the *Gazette* aside and shot to his feet as she returned to the parlor, the butler following with her valise. "That was quick. Any other woman would have taken until midday."

"I suppose a woman with few possessions, accustomed to doing things herself is a bit more efficient than one who has been pampered all her life."

"Are you saying my mother isn't efficient?"

"I have no grounds upon which to judge, but I'm guessing she would spend a great deal of time deciding which gowns to bring, which shoes, hats, gloves, jewelry, fans…need I go on?"

Ravenscar took the portmanteau from the butler. "We'll be slipping out unawares, so I will do the honors, thank you."

Bria led the way to the servants' stairs. "You seem like any normal man when you carry my things."

"Normal? How do I appear otherwise?"

"You know what I mean. You're a duke…one of the untouchables."

"Hmm. I'll have you know, I certainly have carried my share of crates and trunks over the years."

She giggled, unable to picture Ravenscar trudging along a footpath with a trunk on his back. "I find that difficult to believe."

"I haven't always been a duke. And I didn't receive any preferential treatment when I was at Eton or at Oxford."

By the time they reached the mews, the carriage was rigged, its doors turned to the shiny, black panels without the Ravenscar crest and the coachman was standing at the block ready to lend a hand.

***

They'd been traveling for hours when, the town car jerked and wobbled from side to side. With a gasp, Bria braced her palms on the velvet seat.

"Ho!" hollered the driver.

Drake pounded the pommel of his cane on the ceiling. "What the devil is—?"

"Aaaaaaaack!" Bria cried as the carriage jolted and came to stop, sending her flying through the air, straight toward His Grace.

Before she could grab something to stop her momentum, his arms wrapped around her. "I have you," he grunted in her ear.

Yes, he did.

Breathless and stunned, Bria looked into his eyes. Beautiful, expressive eyes stared back, concerned, and a deeper emotion she couldn't put a name to.

"Are you all right?" he asked, his voice husky.

He cared. Yes, she knew he held her in high esteem, but now she was certain his regard for her extended much further than friendship. His concern made her want to embrace him and never let go.

She nodded, not bothering to look back to her seat. If only she could stay in his arms for the duration of the journey.

Outside, the clatter of horses passed them.

"Apologies, Your Grace," the driver hollered from above. "We barely avoided a collision."

"Carry on," Ravenscar replied before returning his attention to Bria. "I rather like this new seating arrangement."

Unable to help herself, she brushed her fingers over his exquisite silk neckcloth. "It is…um…cozy."

Black eyelashes fanned his eyes while he slid his palm along the curve of her waist. "And my hand fits ever so nicely right here."

A tiny gasp escaped her throat. "Your Grace—"

"Britannia, when we are alone, I want you to call me Drake." Licking his lips, his gaze shifted to her mouth. "You may not realize it, but ever since you asked me to kiss you at Mother's soiree, I've thought about that moment at least a hundred times a day."

Was she floating? Bria could have sworn she'd just turned weightless. "Only a hundred?"

"Is it not obvious? Though propriety insists I remain aloof, I always seem to lose myself when we are alone."

"Y-you do?"

"Mm hmm."

The inside of the carriage turned into the Sylph's magical forest as their gazes held with an awareness deep with meaning. How could she resist him when he looked at her with such fierce desire? How could she resist a man who'd protected her and shown her boundless kindness at every crisis? Drake had established her in a suite of rooms without asking for anything in return. And now they were traveling to Brighton for the single task of querying his mother about the identity of the mysterious *Grande-Duchesse* at long last. What other nobleman would go to such lengths?

He dipped his chin, his lips nearing. And the moment he kissed her mouth, the invisible thread binding them tightened. As his lips opened against hers, insatiable longing coursed through her blood. Heat spread low in her belly. Need claimed her. Greedy for more, Bria shoved her fingers into his thick hair and drew him closer.

They clung to each other, their tongues entwined in an intimate dance meant only to be shared in the confines of the tiny carriage. Bria sighed as his lips trailed to the arc of her neck.

Throwing back her head, she arched, her body screaming for more. "Every day I grow more powerless to resist you."

"Then do not."

"But—"

"Hush," he whispered, his lips moving lower as his fingers swept over the sensitive skin at the scooped neckline of her bodice.

She tried to focus her mind—grasped at sanity. "We have no future."

"We have this moment." His voice rumbled against her skin, filling her with ravening desire. "I swear I will not try more with you than you are prepared to receive."

"Then kiss me over and over. I long to stay in your arms and savor the taste of your lips."

His tongue trialed along her jaw. "I'll kiss you all the way to Brighton if that is your wish."

For the first time in her life, Bria couldn't think about tomorrow. She was melting in Drake's arms and that's the only place she wanted to be. "Yes. Oh God, yes!"

Ravenscar's strong fingers stroked and kneaded while she floated upon a cloud of pure bliss. His languid kisses beguiled her with hot, deep glides of his tongue. Ever so slowly, he slid his hand from her hip, over her thigh and down to her exposed ankle, covered only by her stocking.

Bria gasped, stilling his hand. "You mustn't."

His fingers squeezed as vivid eyes arrested her. "On stage you enchant me with your shapely ankles. Surely you will not deny me the pleasure of a mere caress of this one."

She slid her hand to his beguiling fingers, her tongue slipping to the corner of her mouth. "On stage I am not myself."

The pads of his fingers swirled around her ankle. "No? Then who are you?"

"In *La Sylphide* I am the Sylph. I am a mythical creature not of this world."

"I disagree. You are the only woman who can breathe life into the character who happens to be the Sylph."

"But you wanted Marie Taglioni."

His lips traced the tops of her breasts, sending shivers of joy across her skin. Everywhere he touched her brought a new swarm of mind-boggling sensations. "That's because I hadn't yet seen you dance," he growled. "No one can touch your grace, your passion. I am in awe of you."

She took in a gasp. "I am still learning, still growing."

"Never stop." Drake's hand moved up her calf sending her insides into a slick torrent of want. "Kiss me."

Chapter Nineteen

Late afternoon, the butler ushered them into the drawing room of Ravenscar's Brighton town house. Standing stiff as a board, Drake clenched his fist. Bloody hell, Her Grace was keeping company with Edwin Peters.

Scandalous!

The man was a rotten gunsmith, not a gentleman. He held no peerage. He wasn't the son of a nobleman. Hell, the bastard hadn't even been knighted.

I will put an end to the man's gold digging as soon as I have Mother alone.

Her Grace looked at him with a cool arch to her brow. "Son, I did not expect to see you here. Is something wrong? Is your sister well?" Mother's gaze shifted to Britannia as if it were perfectly acceptable for the dowager duchess to engage in indiscretions. "Has Chadwick Theater burned to the ground?"

"Nothing quite so drastic." Drake nailed Peters with a hard stare and scowled. "And last I heard, Ada was in good health."

"Indeed. Nonetheless, it is lovely to see you Miss LeClair. I hope you are well?" Mother asked, her lips turning white—a sure sign she was furious.

Britannia curtsied, hiding any hint of shock she might have felt. "I am, thank you."

"Please, join us." After making the introductions, Her Grace rang the bell. "I'm curious to hear what brought you to Brighton without sending advance notice."

The butler stepped inside and bowed. "You rang, Your Grace?"

"Please have the housemaid bring us some cordial and cucumber sandwiches."

"Straightaway, madam."

Mother leveled her gaze upon Drake. "And do sit down. Looking up at you is making my neck sore."

Taking a seat beside Britannia on the settee, Drake reassumed his glare at Peters. The man pulled out his pocket watch and flicked it open.

"Do you have somewhere you need to be?" asked Drake.

Peters didn't make eye contact, the coward. "Perhaps I'll take a stroll to the shore."

"It is a splendid day for it." Drake pulled the cushion from behind his back and squeezed it while he watched the gunsmith leave. Once the man disappeared, he tossed the pillow aside and turned his attention to the dowager duchess. "We shall talk later."

"If we must." She fluffed her skirts as if she hadn't a care. "Now tell me, why are you here?"

Before he produced the miniature, he summarized all that had transpired leading up to the fact that he believed his star performer was being targeted by a madman. He explained about Britannia's keepsakes and only then did he pull the tiny portrait from his waistcoat pocket.

"Yes." Her Grace looked to Britannia. "You should have approached me about this sooner. I daresay it might have saved everyone a lot of todo."

"Who is it?" asked Drake.

"You know her, Son. I cannot believe she has changed so much you didn't recognize Lady Charlotte Somerset, now Lady Calthorpe."

"Calthorpe?" Britannia scooted to the edge of the settee. "She is the last person I would suspect."

"But she did spill wine down your dress," said Drake.

"The incident was an accident after which she apologized profusely." Standing, Britannia began to pace. "She even established a credit in my name at Harding, Howell and Company."

"Possibly to displace blame?" suggested Her Grace.

"I do not believe it." The ballerina stopped in front of the hearth and threw out her hands. "Not long ago, she invited us to her home for a recital and paid us handsomely."

The housemaid brought in a tray, distributed glasses of cordial and hastened away. Obviously, the servants were as abhorred by Her Grace's indiscretion as Drake.

Mother reached for her drink. "Did anything untoward happen while you were at Her Ladyship's town house?"

Dropping her arms, Bria returned to the settee. "Nothing."

Drake swiped a miniature sandwich from the plate. "Miss LeClair was born in February of 1814. Did Her Ladyship have an affair with George during the season of 1813?"

"That was quite a long time ago. Who remembers who was tupping whom? I had two young children at the time." After filling three teacups, she picked up the dainty china pitcher. "Milk?"

"Please, for us both, no sugar," Drake replied before continuing, "But you were still involved with the Season at that time."

"True. Lady Charlotte, hmm…" Mother placed one of the finger-sized sandwiches on a plate while her lips disappeared into a thin line. "I vaguely remember her first

Season. She was lovely and terrified, just as we all were our first time out."

The dowager duchess grew silent for a time while she nibbled. "Come to think on it, I do not recall hearing anything about Charlotte again until Beaufort announced her betrothal to Calthorpe."

"What year was that?" asked Drake.

"Now you're stretching my memory." She pushed her plate away.

Britannia stilled her glass halfway to her lips. "Do you think her generosity might be because she knows something about my parentage?"

Giving Drake a nudge, Britannia looked flummoxed. "Could be. The only way to know for certain is to ask her."

"But why wouldn't she say something to me?"

"Chances are there would be a mortiferous scandal. Even after twenty years." Mother flicked a bit of lint from her red velvet sleeve. "Why else would someone be sending you threatening messages?"

Drake stood and offered his hand to Britannia. "Miss LeClair, would you mind leaving me alone with my mother for a moment? You'll find a library the next floor up."

She hesitantly placed her hand in his palm, her gaze shifting between them. "Very well. But you'll tell me if you uncover anything else, won't you?"

"Of course." Needing something more powerful than cordial, Drake poured himself a tot of brandy while he listened to Britannia climb the stairs.

Mother whipped open her fan and briskly cooled her face as if hit by a sudden blast of heat. "Please tell me you are not thinking of confronting Lady Calthorpe. If she is that ballerina's mother, the poor woman's life could be ruined by exposing such a scandal...and after twenty years. My word!"

Drake rested his elbow on the sideboard. "I'll speak to Her Ladyship in confidence. No one else needs to know.

Britannia doesn't want anyone to suffer because of her inquiries. She merely desires to uncover the truth."

Mother nearly coughed out a laugh. "So you think."

"So I know." To drown his irritation, he tossed back his drink, consuming it with one swallow. "With that decided, I cannot tell you how shocked I was to find you keeping company with Mr. Peters."

"Shocked? He's attends my every event at Ravenscar Hall. Surely you suspected."

"Good God, Mother. He's a bloody gunsmith. He has no title, no lineage."

"He has money."

Drake batted his hand through the air. "New money."

"Yes, well, after you put my house up as collateral for your risky theater venture, I needed some assurances, did I not?"

What the devil? His stomach squeezed. "You knew about that?"

"Please." Mother wielded her fan as if it were a saber. "I have more social connections than anyone in London. I knew what you were up to before the ink dried on your contract."

"Forgive me." He sauntered over and dropped onto the settee. "I never intended for Ravenscar Hall to be on the chopping block. At the time of signing, I was convinced I couldn't lose."

"And you didn't."

"No."

"But you were worried."

"I was."

Mother tucked the damned fan up her sleeve as if she'd won the battle. "If your theater venture had failed, Mr. Peters was my insurance."

But Drake wasn't surrendering that easily. "Explain."

"I had a wager of my own. Had you lost my beloved home, I would have married Mr. Peters."

"Married his money, or the man?"

She patted her perfectly styled coiffure. "Both."

"Do you care for him?"

"I do."

"But not enough to marry him?"

"Well, as you said, he has no title. Such a union would be egregiously frowned upon."

"So is taking a lover."

Mother huffed. "I am a *widow* and have been for ten years. Would you have me live as a nun? Besides, rules are not as strict for widows as long as they are discrete." With an indignant air, Her Grace poured another glass of cordial. "I am entitled to live a bit before you dig my grave."

She held out the pitcher with a questioning glance and Drake refused with a wave of his hand. "Live, yes," he bit out. "But entertaining a gunsmith with such intimacy is…well, in poor taste."

"Oh, you believe so?" She flicked her hand in the direction of the library. "And what about the strumpet you brought to Brighton? Are you bedding Miss LeClair?"

"No, I am not, and how dare you ask."

Mother sipped daintily, though the gesture minimized his outrage. "Surprising—though people are talking, regardless. Thank heavens the ballet is coming to an end and, soon, Miss LeClair will be returning to Paris. You will never settle down as long as that woman holds your attentions."

Drake provided no reply. Yes, Britannia commanded his attention. Since she'd pirouetted into his life he hadn't given a second look to any other women.

"I cannot believe you look fondly upon that chit."

"You're dancing a precariously thin line, Mother."

"At least Mr. Peters has made a name for himself and he's nearly as wealthy as we are."

"If you haven't noticed, Miss LeClair has made quite a name for herself as well."

"A foundling? A ballet dancer? That girl was ruined from the day she was born." Mother shook her head. "The best you can hope for is to keep her as your mistress as much as I hate the idea."

"Why?" Drake asked through clenched teeth. She dared criticize him when she was out carousing with Mr. Peters? Wasn't there a widowed nobleman out there who could take her fancy? And how dare she say a single judgmental word against Britannia?

"Because you will be a husband and have a family soon. 'Tis not easy on a family when the father's eyes stray, no matter how nobly born. Thank heavens your father never wandered far from the path."

"You were fortunate, then."

"I was and will always consider myself blessed."

Before he lost his temper, Drake stood.

Mother seemed not to notice. "I suppose it would be no surprise to you that Lady Blanche is engaged to be married."

"Is she?" he asked in a monotone.

"I knew she would be."

"Then I wish her and her suitor well." Drake bowed and stepped out of the drawing room in time to see Britannia sprinting for the front door.

Chapter Twenty

"Britannia, wait!"

Bria paid Ravenscar no mind as she fled out the door. She mightn't have heard it all, but she'd heard enough. His Grace's own mother thought her a trollop.

"Where are you off to?" the duke demanded, gaining as he followed, blast him.

"Leave me alone!" Spotting a park, she changed course, picked up her skirts and ran as fast as she could. How could she have been so dimwitted? She'd told herself a hundred times not to lose her heart to the duke. He could never be hers. The man was dallying with her in the carriage and every other time he'd ever offered a kiss.

Well, no more! Bria refused to stay where she wasn't respected for one more minute.

"Britannia," Ravenscar called again.

As she dashed under a canopy of trees, she glanced behind. "Go away," she yelled just as her toe caught the root of a tree. Throwing her arms forward, she tumbled to the ground. Searing pain shot up her wrist. She clutched her arm to her midriff as she rolled to her derriere.

Curses! The blasted duke stood over her like a court judge.

"Why the bloody hell didn't you stop?" He dropped to one knee and reached for her wrist. "Are you injured?"

She jerked away, the movement making her arm hurt all the more. "No." She squeezed her eyes shut against the tears. "Please. Leave me alone."

"I'm afraid I cannot do that." He sat beside her. He, a duke, sat on the ground, not only in public, but in broad daylight.

"By the way you're holding your wrist, I suspect you may have answered my question a tad hastily."

"I did not. And what do you care if I am injured? Are you afraid to see your greatest commodity *bourrée* onto the stage wearing a sling?"

"Greatest commodity? What the devil are you talking about?"

"The only reason you're nice to me is because I saved your theater. If I'd come to London and had been an embarrassment, you would have sent the entire troupe back to France. And do not deny it. I heard what you said to Monsieur Travere."

Ravenscar leaned his elbows on his knees, looking even less like a duke. He didn't respond right away, and Bria didn't expect him to. He didn't care for her, not in the same way she cared for him, and it was time she stopped fooling herself.

"Initially, yes," he said slowly, contemplatively. "If you hadn't proved you were capable of dancing the Sylph I would not have allowed the ballet to premiere. But that was before I came to know you."

"Know me or not, we can never be more than master and servant."

"Until the Season is over, no."

"Oh, please. Spare me the inkling of hope. Your mother was right. I was ruined on the day I was born. I can never be more to you than an *amusement*."

"You're wrong. You already mean far more to me than any woman I have ever met."

Her heart melted. "Then I pity you because you can never have me. Not because I'm unwilling, but because your class will not allow it."

"Sometimes I would give away my fortune not to be a duke."

"But you are and there's no changing the fact." Bria groaned, picked up a pinecone and threw it. "And why are we discussing that which cannot be when we ought to be talking about how to approach Lady Calthorpe?"

"Because this, us, we...needs to be discussed."

"I think not."

"Perhaps not in the open. But, mark me, I am by no means giving you a pass."

A couple strolled by, arm in arm. Bria's insides twisted in a hundred knots. Why couldn't Drake be a normal man? Someone with whom she could start a family? Why couldn't she fall in love with a stage hand or a dance master or the blasted orchestra conductor?

"And Lady Calthorpe?" she asked, praying the duke wouldn't forbid her from mentioning the baroness.

A furrow formed between those black eyebrows. "I will have a word with her first."

"Do you think it best?"

"It would be the proper thing to do. Allow her to explain how you might have come into possession of the miniature."

"What if she lies?"

"Then she is a lesser person than I believe her to be."

"Me as well." Now that the throbbing in her wrist had eased, Bria plucked a daisy and began pulling out the petals. "Ever since I met Her Ladyship at the soiree, I thought her gracious, perhaps more so after the incident with the wine."

"Well then, neither of us care to see her hurt."

"Definitely not. I only want a private audience with her. *Once*. We never have to discuss the issue again. After which, my lips will be forever sealed."

"I hope she is willing to talk."

"I pray she is."

Scraping her teeth over her bottom lip, the sound of laughter turned Bria's attention to a pond. Three children played with wooden boats—a girl dressed in yellow with lacy pantaloons peeking beneath her hem. Bria guessed the boys with the lass were her brothers. One taller and one shorter.

Using sapling limbs, they pushed their boats as they skipped along the shore.

When the girl inched up and took the lead, the larger boy pushed her out of the way and jumped ahead. Bria straightened, about to spring to her feet when the girl clonked her brother on the backside with her stick and ran for the finish line.

"I won, I won!" she hollered, jumping up and down.

"She reminds me of Ada," said Drake, a distant glint in his eye.

"It must have been fun to have a sister."

"She was a vixen."

"But I'll wager she loved you."

"Aye." He snorted thoughtfully. "She did—still does."

Bria watched as the children squealed, now playing an impromptu game of tag. "I'd like to have a family of my own one day."

Drake plucked one of the daisies and brushed the petals along her jaw. "And give away your life on the stage?"

"Not today, mind you." She shivered at the light touch. How could she remain angry with him when he had done so much for her? "But yes. In a heartbeat, I'd give it all away to have children, a husband, perhaps live in a provincial cottage."

"Every time we are together, something new about you amazes me."

"I wouldn't think a girl expressing her desire to have a family would be astonishing to you in the slightest. Isn't the marriage mart full of such women?"

"None like you."

Bria plucked Drake's daisy from his fingers and twirled it. She guessed there were fewer men like Ravenscar. And yet, she harbored no doubt that he was as attracted to her as she to him.

Why not allow herself an affair—an interlude? She was nearly twenty years of age. What was she saving herself for if not someone she loved?

Out of the corner of her eye, she examined her duke. Who would have thought a man as powerful as he would sit in the grass beside a dancer and speak with her as if she were a confidant? With his arms across his knees, he might look like a normal fellow, aside from his neckcloth perfectly tied in an Oriental knot, the exquisite cut of his coat, silk waistcoat, not to mention gleaming Hessian boots topping off his traveling buckskins. One look at Ravenscar and anyone within miles knew he was a member of the aristocracy.

But right now, sitting beside her, caring about how to approach the baroness, Bria saw him not as a duke, but as a dear friend. He'd hitched up his carriage and took her to Brighton just to ask Her Grace if she could identify Bria's mystery mother…woman…relative. Whatever role Baroness Calthorpe ended up playing in all this, it was a relief to know, at long last, Britannia could put a name to the lovely face in the miniature.

She placed her hand atop His Grace's. "Thank you. You have been generous and kind and I am truly grateful."

He smiled, a faraway look in his eye. "You must know, regardless of your worth to Chadwick Theater, I would have willingly brought you to Brighton."

"But…"

He took her hand, closed his eyes and pressed his lips to her skin. Soft, moist, warm, and filled with intense and unspoken emotion. "There is something I need to ask. But I do not want you to misunderstand."

"What is it?"

"You have been very clear about maintaining your virtue."

She bit her lip, her stomach squeezing. "I have and—"

He held up his palm. "Please allow me to continue."

"Very well."

"I'm not going to profess that I haven't had impure thoughts. All men have them. But I will always honor your wishes whatever they may be. Just help me to understand: When so many women as well as men in your profession take lovers, especially the French, why are you so averse to it?"

"Do you have all afternoon? Because it will take some time for me to explain."

"I have as long as you need. Please. Humor me."

"First of all, you may remember I was raised in a nice manor in a good Catholic home."

"Catholic?"

"*Oui.* I had my first communion before Monsieur and Madame LeClair perished and, when I was turned out, I swore I would always honor them for the love they showed me."

"Respect for the dead. That is justification enough."

"But it is far from the only reason."

"Go on."

"I need to be true to myself, my dreams."

"But you have already achieved far more than most dancers could ever hope to."

"You do not understand. Not at all."

"Then help me."

"Monsieur Marchand nearly turned me away."

"When?"

"After I left Bayeux, the Paris Opera Ballet was the only place I could think of to go. I know I mentioned that *Maman* had been in the *corps de ballet*."

"Yes."

"When I arrived in Paris I waited outside Monsieur Marchand's studio for hours before he granted me an audience. When I explained about *Maman*—Sarah Parker was her maiden name—he laughed at me. 'So now you think to follow in her footsteps?' And then he pointed to the door. 'We only take the elite. Children who have been born to the master performers or who show uncanny ability. Mademoiselle Parker was merely a member of the *corps*. I'm afraid I must ask you to leave.'"

"You must have been frantic," Ravenscar said, rubbing her hand and kissing it.

She squeezed his fingers as she continued, "I was ready to drop to my knees and beg, but I blinked away my tears, squared my shoulders, and insisted he watch me dance."

He brushed a wisp of hair away from Bria's face. "And he thought you were brilliant, just as I did."

"Not exactly. Marchand even tried to grab me. But I twirled away and danced a passage from a scene in the opera *Nina, ou La Folle par Amour*, one I'd perfected, a part *Maman* had thought was stunning."

Drake chuckled. "I'd wager she was right."

"I don't know about that. Monsieur Marchand began to object, but before he could stop me I executed an *entrechat cinq*, a jump only ever performed by a danseur…that's when he asked my age."

"You showed him, did you not?"

"No, he told me fourteen was far too old, I needed polish, and I would never be a ballerina."

"The uncompromising mule. I knew I didn't like the man from the outset." He slammed his fist into his palm. "So, how did you convince him to give you a chance?"

"After a fair bit of groveling and pleading, he gave me a challenging combination—one I believe was meant to confound me."

"Nothing could confound you."

"Right." Bria couldn't hold in a laugh. "And when Monsieur Marchand saw how quickly I learned, he gave me a month to prove I was worthy of becoming his student."

"I'll wager you didn't look back after that."

"The journey was never easy. Remember when you asked about my pedigree?"

"How could I forget?" The dashing duke hung his head. "My moment of shame."

"I wouldn't say that, but you were right. Everyone at the school has one but me. Most have famous parents. Many are wealthy. I had neither parents nor wealth. Dance became my master, the only consistent thing in my life."

"And you feel you must remain true to your art?"

"I do. Dance was my first love. There were times when it was the only thing standing between me and utter misery. You cannot know what it is like to watch your schoolmates join their families for the holidays while you stay in the cold and silent corridors, alone with nothing to do but practice."

"That must have been awful for you."

She shrugged. "At least I had a roof over my head, which is a lot more than many foundlings can claim. But I digress." The rest was so painful, Bria couldn't look him in the eye. "From fourteen to eighteen I was scorned for being different. Teased, of course. And dance remained the only consistent thing in my life. I watched the others more than they thought I did. As time passed I observed as they became distracted by wealthy men who promised to take care of them and, in time, they lost sight of what was truly important."

"Dance?"

"Yes. Ballet, the theater, the body's movement as a form of art."

He tapped his pointer finger on her hand. "That's why you dance with more passion than anyone I've ever seen."

"I'll admit, performing is in my soul. I cannot walk away from it, just like being a duke is your duty."

"Perhaps to you they are the same, but I may be more trapped by my station than you are by yours."

"I don't understand. Have you not heard me?"

"I have, and I respect your dedication. But, let's say you were offered another position—say a—"

"Patroness of an elite ballet school?"

"Excellent, let's go with that, and you decided to leave the stage—perhaps you are getting on in years and you decide it is time for a change."

"But I would still be involved in ballet."

"True, though your role would change, would it not?"

"It would."

"You see, my role cannot change. I am a duke and, as such, there are responsibilities and expectations I must shoulder for the rest of my days."

"You must produce an heir."

"Yes, but not only must I sire gently-bred children, I must provide shelter, wages and meaningful work for the people in my care. I am expected to behave like a duke with my every breath. I must sit in the House of Lords, support the king, maintain my lands and my fortune so there will be a legacy for my heir."

"What would you do if you didn't give birth to an heir? Doesn't that happen all the time?"

"It does." He picked up her hand and laced his fingers through hers. "Either a couple has only female children or the woman in barren."

She liked to have him hold her hand and with their fingers woven, it was more intimate. "What then?"

He lifted her hand to his mouth and kissed. "The estate passes to the next in line or the title could become extinct."

Watching his lips, she longed to be back in the carriage where they'd kissed unabashedly for hours. "If you were to perish on the morrow, who would inherit?"

"My nephew. Fortunately, Ada has a son. He's only three."

Bria smiled. "I'd like to meet him someday. Children are so dear."

"They are." He released her hand and gave it a pat. "But earlier you said you would give it all away for a family."

Bria's cheeks burned. Before today, she had never spoken the words aloud, but in her deepest heart of hearts, she wanted a brood of her own. Heaps of children to love and hold. To nurture and cherish. "I don't always want to spend my holidays alone."

"Then, you plan to marry."

"*Alors*, I know I will not always be young and spry enough to perform. One day I hope to."

"Then I am already jealous of that lucky man." Drake stood and offered his hand. "Come. Let us go back to the house. My mother owes you an apology."

Bria let him pull her up but once she was on her feet, she dug in her heels. "I don't want to go back there."

Looking away, Drake rubbed his chin. "I suppose I'm not too fond of the idea either. Especially with Mr. Peters loitering about."

"'Tis a shame the roles aren't reversed."

"Whatever do you mean?"

"If you were an elderly widowed duke, and I was a wealthy ballet patroness of some sort and Her Grace young and not yet wed, then we could enjoy each other's company without all of society being outraged by our every move."

"Perhaps that's why I like you so much. You have such a pragmatic way of looking at things." Drake offered his elbow. "If you are averse to staying under the same roof with Her Grace, our only option is to find a suite of rooms at one of Brighton's hotels. It is too late to start back to London now. There are, however, many nice places near the shore."

"But won't people know you at those places?"

"Indeed they will."

"What will they think if you book rooms for the pair of us?"

"If I book two rooms, I doubt my reputation will be sullied." He grinned. "I cannot speak for yours however."

She gave his arm a thwack. "It is not fair that men can carouse all they want while women are held to an entirely different set of standards."

"At least you're not being paraded before polite society every Season looking for a husband. I say, I respect you far more for making your own way while holding on to your principles. It is not easy to do with temptation loitering around every corner."

"Though I do like kissing you, Duke."

"I shouldn't be, but I'm awfully glad to hear it." He gestured to the footpath. "Shall we?"

Chapter Twenty-One

Sitting in front of the hearth in the king's chamber of the Royal York Hotel, Drake sipped his brandy while he stared at the forbidden door. The portal leading to Miss LeClair's bedchamber. The place where he ought to be sleeping if it weren't for Britannia's presence within. But she'd been rather insistent and if Drake had learned anything, it was to be selective about choosing his battles where she was concerned. If she wanted to stay in the smaller chamber, then so be it. Besides, since it had grown dark, the lovely view of Stein Gardens out the bay window no longer mattered.

He'd sent his apologies to his mother but, honestly, this arrangement was for the best. He couldn't bear to stay under the same roof when Mr. Peters was having his way with Her Grace.

Drake shuddered.

For the love of God, had Mother mentioned her loneliness sooner, he would have endeavored to find her a suitable companion and husband—a man worthy of her affections. He didn't know Mr. Peters well, but in no way could the gunsmith be good enough for Her Grace.

Faint noises came from the adjoining room—footsteps followed by a brushing sound. Drake's ears piqued.

She's rehearsing.

The sounds of rhythmic movement continued while he closed his eyes and pictured his nymphet. That's what Britannia had become to him—a very attractive and alluring young woman. *Plié, tendu, frappe, rond de jambe.* He knew the names of many ballet steps and could execute them, but Britannia made every movement appear effortless as if she'd been born with the grace of a feline—the beauty of a goddess. She did not only execute the steps, she breathed life into them, became one with her surroundings and turned dance into an art. They could be standing on a footpath and, with a gesture of her arm, a dreary day became bright; melancholy melted into joy.

Was the nymph practicing in her gown or in her shift? Were her ankles bare? Drake rubbed the pads of his fingers along the velvet upholstery on his seat. Earlier that very day, he'd savored the silkiness of her slender ankles, the suppleness of her calf, and, heaven help him, her glorious, muscular thighs. Thighs he'd craved to have wrapped around him every time he'd watched her dance. Thighs he glimpsed ever so fleetingly when on stage the Sylph would leap or kick or raise her leg in *arabesque.*

A loud bang followed by a high-pitched gasp made Drake jolt to his feet. In two steps he barreled through the door. "Brit—"

She stood beside a chair, a sheen of perspiration glistening while her breasts rose and fell with her deep breaths. "It fell."

"Huh?" he asked dumbly. Staring. The woman wore nothing but a silk chemise.

"The chair. I'm sorry, did I startle you?"

"No. Er, yes. I thought you might have taken a tumble." Unable to help himself, Drake's gaze meandered lower. The faint shadow of her nipples teased him from beneath the sheer white fabric. Though the garment was shapeless, it couldn't hide Britannia's figure. At his sides, he stretched his fingers, longing to wrap them around her waist, slowly sliding them down the trim arc of her hips.

On a delicate, stockinged foot, Britannia stepped nearer. "It has been a long day. I'm surprised to see you're still awake."

Did she have any idea how alluring she sounded? If he reached out, he could grasp her hand and tug her closer, wrap her in his arms and kiss her, potently aware the bed was only paces away.

She took another step, beguiling him further. "Forgive me, Your Grace. Though the hour is late, I mustn't overlook proper courtesy."

"Alone, we have no need of convention, you and I," he rasped.

Near enough to embrace, she placed her palm over his heart. "I wish it were so."

His heart hammered against the coolness of her fingers, yet Drake was fevered with desire. Every part of his body was rigid, ready for a night of passion, everything but his boneless knees. With whisky eyes, she gazed up at him, her bow-shaped lips shining like cherries in the lamplight.

"Britannia," he hoarsely whispered. "I want you."

As if his words became a hypnotic elixir, she slid her fingers around his waist and raised her chin. "I do, too. I crave you."

Oh yes, heaven opened her gates.

Before she could change her mind, he devoured her, intently backing her toward the bed.

"But…"

"Yes?" Drake strained to draw air into his lungs. She couldn't refuse him. Not now. He knew she wanted him.

"Can we take precautions? I desperately want children but not until I am wed."

Grinning, he pulled a tidy French letter from his waistcoat pocket—one that he'd found in his travel kit—and set it beside the bed. "Do you know what this is?"

"I do."

He wasn't surprised. Britannia might be an innocent, but she'd been in the theater for too long not to know…certain things.

"Are you sure you want to do this…ah…with me?" It killed him to ask, but if she wasn't absolutely sure, he needed to stop now before he was unable.

Though she didn't answer, a pink tongue slipped to the corner of her mouth while she stepped into him and began unbuttoning his waistcoat. On fire, Drake kicked off his shoes, tore away his neckcloth, unfastened his falls. In the blink of an eye his clothes fell to the floor leaving him standing naked and hard before her.

She made a small sound as she drew a hand over her mouth and stepped back. "You are too beautiful for words."

Unable to speak, he reached for her chemise and tugged it over her head.

As he beheld the creamy silkiness of her skin, she wound her arms around his neck, tilting her head up, kissing him, plundering his mouth thrusting her tongue deep. By God, her passion on stage was nothing compared to the temptress seducing him.

He drew his mouth away and gazed down. "My word, you are divine."

Unbelievably desirable, Britannia's only remaining garments were ivory silk stockings secured by garters with pink bows. Up a tad higher, sleek thighs pressed together, just below the cinnamon tuft of hair covering her most sacred treasure.

Womanly hips—far curvier than he'd imagined, a tiny waist, and breasts the perfect size for his mouth. "No words could possibly describe you," Drake said, his voice low and gravelly. Sliding his hands along her shapely hips, he dropped to his knees. Awash in the fragrance of woman, a bead of his seed leaked from the tip of his cock.

Britannia sank her fingers into his shoulders, her grip on the verge of painful. "W-what are you doing?"

"This." He lapped his tongue along her parting.

"*Mon Dieu!*" she sighed with a quiver.

"I love it when you say that." Sliding his fingers between her thighs, Drake coaxed her legs apart and licked. Britannia's gasps drove him mad as he suckled her tiny button, sliding his fingers into her core.

"Please," she begged, but Drake refused to relinquish control. Her sighs and gasps taught him what she liked.

"Please," she said again. "I want my hands on your body."

In one motion, he swept her into his arms and onto the bed. Rolling beside her he stroked himself. "See what you do to me?"

Bria's thighs trembled as she watched his hand move up and down his shaft. "May I do that?"

"Would you?"

She closed her fingers around him—hard, but velvety soft. "I want to."

He guided her wrist up and down. "Don't squeeze, but let it slide in your hand."

In an instant his breathing grew ragged.

Bria drew her hand away "Are you in pain?"

"God, no. But I won't last much longer. You are a fast learner."

"One of the fastest." She lowered her lips to his and kissed. "I think I've mastered this part."

"And your first one was rather rushed."

"I'm ashamed to say that fleeting moment whet my appetite for more...*you* whet my appetite."

He slid his hand down her side, his finger slowly tracing over the curve of her hip. "I adore this part."

And then he continued between her legs to the place driving her insides wild for months, the spot that craved more of him. The center of her being that ached deep inside when she looked at him. Bria's breathing grew faster as he teased her, climbed over her, kissed her lips, her throat, her breasts. Oh God, her breasts.

She bucked when he rubbed his member along her wetness. As she wriggled and gasped, he rocked back and let her gaze upon him. Again, he touched himself. "Do you want this inside you?"

"I will die if you don't make love to me."

"It might hurt."

"I'm no stranger to pain."

He slid the French letter over himself and tied the pink bow. Bria lay back as he climbed over her, kissing, suckling, rubbing. In an attempt to satisfy the hunger, she writhed beneath him, wanting more, but not exactly certain how to ask.

"Britannia, look at me."

She opened her eyes and gazed into the most handsome face she'd ever seen. And then he pushed against her, slipping into her just a little. "You are a goddess."

She tried to talk but her voice caught as he slid deeper. Pain seared around him—heavens he was enormous.

"And I worship you."

"I…" she sighed, clamming her fingers into his buttocks.

"I'm filling you completely."

"I didn't think you'd fit."

He held very still and devoured her mouth until she began to move again as if some primitive force deep inside her demanded a seductive dance only for Ravenscar.

"Are you ready for more, my love?" he whispered.

"Yes. More. Yes, yes, yes!" She rocked her hips faster, the raggedness of her voice begging him for more as she held on for dear life.

Drake's face strained as if he were trying desperately to maintain control.

And suddenly the cravings peaked, making her soar, making her ravenous. "Drake!" she screamed while her body exploded into tremors of euphoria.

His hips pumped like a wild man until with one deep thrust the tension caught in the air like a gasp of breath. He threw back his head and roared as his body shattered.

Chapter Twenty-Two

The return trip from Brighton had passed too swiftly for Drake. Had he known the love of his life would open to him, he would have booked the entire hotel for a month. That one night spent in her arms would stay with him until the day he took his last breath.

But alas, the ballet must go on and the mystery of Britannia's parentage must be solved. Then perhaps he might find a way to expose her stalker.

Seated at his writing table, Drake read the response from Lady Calthorpe, agreeing to his visit. Pennyworth entered with the morning's papers. Most likely it wasn't an accident to see the scandal sheet on the top. Bold, black letters announced: *Ravenscar Spotted in Brighton with his Lady Bird*.

"Good God." Drake put the missive aside and grabbed the paper as he eyed his butler.

"Exactly my reaction, Your Grace."

He quickly scanned the article while the back of his neck burned. He could weather slights against his character, but the damned *Gazette* referred to Britannia as base-born, a by-blow, and called her "*the duke's bonny ballerina*". Not surprisingly, it went on to bemoan the plight of the *ton's* gentlewomen who would "*not be waltzing with His Grace this Season, the most eligible bachelor in London*".

Drake slapped the sheet on the table. "Bloody rubbish. I ought to pay a call on the *Gazette's* offices."

Pennyworth sniffed. "If you did, I think they might finagle a story out of it—smear your reputation further if I might be so bold to say."

"That's why they can get away with such slanderous drivel."

"They'll receive their due, even if they have to wait until Judgement Day." Pennyworth picked up Drake's cup and saucer. "Will there be anything else, Your Grace?"

He tapped his finger atop Lady Calthorpe's response, anxious to gain an audience with her. Needless to say, the reasons he'd given for the meeting had been rather vague. "Just my hat and cane. I will be paying a visit to Ravenscar Hall."

"Has Her Grace returned from Brighton?"

"That is what I aim to find out."

"I could send the lad. You needn't bother—"

"That will not be necessary. I have my reasons and I will be leaving within the quarter hour."

***

Having slipped into Mother's house by way of the mews, Drake was waiting in the salon when Lady Calthorpe was announced. According to the housekeeper, his mother would be returning from Brighton this afternoon which suited him perfectly. He neither wanted Her Grace to know about his meeting with the baroness, nor did he want her eavesdropping.

After the niceties were exchanged and the tea poured, Lady Calthorpe took one sip, then gracefully set her cup in its saucer and regarded Drake with a sober stare. "I remember you sitting in that very spot when you were but nine years of age."

"Do you? I was just trying to figure out how long it has been that I've known you, my lady."

"At least sixteen years, I'd say."

Drake stared at his untouched cup of tea while he collected his thoughts. "I'd like to talk more about the past. It is exactly why I asked you here today."

"Oh? I thought the missive was rather clandestine of you, especially now that I've discovered your mother is not here. Truly, I ought to make my apologies and go."

"Please don't. Not until you've heard what I have to say." Having perseverated long and hard about how to broach the subject as gently as possible, Drake produced the miniature from his waistcoat pocket. "Have you ever seen this?"

As Her Ladyship took the portrait in her palm, her mouth dropped with a shocked gasp. "My word." Her face lost all color then changed to fiery red. "Where did you find it?"

"The piece belongs to Miss LeClair."

Covering her mouth, she nodded as if she might already know to whom the miniature belonged.

"If I may interject, it is a lovely rendering. I should have recognized the likeness straightaway." There were so many things he should have noticed, the whisky eye color, both women were petite and lovely though Her Ladyship's hair was a darker brown.

Drake relayed Britannia's story from the beginning—the LeClairs taking in a foundling, the tragedy of smallpox, the christening record, and why Britannia had fled to Paris. He told her about the years the young lady had spent alone at the Paris Opera Ballet, and how she'd strove to discover the identity of the person in the miniature.

Throughout his soliloquy, tears streamed down Her Ladyship's cheeks.

When Drake finished, she dabbed her eyes with a handkerchief, then looked at him directly. "There was something else with the miniature. Are you aware of what it was?"

He didn't blink. "A handkerchief bearing the seal of the Prince Regent."

"Then it truly is she."

"Tell me what happened."

"Reveal my shame? Tell the Duke of Ravenscar about the ruination I have spent my entire life trying to forget?"

"That is why we are meeting under utmost secrecy. I entered Mother's house by way of the mews, out of sight from passersby. Moreover, you have my word that what is said within these walls will remain here—I will even withhold the information from Miss LeClair if you desire, though she wishes to know the truth." Drake took a breath. "I'll say here and now; the young lady is not asking for money. She will not ruin your name or create a scandal. I stake my reputation on it."

Lady Calthorpe rubbed the miniature between her fingertips. "Very well. If you will bear with me, I must go back to my debut Season if you will."

"Please do."

She clutched white-knuckled fists against her midriff. "My first ball was a masque at Carlton House. The Prince Regent was there, of course. It was his illustrious and pretentious home. He danced with me more than once, which was untoward. And truth be told, I wasn't sure it was he until later. Toward the end of the evening, after a great deal of wine had been served, he coaxed me into a bedchamber, under the pretext of joining an exclusive game of charades."

Drake cracked his thumb knuckles while rage burned in his chest. "The unmitigated rake."

"True. I cannot bear to go into further detail except to say that in the midst of the deed, I ended up with the prince's handkerchief in my fist, a baby in my womb, and I was ruined." Her Ladyship again wiped her eyes.

"I feigned a malady of an incurable megrim and refused to attend another soiree until my father sent me home to

Gloucester. You see, it was a few months before I knew I was with child. But I wanted nothing more to do with the *ton* or London or polite society."

"I'm so very sorry," Drake whispered.

With a release of a pent-up breath, she waved a hand through the air as if to brush away the past. "It was a long time ago, and I obviously have fared far better than my daughter."

"But you said you went home to Gloucester. How did you end up in France?"

"When Napoleon was captured, Father thought provincial France was the ideal place for me to hide without being recognized. He sent me to Bayeux with a manservant and a lady's maid—which is why I was so interested to hear the year of Miss LeClair's birth at your mother's soiree. How many children named Britannia are there from Bayeux?"

"I wouldn't be surprised if she's the one and only. But how did she end up with the LeClairs?"

"That's where I lost her. I gave birth and named the child Britannia. A fortnight later, my lady's maid and the manservant took the baby to have her christened. Suspecting they were up to something—I'll say a daughter of the Duke of Beaufort remains vigilant—I secretly wrapped the miniature and handkerchief around the infant's ankle, praying that, one day, those tokens would lead her back to me. I knew my father wouldn't allow my illegitimate child under his roof." Shaking her head, Her Ladyship drew a hand to her temple. "I was right, you know. I never saw Britannia again. And that hideous Mr. Gibbs—"

Drake's gut clenched. "Did you say Gibbs?"

"I did. He has been father's man since his Bow Street days."

He took a bit of tea in an attempt to swallow his ire. Britannia had sought help from Gibbs as well. The scoundrel had a reputation as a man whose muscle was for hire, and he didn't care whom he crossed. Word was Gibbs mightn't have voluntarily left Bow Street either, but no one knew the truth. "Forgive me. I interrupted. Please go on."

"As soon as I was able to travel, we returned to England. And though I begged, they refused to tell me where they'd taken Britannia, aside from saying, 'she'll be well cared for'. My father sent my lady's maid somewhere in the north. And Mr. Gibbs? Well, he's still carousing around London as you are aware. I loathe that man."

When Drake arranged this meeting, he'd expected far less frankness from Her Ladyship. He'd even suspected her of being a party to the skullduggery plaguing Britannia, but now he had overwhelming doubts. "Are you aware that since Miss LeClair's London debut, someone has been stalking the poor woman?"

The shock on Lady Calthorpe's face was undeniable. "Oh, my heavens. You cannot be serious."

"Unfortunately, it is true and it all seems to have started with the port wine incident at my mother's soiree."

"You're not saying you blame me?"

"I have no idea whom to blame. I know Miss LeClair believes the spill to have been an accident."

"It was. I was mortified." Suddenly gasping, Her Ladyship drew her hand over her mouth as if she'd had an epiphany.

"What is it?"

"My father was standing beside me. It was his glass of port I knocked."

"I recall. And, come to think of it, he said something discourteous under his breath. Something I didn't quite understand."

"I cannot be certain, but I now wonder if he shifted his glass on purpose, as if he wanted me to bump it."

"I wonder." Drake reached for the plate of biscuits and offered them to the baroness. "Perhaps I should pay a visit to His Grace."

"My father wouldn't tell a man the time of day unless he thought he might profit from it." Lady Calthorpe took a morsel with white castor sugar and nibbled. "I will confront him myself."

"Do you believe him to be the culprit?"

"I believe he is capable of any manner of malice. However, the only way to know for sure is to ask him."

Her Ladyship returned the miniature which Drake, in turn, slipped into his pocket.

"May I have your permission to tell Miss LeClair about our conversation?" he asked.

"You may, but then I would like to schedule a private meeting with her. Perhaps at my town house?"

"Will that not be awkward for Lord Calthorpe?"

"Yes. Though it is neigh time I confessed to him what happened. I've hidden the shame of my past for too long."

Drake pushed to his feet as the lady stood. "Are you certain? Perhaps we should remain vigilant. After all, why should we dig up the past only to mar your good standing, not to mention put your marriage in jeopardy?"

"No. Now that the truth has come about, it is time to stop living a lie. I will send Britannia an invitation to tea...perhaps once the dust settles."

"I think Miss LeClair would like that very much."

"You care for her, do you not?"

"I do, indeed."

"'Tis a pity..."

"I beg your pardon?"

"Forgive me. I spoke out of turn. From my interaction with Miss...ah...*my daughter*, she has grown into a true gem."

***

"Ravenscar to see you, miss," announced the butler.

"Thank you." Bria set her book aside as the duke strode into the parlor with an enormous grin.

Her heart skipped a beat while she rose. If she lived to be a hundred years of age, she would never find a man with a smile as endearing. "You're early." He usually came for a sip of sherry before she had to leave for the theater. But after Brighton…

He clasped her hand and kissed it. "I've missed you."

"Missed me? I cannot manage a complete thought for pining for you." She thumped the book. "I've read the same silly page over and over and still have no idea what it says."

Laughing, he grasped her waist and twirled her in a circle. "I have stupendous news!"

She braced herself on his shoulders. No, she shouldn't let His Grace pick her up and spin her around, but it was too fun. "Stop," she said, giggling.

He wrapped his arms around her while she slowly slid down his body. "Lady Calthorpe gave me leave to share the contents of our conversation with you."

"Oh my!" Tears stung her eyes as she drew her fingers to her lips. "You've seen her already?"

Drake led her to the settee. "I have, and you'd best have a seat."

As Bria listened to the duke's story about his meeting with the baroness, tingles spread across her skin. "Lady Calthorpe is my mother?"

"I suspect you're not surprised."

Warmth spread through her—after all these years the mystery of the *Grand-Duchesse* had been solved. "No, though I barely allowed myself to hope."

"She not only admitted to being your mother, she freely told me what happened."

"I cannot believe they took me away from my mother at two weeks of age."

"It is remarkable you survived. Moreover, you are the daughter of a king and a baroness. I knew you were too extraordinary to be a guttersnipe."

"How can you say such a thing? The news confirms I am the by-blow of a prince who became a king who wasn't well-liked, and a lady who hid her shame for over nineteen years." Bria clutched a handkerchief over her heart while hundreds of emotions coursed through her. "I cannot tell you how elated I am to know who my parents were…*are* in Lady Calthorpe's case. Though, doesn't being a bastard lower me in your esteem?"

"You'd be surprised the percentage of bastards who mingle amongst the gentry. In my estimation, your parentage has merit."

"I understand George sired a number of bastards, none of whom he legitimized."

"That's because he was a profligate spendthrift who cared only for himself."

"Not exactly the type of man I want to refer to as Papa."

"Whyever not? He did little to improve England whilst he sat on the throne, why not grant him a good deed from the grave?"

A tear spilled onto her cheek. "I love how you can twist every situation toward your favor."

He winked. "'Tis a prerequisite for dukedom."

Bria laughed. "Well, I suppose you can make your own rules."

"Some. Not all." Drake brushed a lock of hair from her forehead as he grew serious. "Regardless if we've solved the mystery of your parentage, we still have no idea who is behind the attacks on your person. Lady Calthorpe intends to discuss the matter with her father, but—"

"The Duke of Beaufort?"

"Yes."

"Did he not have something to do with my placement with the LeClairs?"

"I imagine so. He's the man who arranged for your mother to spend her confinement in France."

"If Beaufort is responsible having them foster me, then surely he cares?"

"I wouldn't be hasty to trust His Grace. And in the interim, I'm not letting you out of my sight for a moment."

Chapter Twenty-Three

Charlotte found her husband reading the *Gazette* in the drawing room while he sipped his morning coffee.

She cleared her throat. "I've asked the coachman to bring the carriage around."

"Very well, dear." Frederick Gough, Lord Calthorpe, didn't bother to lower his paper.

As her finger traced the line of a table sculpture of two dancing nymphs, Charlotte's heart raced. Last night, she'd paced her chamber for hours. She'd lived a lie for so many years. If only she could reveal the truth, if only she could square her shoulders and tell her husband about her transgressions and have it done with. They hadn't been blessed with children—doubtless God's penance for her sins.

Her fingers slipped on the statue, gravely aware that with her next words her life would change.

Charlotte still had her dower funds at her disposal. If Frederick cast her out, she could move to a cottage in the north and live out the rest of her days. Perhaps Britannia would even see fit to pay her a visit now and again.

"I'm off to call on my father."

"Brave of you." Freddy flipped the page over. "Have you received a summons from His Grace?"

"No. As a matter of fact, he is unaware of my impending visit."

Again, the *Gazette* rustled. "Good strategy, my dear. Attack unawares. You would have made an excellent field marshal."

"You may be right, especially since I'm going to speak to him about my *daughter*." She froze, her hand gripping the statue, her heart thundering in her throat.

While Frederick lowered his paper, managing to breathe was impossible for Charlotte. Gray eyes focused on her, a myriad of emotions passing through them—confusion, shock, anger, horror and more. Her husband's Adam's apple bobbed as he slowly drew his finger across the right side of his moustache, then did the same to the left.

"*Daughter*, did you say?"

"I did." With a sharp inhale, Charlotte raised her chin and squared her shoulders. "I am not proud of my youth. I fully accept that you have every right to turn me out, thrust me from your life, and never wish to see me again. But I can no longer hide the truth. In the year of our Lord 1814, I gave birth to a girl in Bayeux, France."

Frederick coughed. "Why are you telling me this now?"

"Because, at long last, the young lady has found me. I was a coward not to have searched for her, but now that we have been reunited, I will *not* turn my back on her."

"I see." Frederick set the newspaper aside and strolled to the window. "Do you believe I did not know what happened?"

Charlotte pressed her palm into the figurine. "Of course you didn't. How could you have known? Father ensured my shame—the family's shame was tidily brushed under the carpet."

"Indeed, Beaufort worked diligently to see that your reputation was not marred." As if mesmerized with the rain outside, Frederick clasped his hands behind his back, refusing to face her. "I was there, Charlotte. Remember, we had the first dance of the evening?"

"At Carlton House?"

"All it took was one smile from you and I was smitten beyond saving."

"But I thought my father—"

"He arranged everything, of course, but not before we discussed what had happened and why you suddenly disappeared. You see, I already knew. I overheard George's audacious babble before he took you above stairs for your game of charades. I heard his lies. I heard you question him as you ought. He lied about there being a gaming room up there. But I had no idea what he would do."

Charlotte's fingers slid from the statue and clamped around her midriff. "No…"

"I did, however, suspect what had transpired when, later, you raced out the door, your hair askew, your eyes filled with tears."

"You saw me?" she asked in a chilled whisper.

"I bore witness, and if George were not the Prince Regent, I would have challenged him to a duel." Frederick turned, his eyes tortured and glistening. "I loved you then and I love you more now. I am not a handsome man, Charlotte. I am not a dandy like so many debutantes desire. When it was clear you would not be returning to London, I approached your father with an offer and he accepted."

A tear slipped onto her cheek. "All this time you knew I had a daughter, but never told me?"

He, too, wiped his eyes. "Your father said the child had been well placed and it was best to let the past lie. I had no reason to doubt him, or his wishes to never mention her. Beaufort felt doing so would cause you too much pain."

"But the people who fostered her died." Moving closer, Charlotte kept her hands clenched at her middle. "At the age of fourteen, the fosterer's brother told her she was a foundling and turned her out with nothing."

"Good God."

"That's exactly how I feel." She took her husband's hand. "And you're wrong. You are the most handsome dandy I've ever known, and you have made me happy every day of these past years."

He raised her fingers to his lips and kissed. "Then I will not keep you. Go make your peace with the duke. Would you like me to come along for moral support?"

No matter how much she wanted to lean on Frederick's arm, it would be cowardly to do so. "I'm a grown woman now. I will face my father alone."

"Then I shall honor your wishes. Send up a white flag if you need my assistance."

***

As Bria prepared for the final performance of *La Sylphide*, not only sadness but worry stretched her heart.

Out of breath, a lad popped his head inside the dressing room door. "She's not at the boarding house."

"*Zut alors!*" Only a half-hour until the overture was due to start, Bria looked to Pauline's untouched toilette. She could wait no longer. They always covered for each other but, this time, her friend had left things too late.

She found Monsieur Travere on stage, rehearsing something new with a few of the girls from the *corps*.

"Monsieur, may I have a word?"

"What is it?"

Bria pulled him aside. "Pauline isn't here. It's not like her to be this late. I'm worried."

"Do you have any idea where she might be?"

"None. I sent a lad to the boarding house to fetch her, but she's not there either." Mentioning Pauline's arrangement with Lord Saye would only put her friend in more trouble, so Bria turned the blame to herself. "Ever since I moved into my rooms, Pauline and I have not checked on each other as we ought."

"And she's been keeping company with a viscount."

"You knew about that?"

"Of course, I make it my duty to know all of my dancers' affairs, especially yours."

"I see." Bria stopped herself from commenting further. Momentarily, there were far more important things to discuss than Monsieur Tavere's snooping. "Then do you have any idea where we can find Pauline?"

"I'll send someone to follow up with Lord Saye. In the meantime, notify the *corps*. We must put plans in motion to cover for her absence."

"Yes, monsieur."

"And Britannia?"

"*Oui*"

"I am not happy about this. When you do see Miss Renaud, send her to me."

A half an hour later when the curtain opened, Pauline was still nowhere to be found. Worried half out of her wits, Bria danced with clipped and frantic movement, her eyes darting to the wings as often as possible, praying she'd catch sight of her friend.

At intermission, there was still no sign of her.

In Act II after James chased the Sylph off the stage, Bria raced to the dressing room for what seemed like the hundredth time. Pauline's toilette remained untouched, but Bria froze when her eyes trailed to her own table. A missive rested against the mirror, addressed to Miss LeClair and written in a bold hand.

Prickles fired across her skin as she rose on her toes and tiptoed toward the letter. With trembling fingers, she snatched it, turned it over and examined the seal.

A blank.

Clenching her teeth, she broke the cowardly seal and read:

We have Miss Renaud. If you want to see her again, come alone. If you tell a soul, she will die. A carriage will be waiting beyond the stage door upon the last curtain call. Do not hesitate. Speak to no one. Do not stop to change or Miss Renaud will meet her end.

Clutching the missive to her chest, Bria searched the room. Someone had been inside after intermission while she was on stage. Who? Who could move past the guard without being questioned?

She didn't dare ask. Doing so would raise an alarm for certain.

And why were these beastly people doing this? Pauline had never harmed a soul. Why did this monster choose her? Why not confront Bria directly?

Who was behind these reprehensible deeds? Why? Lady Calthorpe had invited Bria to tea on the morrow, and Drake had said she was ever so anxious to meet. It seemed unlikely for Her Ladyship to be involved. Didn't it?

Beyond the dressing room, the orchestra continued, almost to the finale. Bria only had moments before she needed to be on stage. Shoving the missive into her bodice, she pulled her cloak from the hook, rolled it into a ball, and smiled at the guard as she skipped toward the stage door trying to look as if nothing had gone awry. She glanced over her shoulder to ensure she was out of the guard's sight before draped her cloak over the handrail. Then she checked over both shoulders and skipped toward the wings at stage right.

"Are you all right?" asked Claudio after she took her place beside him, ready for her next sequence.

As Bria shook out her legs, she gave a curt nod while the girls in the *corps* danced on stage for the finale. "Worried about Pauline."

"You look as if you've seen a ghost."

"Perhaps I have."

Thank God the music demanded her entrance. If she'd stood there for a moment longer, she would have broken down into a weeping mess. She had to be strong for Pauline. *Entrechat, pas de bourrée.* The poor girl's life was in danger. Bria must do nothing to arouse suspicion. No one must know.

Bria painted on a smile and danced with more emotion than ever before.

It took an eternity for the finale to end. The curtain calls were torture, but she forced herself to smile, her gaze shooting to the wings, searching for a villain. Was the carriage out there now? How fast could she run for the door? Who might see her?

When the curtain finally closed, Gérard grasped her hand. "*Ma chére*, what is the matter? You were dancing as if blown by a tempest."

Bria snapped her fingers away. "Of course I was. Pauline is missing."

Before anyone could interject, she ran. It hardly took more than a heartbeat to pull her cloak from the rail and swing it over her shoulders. Outside, a coach waited only steps away, the door ajar.

I will save you, Pauline!

Chapter Twenty-Four

"What in God's name are you saying? The woman disappeared from under your nose?" Drake boomed. Now they not only were missing Miss Renaud, but Britannia hadn't been seen since the curtain closed.

The air backstage stifled him. Either that or his valet had tied his neckcloth too tightly.

"N-no," the guard stammered, thrusting his hands up as he shrugged. "She took her bows and I stood right where I always do. She either vanished into thin air or she exited stage right."

Had Perkins hired a complete imbecile to guard the theater's most important performer? "Your job is to see that Miss LeClair remains in your sight at all times."

"Yes, Your Grace."

"Did anyone see Miss LeClair leave the theater?"

"No, but I thought she seemed upset before she entered for the finale," said Gérard. "I asked her what was wrong, and she said she was worried about Pauline."

"Of course we're all upset about Miss Renaud as well." Drake slapped his gloves in his palm. "Was there anyone backstage who shouldn't have been? Did you see anything unusual? Anything at all?"

The guard scratched his head. "The lad took a missive into Miss LeClair, but it didn't seem unusual—he's done it before."

Drake's gaze shot left then right. "Where's the boy?"

Mr. Perkins led the boy onto the stage.

Eyes round and scared, the stage boy gripped a cap in his hands. "'ere, sir."

Drake marched toward the lad. "Who gave you the missive?"

"I didn't do nofin' wrong."

"Of course not," Perkins placed a hand on the young fellow's shoulder. "Just tell His Grace what he asked."

The cap twisted. "I was tendin' the gas lights like I always do. A man came in and 'anded me the note—told me to put it someplace where Miss LeClair would see it straightaway, 'e did."

"What did he look like?" Drake asked trying not to growl while he clenched his fists behind his back.

"Dunno. Tall and old…a-and 'e 'ad a big nose."

"Most likely a messenger," said Perkins.

"It seems you've managed to lose two dancers in one night." Drake glared at the theater manager. "Have you received any word regarding Miss Renaud?"

"Bow Street hasn't reported back as of yet. But she's only been missing a few hours."

"A few hours can mean the difference between life and death." Drake's gut clamped into a lead ball. "Go camp on Bow Street's doorstep—take the boy. Tell them about Miss LeClair and have the lad give them the description of the messenger. I want to know as soon as they have the remotest clue."

"I'll put a man on it straightaway." Perkins bowed and started off.

"Wait." Drake stopped him. "Did you ask the driver to bring my carriage around?"

"Yes, Your Grace. I've been advised it is waiting out back just as you requested."

"Good. I'll be chasing a few leads—but they're only hunches." He made a point of looking everyone in the eye. "If you received any clue at all, I want notification immediately, is that understood?"

Perkins, Travere and the entire cast—less two ballerinas—all nodded. With a swing of his cape, Drake marched out the door and gave his coachman instructions to drive directly to Lord Calthorpe's town house.

He didn't care about the lateness of the hour. He didn't care if he exposed Her Ladyship. For all Drake knew, she could be the one behind the missing women.

Damnation, if anyone tried to hurt Britannia, he would carve out their heart and show no mercy. *Both* women had best be unharmed or there would be hell to pay.

Being caged inside his carriage was pure torture. He pounded on the ceiling with his cane. "Faster, you bloody laggard!"

"We're at a gallop, Your Grace!" bellowed the coachman.

Drake ground his back molars. For the love of God, he could run faster. He had a matched pair unsurpassed by anything Tattersalls might offer up for auction.

With no other recourse, over and over again, Drake slammed the pommel of his cane into the seat opposite. By the time the carriage came to a stop outside the Calthorpe town house, the velvet had been bludgeoned to shreds while sweat soaked the band of his top hat. Not waiting for the footman, Drake barreled onto the footpath, up the steps, and pounded on the door. "Open at once! This is a matter of life and death!"

The gaunt butler popped his nose out the door. "Ravenscar is it? What the devil, Your Gr—"

Jamming his card into the insolent boob's palm, Drake shoved his way inside. "Two dancers have been kidnapped from my theater, that is what, one of whom has a rather close attachment with Lady Calthorpe. I'm certain she will be quite anxious to know of this calamity."

The man held the card to the candlelight. "Close attachment, Your Grace?"

"Notify Her Ladyship of my presence forthwith."

"Straightaway. Please wait in the parlor."

"What is going on?" asked Lord Calthorpe as he plodded down the stairs, wearing full evening dress and looking as if he'd recently returned from a night at a ball.

"Ravenscar?" Her Ladyship's startled voice came from behind the baron. "Branson, please open a bottle of claret for His—"

Drake held up his palms. "Not on my account. Something dire has happened."

"At the theater?" asked Calthorpe.

Her Ladyship drew her hands over her heart. "Oh heavens, please tell me all is well with Britannia."

Drake's gaze shot to the baron. Did he know? This was no time for secrets. "I wish to heaven I could tell you she is well."

The countess gasped. "No!"

Drake glanced between the couple, his lips thinning. Uttering more might very well ruin the woman for the rest of her days. "May I speak freely?" he asked, well aware he'd already said too much.

Her face stricken, she nodded, looking like the Maid of Lorraine, ready to lead her army into battle. "I've told my husband all."

Calthorpe gestured to the adjoining room. "Please step into the parlor."

Drake moved inside, but he didn't sit. None of them did. Using as few syllables as possible, he explained how Miss Renaud had gone missing before the final performance of *La*

Sylphide and how Britannia vanished afterward. "All we know is someone gave a missive addressed to her to the stage boy."

"Doubtless, it had something to do with Miss Renaud's whereabouts," said Calthorpe.

Drake slammed the ball of his cane into his palm. "That is my presumption as well."

"Oh, my Lord in heaven, no." The baroness' skirts skimmed the Oriental rug as she paced. "He threatened, but I never thought he'd be mad enough to act. And he brought Miss Renaud into his delusion as well."

Shards of ice pulsed through Drake's veins. "You're speaking of Beaufort?" Her ladyship nodded while he gripped his cane with iron fingers. "What. Exactly. Did he threaten?"

"I thought he was just having one of his tirades." Her Ladyship braced her hands on the back of a chair. "H-he ranted about sending my bastard so far away from England no one would ever find her!"

Drake's gut turned to lead. "Good God."

"We must make haste. Confront the old fool before he has time to act on his threats." Calthorpe started for the door. "Ravenscar, your carriage is outside I presume?"

"It is." Leading the way, Drake raced out the door.

***

Mr. Gibbs sat across the carriage from Bria, his face cadaverous in the dim light.

"Why is it taking so long?" Bria insisted, grinding her fists into the seat cushion. "I must see Pauline this instant!"

Never in a hundred days would she have suspected Mr. Gibbs, a former lawman, to be involved in kidnapping. But presently, he seemed to rather enjoy making Britannia uncomfortable. "She's quite well."

"What are you saying? What did you do with her?"

He pulled the curtain aside and looked out. They weren't in London anymore. The moon shone blue on the grass as they passed. "I reckon she ought to be waking up about now."

"Waking up? She missed the final performance. Pauline would *never* do that. Not unless someone poisoned her."

"Not poison. Just something to make her sleep. Soundly. She'll wake in some room in the boarding house none the wiser."

"The boarding house? Why, it is only three blocks from the theater." Britannia slid toward the door. "Sir, I demand you tell me what you are playing at this very instant!"

He grinned, sliding his fingers into his pocket. What was he hiding in there? Blast, it was too dark to make out much of anything. "You see, someone is paying me a great deal of coin to ensure you never trouble Lady Calthorpe or her family again."

"Her Ladyship—?" Before Bria could say another word, Mr. Gibbs lurched across the carriage, grabbed her wrist and brutally twined a rope around it.

Thrashing and kicking, she fought to push him a way. "Stop!"

He reached for her other wrist, but Bria was faster. Fighting, she slammed her fist into his jaw. The cur snarled and caught her hand, throbbing knuckles and all.

"That was very unwise," he growled, winding the rope tighter. He opened his mouth wide and stretched his chin from side to side while he knotted the bindings so forcefully her fingers grew numb.

Bria tugged and twisted, only making the bindings bite into her flesh. "You're mad!"

"Perhaps."

"Ravenscar will never let you get away with this. Pauline and now me? You will swing from the gallows!"

"I think not. I am very efficient at covering my tracks. Even if he does figure it out, you'll be on a convict ship headed for Australia before he can ride to your rescue. And I will be under the protection of my patron."

An icy chill thrummed through Bria's veins. Australia? Convict? *Mon Dieu, je suis condamnée!*

With her next inhalation, the parchment in her bodice crinkled. If only she'd left the missive on her toilette, someone might deduce what had happened. How could she have been so naïve to blindly follow the directive in the missive? How could she think she could save Pauline? She, a petite ballerina take on a behemoth the size of Mr. Gibbs? Heaven's stars, she was smaller than most women let alone men.

Australia?

She'd heard terrible things about people who perished, the abysmal conditions, the sickness, the—the rats!

Oh God in heaven, please tell me this is not happening!

Chapter Twenty-Five

It was nearly eleven o'clock when Drake led Lady and Lord Calthorpe into Beaufort's salon, complete with a mahogany billiards table.

"Not yet abed, Beaufort?" he asked, sauntering inside.

"Ravenscar?" The elderly duke stumbled away from the table, cue in hand. "Charlotte? Have you completely lost all sense of propriety? How dare you force your way into my home unannounced?"

"Beg your pardon, Your Grace. They were too fast for me," wheezed the butler from behind, who couldn't be a day younger than eighty. "Shall I bring up a tray?"

"No, you should not—"

Ready to beat Beaufort to within an inch of his life, Drake sidestepped along the table. "There won't be time for niceties."

Inclining his cue stick Drake's way, Beaufort assumed a defensive stance. "Do not move another inch closer."

"Or what, pray tell, will you do? Brain me with that skinny piece of maple?" Before the duke could answer, Drake closed the distance, snatched the cue from Beaufort's hands, cracked it on the side of the table, and broke the damned stick in two.

Lady Calthorpe gasped. "Please, Father—!"

"Where is she?" Drake demanded, brandishing the splintered end.

Beaufort spread his palms as if he were an innocent monk heading for compline. "To whom are you referring?"

Her Ladyship tsked. "Father, lying does not become you."

"Whyever not?" asked Lord Calthorpe with a bold display of backbone. "His Grace has been shamming it for so long, I don't think he knows the difference between truth and fiction."

Beaufort shot the baron such a deadly glare, Drake had no illusions as to the truthfulness of the baron's accusation. He smashed the butt end of the cue stick onto the table. "I'm going to ask this once and if I do not receive a satisfactory answer, my next swing will be at your balding head."

The duke narrowed his eyes. "You dare threaten—"

"It is not a threat. 'Tis a certainty." Stepping forward, Drake pointed the jagged weapon at the man's nose. "Where. Is. Miss LeClair?"

"I have no idea—"

Her Ladyship threw out her hands. "Please, Father. Help us."

Beaufort thrust his finger at his daughter. "Why are you putting this on me? You have no grounds!"

"Actually, we do have evidence and it all points to you," said Lord Calthorpe.

The coward scooted behind a small writing table—little protection it would give if the man didn't start cooperating. "No one would dare prosecute me. I am a duke."

"As am I." Drake closed in, itching to strike. "And I tell you true, judge and jury are standing before you this night. Now where *the hell* have you taken Britannia LeClair?"

Her Ladyship neared. "Where, Father?"

Beaufort's gaze shot from one scowling face to another. "Y-you won't harm me."

Rage shot through Drake's blood like the ignition of a cannon's fuse. Lunging around the damned desk, he swung back with the weapon, eyeing Beaufort's neck. He needed the man lucid until he confessed—a strike to the throat wouldn't knock him out. But the blow would drop him to his knees.

Squealing like a woman, Beaufort threw up his hands and ducked beneath the hissing cue stick. "She's sailing to Australia!"

God on the cross, the words took Drake's breath away. "*Aust-ral-ia?*"

"No!" cried Her Ladyship.

"Which ship?" asked Calthorpe with calm ire. "There's none sailing from London. Hasn't been in over a year."

Drake spun on his heel. "You know this?"

The baron's shoulder inched up. "I play cards with the Governor of Newgate Prison."

As Beaufort tried to sidle away, Drake caught the bastard's wrist. "Which port?"

"I have no idea." Twisting his arm away, Beaufort collapsed into a chair. "I told my man to send her to Australia on a convict ship. Then I washed my hands of the whole abhorrent affair."

"Your man?" asked Lady Calthorpe. "'Tis that scoundrel Gibbs, is it not?"

Though her father did not reply, it was clear by his expression his daughter's guess was right.

Her Ladyship drew praying hands to her lips. "For the love of all that is holy, you must tell us where he's taking her."

Beaufort jolted in an attempt to break free. "I know not. That I can admit with utter honesty. Now leave an old man to his peace. I have nothing more to say, especially to you, Ravenscar."

Drake loomed over the scoundrel—a bane to the aristocracy. "You'd best pray I find her, or I swear I will see to it you set sail on a sinking ship to hell."

"Come," Calthorpe beckoned. "And let us hope the governor is at home."

Reluctantly, Drake stepped away from His Grace, and gave the baron a nod. They were losing time with every tick of the clock. No longer able to withstand the sight of this piss-swilling boar, he turned and hastened for the door.

Once they reached the carriage, Drake pulled one of his footmen aside. "Haste to Half Moon Street. Saddle my horse and ride like hellfire to Newgate Prison."

"You want me to ride your horse? W-with *your* saddle, Your Grace?"

"That's what I said, and have Pennyworth fetch my pistols and dagger. Now run. There'll be extra wages for you if you have the beast waiting by the time we arrive."

With a hasty bow, the lad sprinted away.

Inside the carriage, Lady Calthorpe sat as primly as the Dowager Duchess of Ravenscar. She held her back erect, though the corners of her mouth were taut with worry. "You do not believe that young man can make it to Newgate before our carriage?"

"My town house is ten blocks away. And that boy is the fastest man in my employ—was a messenger when he was younger. And never underestimate the power of money. He'll be there. Mark me."

Drake clenched his teeth, ready to jump out of his skin. Britannia might be a spitfire, but she was no match for a crew of seedy sailors on a three-month voyage to the south seas. A convict ship to boot. Look at how she'd wilted and swooned after merely crossing the channel! Healthy men perished at sea all the time. And she was so damned frail.

Worse, the crew would throw her in the hold, feed her slop—Lord knows what more they would do.

Drake's stomach roiled.

By God, he refused to consider it. He would find her. There was no question. He must.

I love her with every fiber of my being.

***

Drake had been right. The footman arrived at Newgate Prison just as he and the Goughs alighted from the carriage.

"I have news, Your Grace," said the lad.

Drake's heart leaped. "Yes?"

"Miss Renaud has been found. Pennyworth thought you would want to know."

"Thank you." Drake eyed Her Ladyship. "Well, at least we're only searching for one woman."

"One too many," she agreed.

The lad waited outside, holding the horse while Calthorpe gained entry to the governor's quarters. Of course, they were met with exasperation due to the lateness of the hour. But it couldn't be helped.

Once the governor realized he was not only being addressed by a baron, but a duke had taken pains to darken his door at this hour, his sleepy demeanor perked considerably. "Indeed, I have a schedule of all convict ships sailing for Australia. 'Tis in my offices. Follow me."

Drake marched behind the man. "Lord Calthorpe tells me there hasn't been a convict ship sail from London for quite some time."

"That's right. To make the crossing, large ships are necessary, and the Thames just isn't equipped—there are far too many merchant ships, I should add. Society doesn't care to have a vessel laden with ne'er-do-wells anchored in the Pool of London. It just isn't good use of prime moorage."

"How do you transport the prisoners to the ships?" asked Drake.

"By wagon mostly." Stopping outside a big oak door, the governor grappled for a ring of keys tied to his belt.

"And from which ports do they usually sail?" asked Her Ladyship.

"All of them, honestly. I sent a wagon full of thieves all the way to Maryport last month."

Drake followed the governor inside, praying for a closer port…but not too close. The further away, the better chance he'd have of intercepting her kidnapper before he reached its destination.

"The book is just here. My clerk enters the ship's name and expected date and port of departure."

"Expected?" asked Drake.

"Well, all manner of things can go wrong, what with the weather and the like."

Lady Calthorpe crossed herself. "Jesu save us."

The governor opened a large, bound volume atop his table. "Let me see," he hummed as if he had all night to turn the bloody pages.

Drake was about to rip the book from the man's grasp when the governor's pointer finger stilled. "Here we are. The *Lloyds*, a four-masted barque sails from Portsmouth on August 19th."

"That's two days hence."

Calthorpe glanced to the mantel clock. "One, actually, given 'tis just past the witching hour."

"At a fast trot I can reach Portsmouth in ten hours." Drake tugged on his gloves. "I shall leave at once. If I ride all night, I'll be there before midday. I'll find her well in advance of the *Lloyds* sailing time."

"A moment." The governor scanned down the page a bit. "There's a brig, the *Amphitrite*, scheduled to depart Plymouth on the twenty-first."

"Plymouth?" Her Ladyship fanned her face. "What if Britannia is not in Portsmouth? Can His Grace reach Plymouth in two days?"

"If nothing goes awry," said Calthorpe.

Drake shot the baron a stern look. "I will allow no one and no obstacle to stand in my way."

Oblivious to the conversation, the governor continued, "Furthermore, there's not another ship sailing for Australia until the *Royal Sovereign* departs Port Chatham on the sixth of September."

Drake leaned over and read the entry. "Then it's either Portsmouth or Plymouth."

Her Ladyship did the same. "Very well, count on the Goughs to do our part to save Britannia. Calthorpe and I will travel on to Plymouth in the morning. 'Tis a two-day carriage ride, is it not, Freddy?"

"A long two days, but even if it takes us three, we'll arrive in plenty of time to locate both the *Amphitrite* and Miss LeClair," said the baron. "Jolly good idea, my dear."

"You would travel all that way, my lady?" asked Drake.

"She's my daughter. After nineteen years, I'm not planning to lose her yet again."

Drake bowed. "Then it is settled. I'll ride to Portsmouth. If I find Britannia along the way, I'll send word to Plymouth. If, heaven forbid, I do not intercept her, I'll continue on and meet you there."

"We'll stay at the King's Inn. Send your correspondence there."

"Your Grace." The governor clasped his hands. "Might I suggest you wait until morning and give me a chance to organize His Majesty's dragoons to accompany you to the coast?"

"There won't be time. I must leave straightaway. Miss LeClair is in dire straits and I cannot bear to see her suffer any longer than necessary."

"In the meantime," said Her Ladyship. "Can you issue a warrant for the arrest of Mr. Walter Gibbs? He's the man who has abducted Miss LeClair. I do not want to leave anything to chance."

"Gibbs? The runner?" the governor asked in disbelief.

"He's the one," replied His Lordship.

"Very well. I shall attend to it straightaway."

Chapter Twenty-Six

It was still dark when the carriage rolled to a stop. "Where are we?" Bria asked, her hands tied to a metal handle beneath the window.

Gibbs pulled down on the latch. "An inn. We'll stop here for the night. But right now, I expect you to wait here without making a sound." He hopped out and slammed the door.

"Mr. Gibbs," a man called while footsteps approached. "I haven't seen you around these parts for ages."

"I've moved on from Bow Street. Opened my own establishment. But presently I'm escorting a lady convict—a special case, if you will."

"Oh, my. Is she dangerous?"

"A thief—headed for fourteen years transport."

"I am not a thief!" Bria shouted. "My name is Britannia LeClair. I am the principal ballerina in *La Sylphide* at the Chadwick Theater in London!" Curses to remaining quiet. She'd profess her innocence to everyone who'd listen.

"And she's a tad delusional," the scoundrel's reedy voice seeped through the carriage walls.

"You're the one who has lost his mind, Mr. Gibbs. Help me! Please!"

"I should have gagged her."

"Are you certain?" asked the new voice. "She sounds convincing."

"You would go against the ruling of the Circuit Court?" Gibbs countered, the lout.

"Of course not."

"There is no ruling! There has been no arrest! I have been *kidnapped*!" Bria screamed so loudly, her throat burned.

"Do you still have the holding cell out the back?" the bastard continued.

"Aye, sir."

"And the key?"

"Where it always is."

"Please!" Britannia tried again. "You must believe me. I am innocent. This man kidnapped me from the theater and is holding me against my will." Under her breath, she cursed Gibbs to hell in both Latin and French.

"She sounds awfully young," said the man. "Do you think she'll survive fourteen years?"

"She should have thought about that before she stole the necklace from the Duke of Beaufort. I've been assigned with seeing her to the ship. After that, only her wits will keep her alive."

In the blink of an eye, Bria's skin chilled with the coursing of ice through her blood.

Beaufort? Lady Calthorpe's father?

"What are you saying?" she shouted. "The miniature is *mine*! I found it in Bayeux in a box with my name inscribed atop."

Gibbs opened the coach door. Her heart raced as she fought against her bindings.

She spat in his face. "You deceitful blackguard! First you took my payment, then you lied about Lady Hertford, and now—"

He worked loose the knot tying her hands to the handle. "I didn't lie about the dowager marchioness. She was embroiled in an affair with George just as I reported."

"I think you knew who my mother was from the outset. I think you—"

He slapped her. "Shut up."

"How dare you?" Bria's cheek stung like the attack of angry bees. Her eyes watered. "I will never forgive you as long as I live."

Uttering not another word, Gibbs yanked her down the steps and dragged her toward a stable. "Pull the carriage off the drive and put up the horses. We're leaving at nine o'clock on the hour."

"Yes, sir," said the coachman.

"Do you want to be a party to kidnapping?" Britannia barked at the driver, her words met with a backhand. The strike only served to ratchet up her anger. Gibbs could manhandle her all he dared. She would die before he pushed her aboard a convict ship bound for ungodly Australia.

"Do you know who pays my wages?" she looked directly toward the driver, the whites of his eyes prominent in the moonlight. "The Duke of Ravenscar. And if you are a party to this madness, you will swing from the gallows with Mr. Gibbs, so help me God!"

Turning away, the man took up the reins as if he were deaf.

Gibbs shoved her into a shadowy, dank cell with nothing but iron bars in place of windows and doors.

"You will not get away with this!" she shouted.

He slammed the door and affixed a padlock. "Oh, but I will."

Wrapping her fingers around the bars, Bria shook with all her strength. "Why? Why has my *grandfather* done this? I did nothing. I hurt no one!" A new bout of chills spread across her skin when she referred to Beaufort as her grandfather. If he was the patriarch of her family, she'd choose being a foundling!

***

Near half-past three, Drake jerked up from being hunched over his horse's withers. Shaking himself awake, he reined the stallion to a stop in Guildford to pound on the innkeeper's door. A man opened with a string of expletives that would have put a jack tar to shame.

Drake apologized, announced himself, and asked about Britannia, giving a description of Gibbs.

"The only guests we have at the moment are a merchant and a couple from Southampton." The man gestured inside. "You look as if you could use a rest. The king's chamber is let, but I have a soft bed in a respectable room."

"Thank you, but no. I must continue on."

"Wait a moment, Your Grace. I've a bit of cheese and some bread for your journey."

"Such a kindness, I did not expect. Please allow me to pay for the meal."

"Not necessary. People will come for miles to hear a good yarn." The innkeeper beckoned him inside. "I couldn't have dreamed this up, having the Duke of Ravenscar pull me out of bed in the middle of the night in search of a woman."

The man led him to the kitchens. "Is she highborn like yourself?"

Drake wiped the sleep from his eyes. "Higher."

After slicing a chunk of cheese, the innkeeper wrapped it in some parchment with a half-loaf of bread. "Higher than a duke?"

"I'd say so."

"Lord blind me. And some cad has off and kidnapped her?"

"The man's name is Gibbs. The woman is no taller than the center of my chest. Petite. Cinnamon hair. Eyes like aged whisky. If you see anyone fitting my description, send word to Portsmouth straightaway. There will be a reward."

The innkeeper held out the food wrapped in leather and tied with a thong. "How much of a reward?"

"Sizeable." Drake took the parcel. "Thank you for this."

***

He ate the food as he rode which helped subdue his fatigue. A few miles on, the hint of cobalt illuminated the eastern sky. In another few hours, he'd arrive in Portsmouth. Had Gibbs ridden all night? Had Drake passed them? Was the scoundrel taking a circuitous route? Surely, he wouldn't veer far from the turnpike?

No sooner had doubt filled Drake's mind, when he passed a signpost pointing to the left, indicating the Stag Inn was a mile down the road. He slowed his horse when he spotted fresh carriage tracks, at least by the darker shadows, they looked to be fresh. One wheel had swerved off the road and made a rut in the grass.

Prickles fanned out across his nape as he dismounted and studied the tracks—they were newly carved, all right. The mud around the edges hadn't yet begun to curve inward.

Even on the turnpike, there were stretches of road in poor repair. Drake had seen ruts and hoofprints galore, but due to the traffic, there was no possible way to guess which ruts had been made by Gibbs' carriage.

Was he utilizing a carriage?

Most likely.

Was this rut caused by Gibbs' carriage?

The only way to find out was to take a detour.

Dawn came, illuminating the narrow road cutting through a canopy of trees with misty shadows of foreboding. Drake checked his pocket watch—a quarter to six. Riding down a mile to have a look around would cost him fifteen or twenty minutes. His gut squeezed while a shiver coursed up his spine.

Damnation, it was dawn on August 18th and the *Lloyds* wasn't scheduled to sail until the 19th. He could spare twenty bloody minutes for a hunch.

A pistol at each hip and his dagger at his back, Drake cued his horse forward, but he didn't ride on the road—he opted for the grass. Though the road was dirt and rock, his horse's hooves could be heard yards away each time the stallion's shod hooves kicked a stone.

The mist had grown thicker by the time he reached the Stag Inn. On first glance, nothing seemed amiss until he rode around the side of the stables. There was a carriage all right, an expensive one. A conveyance not unlike the town coach Drake owned.

He dismounted, tied his horse and crept to the carriage. Inside, he found a length of rope on the floor. *Rope?*

It wasn't all that unusual, though the piece was too short for tethering a horse.

A thud sounded.

Drake froze.

Another thud.

Someone's chopping wood.

At a crouch, he tiptoed toward the sound.

A boy no more than ten years of age swung an ax, splitting a log in two. Drake waited while the lad collected another stick and set it on the block. As soon as he raised the ax for another chop, Drake lunged in, seized the ax and clapped a hand over the boy's mouth.

Screaming and thrashing, the lad fought.

"Silence!" Drake growled. "I am not here to hurt you. I am searching for a woman who was kidnapped in London last eve."

The boy froze, his eyes wide and afraid.

"When did that carriage arrive?" He slid his hand down to the boy's jaw to allow him to talk. Though God save him if he tried to holler for help.

"Last night. L-late. Well past dark."

"Did you see a woman?"

The lad's eyes shifted.

Drake tightened his grip as he followed the young fellow's line of sight. "Jesu. Is she in there?"

Looking as if he was about to release his bowels, the lad gave a single nod.

"As I said before, you'll not be harmed. In fact, you will be rewarded. I am a duke. I can ensure your life takes a turn for the better."

"A d-duke?"

"Ravenscar. Seventh in line to the throne." Drake took a chance and released the boy. "Will you keep mum?"

He nodded.

Drake reached inside his coat and pulled out a crisp one pound note. "Have you seen one of these before?"

"Seen, but never held one."

"This is yours if you saddle a horse for the lady."

"I-is she a duchess?"

"She's better than a duchess."

"Cor."

Drake put the money in the boy's hand. "Tell the innkeeper to send me an accounting for the horse and saddle."

"Yes, sir. I mean, yes, Your Grace."

"Now haste."

Drake strode to the barred box that looked to be a one-man jail cell sitting at the rear of the stables.

"Britannia?" he said in a strained whisper, peering into complete darkness.

"Drake?" Gasping, she stood, grasping the iron bars. "I-I, they, he, you—"

"I know." He brandished the ax. "Stand back."

"It's Gibbs. He's taking me to a convict ship. G-g-going to *Australia*!"

"The only place you'll be going is to the north of England. I swear it." With one swing, he smashed the lock from its fastenings.

Drake tossed the ax aside and swept Britannia into his arms. "My God, I was terrified I'd lost you."

"I can't believe you're here."

"Hell would freeze before I'd let you board a convict ship."

"How did you know?"

He cupped her beautiful cheeks between his palms. Warm, delicate cheeks he never wanted to release. But he must. Closing his eyes, he imparted a ferocious but passionate kiss. "Lord and Lady Calthorpe helped me persuade Beaufort to tell us what had happened."

"Beaufort."

"Gibbs is his man."

"But—"

"We'll talk more later." He clutched his arm around her shoulders and started for the stables. "Are you well enough to ride?"

"A horse?"

"Yes."

"I haven't for years, but I'll do anything to—"

"Halt!" bellowed a deep voice from the direction of the inn.

Turning, Drake pulled Britannia behind him. "Gibbs. I might have known you were a light sleeper."

Secure in the scoundrel's hand was a Wogdon and Barton pistol. It had only one shot but was deadly accurate when fired by the right man. And Drake had no illusions about Gibbs. His reputation as a Bow Street Runner alone heralded the man's skill.

"And I might have known you were a fool," said the cur with a smirk.

"I think not." Buying time, Drake guided Britannia backward, edging closer to the barn. "You see, I had a word with Beaufort. He gave you away. Sang like a sparrow and accused you of being a kidnapper." It wasn't the complete truth but was intended to plant doubt in the blackguard's heart.

The former runner smirked. "I'm following orders. That is all."

"You're a liar," Britannia seethed.

Out of the corner of his eye, Drake spotted the stable door. "Oh? If anyone knows the law, it is you, sir. And abducting a woman without cause is absolutely a hangable offense."

Gibbs raised his pistol. "Only if you're still alive."

As the flintlock fired, Drake dove through the gap, pulling Britannia beneath him, shielding her with his body.

She grunted as they hit the ground.

"Are you hurt?" he whispered.

"No."

He looked up to see the boy standing wide-eyed, saddle in hand. Before he drew his pistol, he helped Britannia to her feet. "Take the boy. Hide in the loft."

With no time to help them, Drake led with the barrel, suspecting Gibbs' pistols were a matched pair just like his. "Do you honestly want to pay fealty to a man who would sell you out?"

"Shut your gob." The blackguard's voice was nearer now.

"What do you aim to do once you've killed me?"

"I'm finishing the job. Charlotte's by-blow never should have been born. If it had been up to me, I would have drowned the bitch in Bayeux."

Britannia's gasp came from above.

Swallowing his rage, Drake stepped out. His pistol held secure in his right, he swung the weapon toward the sound of Gibbs' voice.

Nothing.

A twig snapped.

Drake dropped into a crouch.

But not far enough.

As a blast boomed in his ears. Suddenly, his world turned black.

Chapter Twenty-Seven

"Drake!" In a heartbeat, Bria flew down the ladder and dropped to her knees beside him. He wasn't moving. Blood seeped everywhere. She grabbed his shoulders and shook. "Wake up! Please!"

A trickle of blood streamed from his temple while his eyes remained closed.

"No!"

Throwing herself over him, she wrapped him in her arms. "Please. You can't be dead."

"Release the bastard," said Gibbs, moving beside her.

"No," Bria's voice strained as she clung tighter. "I'll never leave his side."

Gibbs grabbed her arm and tugged.

With all her strength, she twisted away. "Let me go!"

"We have a ship to catch." He wrapped his hands around her waist and tore her away from the love of her life.

"Drake! No!" Bria kicked her legs. "Put me down!"

"Glad to," he said, carrying her to the coach.

She thrashed, fighting with all her strength. "You won't get away with this. Too many people know that Ravenscar was after you."

His arms squeezed tighter. "Shut your mouth."

"You'll be hanged. My mother will see to it!"

"If you don't stop talking, I'll shut your mouth for good."
He opened the carriage door and tied her wrists to the bar.
Then he pulled a kerchief from his pocket and gagged her.
"You'd best forget about Ravenscar. Besides, dukes don't
marry by-blow trollops. They tup them and leave them in the
gutter. God's bones, woman. A stage dancer? You might as
well have been a lady of the night."

Tears burned the back of Bria's eyes as she struggled to
twist her arms free. But the hemp rope only cut deeper welts
into her wrists.

As the carriage got underway, Bria strained for a glimpse
at Drake. The boy from the stable was kneeling over the duke
while a man rushed from the inn.

If only she could take care of him. If only Gibbs had
listened.

Was the only man she had ever loved badly injured or was
he dead?

No, no, no, no, no!

The worst thing? She would never know.

***

Well before the carriage came to a halt, odors from the
wharf seeped through the walls. The foulest was that of
rotting fish, followed by filth. Only the wafting overtone of
the sea made the stench bearable.

But Britannia didn't care. One moment she had been the
darling of London with her name in the papers several times
a week. In her haste to save Pauline, Bria had erred and now
she was lost. Overpowered by a tyrant, she'd been bound and
gagged and now she was headed to Australia for fourteen
years transport, accused of a crime she didn't commit.

When the carriage stopped, the smell grew worse. Gibbs
opened the door, untied her hands from the rail and pulled
her outside. Bria pulled down her gag and blinked at the
bright sun hidden by a thin layer of clouds. Right beside
them, a large ship bore the name: *Lloyds*.

"Come on, then," Gibbs said, marching her up the gangway.

The plank's timbers creaked and groaned, making a shiver snake up Bria's spine.

Behind her, Gibbs sniggered. "You'll have a three-month voyage to wallow in the bowels of this cesspool."

A sailor on deck whistled. "Don't tell me we'll 'ave a bit of muslin to keep us company during the long nights of our cruise."

"Aye, a cruise to bleedin' 'ell," another added.

Gulping, Bria kept her gaze downcast. From the arms of a duke into the talons of the bane of society. Could she fall any further?

"Who's this?" asked a man, sounding official. He wore a navy-blue uniform. Behind him stood a stout but well-dressed officer who had gray hair and a double chin.

The captain?

"Miss Britannia LeClair." Gibbs handed over a parcel of documents. "You'll find her transport documentation in order."

The first man frowned and leafed through the papers. "What is her crime?"

"Thievery."

"Lie!" Bria jerked her fists against her bindings. "I've never stolen a thing in my life."

The feminine pitch of her voice hung over the deck like sultry air. All work stopped as every pair of sailor's eyes shifted her way.

The officer knit his brows. "An upper-class accent? She doesn't sound like a thief."

Gibbs pointed to the document. "She stole a necklace from Baroness Calthorpe."

"You told the innkeeper it was Beaufort's. You cannot even manage to keep your story straight." Bria turned to the officer. "Bless it, the miniature was mine! Given to me by Her Ladyship at my birth."

"Likely story. She's been professing her innocence since we left London." Gibbs snorted. "But the Duke of Beaufort has attested to LeClair's guilt."

"A baroness and a duke?" Eyeing her, the officer passed the papers to a younger man dressed in a similar uniform. "You keep lofty company for a convict."

"I haven't been convicted of anything." Bria stamped her foot. "Nor have I received a trial."

"No trial?" asked the man who looked like the captain.

"Ah…" Gibbs stammered, turning red in the face. "His Grace wanted this situation to be dispatched swiftly. It was a matter of security. Utmost confidentiality was needed."

"Beaufort, hmm? I see." With the tenor of an educated man, the captain stepped in and looked Bria from head to toe. "What has been your occupation?"

"I am a dancer for the Paris Opera Ballet. I've been in London performing the role of the Sylph in *La Sylphide*." Understanding the captain as educated, she leaned toward him. "*S'il vous plait, aidez-moi!*"

The man's eyes widened at her request for help.

"If there's nothing else, I'll be on my way," said Gibbs, backing down the gangway.

"How did you come to know the Duke of Beaufort?" the captain asked in a whisper.

"He's my grandfather."

That made the man's wiry eyebrows draw together. "Lieutenant Barrow, let me see Miss LeClair's documents."

"Aye, sir."

The captain studied them more closely than the first officer had. "This is signed by Beaufort himself. If you are his kin, why in God's name is he sending you off for fourteen years transport?"

"Because I've only just discovered that His Grace's daughter is my mother. Merely two, no three days ago, I thought I was a foundling." Bria pursed her lips. She wasn't about to say anything else. Though the captain could put the pieces together, admitting that she was illegitimate would do nothing to help her survive the voyage—if she managed to endure three grueling months at sea.

"Well, your paperwork appears to be in order. Lieutenant, put this *lady* in the cell with the boy." The captain raised his voice and faced the crew. "Any man who raises a finger against Miss LeClair will have said finger severed from his hand. Am I understood?"

"Aye, Captain!" the men shouted, still staring.

"Return to your duties. The *Lloyds* will not sail on its own."

The lieutenant tapped Britannia's arm. "We'll proceed below, miss."

Below. The word made her swoon.

Without the use of her hands, she managed to descend the narrow steps into the dim hold, smelling worse than had anything along the wharf. "It stinks."

"You'll grow accustomed to it. We've no choice but to bring livestock aboard, else we'd all starve."

Presently, starvation seemed like a merciful escape. Drake was gone. Left bleeding in the grass. Who would tend him?

He cannot be dead. I will not believe it.

But there had been so much blood.

No!

A hole the size of a cannon ball stretched her heart.

Fourteen years in Australia? She'd be thirty-three by the time she was given leave to return—well past her prime. She'd never dance again. She'd never marry, never have the family she wanted so badly.

God save her. Bria couldn't care less about the stage or the papers or the applause. If only she could breathe life back into Ravenscar—sit by his sickbed and tell him how much he'd come to mean to her. If only he were taking this voyage with her it might be bearable. Who cared where they lived as long as they had each other?

But nothing and no one would help her escape.

She was doomed to a life in hell.

The lieutenant removed her bindings and nudged her into a small room. Bria's eyes welled with tears as she slid down the wall. She buried her face in her hands while sobs wracked her body. Why did this happen to her? Why was her grandfather so evil? What horrors had she ever committed against him?

Something moved in the far corner. Bria blinked, trying to clear her vision. "Who's there?"

"It's Johnny," the figure said, his voice raspy, but childlike and not yet changed to a man's.

Bria wiped her face. "Are you a convict?"

"Uh huh." The boy didn't sound very sure about it. As her eyes adjusted, she spotted him sitting in the corner, his arms wrapped around lanky knees. His face streaked with dirt, the lad had unkempt sandy-colored hair.

"Tell me, Johnny, how old are you?"

"Nine, I reckon."

"You don't know?"

"I'm pretty sure."

"Where are you from?"

"Here and there. London mostly." He picked his teeth. "You ask a lot of questions."

"Do I?"

"Weigh anchor!" shouted a voice above decks.

"God save us," Bria whispered.

Johnny bit his lip. "What's your crime, miss…ah…"

"LeClair." The ship's timbers groaned as the vessel pitched to the side. Bria braced her hands on the floorboards.

Johnny rolled to his knees and scooted closer. "So, what'd you do?"

"I am innocent."

"Right-o. Me as well…aside from being hungry."

"Hunger is no crime."

"Aye, but the baker saw it different when I pinched a loaf of bread."

"Nine years old and you're being sent to Australia merely for taking bread?"

"I reckon Botany Bay will be better than the foundling home in the long run."

"Oh, my heavens." Her heart twisted into a hundred knots as she let out a sob. "It seems more than one person on this voyage has been wronged."

The boy scooted over the timbers until he sat beside her. "Don't cry, Miss LeClair. Everything will work out in the end."

"How can you say that? How can you be so assured? A foundling at the age of nine sentenced to fourteen years transportation which will doubtlessly include back-breaking hard labor." Yes, Britannia's predicament was precarious and frightful, but what chance at life did this young boy have?

"I got to believe the future will be brighter, else there would be no use thinking at all."

Chapter Twenty-Eight

Aware of a bright light and a pounding headache, Drake groaned. "Stop blinding me with the bloody lamp."

When nothing happened, he drew a hand over his eyes. Until he remembered his purpose. He jolted to sitting, the fast movement making him heave. Fie, he felt like shite. Gripping his hands across his gut, he looked from wall to wall.

Where the blazes am I?

More importantly, where was Britannia?

He staggered out of bed and looked out the window, immediately recognizing the grounds of the inn and stable. Not surprisingly, the carriage was gone. And after he'd been shot, they must have dragged him upstairs. Indeed, his entire body ached as if they'd dragged him.

Quickly, Drake filled the bowl with water and splashed his face which did little to help the throbbing pain in his head. He grabbed a cloth and looked in the mirror. His skull was wrapped with a blood-seeped bandage. Pulling it off, he examined the wound. A deep scrape the length of his little finger cut a channel at the side of his temple. Holy hellfire, had the musket ball hit a fraction of an inch nearer, he'd be dead.

Worse, his beard more than peppered his face. There was two, perhaps three days growth. Drake threw the cloth aside. Dash decorum, he'd take time to shave when Britannia was in his arms.

He shrugged into his coat and loosely tied his neckcloth as he bounded out the door.

At the bottom of the stairs, the boy who'd been chopping wood peeked around a door jamb.

"You there, where's my horse?" Drake demanded.

"In the stable, Your Grace."

"Saddled?"

"I don't think so."

"How long have I been abed in that chamber?"

"They carried you up yesterday morn," the boy said as if it were nearly dark.

Drake pulled his watch out of his pocket and held it to his ear. Blast it all, the damned thing had stopped. "What time is it?"

The boy pointed to a floor clock at the end of the hall. "A quarter past three."

"Three?" He had no time to waste. "Run—see to it my horse is saddled. Where is the innkeeper?"

"Here, Your Grace."

"I demand to know why you were harboring that fugitive, Walter Gibbs."

"Fugitive?"

"He kidnapped the Duke of Beaufort's granddaughter."

"Kidnapped? That doesn't sound like—"

To steady himself, Drake pressed a hand against the wall. To make matters worse, he was as weak as a babe. "You believe the word of a festering pustule like Gibbs over that of a duke?"

"N-no, Your Grace."

"If you see Gibbs again, I want you to report it to the authorities. And say nothing to him. There has been a warrant issued for his arrest."

"But Mr. Gibbs is a Bow Street Runner."

"*Was.* The lout has since left the service and turned to kidnapping innocent ballerinas."

The innkeeper's jaw dropped. "God blind me—the woman was telling the truth."

"Indeed. The only person in this calamity going about spreading lies is Walter Gibbs. And if I hear one word—any rumor whatsoever that you have aided that blackguard, I will personally see that you are led to the gallows and hang beside him."

Drake didn't wait for a reply. He stormed out of the inn and mounted his horse, riding at breakneck speed, praying the *Lloyds* had not yet sailed.

***

Admiral Sir George Cockburn placed his quill in its holder and rose when Drake was introduced. "Your Grace, I am quite taken aback to see you without prior announcement."

"This is a matter of national consequence. I've been told the *Lloyds*, a barque, sailed for Australia yesterday morning."

"Indeed. I was on the pier myself when her sails unfurled."

"We must stop that ship immediately."

"I beg your pardon?"

"A man named Gibbs kidnapped the Duke of Beaufort's granddaughter and falsified convict papers." The harbormaster had confirmed that Britannia had boarded the *Lloyds* as a convict.

Cockburn's jaw slackened with a stare of disbelief. "Why would someone do such a thing?"

"It is a very long story, one that would embarrass several members of the nobility. By removing Miss Britannia LeClair from Britain, the guilty parties schemed to prevent their own ruination." It was as much of the truth as Drake cared to reveal. Baron and Baroness Calthorpe were completely innocent, and he would not tolerate any slight to their names."

"I imagine you are not about to let that happen."

"I will die before I do."

"Hmm. By the look of the gash on your head, it looks as if you nearly did die."

"A near miss by Gibbs himself."

Cockburn rang the bell. "Let me see what I can do to help."

"Thank you, sir."

"Did you know I served under your father in Napoleon's War?"

"I did not." Drake catalogued that piece of information. It might very well be of use.

"Good man he was."

"He was, thank you."

The door opened, and a lieutenant stepped inside. "You rang, sir?"

"I did. The *Lloyds* sailed yesterday destined for Australia."

"Indeed, she did—two and fifty convicts aboard."

"How many women?" Drake asked.

"One—arrived at the last moment."

Drake's knees turned boneless. "Dear God."

"I beg your pardon?" asked the lieutenant.

"The woman was kidnapped," said the admiral. "Do you know where the *Lloyds* will be resupplying?"

"The boatswain told me Jamestown on the isle of Saint Helena, then not again until they reach Botany Bay."

The admiral moved to a globe and pointed to a tiny dot off the coast of Africa. "Saint Helena is a British isle—a favorite respite for most ships before they sail around the horn."

Drake examined the distance between England and the tiny dot off the coast of Angola. "It would take a month of sailing to reach that island."

"Five to six weeks minimum," said the admiral.

After tracing his finger along the globe's arc, Drake turned it, estimating Saint Helena to be just shy of the halfway point. "Can we catch her there?"

"What say you, Lieutenant? What are the fastest ships in the harbor?"

"Well, the *Lloyds* is heavy bodied, though she isn't carrying the cannon of a warship. What would be ideal is a schooner."

"A pirate ship?" asked Drake. "Are there any in the fleet?"

"Not in Portsmouth," said the admiral. "But we did acquire the *HMS Hastings* from the East India Trading Company. She's a cutter."

The lieutenant threw back his shoulders. "But she's a third rate, sir."

Cockburn gave the globe a spin. "No, I should have thought of her sooner. She's the fastest vessel in England."

"Can she make up enough time to meet the *Lloyds* in Jamestown?" Drake asked.

"That depends on the wind."

He didn't have many options, but one thing was for certain. If he didn't act now, he'd be sailing clear to Botany Bay. "When can she be ready to set sail?"

The admiral moved around his table and reached for his quill. "I'll give the order for morning."

"That won't do. Two hours," said Drake. "By order of His Majesty the King, I commandeer the *Hastings* to sail at once."

The lieutenant coughed out a stammer. "B-but she'll need provisions and proper inspections."

"We sail as soon as provisions are aboard." Drake tugged on his gloves. "Make it a priority. This is the Royal Navy. My father fought alongside you, Admiral. Are you not prepared to sail for king and country at a moment's notice?"

Cockburn scrawled out an order. "We shall do our best to weigh anchor before dark." He handed the missive to Drake. "Take this to Captain Schiffer on the *Hastings*. He's one of my best. He'll see to your needs."

"Thank you." Drake bowed and left with the lieutenant. "I have urgent correspondence to dispatch. Where can I find a quill?"

"You may use my writing table, Your Grace."

Drake took a seat, hastily scribing missives to Calthorpe and Perkins. He sealed them with his signet ring bearing the Ravenscar coat of arms and left them in the admiral's care.

***

Bria had thrown up until there was nothing left, but Johnny had borne the worst of it. She cradled the boy's head in her lap as he lay on his side and moaned.

"Make the rocking stop," he whimpered, gripping his arms across his little stomach.

Bria smoothed her hand over his head. "I wish I could. You ought to feel better soon. I did. It is your turn next."

"I don't think I'm ever going to feel well again."

"Close your eyes and try to sleep. You won't feel so ill when you're sleeping."

Johnny gave a nod and snuggled closer. "I'm c-cold."

Bria gave the pile of musty hay a forlorn look. They'd barely survived last night by sleeping together and using her cloak. Johnny's clothes were in tatters, his legs too long for his trousers, and he was nearly bursting out of his moth-eaten coat. The boy didn't even have a pair of shoes.

When Bria was Johnny's age, she had been well looked after by the LeClairs. Sure, she'd struggled after they'd died, but she always had a place to sleep and a dress that fit. And

Monsieur Marchand provided her with dancing slippers and costumes. When she looked at this boy, she realized how blessed her life had been. If she hadn't joined the Paris Opera Ballet, she might have ended up like Johnny.

Before the seasickness had taken hold, he'd told her he'd been found at the foundling home as a toddler—they'd estimated his age between one and two. Worse, the boy's bottom lip had trembled when he'd explained no one had ever come for him.

The door opened. "I'm Mr. Baldy, ye'll be answering to me on this voyage and I don't want no trouble, else ye'll be fed to the sharks." He pushed in a tray laden with broth and bread, then held out a bucket. "Empty yer slops in 'ere."

Bria carefully slipped out from under Johnny's head and picked up the bucket they'd used as a chamber pot. "It's disgusting to bring food at the same time."

"Mayhap next time, I'll just bring around the bucket and let ye starve."

Bria pursed her lips and poured out the contents. "The boy is seasick. Would it be possible to take him above decks for some air?"

"What's this? Do ye think ye're on a pleasure cruise? Jesu on the cross, ye're lucky not to be thrown in the 'old with the other miserable sops. They're wallowing in the bilges with the rats."

Cringing, Bria glanced back to Johnny. "Are the convicts ever allowed to go up top?"

"Not usually. Not unless the captain gives leave."

"Could you please tell the captain the boy is sick? Surely he doesn't want to lose him to the flux."

"Oh, aye. I'll just mosey into his cabin and request a bloody audience. Tell em *'er ladyship* is worried about a wee thief who should 'ave been 'ung in Newgate's yard."

She crossed her arms. "You, sir, are repugnant."

"Re-pug what? Don't be using them accursed words around 'ere. Ye might have been a lady once, but on the *Lloyds*, ye're nothing but a condemned thief. And I'll tell ye true, if it 'adn't been for the captain's orders, 'alf the crew would have already sampled yer wares."

"No!" Johnny hollered from his pallet, trying to push himself up. "Don't bleeding touch 'er."

Mr. Baldy smirked. "The 'arlot and the urchin. What a pair. No wee lad will protect ye if the captain has a change of mind." The sailor chuckled and gabbed his crotch. "And I'll be the first to claim me due."

Bria shut the door in his face, not about to tell him she'd never been a lady. Besides, being locked in a tiny closet below decks was far better than listening to rot from such a vile rapscallion.

The man popped his big nose through the barred viewing panel. "Ye'd best watch yerself, wench."

Before she could answer with a retort, the sailor's footsteps clomped away.

"I won't let him touch you." Johnny curled over. "As long as the sickness doesn't do me in."

"This dratted boat will not get the better of either of us." She resumed her seat, smoothing her hand up and down the child's shoulder. "I swear it."

Chapter Twenty-Nine

After several days of bad weather, Drake stood on deck, looking out over an endless sea. He'd traveled to the Continent, but never had he been on a voyage of such length, nor had he ever desired to do so. And there he stood on the deck of a ship heading for some ungodly place called Jamestown on the isle of Saint Helena, traversing a quarter of the globe while Britannia suffered unconscionable circumstances.

He would never forgive himself if she were to perish. Over and over, he'd replayed the incident with Gibbs. He should have acted more quickly, he shouldn't have worried about the second horse. Damn it, if he had put her on the back of his mount, they could have hastened to the inn in Guildford and summoned help from there.

He pulled Lady Calthorpe's miniature from his pocket. Though there was a likeness, Britannia was prettier. God, he missed her. What horrors must she be enduring on that vile ship? Drake's gut churned at the thought of dastardly tars and how they could mistreat a maid. The tiny dancer was so frail, she was no match for a mob of convicts or rutting sailors, for that matter.

By God, I'll court-martial anyone who raises a hand against her.

His jaw clenched as he looked south, praying for a stronger wind.

The heels of Captain Schiffer's shoes tapped the deck as he moved toward Drake. "Your Grace, it seems the sea suits you. Most passengers unaccustomed to sailing wouldn't have gained their sea legs as of yet."

Drake gave the man a sideways glance. "So that explains the roiling in my gut."

"Well, we did set sail in a nasty squall. Even some of the crew fell ill."

Schiffer obviously knew that Drake had kept to his stateroom for the first few days and his comment about sea legs had been an attempt to be kind.

"Have your men all returned to good health?"

"They have." The captain leaned on the rail. "And you? The fresh air and smooth seas ought to be a welcome respite."

"No respite will be welcomed by me until I find Miss LeClair."

Schiffer pointed to the miniature. "Is that her portrait?"

"It's a rendering of Lady Charlotte, Miss LeClair's mother." To remain ambiguous, Drake used Lady Calthorpe's title before she became a baroness. There could be any number of Lady Charlottes but only one Calthorpe. He held up the painting.

The captain looked closer. "She's lovely."

Drake pocketed the miniature. "Yes, and her daughter is lovelier."

"I understand you left London quite hastily." The captain rubbed his chin. "Your beard is looking a bit primitive. I have a spare kit I could lend you."

"Thank you, but I swore I wouldn't shave until I found Miss LeClair."

"Oh my, you could end up looking quite un-duke-like, if you don't mind me saying, Your Grace."

Drake shrugged, resting his elbows on the rail. "This far from civilization, I doubt it matters."

"Well said." Schiffer, who wore a tidy beard, pulled a compass out of his pocket and gave it a tap. "With the wind in our favor, we ought to be able to make up some time."

"Then I hope it continues for the duration of the voyage."

"One thing about the sea, it never stays the same. No one knows what Mother Nature has in store on the morrow—or even the next hour for that matter."

"Comforting," Drake said, looking up to the crow's nest and wishing he were up there with Buggie the cabin boy who spent his days scouring the seas.

"If I may be so bold to ask, would you tell me about this woman you're after? It does seem rather odd to see a duke drop everything and commandeer a vessel in the king's navy with two hours' notice."

Drake cracked his thumbs. True, he didn't ask the king's leave to chase after Britannia, but this was a time of peace. Besides, if he was questioned upon his return to England, he'd beg forgiveness and that would be the end of it. "You haven't anything better to do?"

"Not at the moment."

May as well tell a good tale.

"Well, I suppose it all started when I contracted *La Sylphide* to premiere at my new theater in London…"

There was really no reason to keep the story under wraps. Most of it a man could uncover just by asking a few questions in London.

"I've heard of Walter Gibbs," said Schiffer after Drake had divulged most of it. "Always thought he'd fall victim to his own skullduggery one day."

Gripping the rail, Drake's knuckles turned white. "It would give me great satisfaction to watch that man swing from the gallows."

"I'd think you'd want to shoot him after giving you that scar."

The gash still throbbed. "A musket ball to the head would be too merciful."

"Perhaps you're right. 'Tis a pity drawing and quartering has been banned."

Drake almost smiled. "I think you and I will get along well on this voyage, providing you ferry me to Saint Helena whilst the *Lloyds* is still anchored in James Bay."

***

Bria had lost track of time. The dim light in the cell didn't change much between day and night, though her eyes had grown accustomed to it.

She drew the letter P through the dust on the floor. "What words start with P?"

Johnny twisted his lips, his face contorted in thought. "Potato, parrot—do you think there might be parrots in Australia?"

"Perhaps. I've seen drawings of Australian birds. They're very colorful compared to European ones."

"I think I'll catch one and train it."

"Good idea. With your confidence, I'll wager you'll have a pet parrot in no time." Bria rubbed out the P. "Now, show me how to spell John." She'd taught him John first to keep it simple.

The boy slowly drew a J and an O. "But why is the next letter an H? I don't hear H when I say it."

"The H is silent." Bria drew the letter for him. "Then which letter makes the nnn sound?"

He sat there tapping his fingers for a moment. Then he hung his head. "I can't remember."

"Not to worry. Letters take time to master." She drew the N. "Now you do it. Write your name below that one ten times."

"Ten?" he moaned, sounding as if she'd just asked him to carry ten buckets of slops from the bilges.

Halfway through Johnny's lesson, Mr. Baldy peered through the viewing panel bars. "Ye lot must be blessed by the water fairies. Captain granted ye a quarter-hour on deck." He held up two pairs of manacles. "But ye 'ave to wear these."

"Even Johnny?" Bria asked. "He's just a child."

The boy gave her a nudge. "I reckon I'd wear a ball 'n chain for a chance to go up top."

Honestly, she felt the same. Her entire body was stiff from lack of exercise.

Irons secure, once they reached the top deck, Mr. Baldy shook his finger under Johnny's nose. "There's water on the timbers and that makes 'em slippery. No running do ye 'ear?"

"Yes, sir."

Blinking to adjust to the painfully bright light, Bria whispered in the lad's ear. "Stay close to me."

"Don't worry, miss." Johnny inclined his head toward the helm. "The captain's on deck. I doubt there'll be any plundering whilst he's watching."

Bria let out a breath. The boy might need a proper education, but his rough beginnings had taught him cunning no one could learn attending lessons. Still, she needed to have a word with the captain, and there was no time like the present.

All across the deck, sailors worked, coiling rope, pushing mops, hauling buckets and dumping them over the side. Every single one of them stopped and leered, though they kept mum for the most part.

A man tossing something rather foul over the rail gave her a scowl. "I can smell ye clear across the deck."

"Surprising," she whispered so few could hear. "The stench from your bucket is so overpowering, I'm surprised you can withstand it."

The man lunged toward her and grabbed her arm, his fingers, vise-like and rough. "I ought to give ye—"

"Mr. Cunnington, unhand the prisoner," said the lieutenant who stood beside the captain on the quarterdeck.

The cur released his grip, giving Bria a glower before sauntering off.

Bria hastened aft. "Captain, if I may have a word."

The lieutenant moved to block the stairs. "Convicts are never given leave to speak to the commander of the ship."

"Very well, Lieutenant, then I shall address you."

Johnny tugged her sleeve. "Sh. Else we'll never be given leave to come up again."

She ignored the boy. "Master John's clothes are so small, he's about to burst the seams. If anyone has castoffs, I'm skilled with a needle and thread and can tailor them to suit."

"You want clothing for the boy?" asked the lieutenant, flabbergasted as if she'd just requested a three-course meal.

"And a blanket. The child needs a blanket."

"Is there anything else, Your Highness?" The lieutenant puffed out his chest while the captain pretended to be preoccupied with the calm seas ahead.

"Niceties would be a basin for washing and a comb, though by your tenor, I am highly suspicious this lowly convict's requests for a child have fallen on deaf ears." There was no time like the present to stand on her own two feet. She didn't have a duke to protect her and never would again.

Mr. Baldy shoved her in the back. "Move on, wench. No one gave ye leave to speak."

Johnny hastened along beside her. "You shouldn't have said anything. Now they'll cut our rations or worse."

But the lad was wrong. The next day, Mr. Baldy presented her with a pair of canvas trousers and shirt for Johnny, needle, thread, a pail containing an inch of clean water, a sliver of soap and a wooden comb.

"Ye'd best wash good," said the sailor. "Captain Sands expects ye in his cabin for supper this eve."

Johnny caught Bria's eye, his face scrunched in a cringe.

Though trepidation clawed at her insides, she needed to put on a brave front for the boy. "Not to worry. I can manage an entire theater filled with hundreds of patrons. I ought to be able to handle one measly ship's captain."

"Aye, but that was afore. Now you're a convict."

"Never you mind." She reached for the shirt. "Put this on. I'll make a few tucks and it will be like new."

Chapter Thirty

Bria followed Mr. Baldy to the captain's cabin, trying to convince herself to be optimistic. What motives could the man have for requesting an audience? Perhaps he wanted to converse in French. Perhaps he wanted her to thank him for the soap and the clothes for Johnny. She'd sewn all day and her fingertips were rough, but the boy now had trousers and a shirt with a bit of growing room.

Regardless of soap or clothes or any comfort the captain might provide, Bria was bereft with worry. The only thing that had kept her sane throughout the endless days was Johnny. And when she wasn't helping the boy, Drake consumed her every thought. And by God, she would do anything to be in his arms again.

There was no escape from the hold. Even if she could overpower Mr. Baldy, she'd fall into the hands of abhorrent sailors, most of whom looked at her as if she were a prostitute, waiting for their chance to spirit her into the shadows and have their way with her. At sea in the middle of the ocean, she couldn't run, hide or beg for mercy.

Why must her life always be one battle after another? She'd been lost and alone after the death of the LeClairs. In Paris, with nowhere to go, she thought she'd hit the lowest of lows. But she'd been wrong. The voyage to Australia took three months, and it had only begun. She shuddered. What if something happened to the captain and she no longer had his protection? Things might grow worse—oh so very much worse.

If only Bria could convince the captain to turn the ship around and head back to England. But that was as likely as the Duke of Beaufort embracing her as his long-lost granddaughter.

Mr. Baldy opened the door at the end of the corridor. "Her Ladyship…ah, Miss LeClair, sir."

"Ah, yes. Show her in."

Bria stepped inside cautiously. The captain of a convict ship did very well for himself. Her gaze was first drawn to the arcing row of windows overlooking the ship's stern, each one framed with red velvet curtains. The cabin was paneled in teakwood with a small library, a berth, an elegant writing table and chair, and in the center of the room stood an ornate dining table. That it was set for two didn't escape Bria's notice.

She startled when the door shut behind her.

"How has the voyage been thus far? Has Mr. Baldy been treating you fairly?" asked Captain Sands with a wry smile, as if he knew conditions below decks were deplorable yet expected her to offer a respectful reply.

Not about to mince words, Bria stood proudly as if she weren't still wearing the costume of the Sylph, covered only by her muddied cloak. "Mr. Baldy is a vile scourge."

"I'll admit it isn't easy recruiting sailors to man a convict ship heading for Australia. Unfortunately, the crown doesn't see fit to offer wages high enough to entice the cream of the crop."

"Clearly not."

Standing not much taller than she, Sands gestured toward the table with stout, pudgy fingers. "Will you sit? Cook has prepared a fine meal for us."

"A fine meal? I should like to take a parcel below for Johnny. He needs sustenance more than I."

The captain held the chair. "You've grown fond of the boy, have you?"

"He's a lost child." Before sitting, Bria glanced toward the door. Nothing felt right about being in the captain's cabin with the table set for two. Though, only four months ago she'd done the same in Ravenscar's town house and that hadn't turned out badly. Perhaps if she remained vigilant, she might win the captain's favor. "Any boy Johnny's age should be attending lessons and flying kites, not fearing for his life in the bowels of a convict ship."

"You're quite opinionated, are you not?"

"A woman in my position must be forthright." She reached for the serviette, unfolded it and placed it in her lap. "Please allow me to share my meal with the child."

"I suppose there's no reason you couldn't slip him a few morsels. If…" Giving her a licentious glance, the captain's winged eyebrows shot up. He wrapped his thick and hairy fingers around a squat bottle of wine and poured, first for Bria then for himself.

Her stomach roiled as she picked up her glass and sipped, trying not to imagine the captain's vile conditions.

Sands followed suit. "It's not customary for me to invite convicts to my cabin let alone to dine."

"But I haven't been convicted of anything."

The captain swirled the liquid in his glass. "Your paperwork is in order, and it claims you are a thief."

"I stole nothing."

"Oddly, I believe you."

"Oh?" Could she hope? "What drew you to your conclusion?"

"Firstly, Mr. Gibbs' admission that you had no trial made me suspicious. Your situation stinks of underhandedness.

And then there was your reaction when he said you were accused of stealing."

"I see." Is this why she'd been put in a solitary cell with Johnny and not in the hold? By the way the captain's beady eyes shifted, the sheen of sweat on his brow, the way his tongue repeatedly licked his bottom lip, no matter how much she wanted to believe a captain of a convict ship might be her salvation, Bria questioned his benevolence.

"Many prisoners profess their innocence, but you clearly had no idea the extent of the charges laid upon you. Furthermore, Gibbs looked the guilty party as he slithered off my ship."

"If you deduced all that, why did you not send me ashore? You could have handed me over to the magistrate and allowed me to plead my case." *And try to escape.* Hasten back to Drake's side—sit at his bedside and tend his every need.

Bria reached for a slice of bread and picked up a knife. Rather than helping herself to the butter, she closed her eyes and pictured those fleeting moments for the thousandth time. Laying in the dirt, his eyes had been closed. When the LeClairs had died, their eyes were open, haunting and staring at nothing. As she looked toward the windows, her heart leaped. Heaven help her, Drake was alive. She felt it in her very bones.

Oh, God please let it be so.

"You seem contemplative."

She blinked and set to buttering the bread. "Just thinking about the events that brought me to this end."

The man rested his hand on her wrist. "I've been wondering about that myself. How does a ballerina from Paris, playing the starring role at one of London's grandest theaters end up being accused of stealing a necklace from an English duke whom she professes to be her grandfather?"

Trying not to cringe, Bria snapped her arm away. "When you put it that way, it does seem a bit convoluted."

A sailor entered with a tray. After weeks of eating broth and bread, the scent made her salivate. He presented her with a pair of tongs. "Chicken and cabbage, miss?"

She gave the captain a wary glance. No, she didn't want to dine with him, but she wouldn't turn down a chance to regain her strength and take a few morsels for Johnny. "Thank you."

The captain sat back while the sailor filled his plate and didn't say a word until the tar left. "When you boarded my ship, you said the duke's daughter gave you the necklace when you were born."

"She did."

"Why, may I ask?"

"So that I would remember her."

"Is that how you ended up in France?"

"Yes."

"I'm beginning to see."

"Are you? Because I have no intention of dragging my mother's good reputation through the mire."

"Mayhap that isn't your intent, but I'm guessing the Duke of Beaufort does not see it that way."

She shoved a bite of chicken into her mouth and almost moaned aloud. "Most likely not. He's never had a kind word to say about me."

"And now you find yourself on a voyage that will take you to hell. I read the *Gazette*. One moment you were the darling of London premiering in a Paris ballet, and now you have been reduced to the lowliest, most reprehensible of humanity."

She gulped down a swallow of wine. "It appears so."

"But I can help you."

"You would do that?" She wasn't exactly sure she wanted to hear more.

"If you agree to help me."

Bria could only imagine the captain's terms. And he had no idea how much she needed to return to London. Where was Drake now? How grave were his wounds? "I'm listening."

"When we arrive in Botany Bay, I have a great many contacts. I can ensure you are placed well."

She opened her napkin and placed a slice of bread on it for Johnny. "I have no intention of staying in Australia."

"Perhaps not, but first you must survive this voyage, and then survive Australia. I can help you with both of those things."

Nipping a leg of chicken, she set it atop the bread. "And what do you expect in return for your generosity?"

Sitting back, Sands smoothed his hands up and down his doublet. "You see, a man grows lonely during a three-month stint at sea." He paused, his tongue nervously sliding across his lower lip while his words hung in the air like a death knoll.

While her stomach turned sour, she'd expected his indecency. The clothes, the soap and water, the blanket, dining with the captain—it was all meant to show her how nice things might be for her on this voyage. Furthermore, he'd tried to trick her into thinking he was kind by providing kindnesses for Johnny as well.

But at what cost?

When Drake had been left bleeding somewhere between London and Portsmouth?

She set her fork aside. "And if I refuse?"

"You'll receive the standard convict fare." He picked at his teeth with his fingernail. "*If* you survive the crossing, you won't see the light of day again until we arrive at Botany Bay. And I imagine a woman as lovely as you won't last long among the ruffians there. 'Tis a different world in Australia. A man's world."

Bria took another drink of wine to wash down her revulsion. What would become of her once they reached

Botany Bay? "What about Johnny? Would you see him well settled once we arrive?"

Sands pulled something ungodly from his mouth and wiped his finger on the tablecloth. "The child is a foundling."

"So was I, at least I thought myself to be at one time."

The ship groaned and shuddered a bit, shifting Sand's attention for a moment, but not long enough. His gaze returned and meandered to her breasts, thankfully concealed beneath her cloak. "You have little ground on which to negotiate."

Bria crossed one arm over her chest. From what she understood, she was the only female aboard ship—which gave her a great deal more room to negotiate than he'd insinuated—though the thought of using her body to purchase protection was abhorrent. So, Sands' kindness didn't come without a price. The problem was she'd rather jump overboard than submit.

"Must you have my answer now?"

"If not now, by morning."

She hadn't yet played her final card. Though Bria preferred not to use it at this juncture, not knowing when she'd see Drake again, if ever. Not knowing how grave his injuries were. Not knowing if he survived them, she didn't have many options. Somehow, she had to find a way back to England. Was the price worth her dignity? Was it worth putting her relationship with Drake in jeopardy? Worth the risk of conceiving a child? Could she live with herself if she gave in to the captain's demands?

"You're a player," he said as if he knew what she was thinking. "Everyone knows women who join the theater are borne of easy virtue."

"Not everyone." Bria took one more piece of chicken and wrapped up the serviette. "Are you familiar with the Duke of Ravenscar?"

"Any Englishman knows of him. Not only is he in line to the throne, he's the man who footed the bill for Chadwick Theater."

"He is." She tied the ends and slipped the food in her pocket for Johnny.

The man leaned back in his chair with a sly grin. "Ah, so you've sampled the hospitality of a duke?"

"He is my greatest patron. If you help me gain passage back to England, there will be a reward in it. A *sizeable* reward."

Sands stood and moved behind her, running his thick fingers along the curve of her neck. "My, my, how you've been misled. I'd be more likely to believe Ravenscar colluded with Beaufort to send you to Australia." He chuckled. "You had a bit of a *tête-à-tête* with His Grace, and now you've been sent away, cast aside, so to speak."

Bria's skin burned hot. How dare he insinuate the love between she and Drake was sordid? "As a matter of fact, he attempted to rescue me...until Gibbs shot him."

"Shot? You story grows more preposterous by the moment." Removing his hands, the captain moved toward the windows and gazed into the darkness. "Is Ravenscar still breathing?"

"He is, and I have no doubt he will be coming after me. As soon...as soon as he is able."

"Where was he shot? It's not uncommon for a man to succumb to a lead ball lodged in his flesh."

"Does it matter?" she hedged. "I'm telling you there will be a reward for anyone who helps me return to England and I'm asking for your help."

"You're trying to sidetrack me."

The ship lurched, making the glasses teeter.

"Captain!" The lieutenant burst through the door. "A warship is in sight and gaining."

Chapter Thirty-One

Thank God for the young spotter in the crow's nest. Buggie spent every daylight hour up the mast with his spyglass, so high in the air Drake had no idea how the lad managed to maintain his relentless vigil without suffering vertigo.

But once the boy spotted the heavy barque, it took no time to set a course directly for the *Lloyds* and flag her with an order heave to. Spun tighter than a noose's knot, Drake paced the deck while both ships underwent the process of being tied together with a plank spanning the gap between them.

He followed Captain Schiffer across. Waves slapped the hulls while the two vessels rocked, making the footing precarious at best. Drake glanced down once, his stomach flying to his throat. One misstep and he'd be at the mercy of the eddies below.

Once across, he took note of the convict ship's crew while the two captains exchanged pleasantries. The bedraggled men looked as if they all belonged in irons. *This lot of miscreants has Britannia locked away?* Behind his back, he cracked his knuckles and leveled his stare at the miserable welcoming party just as Schiffer gestured Drake's way.

"Allow me to introduce His Grace the Duke of Ravenscar."

Captain Sands' eyes widened for a moment. The look contained more than respectful regard for Drake's rank. The man knew something, harbored something. Sands bowed. "What would bring a duke out to the middle of the Atlantic, chasing a ship laden with convicts?"

So, the dastardly captain opted to play his cards close to his chest? Drake eyed him. "I'm guessing you already know the answer."

The man licked his lips while a trickle of sweat bled from his brow.

"But to allay all doubt, a ballerina named Britannia LeClair was kidnapped from my theater on the night of August 17th. Acting swiftly, I made inquiries and traced her to a remote inn just south of Guildford. There, I attempted to stage a rescue when her kidnapper, a Mr. Walter Gibbs, shot me, grazing my temple." Drake removed his hat and turned his head, showing the newly-formed scar.

The captain leaned in with a squint. "Good Lord, 'tis a miracle you survived."

"The shot rendered me unconscious for a time. When I came to, I rode straight for Portsmouth, but the *Lloyds* had already sailed."

"And Admiral Cockburn assigned my ship, the fastest in the fleet to hasten after you." Clearing his throat, Schiffer unrolled the missive with the orders scribed by the admiral. "By order of His Majesty the King, you are herby required to release the prisoner, Britannia LeClair, into the custody of the Duke of Ravenscar."

Drake entrusted his hat into the hands of one of the officers from the *Hastings*. "Please lead me to the lady's berth at once."

"Below decks is no place for a man of your station, Your Grace." Sands gestured to the quarterdeck stairs. "I bid you remain at the helm with me whilst my man fetches the lass for you."

"I will not be mollycoddled. And Miss LeClair had best be in good health."

"I assure you she is fine. In fact, she dined with me this very eve."

"Do you make it a habit to take the evening meal with convicted criminals?" asked Schiffer.

"N-n-no. But Miss LeClair seemed an unusual case. When her jailor—ah Mr. Gibbs—brought her aboard, she insisted she had received no proper trial."

Drake's fingernails bit into his clenched fists. "Good God. It took you a fortnight to ask her what had happened?"

"I—"

"Enough. Lead the way, sir, and pray I do not find anything amiss."

The stench of excrement and filth wafted from below as they approached the stairs. Drake swallowed his gag reflex and ignored the urge to cover his face with a kerchief. If Britannia was suffering these conditions, he would not allow her to see him repulsed.

On the second level, they stopped outside a door. Something scurried on the other side.

"Mr. Baldy, unlock the door," commanded Sands.

A man with a full head of hair and a pock-scarred face sauntered forward with a fist full of clanking keys and held up a lantern as the door swung open.

Britannia stood in the center of a tiny room, shielding a child who was peering from behind her cloak. Chin held high, she threw her shoulders back as if she were the last defense between her and a crowned prince. "You told me you would allow me until the morrow to make a decision!"

Sands took a cowering step back.

After giving the captain a scowl, Drake moved into the light. "Britannia."

"Drake?" She drew her hands over her mouth, stepped forward, then back again, her eyes brimming with tears. "Your Grace. I-I…you're alive!"

Drake turned to the others. "Leave us. I require a moment alone with Miss LeClair."

Tears streamed down her face as they waited for the men to go up top. And then he opened his arms. "My love, I cannot believe we found you."

"I am astounded to see you here. They accused me of stealing my miniature—that was my crime—thieving a picture that has belonged to me since my birth."

"I know, my darling. But I'm here to take you home now."

"At the inn—I was terrified. There was so much blood, and then Mr. Gibbs refused to let me see to your wounds. A-a-a-and I thought you might be deaaaaaad."

Britannia's body shook as she sobbed into his shoulder. Drake, too, couldn't help the tears welling in his eyes as he clutched her tight to his body. At long last, he could protect his ballerina from harm for the rest of his days. "I'm never letting you go. I love you. I've loved you since the first time I laid eyes on you when you were but a silhouette performing in your traveling clothes."

"I-I-I." So overcome with emotion, the dear woman couldn't manage to utter a comprehensible word. But she needn't say anything. Drake's soul brimmed with love, enough for the both of them.

"Excuse me, sir," said a tiny voice, accompanied by a tug on Drake's overcoat.

Trying to catch her breath, Bria wiped her face on her sleeve and turned toward the child. "J-Johnny. This is the D-duke of Ravenscar, you call him Your Grace, not sir."

The boy's bottom lip quivered. "Are you taking Bria away from me, Your Grace?"

"No!" She dropped to her knees and wrapped her arms around the child. "You must come with us. I will take care of you, I promise."

Drake looked between the two. "Britannia?"

She stood, taking the boy by the hand. "This is Johnny. He is a foundling and he was sentenced to fourteen years transportation for stealing a loaf of bread merely because he was hungry."

"Christ."

"Please. I cannot leave him behind."

"Of course not." Drake looked at the lad's eyes. Hell, his damned heart twisted. Who could resist eyes of the innocent and angelic? "Perhaps Mr. Schiffer can find him a position on the *HMS Hastings*."

Bria pursed her lips and gave a nod, clearly not in favor of the cabin boy idea. "As long as we can take him off the ship, you and I can discuss his future after."

"Can I discuss it, too?" asked Johnny. "I reckon I might be interested in my future."

The boy had gumption for a tike no higher than Drake's waist. "Come. I'll have the crew aboard the *Hastings* draw baths for you both."

"Must I have a bath?"

"Yes." Britannia took the boy's hand and followed Drake to the main deck.

"There was nothing in the order that mentioned the boy," said Captain Sands.

It didn't surprise Drake to come up against resistance. "Do you often ferry small children to penal colonies?"

"If their crimes warrant it. I'm no judge, I merely provide transport."

"Merely is a good descriptor, though I might have chosen barely."

Sands jowls shook with his snort. "Nonetheless, I am duty bound to see that boy is delivered to Botany Bay."

"What if he were to die en route?" asked Drake.

"Then I'm out ten quid."

"Merely ten pounds? For a human being?"

"For transporting a criminal over the high seas and delivering them to the governor in Australia."

"I'll pay the boy's fee."

"But what will I tell the governor?"

"I'll double Johnny's bounty and you can tell the governor what you like." Drake signaled to Captain Schiffer. "Shall we sail home to England, sir? We need passage clear to Robin Hood's Bay, mind you. The detour shouldn't be a bother. After all, you're no longer facing the challenge of sailing to Australia and back."

***

On the *Hastings*, Bria enjoyed the freedom of a small cabin with a narrow bed, a table and a chair, a chest and a mirror on the wall. The captain's valet had brought in a wooden tub for her bath though it was only filled with a few inches of water—a precious commodity on a ship. She didn't mind. The valet had also given her a bar of soap scented with lemongrass.

Though a tad cramped in the tub, Bria was in heaven. She drew the soap to her nose and inhaled, clearing the stench from the *Lloyds* from her nostrils. The past weeks of terror melted away as she relaxed. No, she wouldn't soon forget her ordeal, but the shock of her abduction and the horrors that followed paled in comparison to the thrill of seeing Drake alive and in her arms. He'd wielded his power and took command of a navy ship and sailed to her rescue. She still couldn't believe he'd found the *Lloyds* in the middle of the sea.

Britannia loved Ravenscar—the duke—Drake—the man. He came for her. He fought for her. He loved her. If only they could spend the rest of their days together. But doing so would only bring them more misfortune and Bria could never burden the man she loved with Beaufort's threats or with the scandal of her birth. Too much adversity prevented her from remaining in England. Yes, they were sailing to Peak Castle, but she wouldn't stay—doing so would be inordinately selfish and she couldn't risk putting Drake in danger any longer. For the love of God, he'd been shot—nearly killed.

How could she let such a thing happen again? Her only option was to take Johnny back to France. They'd be safe there. And the boy was young enough to earn a place at the Paris Opera Ballet School.

But until she had to go, Bria intended to savor every moment with His Grace.

The door cracked open. "May I have a word?" asked the man who consumed her thoughts.

"Ack!" Crossing her arms over her chest, Bria sank lower in the tub. "I'm bathing."

"I promise to keep my eyes averted."

"What if one of the sailors or Johnny—?"

Drake stepped inside. Closing the door behind him, he looked at her with the intensity of a man starved. "Forgive me. I could stay away no longer."

A flutter of yearning spread low in her belly. Oh, how she loved this man. And he grew more handsome every time she saw him. "Is Johnny settled?"

"He's fit right in. The lad is exploring with Captain Schiffer's cabin boy. Buggie is twelve and Johnny is following him like an enamored puppy."

"After his ordeal on the *Lloyds*, the lad deserves to have some fun. He's such a sweet child. I cannot bear to think of how difficult things have been for him."

Drake sauntered forward, making her ache for him all the more. "Not unlike your beginnings, I imagine."

"Far worse. You forget I lived in relative comfort until the age of fourteen." A slow grin spread across Bria's lips as her gaze slowly meandered up his body. "Your beard combined with your scar makes you look dangerous."

The corner of his mouth ticked up. "You reckon? I think I look like a pirate."

"I like it."

He stroked his fingers along his jawline. "It is not exactly the fashion, but I swore I wouldn't shave until I found you. It served as an ever-present reminder of my purpose."

"You did?" Her heart twisted. It ached, melted, and pined. Oh, how she'd missed the intensity of his stare—blue eyes that, had she not been sitting, would have made her grow weak at the knees. "For me?"

"Only and always for you, my darling."

He sat beside the tub. "I wish I could join you."

"Scandalous."

Leaning forward, he pretended to peek around her crossed arms. "A scandal worth exploiting." He grinned as he reached down and grasped the sponge. "Allow me to wash your hair, my lady."

Relenting, she fished for the soap and handed it to him. "You are shameless."

"When it comes to you I have no shame. Now lean forward."

Bria covered her face with her palms while Drake sopped up water with the sponge and drizzled it over her head. "Have I ever told you how much I adore your hair?"

"Just my hair?"

Gentle but strong fingers began massaging the soap into her scalp. "It is only the icing on the cake."

"Sweet cake?"

"The sweetest."

He helped her rinse, then swirled the sponge around her back. "Britannia, you must know how much I love you."

"I do. I love you as well but—"

"I want to marry you."

Curving her back, she drew her hand over her mouth. If only it could be so. If only rules and society were different. "But you cannot."

"What say you? I can marry whomever I please."

"Aren't dukes supposed to marry highborn women from reputable families?"

"Theoretically, yes. But Moses brought no tablets down from Mount Sinai commanding all dukes to marry daughters of peers and gentlemen. Besides, you are the daughter of a British monarch and a baroness."

"An illegitimate daughter, mind you."

"So, who gives a fig?"

"The whole of London society."

"Oh, just them."

"Aren't you worried? Won't you be ostracized?"

"The British aristocracy places far too much importance on how things look." Drake swirled warm fingers across her back. "Will people gossip? Yes. Will the papers have their heyday? Yes."

Bria closed her eyes and leaned into his touch. "But what about Chadwick Theater? Won't ticket sales plunge?"

"Possibly." He kissed her temple. "But people will not be able to stay away from talent. And I have every intention of continuing the success of our first Season."

"With ballet?"

"And opera." Drake grinned irresistibly, while his tongue tapped the corner of his mouth, his eyes growing dark and seductive. "But I don't want to talk about the theater right now. I want you to agree to be my wife." Grinning irresistibly, his kisses nibbled from her ear to her neck and finally around to her mouth.

As their lips met, her heart broke. Drake had so many lovely dreams, but he was forgetting one critical factor. "I want to marry you more than anything, but…"

"But?"

"How easily you forget I was kidnapped, falsely charged and shipped to Australia by my own grandfather. What might he try next? Not only am I not safe, I fear for your life as well."

"Believe me, your grandfather will never again come near you. I don't care if I have to make an appeal to the crown, he has behaved despicably and without cause."

"All to protect the honor of his family name."

"He is a deceitful prig. And his henchman is worse. I intend to have Gibbs brought up on charges."

"Do you think he will be convicted?"

"There is enough evidence against him." Cupping his hands on her cheeks, Drake kissed her again, slowly, seductively. "Agree to marry me right here and now. I'll die if you go back to France"

Right there. Soaking wet without a stitch of clothing on her body, he rendered her powerless to resist. "One more thing," she whispered, all thoughts of France vanishing.

"Anything."

"You won't like it."

"How do you know unless you ask?"

"Very well. I want to take Johnny as my ward. I have a little money now. I can see to his education and ensure he grows up to be a fine man—not a thief."

His smile grew warm and filled with love. "You have really grown attached to the lad, have you not?"

"I feel it is my duty to protect him."

Drake let out a long breath. "Then I must have a condition of my own."

"Yes?"

"That Johnny must become a ward of us both. Once a woman marries, by English law, her ward becomes her husband's ward."

Bria threw her arms around his neck. "Oh Drake, I love you more with each passing day."

"Then we have only one more thing to settle."

"And what would that be?"

"Do you want to have a scandalous elopement and wed aboard the *Hastings*, or shall we wait and marry in the chapel at the castle?"

Chapter Thirty-Two

Drake wasted no time making the wedding arrangements with Captain Schiffer. Thank heavens. If Bria had to spend one more night without being in his arms, she'd burst.

She stood in front of the looking glass and pressed her hands to her stomach. There she stood, about to marry a duke with only her ratty old costume to wear, not to mention the skirts were scandalously short. One of the sailors had come up with a handful of hairpins, so at least her hair was tidy. She had no rouge or face powder, nothing to improve her appearance.

And yet, when she'd argued all these points, Drake repeated three words: "I don't care".

"Bria!" Johnny burst through the door and charged inside with Buggie, the cabin boy on his heels. "Look what we have for your wedding."

No matter how excited and adorable the child appeared, as his guardian, she mustn't abide his audacity—not to mention hauling a friend into a future duchess' cabin without so much as a knock. "I beg your pardon, but before you show me one single thing, I insist you go out to the corridor and knock. A young man never bursts into a lady's or anyone's chamber without first requesting permission."

"But—"

Bria thrust her finger toward the door. "Do it, I say."

Johnny rolled his eyes at the older boy. "Bleeding hell."

"And without the colorful language," she added before they skulked away, shutting the door behind them.

An impatient rap sounded. "May we please come in, milady?" asked Johnny, followed by a considerable amount of giggling.

"May we come in, your worship?" Buggie barely contained his laughter while his voice resounded through the timbers. The troublemaker.

"Your magnificence," the younger miscreant chortled.

"Oh, please." But Bria had asked for their sauciness. She cleared her throat. "Enter."

Again, the door burst open. "Buggie told me one of the sailors makes flowers out of paper." Johnny thrust his arms forward with an enormous grin. He held at least a dozen paper roses that looked as if they'd been made from castoff letters. "Now you'll have a posy to hold for your wedding."

Bria took one and held it up. It really was a work of art and if not for the ink, the flower would have looked like a real rose. "These are splendid."

"I knew you'd like them."

"I do. Very much."

The boy grinned as if it were Christmas morn. Then he nudged Buggie. "Go on. 'Tis your turn."

The older lad shoved a bundle of lacy cloth into Johnny's hands. "You do it. I'm not accustomed to speaking to girls."

"All right then." Giving Bria a bow, the lad held up the lace. "This is the captain's tablecloth. He said you could use it for a veil."

"It's good as new," added Buggie. "And no one will be the wiser."

"Why, thank you." Bria imagined gravy stains accompanied by a spot of red wine or two, but she shook out the cloth, grateful to have something to cover her costume. "You're right, it looks new."

"You'll have to give it back after the ceremony," said Buggie. "The captain needs it on account he is hosting the wedding feast in his cabin."

"I don't mind. Thank you for being so very thoughtful." Swinging the cloth around her head and shoulders, Bria performed a *pirouette*. "A bride always wears something borrowed when she's married. This is perfect, and I doubt anyone will know it is really a tablecloth."

Johnny beamed. "I think it's beautiful."

***

How did she manage it?

Drake expected to see the love of his life appear on deck dressed like the Sylph. But she'd found some ivory lace and had it wrapped around her head and shoulders like a shawl. Smiling, her face pure and radiant, no other woman had ever looked as beautiful.

In her hands she carried roses. Paper roses, but they looked so real, he could practically smell them. Johnny strutted beside her protectively as if he might kick anyone in the shin if they tried to touch the bride. "I'm giving her away."

Drake patted the boy's sandy curls, which were almost clean now he'd had a bath. "You're doing a fine job. Thank you." But he didn't linger long on the lad. Today was Britannia's day and he wanted to shower her with adoration. "You look stunning."

She smiled. "Delicious, perhaps?"

"Delicious, stupendous, wonderous, divine…"

"I suggested delicious because I'm festooned with a tablecloth."

He stifled a laugh. "No woman hath ever put mere drapery to so good a use."

"I'm glad you approve. Though I must say the groom is far better clad than the bride."

"I have nothing but my theater attire from that fateful night and a spare shirt I borrowed in Portsmouth. But I would marry you no matter what you chose to wear."

Her gaze slid to his chin. "You shaved."

"Only for you, my love."

"Shall we begin?" asked the captain, holding the Common Book of Prayers.

Drake gave the man a nod. "Please."

"Dearly beloved…"

He barely heard another word. As Captain Schiffer droned on about the sanctity of holy matrimony, Drake stared into the whisky eyes he'd grown to love, the pert lips he was dying to kiss, the radiant smile of a woman who would be his for the rest of their lives.

"Drake Alexander Thomas Chadwick, wilt thou have this woman to be thy wedded wife, to live together after God's ordinance in the holy estate of matrimony? Wilt thou love her, comfort her, honor, and keep her in sickness and health; and, forsaking all others, keep thee only unto her, so long as you both shall live?"

When Bria's expression became inquisitive, Drake realized a response was necessary. "I will," he croaked.

"Britannia LeClair, wilt though have this man to be thy wedded husband, to live together after God's ordinance in the holy estate of matrimony? Wilt thou obey him, and serve him, love, honor and keep him in sickness and in health; and, forsaking all other keep thee only unto him, so long as you both shall live?

"I will," she said as if no one on earth possessed the power to change her mind.

The captain looked across the crowd of sailors. "Who giveth this woman to be married to this man?"

"That's me, Johnny. I don't have no surname. But I give her in holy man-a-mony all the same."

Drake chuckled and gave the boy a wink.

"Sorry," Britannia whispered.

"Not at all. He's perfect."

"You're perfect."

"May I continue?" asked the captain with a sober frown.

Johnny gave the bride a very inappropriate nudge. "There's more?"

"Yes, and now you must go stand by Buggie."

Drake pulled upon all his ducal training and swallowed a laugh. There he stood, seventh in line to the throne, eloping with the love of his life who was wearing a tablecloth, who happened to be of questionable birth, given away by a foundling who had been convicted of thievery and sentenced to fourteen years transport.

And I couldn't be happier.

The rest of the ceremony continued without further incident and, when it came time to place a ring on Bria's finger, Drake removed the unicorn signet. "With this ring I thee wed, with my body I thee worship, and with all my worldly goods I thee endow…"

Britannia gasped as he slid the ring onto her finger. "Your seal?"

He bent down and whispered into her ear. "Until I find a proper jeweler."

"Without ado, I pronounce you man and wife!" The captain closed his prayer book. "Open a barrel of rum for the crew. Two drams per man, mind you. I'll tolerate no drunkenness aboard His Majesty's ship."

As the *Hasting's* deck erupted into mayhem, Drake drew Britannia into his arms. "You have made me the happiest man in Christendom."

"And me the happiest woman."

The noise from the celebration ebbed as he lowered his chin and kissed her. "There will be far more kissing in our cabin this eve."

"Must we wait?"

"The captain has a feast planned with the officers, otherwise, I'd make our excuses."

"Oh, yes." She removed her veil. "He needs this back for the table."

Chapter Thirty-Three

A few hours later, Drake closed the cabin door and faced her. Bria's breath quivered with anticipation as he stepped forward and grasped her hands. "You are a duchess now."

"I am?"

His hands slid around her, enveloped her. "You are my duchess and I will have no other."

"I cannot believe it."

"I cannot believe I found you without sailing all the way to Australia."

"I'm so glad you did. Captain Sands tried to…"

"Did he force you?"

"No. He gave me an ultimatum—used Johnny against me, but you came before I had to make a decision."

"Thank God."

She smoothed her hands up the front of his chest before her fingers slipped around him. "I never want to be separated from you again."

Melting into his arms, she closed her eyes and savored him. And when he captured her mouth, she went boneless, scarcely able to support her weight.

With one hand pressed into the small of her back, Drake supported her while he slipped the gossamer gown from her shoulders and let it to drop to the floor. "Are you warm enough?"

Hardly aware of her surroundings, she smiled at him. "Your warmth is plenty for the both of us."

He sucked in a sharp inhale and unlaced her stays. "I want to see you bare."

Bria shuddered. It seemed like an eternity since she'd last lain with this man who'd stolen her heart. So many times when she'd lain in the dark cell below decks, she'd ached to be with him, ached to join with him as God intended a man and a woman to share passion. She wanted Drake Chadwick to hold her in his arms forever and make love to her like she was the only woman in the world.

The insides of her thighs quivered while the scant pieces of her clothing dropped to the floor. When all that remained were her threadbare stockings and garters, he grinned, slowly lowering himself to his knees. "This is my favorite part."

She threaded her fingers through his thick, black hair. "And why is that, Your Grace?"

He brushed his thumb through the triangle of curls at her apex. "Because the most intoxicating scent in all the world is hidden inside this treasure." He tugged one garter bow. "And I can sample the fragrance whilst I unmask the most perfect, most shapely legs I've ever seen in all my days."

Bria reached for him but caught her fingers and kissed them. "One more garter, my love."

When she was completely naked, he took her hands, rose, and stepped back. How erotic it felt to be completely bare while he was still clothed. Drake's gaze raked along her body. She shivered when his lips parted, his eyes grew dark and the big duke gasped.

With a sultry chuckle, she stepped into him and smoothed her hands down his lapels. "You've made love to me with your eyes, now I want to feel the flesh of my husband take me to the stars."

A devilish chuckle rumbled from deep in his chest. "Ask and ye shall receive."

In less than half a minute, shoes, doublet, waistcoat, neckcloth, shirt, breeches, hose and drawers all dropped into a heap.

Bria's hips swayed as she stepped into him, running her fingers through the downy soft hair on his chest. Good glory, he defined male perfection. "And men like you think they need a valet."

"A valet is a requisite for any gentleman." He pulled her into his arms, running kisses along her neck. "But I have far more important things on my mind, Wife."

All of him pressed into her flesh, igniting a ravening fire deep inside her. Unable to resist touching him, Bria slipped both hands over his velvety soft skin, swirling her fingers down the dark trail of hair running from his navel to the tight curls above his swollen manhood.

But she didn't touch it—not yet. Leaning back, she placed a finger in the center of his chest, as she drew in a hiss. "I want to ravish you."

He growled—a low, feral moan that told her how much he liked her idea.

She moved her finger down, down until she met his navel, then bowed and kissed him there.

Again, he let loose a rapturous moan—a sound that thrummed through her body as if he'd touched her between the legs. "I'll come undone if you keep teasing me like that."

Drawing out the moment, she slowly moved her tongue lower and chuckled. "*Oui*, I want to watch you lose control." Her voice came out deep and breathless.

When she wrapped her fingers around his manhood, his eyes rolled back and his knees flexed. "My God."

She could scarcely inhale as she smoothed her hand up and down. "Can I kiss it like you did to me?"

His thighs shuddered as he looked into her eyes. "Would you?"

Licking her lips, Bria dropped her gaze and lapped.

"This way," he whispered, taking her by the shoulders and backing to the bed. He pulled her beside him. "Are you sure?"

"Positive." She slid down and took his enormous member in her hand. "It's so soft and beautiful." Bria pressed her lips to the tip.

"Mm," Drake moaned, his hips swirling. The movement was like a bellows to the flame in her belly while she took him into her mouth.

"Yes, oh yes."

Emboldened by his encouragement, Bria swirled her tongue around and around, up and down. His breathing grew labored, his moans more frequent, as he shuddered in concert with her licks. As his passion rose, so did her need.

Panting, Drake pulled her over him. "I can wait no longer. I must be inside you."

"Me on top?" she asked, moisture pooling between her legs.

"Yes. You on top, you from behind, you beneath, you standing against the wall. Any way you want it, I'm yours."

Her body completely afire, Bria slid over him, imagining all he had said and wanting it now. Rocking her hips, she rubbed her wetness along his length. "Top this time," she managed to say while he slid his finger over her. "Mayhap the wall next."

"You're so wet." Grasping her hips, Drake moved so his member pushed against her, hard and thick. "Are you ready?"

Frantic for him, she grasped his shoulders and lowered herself onto him until he filled her. Looking him in the eyes, she rocked her hips. "The question is, are you ready, Your Grace?"

Laughing, he met her pace. "If it pleases you, Your Grace."

Unable to stop, Bria took her weight on her arms as her body took over in the dance of desire.

His eyelids heavy and full of lust, he looked like the god of passion. "Do. Not. Stop," he growled, commanding the tempo with powerful fingers sinking into her buttocks.

Ripples of wild need quaked through her body while, faster and faster, her hips rocked in a frenzied motion.

"I'm coming," he said, bucking into her, sinking so deep, she cried out with the most thrilling passion she'd ever felt in her life. And with one more thrust of her hips, the world shattered into ripples of stardust.

Completely spent, Bria collapsed atop his chest.

Drake softly swirled his hands around her tight bottom. "You will be the death of me, but I will go a happy man."

"Hmm? I think you will give me a challenge at every turn." He had no idea how much so. Feeling as if she'd just danced the role of the Sylph twice, Bria's insides still quivered.

"Thank you for loving me," she whispered, her heart filled with more joy than she ever dreamed possible.

Chapter Thirty-Four

"Ah, Master John, come in." Drake beckoned the boy into his stateroom. After the wedding, he'd made the announcement that Johnny was now the ward of the Duke of Ravenscar and would henceforth be referred to as "master".

The lad crept inside. "Is it truly our last morn aboard ship…er…Your Grace?" He hadn't quite come to grips with the new turn of events and things would be even more confounding once they disembarked.

"It is, indeed, and soon Peak Castle will be looming on the horizon."

"And I'm going to live in a real castle?"

"That you are." Drake took the boy by the hand and led him to the bed where they sat together. "Do you know what it means to be the ward of a duke?"

"Weeell. I'll have plenty to eat and I'll have my own bed and toys and I can tell the servants what to do."

"That's not exactly correct. We must respect servants at all times. They help us and have particular skills that are very important."

"What kind of skills?"

"The cook prepares our meals. The livery staff looks after the horses, carriages and the stable. The butler oversees the servants, takes care of the silver, and manages the wine…"

"Being a butler doesn't seem all that difficult."

"Mind you, it is a very important job, and few develop the panache to become one."

"Pan-what? You sure use a lot of big words."

"I'll not apologize for that. Dukes *and* their wards must be well-educated. For now, let us say a butler has style and ability to which few others can aspire." Drake started to twist his ring and smiled when he realized it was on Britannia's finger. "When we go ashore, things will be very busy. You will be overwhelmed."

When Master John scrunched his nose, Drake changed his tack. "I do not ever want you to fear me. I have committed to be your guardian. That means I will act as your parent."

"And Bria, too."

"Her Grace will definitely care for you as well. Things will not always be easy, and I want you to know that you may come to me at any time."

"Very well, but nothing could be worse than living on the streets and going hungry."

"You're right there." Drake scrubbed his fingers over the lad's hair. "Now, have you said your goodbyes to Buggie?"

"Can't he come with us?"

"I'm afraid not, though you may write to him. I've seen how you write your letters. Her Grace has done a fine job commencing your education. Soon you'll be off to Eton with other boys your age."

"Can't Bria teach me always?"

"She will be far to busy. Remember what I said about the servants all having an area of expertise?"

"Mm hmm."

"Well, so do dukes, duchesses and instructors. A young man cannot gain a better education than that which he acquires at Eton. But let us not put the cart before the horse. And today you will be seeing your new home for the first time. I want you to enjoy this day and remember it always." Drake stood and offered his hand. "Are you ready?"

Master John grinned, his eyes shining with excitement. "I sure am."

***

Bria gripped the rail so tightly, her knuckles turned white. "That's not a castle, 'tis a palace."

Dominating a promontory that stood proudly above the sea, conical roofs on the corner towers stretched to white clouds sailing overhead. Between the towers spanned an enormous building of four stories with windows clear up to the top. At the far end, peeking above the southernmost tower stood a baronial keep complete with a crenelated wall walk.

Pride etched Drake's features. "Perhaps, though it has been referred to as a castle for nineteen generations. My ancestor was granted these lands by Edward the First. He built the initial tower intending for the estate to be a hunting lodge, though every duke who followed fell in love with the region and added his own legacy. I believe we made it our principle residence after the fourth duke completed the east wing."

"It looks like the king's castle in London," said Johnny.

Bria didn't bother to ask which one. "I'll wager you cannot wait to go exploring."

"I'd like it better if Buggie could go with me. I might get lost in there."

She had worried over Johnny's attachment to the cabin boy. However, taking in another ward was out of the question. Not to mention that over the past month the older boy had taught Johnny some very colorful language.

"You'll get on fine," said Drake.

Being lowered to the skiff was a bit harrowing, but once they were seated, rowing ashore took no time. As they reached the shore, quite a welcoming party had assembled with more coming down the path leading from the castle.

Drake carried Bria to dry land, while Johnny was happy to make it to the beach on his own.

A woman dressed in a black maid's gown and apron wrung her hands. "My heavens, Your Grace, why did you not send word of your arrival?"

"There was no opportunity. We've sailed from somewhere near the coast of Northern Africa without a change of clothes among us."

"I beg your pardon?"

"I'll explain all later. But first the news." Beaming, he gestured toward Bria, her dress far more tattered than the traveling gown she'd worn on the day she'd met the duke. "Please welcome my new bride, Her Grace, the Duchess of Ravenscar and our ward, Master John Chadwick."

Of course, Drake hadn't the chance to submit the petition to make Johnny's name official, but he intended to do so at his earliest opportunity.

The servants stared, their mouths agape.

He gestured to the woman in black, introducing her as Mrs. Cole, the housekeeper. "I daresay our adventure has been quite harrowing. Her Grace will need an appointment with the modiste immediately. Fetch the tailor for Master John. And we need a governess. Are there any about?"

"I shall make inquiries," said Mrs. Cole before turning to a row of maids. "You heard His Grace. Beds need to be made, the nursery prepared."

"I don't need no nursery," said Johnny.

"No?" asked Drake. "It is filled with toys."

"Toys for babies?"

Drake winked at Bria. "Not at all. Perhaps you should see it before passing judgement."

"I'll show him," said a lad stepping forward from the crowd.

A man dressed in working clothes grasped the boy's shoulder. "James, you mustn't speak out of turn."

"What a grand idea." Drake moved toward them. "Thank you, James, would you mind showing Master John about?"

The boy looked to his father who gave a nod. "Aye, Your Grace."

"He needs a proper bath first," said Bria.

"Oh, hogwash." Their new ward grabbed James by arm. "Let's go afore she douses me."

Bria shook her finger at the lad's retreating form. "A bath. After supper. It is not negotiable."

Drake offered his elbow. "Going is the best idea I've heard today. Shall we, my dear?"

Her stomach leaped. "Is it grander than Ravenscar Hall?"

"Larger and filled with relics, though I'm not certain grander is the right descriptor."

And it wasn't. Peak Castle was a marvel all its own. With over four hundred rooms, each one was decorated with a different theme. The dining hall was painted a light green with French paneling and furniture. The drawing room was lined with pastoral tapestries and gilt furniture. There was an armory displaying years of weaponry with the unicorn family crest at the focal point. A china turret, a salon with a pianoforte, a ballroom for dancing, a library, withdrawing rooms, vast kitchens, and so many bedchambers, Bria lost count.

"I think this is my favorite chamber," she said, dropping to her back on Drake's enormous state bed.

He crawled up beside her, resting on his side and propping his head in his hand. "Not the duchess' bedchamber?"

"Of course not. My favorite is yours. You do not intend for us to sleep apart, do you?"

"I would die if we did." He kissed her forehead. "Because I want to do this any moment I desire." Cupping her breast, he kissed her cheek then growled, nuzzling into her neck

Giggling with delight, Bria scooted aside. "And what about your theater?"

"We could create a scandal and open next season with *La Sylphide*."

"I liked your idea about creating a ballet just for me."

"Hmm." He frowned, brushing his fingers over the tops of her breasts.

"Are you not enthralled with the idea of your wife on the stage?"

"What if you are with child?"

"Then I must have a very talented understudy."

"Have you someone in mind?"

"I do. Pauline is very talented and too sweet to rise through the *corps* on her own."

He squeezed her side playfully. "Are you telling me you're not sweet?"

"Stop!" Bria brushed his fingers away with a squeal. "I'm tenacious."

"That you are."

She tugged on the end of his neckcloth. "Your mother is going to be devastated about us."

"She'll come around in time."

"Do you think so?"

"She'll have to. Besides, once she comes to know you better, she can't help but love you."

"I hope so."

"We must burn this costume." With a sly grin, Drake pulled the sleeves from her shoulders. "Perhaps I'll suggest Mother marry Mr. Peters."

"The gunsmith?"

"We both know they've been having something of an affair. I would be far happier if she married the man than if their liaison became the subject of the scandal sheets."

"He's wealthy, is he not?"

"New money, but mother needs neither wealth nor title. She'll always be the dowager duchess even if she marries a commoner."

"You married a commoner."

"Since women cannot hold titles, in truth, all peers marry commoners."

Bria sat up. "Then why is London's marriage mart such a thing?"

"Because of perceived breeding—*gently-bred* ladies and the like. Though in truth, it always been more about the exchange of wealth and keeping that wealth within certain families than one's lineage."

"Unless the child of a nobleman is born out of wedlock—even if the breeding is superlative."

"As in your case?"

"My father was a king. My mother is a baroness. I am a bastard."

"You are a duchess now." Bria's heart brimmed with joy as her husband pulled her back to his side and kissed her. "Mind you, do not forget it. Now make passionate, unabashed love with me, Your Grace."

Chapter Thirty-Five

"How long has it been since you wrote to Calthorpe?" asked Bria, the reins still a tad unsteady in her hands, though over the past few weeks she and Drake had ridden every morning.

She wore a new riding habit, one fitting for a duchess. Though inside, Bria still felt much the same aside from being content and happier. "I dispatched a letter to them the day after we arrived home. I sent one to my mother as well."

"I'm surprised we haven't heard back."

"I'm more surprised about Mother," Drake said, leading them into open pasture. "I expected to hear from her lady's maid advising that Her Grace had taken to her bed with a mysterious illness."

Bria's knee tightened around the upper pommel of her sidesaddle. "Do you think she will ever accept me?"

"She has no choice but to do so."

"But she may always harbor a grudge."

"Not for long. Mother might put up a fuss at first, but once she realizes she has been beaten, she always pulls in her daggers."

Picking up a trot, Bria rode up beside him. "I've received a letter from Pauline."

"Good news I hope."

"Good and bad. It seems Lord Saye is no longer in the picture."

"I'm not surprised."

"But she's excited about opening the Chadwick Theater Ballet School."

"Splendid—and act as your understudy?"

"Are you still certain I should dance—you once told me dukes don't tread the boards. Will it not be awkward for you if I do?"

"I no longer care what polite society thinks. Besides, your circumstances are entirely different. You were a smashing success last Season—London's darling. I think it will be fitting for you to continue at least until…" He grinned and waggled his eyebrows.

Bria knew exactly what he meant and the idea of starting a family made her insides tingle. She returned his smile. "I think Pauline will be happy to understudy knowing I do not plan to play the lead for long. And she needs a strong supporting role. I'm sure there will be no problem choreographing an extra piece or two for her." She ran the reins through her gloved fingers. "On that note, has Perkins found a choreographer? He'll need to start soon."

"Perhaps there's a whole parcel of mail due to arrive— aside from Pauline's missive. There are too many people who owe us responses, and the last thing I want to do at the moment is travel to London."

A team of horses sounded in the distance. "Look there." Drake pointed. "A carriage is approaching."

Indeed, a shiny, black carriage turned onto the long, sycamore-lined drive. "I think that coach is far too well-appointed for a mail courier."

"Come." He turned his horse toward the castle. "I'll race you home."

Leaning forward, Bria tapped her crop and kicked her heel, but racing the Duke of Ravenscar was nothing short of futile. He was as comfortable in a saddle as she was at the *barre*. Besides, a woman seated in a sidesaddle who was just learning to ride didn't have a chance.

Though Drake could win twice over, he didn't even try. Together, they cantered side by side and reached the entry in plenty of time to be standing on Peak Castle's front steps when the carriage came to a halt.

A footman opened the door.

"There you are at last!" said Lady Calthorpe, accepting the man's assistance. His Lordship followed.

Drake shook the baron's hand. "Her Grace and I were just discussing how long it has been since I sent word of our return to England."

Beaming with a radiant smile, Lady Calthorpe fanned her face. "*Her Grace*...Britannia, your title has such a lovely ring."

"I'm sorry we couldn't come sooner," said the baron. "We were set back by the weather. We should have been here three days ago."

"But I'm still surprised to see you." Bria clasped her mother's hands and gave them a squeeze. *Mother*, the name made her warm all over. "My word, you came all this way."

Her Ladyship return the squeeze and kissed Britannia on the cheek for the first time in nearly twenty years. "I would sail to Australia to see my only daughter."

"And she nearly did," said Calthorpe. "If His Grace hadn't dispatched a missive telling us he was in pursuit, I believe Charlotte would have attempted to swim."

Bria gestured toward the door. "Come inside and I'll order lemonade and sandwiches."

Drake led the way. "Perhaps Calthorpe would enjoy something a tad stronger."

"A tot of brandy wouldn't go astray," said the baron.

"Pennyworth, brandy for the gentlemen, sandwiches for all and lemonade for the ladies, if you please," said Ravenscar, heading to the drawing room.

The butler bowed. "Straightaway, Your Grace."

Her Ladyship pulled Bria onto the settee. "When we were traveling to Plymouth, we had a long discussion about you, my dear."

The baron nodded emphatically. "We did."

"And we decided it was high time to legitimize you as our daughter."

"Yes, yes," echoed Calthorpe, his head still bobbing.

Unable to believe her ears, Bria looked from her mother to the baron to Drake who stood with his hands over his heart and his mouth agape.

Tears stung her eyes as the realization began to sink in.

"Even before you returned to England," Her Ladyship continued, "we had already submitted the documents to legitimize your birth."

"And thus, you are the sole heir to my fortune," said the baron.

Blinking, those pesky tears slipped from Bria's eyes as she gasped. "I-I cannot believe it. This far exceeds my wildest dreams."

"You have made this a glorious day," Drake agreed.

"We're so happy to have our Britannia in our lives." Her Ladyship plucked a lace kerchief from her sleeve and dabbed her eyes. "I only wish we could have been there for the wedding."

"Now that we're on home's soil, we'll have to plan a grand ball. I'm sure my mother will be anxious to make the announcement as well."

A footman brought in the sandwiches while they discussed timing, the guest list, invitations and music. In the distance, Bria heard the wheels of another carriage, and hoped it might be the mail courier with a missive from Drake's mother.

Not long and voices came from beyond the door just before a ruffled Pennyworth entered, tugging down his

34205685R00209

Made in the USA
Lexington, KY
20 March 2019